# Strangers, Lovers
# and the Winds of Time

*Katie,*

*Thank you for reading my story.*
*I hope you find this worthwhile.*
*Also* _____ HAPPY Birthday
2-7-15

# Strangers, Lovers and the Winds of Time

## by

## Dale Lovin

*Dale Lovin*

Oak Tree Press     Hanford, CA

Oak Tree Press
*Publishers Since 1998*

STRANGERS, LOVERS AND THE WINDS OF TIME, Copyright 2014, by DALE
LOVIN.
All rights reserved. Printed in the United States of America. No part of this book
may be used or reproduced in any manner whatsoever without written permission
except in the case of brief quotations used in critical articles and reviews.

For information, address Oak Tree Press, 1820 W. Lacey Boulevard, Suite 220,
Hanford, CA 93230.

Oak Tree Press books may be purchased for educational, business, or sales
promotional purposes. Contact Publisher for quantity discounts.

First Edition, September 2014

ISBN 978-1-61009-161-9
LCCN 2014945325

Author Photograph by Wendy Schott

# Dedication

*Strangers, Lovers and the Winds of Time* is dedicated to the most important people in my life, my family, all of whom have appeared as characters in my writings. Our family memories of mountain streams, alpine lakes, campfire antics and sleeping under the stars are eternal treasures.

My wife, Linda, for unending support and ever-growing love. I could never have made it without you.

My daughter, Amy, for the voice of an angel and bringing music to our family.

My son, Brandon, a quiet, military man of character and compassion.

My son, Brian, who will change the world and so many will benefit.

My brother, Keith, for teaching me the beauty of the spoken and written word.

My brother, Ken, an FBI Agent with uncanny instincts and unblinking courage.

# CHAPTER ONE
## 1997

"Ladies and gentlemen of the jury, the past week has been a journey. It was not a pleasant journey. It was anything but that. Together, we have walked a road that took us down some dark alleys. We had to peer through windows that we all wish were covered and we had to see and hear some things no normal person ever wants to see or hear. Now, here we are this morning. We've made it to the end of the road. What's next? Why did we go through all of this?" The prosecutor ceased speaking. Her calm demeanor, striking six-foot frame, chocolate skin and piercing eyes exuded a commanding presence. Waiting as if she expected someone to answer her question, the courtroom itself seemed to hold its breath.

She spoke again, her voice soft but resonating with authority. "One week ago today I stood before you and told you exactly what this case was about. You were told what evidence the prosecution would present, what to look for and what to listen for. You were told that from a legal perspective this case was about whether or not the defendant murdered James Rush. But, I'm certain that you recall you were also told that the evidence would take you to a realm that is far beyond any technical or legal definition of murder." She paused to gaze at the jury, her voice rising with her next words. "Heaven knows that certainly turned out to be the truth!"

Taking a deep breath, she paused and placed both hands on the podium before continuing. "In the course of this trial you have seen evidence that illuminates a side of humanity that is repugnant. No person with a shred of decency could have sat through this trial without wondering how in the world something like this could ever happen. Not only have you been presented with evidence that the defendant took the life of James Rush simply because of the color of his skin, you endured heartbreaking testimony that told how that life was taken in a calculated, stealth attack from behind. The defendant did not even demonstrate a fundamental courage to face his victim. No, he took the coward's way. He came from behind and, without warning, commenced a ruthless and pre-meditated ambush that snuffed a human life. He snuffed that life with no opportunity for defense. And, the evidence has told you that this horrible deed happened simply because James Rush was a black man."

The prosecutor stood motionless for a moment. And then, with a slight twist of her body and a hardening of her voice, she continued. "Now that, ladies and gentlemen of the jury, is contemptible beyond words. It is behavior that has no place in our society and it must not be tolerated. That is precisely why you have been asked to travel such a dark road this past week. But unfortunately, this case is much more than even that. We are in this courtroom today because the defendant committed murder, that's for sure. But we are also here because that murder was fueled by prejudice, hatred and bigotry." Her eyes fired, "And, let's not forget cowardice." She spat the last words as if shards of glass filled her mouth.

"We have no choice but to be here this morning. How could we not be here? We are here this morning, ladies and gentlemen, as civilized, decent human beings in protection of the most fundamental values that we cherish as citizens. If all of us were not here this morning, if you, the jurors, had not traveled this week's dark road, where would we be as a society? Where would we go, what in the world would we become."

As she stepped from behind her podium, the prosecutor lifted her glasses until they lodged in her hair and then folded her hands across her waist. She stood without speaking in what appeared to be a muted scrutiny of the jurors seated before her.

The jury sat transfixed as she continued. "Now, ladies and gentlemen, this morning brings the closing arguments of this trial. This is the last day that you will hear from the prosecution or the defense. After you have heard what we have to say in our concluding moments together, the judge will give you some instructions and then it is all up to you. You have already heard hours of testimony and listened to witnesses tell their stories. You have seen photographs, observed as exhibits were entered into evidence and you have patiently endured some long-winded, legal wrangling between defense counsel and the prosecution. Thank you. You have been very patient.

"I am not about to bore you this morning with a re-hash of legalities and obscure points of law. All I want to do in these final moments we have together is to step back and take a look at the big picture. What is this case about? What events transpired that led to the defendant being seated here this morning and all of us spending a week of our lives in this courtroom? "

The prosecutor took a side step; once again behind the podium she lowered her glasses onto her face and cast her eyes downward, scanning her notes. A moment passed before she stepped away from the podium, reached for her glasses and held them in her right hand, utilizing them as a pointer, an object of emphasis. "The first and most important thing to remember is that a fine young man by the name of James Rush is dead. James Rush was shot in the back. He was shot not once but three times, at near point-blank range, while he simply walked from his car to a diner where he was to meet his wife-to-be and friends. You heard testimony about how people inside the diner and on the street heard gunshots. People were screaming, confusion was awful and, in the midst of this chaos, a man lay in a pool of his own blood, dying on a dirty sidewalk. You listened to that heart-wrenching testimony from his fiancé and her sister, how they ran from the diner and saw the body of James Rush lying on the ground. You listened as to how they knelt over his broken body, sobbing and screaming, 'Oh God, oh God, oh God!'" The prosecutor stepped closer to the jury box, extending her right hand, piercing the air with her glasses. "That, ladies and gentlemen, is what happened and that is why we are here. That is what we must remember."

She held the moment, her eyes locked with those of the jury. "But sadly, there is so much more to remember. We must remember the police officers who told you about the crime scene investigation, dozens of people interviewed, photographs taken, all painstaking work. They told us how they combed the neighborhood for anything or anyone who could help. They explained how frustrated they were because the only thing witnesses saw was a hooded man leap from a car, shoot the victim in the back three times, jump back into his car and speed away. The police officers testified that the murder was one of the most cold-blooded cases they had ever encountered. In spite of their efforts, they could not find a single person who could give them a description of the shooter or a detailed description of the car."

The prosecutor lifted her arms in a gesture of despair and spoke quietly. "When it was all over, the only lead police had were photographic images from a security camera that was positioned at a nearby business. This camera captured an image of a car that sped through a red light of the intersection just beyond where James Rush had been shot. This all happened at night and, because it was so dark, the camera image was of poor quality. But it was obvious that the speeding car clearly collided with the rear end of another vehicle in the intersection. It was not a severe collision; only a clip and the speeding car kept on going; just a fast-moving, mid-sized, dark-colored car that was bound to have a damaged right front bumper. That's it. That's all they had to work with."

Hands clasped behind her back, she looked to the floor and paced in contemplative silence. Lifting her eyes, she squared her body to the jurors and continued. "Next, I ask that you remember how the police officers testified that James Rush was a hard-working young man who attended night school after working all day as a sales clerk in a convenience store. They also told us of a recent, horrifying incident that had happened inside the convenience store one day while James was on duty. A group of young, white men entered his store. Loud and disruptive, they terrorized customers, mocked James Rush and made racially derogatory remarks. James refused to serve them. He told them to leave and threatened to call the police. But before the men left the store, one of the young men approached the counter and told James that 'no damned nigger was about to refuse service to him.' The man sneered at James Rush and promised that he would stalk him. He said he would 'stalk him until the time was right and would leave him dead.'" The prosecutor dropped her head and again looked at the floor for a moment. She looked up and, with sadness in her voice, delivered her next statement. "Now, ladies and gentlemen of the jury, do you remember how you felt after listening to that testimony?" She shook her head. "Was there anyone in this courtroom who did not feel absolutely sick down deep inside?" She stared into the face of each juror as if she dared someone to respond to her question.

"Well, the store's security camera captured the incident but the man's face was never clearly visible. However, after the murder of James Rush, the police posted photographs from the security camera in the newspaper anyway. They published them because the camera did capture a clear image of a very unusual shirt that was worn by the man who delivered the threat. Unfortunately, they had no luck whatsoever; no calls from a concerned public broke the ice. The case became stagnant and it looked like the tragedy of this horrible murder would go unsolved and, tragically, unpunished."

The prosecutor now paced back and forth, glasses still in hand, her eyes never leaving the jury. No one coughed, no one shifted within their seat.

"And then something happened, something totally unexpected. It came out of left field and new life was breathed into the investigation. You will recall the FBI agent who testified and the amazing testimony he gave about how FBI agents and police officers executed arrest and search warrants in the course of a bank robbery investigation. What an incredible scenario he described when he told of how they broke through the door of a house, just before dawn, and arrested two men for bank robbery. But at the time, even the agents and officers didn't fully comprehend what they had gotten into. Do you recall that the FBI agent sat on the witness stand for an entire afternoon, telling us what happened in that house after they burst through the door? He told us of a large, multi-room house filled with more than a dozen people. The occupants cursed the officers, called them nigger lovers and Jew whores. They even spat at the officers. The agent told us of posters on the walls, posters of swastikas, photographs of Adolf Hitler and the European death camps of the Second World War. He described giant-sized photographs of black men who had been lynched, with insulting and supposedly humorous captions beneath the gruesome photos. He told us about finding books and literature pronouncing white racial supremacy and the necessity to oppress and subdue the races of color and Jewish people." Absolute silence encompassed the courtroom.

"But, ladies and gentlemen, that was not all the agents and officers found. They found guns: guns of many types, sizes and varieties. Guns were found in virtually every room of the house, including the bedroom occupied by the defendant.

The FBI agent told us that finding guns while serving a warrant for bank robbers was not particularly unusual. What made this discovery unique was the exceptionally large quantity and variety of weapons. But, there was another discovery that absolutely was most unusual and it triggered a very loud alarm. The FBI agent related how he searched the bedroom that belonged to the defendant and found a stack of newspaper articles about the unsolved murder of James Rush. He found these articles, carefully clipped from newspapers, bound together and lying on a table in the defendant's room. He told us how that after investigators analyzed all that had been discovered, a line of communication was established among the police officers who were handling the murder investigation of James Rush and the investigators handling the bank robbery.

Now, all of a sudden the ball really started to roll. Once the two cases came together, doors began to open and the investigation gathered steam like a giant train. Through testimony, we learned that ballistics examinations linked one of the guns from the house to the murder of Mr. Rush. And where in the house was that specific gun discovered? The FBI agent told you that it was found in the defendant's bedroom, underneath a magazine, lying right beside the newspaper articles." The prosecutor raised her arms and briefly cast her eyes upward. "After weeks of frustrating stalemate, what an explosive discovery! The weapon utilized in a ruthless murder to be finally discovered in the course of searching for bank robbers was like a gift from heaven." The prosecutor's eyes blazed and a tangible energy radiated from her body. The courtroom was spellbound.

Air conditioning fans engaged, their muffled drone the only sound as she paused. Again, she paced the floor, back and forth, until she resumed. "It is important for you to understand that, as a rule, I would not be able to discuss with you the details of a bank robbery search warrant that was not directly related to the investigation of the murder of James Rush. However, in this instance, I can freely talk about what happened during the search because the defense has offered no objection. They have stipulated to everything that happened. They don't care if I talk about the events of that morning. In fact, the very crux of their defense is precisely that the house that the police and FBI searched was a huge dwelling, holding multiple rooms and occupied by many people. The people living in the house moved about from room to room, often sharing the contents of the house. The defense asks you to believe that the defendant was just an accidental tenant; an accidental tenant in a den of robbers and thieves. More specifically, the defense asks that you ignore several critical items of evidence. They want you to ignore the fact that the newspaper articles about the murder of James Rush were located in the bedroom of the defendant. They want you to ignore the fact that the defendant's fingerprints were found on the gun. And, ladies and gentlemen, they want you to ignore that an examination of the defendant's mid-sized, dark colored car revealed a damaged right front bumper; damage that corresponds perfectly with the accident caught on the security camera seconds after the murder of James Rush."

The prosecutor now stood away from her podium, once again punctuating the air with her glasses as she spoke. "The defense wants you to disregard all of these things and believe that the defendant simply had the misfortune to live in a house filled with robbers and guns and that the damage to his automobile is purely coincidental." She looked to the floor and sighed. "But even this is not the end of the story. The FBI agent and police officers told us more. They testified how after their discoveries inside that house they were able to follow up with more investigation into the confrontation that James Rush experienced while on duty in his convenience store. You were shown the security camera photographs of the man who threatened Mr. Rush inside his store. You saw that even though the image of this man's face was never clearly captured, the shirt he wore was clearly visible. Right there, clear as day, the camera showed the shirt with a skull and bones insignia across the back. Then, the FBI agent showed you an actual shirt with skull and bones insignia. He held it up high so that every person in this courtroom could see it. And where did this shirt come from? He told you that he found it in the defendant's bedroom. He told you that on the morning of the search, he had seized the shirt simply because it was similar to witness descriptions of a shirt worn during several bank robberies being investigated. At the time, the FBI agent knew nothing about the James Rush matter. It was not until later that police and FBI investigators pieced all of this together. Once again, ladies and gentlemen, the defense suggests that you disregard this as simple happenstance, a shirt that any person living in that house could have worn and should not be specifically linked with the defendant."

With a contemplative expression on her face, the prosecutor returned to the podium. She laid her glasses beside her notebook, positioned her hands on the edges of the podium and leaned her body forward, eye-to-eye with a motionless jury. "Please, let me be clear. The defendant was not arrested or charged with bank robbery when the FBI and police entered into that house where he happened to be living. No, that's not what this is about at all. In fact, there is an excellent chance that the defendant even enjoyed a level of smugness that morning as he watched others led away in shackles while he was left free and unchallenged. But little did he realize that the events of that morning had ignited a fuse, a fuse that inexorably burned its way straight into this courtroom.

So, just exactly what has the evidence told us? Well, we have certainly learned that a black man was murdered, assassinated, from behind with no warning. We have learned that the defendant lived in a house that oozed with symbols of racial hatred. We have learned that within the defendant's bedroom were newspaper articles about the murder." The prosecutor paused and stared hard at the jurors. Emotion charged her next words as she spoke with bitterness, "Newspaper articles savored as trophies. Possessions of pride to be shared with others."

Shaking her head in a gesture of incredulousness, she continued. "We have learned that along with the news articles was a handgun; a gun that science tells you was the specific weapon that took the life of James Rush. And, science also tells you that the gun bore the fingerprints of the defendant. No other fingerprints were on the gun, only the defendant's. We have learned that the defendant's car suffered damage to the front bumper; damage that is entirely consistent with what would have been sustained in the accident that took place within seconds and within a few feet of the murder scene. We have learned that the defendant had a shirt in his bedroom that precisely matches the shirt worn by a man who harassed James Rush, made racial slurs and threatened to return and murder him; a threat that was leveled because James Rush, a black man, had the audacity to refuse service to a rude and confrontational person and order that person to leave the store; a rude and confrontational person with white skin."

Picking up her glasses, the prosecutor folded them as she clutched the lenses close to her chest, grasping them with both hands, almost as if in prayer. Silence lingered, the weight of her words and the significance of the moment apparent. "So, ladies and gentlemen, we have a gun, we have ballistics examinations, we have fingerprints, we have a damaged car and we have a shirt. And, do you know what else we have? We have venom. We have venom that has seeped into hearts, minds and behavior until it has poisoned the very fabric of what makes us civilized, decent human beings. Oh, yes, murder is the legal reason that we are here today but that terrible, terrible venom is the human reason we are here."

She paced back and forth, deep in thought, before she again stood still before the podium. For a brief moment she lowered her head, closed her eyes and, with thumb and forefinger, massaged the crease of her brows. Looking up, she spoke. "Why must we lawyers always refer to you as ladies and gentlemen of the jury?" She smiled and shook her head. "I'm going to change that today. May I please call you brothers and sisters of the jury? Brothers and sisters of the jury, fellow human beings of the jury, I am asking that you simply analyze the evidence that has been presented in this trial. Analyze the evidence within the context of your intellect, your common sense and your conscience. The prosecution has done its duty. You have been given compelling and irrefutable evidence that demonstrates beyond any reasonable doubt that the defendant took the life of James Rush." She allowed silence to linger for a moment. "The prosecution has shown you the venom. Now, you must do your duty."

Silence again held before she continued. "I want to remind you of one of America's greatest stories, *To Kill a Mockingbird.* It is a marvelous book that was ultimately made into a powerful movie. I hope you have read the book or seen the movie. If not, after this trial please go home and do so. I promise you won't be disappointed. The story is of a racially charged trial in the days of the old South when segregation and prejudice were ways of life. Gregory Peck performed the role of an attorney charged with the defense of a wrongfully accused black man. If you have seen the movie, you will recall how Gregory Peck stood before the jury in his final plea. Do you remember how he articulated the evidence, laid it out plain and simple? And then, with his horn-rimmed glasses, a lock of hair dangling and in his unmistakable voice, he implored the jurors: 'In the name of God, do your duty.'

Well, I recognize that I am no movie star and I am most certainly no Gregory Peck. I can only wish for his charisma and presence. But, I will use his words once again. None are more appropriate. Ladies and gentlemen of the jury, brothers and sisters of the jury, I ask you to evaluate the evidence, utilize your mind and, in the name of God, do your duty." She leaned over the podium and in little more than a whisper delivered her final plea. "Listen to your heart, my brothers and sisters, listen to your heart, and in the name of God, do your duty."

# CHAPTER TWO
## ACOMA, NEW MEXICO
### Late 1500s

*Strategically positioned atop a sheer, four hundred foot butte of wind-sculpted stone, the pueblo village of Acoma has held life for approximately one thousand years. It may be the longest continuously inhabited city in the United States. For centuries the residents of Acoma have known their cliff-top home above the New Mexico desert as "The Place That Always Was."*

*In 1853, the Spanish Crown, through divine inspiration, authorized conquest of the lands of New Mexico for the purpose of saving souls in the name of God. The Crown proclaimed that the conquest was purely benevolent, the will of God. The proclamation failed to mention the fables that had floated on endless New Mexico winds, reaching even to the palaces of Europe; fables that cities of gold and unfathomable riches lay within the Rio Grande Valley. Thus, the soldiers marched. With a Bible in one hand, a sword in the other and disease spewing from their breath, the Conquistadores began a relentless trek through New Mexico. What they found were not cities of gold, but villages of tan, dried mud and poor people eking a precarious existence from perpetual drought and stony soil. As Conquistadores invaded, they rode horses and brandished weapons that the foot-bound ancient peoples had never even seen. It was the perceived duty of the invaders to convince native inhabitants that their spiritual beliefs and customs were not only wrong but also iniquitous. Conversion to Christianity and submission to the Spanish Crown were the only options offered. Some of the villages of New Mexico and their people did convert and submit, kneeling before a priest and swearing allegiance to Spain.*

*The people of Acoma made a choice that they would neither convert or submit. Three days after Christmas 1598, Spanish soldiers initiated an attack on one side of the sheer rock face. This was a maneuver intended only as a diversion tactic. Simultaneously, a small group of soldiers climbed the precipice from an opposite side and mounted a surprise attack against the Acomans. The Spanish burned what would burn and killed approximately six hundred of the village inhabitants. Wounded Indians were tossed over the cliff's rim. To avoid capture or death at the hands of the enemy, some Acomans killed their own family members and then committed suicide.*

*Ultimately, the surviving citizens of the pueblo were forced from their city in the sky, now in ruin, and marched through freezing winter weather to stand trial. A guilty verdict was pronounced and sentence issued: men over the age of twenty-five had one foot amputated and were condemned to twenty years of personal servitude to the soldiers. Males and females from age twelve to twenty-five were sentenced to twenty years as slaves of the Spanish. Children under the age of twelve were given to friars for Christian schooling.*

*Historians calculate that it took 400 years for the Place That Always Was to recover its lost population.*

## CHAPTER THREE
### July 9, 2012

Colorado's rangeland and brilliant green circles of irrigated fields fell beneath an ascending jetliner, the city of Denver in its wake. Dipping a wing, the magnificent flying machine turned into a spiraling climb for a westerly course, Los Angeles the destination. Brad Walker peered out the window. His preference was always a window seat. He loved to locate familiar landmarks from the air and hoped that he would never lose the sense of exhilaration he felt when suspended in the sky over Colorado. He watched the landscape slip by, Pike's Peak to the south with Denver's foothills giving way to the lofty Front Range Mountains. Soon, Brad recognized the unmistakable profile of the Maroon Bells and the city of Aspen.

Brad turned from the window and leaned back in his seat. The sight of Aspen caused a twinge, a stirring of memories: memories of a kidnapped woman and victimized children that had sucked him into one of the most bizarre episodes of his life. Brad closed his eyes. He didn't want to think about the repugnance of that experience. He was already filled with too much apprehension. He hated hospitals. Elizabeth's illness and death had led to enough time in hospitals for ten lifetimes. But, here he was hurtling through the sky at five hundred miles per hour, a hospital his destination. He had thoughts of antiseptic rooms, white coats, and huddled conferences with physicians. It all rushed back and a sense of dread clutched deep inside. Years of marriage with Elizabeth and a career with the FBI had taken flight from the corridors of a hospital. Like wind over the Rocky Mountains, Elizabeth's life had vanished, carried away to nowhere. Physicians and hospitals, with no answer and no solution, remained in haunting silence as Brad and his three children awakened from their nightmare to a life without Elizabeth. He had left the FBI to be with her in those final, terrible days, a decision he had never regretted.

Brad glanced out the window again, Aspen faded as the jet cruised. He remembered the evil that he had encountered in that mountain town. It was Elizabeth's spirit that had been his strength through the entire experience. He still felt her spirit every day but he knew that she was just as gone as yesterday.

He thought about why he was here, on an airliner enroute to Los Angeles. There had been no choice. After the telephone call, it had taken less than two hours to make a reservation and begin driving to the airport. This was the last thing in the world he wanted to do. Absolutely nothing could keep him from doing it.

Time passed and Brad gazed out the window again; the stark beauty of Utah slipped by in a mosaic of brown and red followed by Arizona's Grand Canyon country, magnificent even from altitude. He felt the tremor of jet engines holding him aloft and heat from the desert five miles below. He thought of Los Angeles. What did this mean? What would he say to her? How was he going to handle what awaited in the hospital?

* * * *

Barking dogs brought end to a night of fitful sleep. Walter was glad to hear them. The barking continued as he opened his eyes and glanced about. Flimsy curtains did little to filter sunlight that illuminated the decay of his surroundings. Cheap, veneered furniture, stained carpet and a ceiling rippled with brown watermarks from the floor above caused him to question why he had selected this particular motel. Oh well, it was time to leave anyway. He reached for his cell phone to silence the barking dogs. He loved that alarm tone.

Walter swung his legs from the bed, stood up and stretched his arms above his head. Sandy grit from the worn carpet prickled his bare feet. He walked to the window and peered outside at the Los Angeles day. The motel parking lot had emptied from the previous night and was now only sparsely filled; check out time was less than an hour away. He verified that his car remained safely parked at the far end of the lot and turned away from the window. Standing over the toilet, thoughts of the past twenty-four hours pushed grogginess aside. Everything had finally come together and worked out perfectly. He recalled the schoolyard and how dark it had been. He had waited such a long time and then everything had happened so fast, over in a flash.

A mental checklist of what lay ahead scrolled through his mind. A shower was next. Walter scrutinized his body as he toweled off before the bathroom mirror. Tattoos wove a twisted labyrinth of color and indecipherable design up and around both arms. Rock-hard muscles rippled as he dried; there was no fat beneath his pale skin. Two days growth of beard sprouted in blonde bristles, the only hair to be found on his perfectly shaved head.

Twenty minutes later, Walter hefted a pack over his shoulder and walked to his car. With the success of last night still pleasantly lingering, he felt a surge of anticipation at what lay ahead. It was a new day.

* * * *

Sounding an occasional horn blast and swerving from lane to lane, the taxicab forced its way out of Los Angeles International Airport and into the madness of afternoon traffic. Brad wasn't sure which caused greater trepidation, clatter of the city or anticipation of the sterile hush of the hospital room that awaited him. Minutes later he paid the driver his fare and cast a hesitant gaze to the imposing configuration of buildings before him. This was the reason he had come. With reluctant resolve, he took a breath and stepped into the hospital.

Following a labyrinth of corridors and elevators, Brad finally made his way to a set of swinging doors, INTENSIVE CARE UNIT, their foreboding welcome. It flashed through his mind that at one time it seemed hospital visits had mostly been happy occasions: flowers and gifts for proud parents, babies, new life. Things were so different now. Elizabeth had died after what seemed to be eternity in a hospital and now this. It was beginning all over again. He felt as though he raced against himself on an unrelenting treadmill that he had no power to halt.

"May I help you?" A pleasant but inquiring voice from the woman seated at the nurse's station brought Brad back to the present. He slowly placed his bag on the floor, stalling for just another moment before replying. "Would you please tell Cassandra Roberts that Brad Walker is here?"

A quizzical expression shadowed the nurse's eyes. "Are you a family member?"

Brad moved his head from side to side, understanding why she would ask. "No, I'm not family but she is expecting me."

The nurse reached for her telephone, "Let me ring for you." Skepticism tinged her voice. Brad listened to the conversation that he knew must be with another medical person somewhere behind the walls of the nurse's station. After a few seconds the nurse hung up the telephone and gave Brad a curious look. "Please wait one moment. Ms. Roberts is on her way."

A side door opened and Brad turned to face the person who had called him and was the reason for him to be here. Her face drawn with stress and eyes bleary from crying did nothing to diminish the beauty Brad had always seen in Cassandra Roberts. As she entered the room their embrace was without a single word and tightly held for lingering seconds. Finally, Cassandra merely whispered, "Thank you so much." Brad broke the embrace, as he whispered back, "No, Cassandra, thank you for calling." Without further word she took Brad's hand and led him back through the door she had just used and into a harshly illuminated corridor of glass walls. Brad felt his heart tighten as he looked into a series of rooms, each holding a human body that was connected to an array of dripping tubes, beeping instruments and blinking lights; ominous electronic vigil of precarious struggle between life and death. Brad followed Cassandra down the hall until she directed him through a doorway where she nodded toward a bandaged form lying motionless in the bed. They stood in silence. Brad struggled to conceal the shock that swept over him. He thought he had prepared for this moment but the reality of what he saw hit like a freight train. This was beyond anything he had imagined. The odor of medicine and sickness filled his nostrils. He felt ill.

Cassandra squeezed his hand and spoke. "They say he is completely unconscious but I talk to him anyway. I don't know if it's for his sake or mine but I have to talk to him." She held her breath, tears swelling. "I think he would love to hear from you too." Brad swallowed hard and stepped away from Cassandra, moving toward the bed. He seated himself in a chair beside the bed, pulled it close and sat in silence for a moment. Gauze strips swathed a cocoon of white and a tangle of wires and tubes snaked from under the bed sheets to overhead monitors. Repetitive, electronic beeps served notice each time the heart managed one more beat. Brad absorbed the scene before he stood and leaned his body over the bed, bringing his face to within inches of the macabre figure. Brad Walker spoke softly into the ear of his friend, Norton Roberts.

\* \* \* \*

Pressing the accelerator felt good. The sensation of speed offered release, putting Los Angeles behind and taking him to what he had to do next. Walter held his eyes on the distant horizon; monotony of the passing landscape or heat of the desert did not even register. The job in Los Angeles had taken longer than he had planned but, in the end, it had turned out just fine. The size and congestion of Los Angeles had made what he had to do difficult and tedious. It had seemed to take forever for just the right opportunity to develop. But things should be easier now. He would grab a bite in Barstow and keep on moving.

Walter spotted what looked to be a decent place to eat and pulled into a parking slot. Just as he got out of his car, dogs barked. He answered his cell phone and listened for a few seconds as Earl gave him some last minute information. After the call, he stepped inside and ordered his meal. While waiting, he looked over a map to orient himself to his route. He had many miles and a vast desert to cross before reaching the mountains of Colorado and the city of Denver.

Visions of the schoolyard had not left him. When he thought of what had happened, his heart quickened and a sweet satisfaction surged through his core. Walter devoured his meal in rushed gulps. He wanted to hit the road so he could get busy to make it happen again.

## CHAPTER FOUR
### July 9, 2012

Cassandra Roberts and Brad Walker sat side by side in the hospital cafeteria. Neither had any appetite but at least it offered respite from the numbing hours Cassandra had maintained while sitting beside her husband. Their daughter, Amy, had arrived and was sitting with her father while Cassandra reluctantly left her husband's bed. This was the first opportunity for Cassandra and Brad to actually converse, but Brad struggled, not knowing how to begin. Cassandra intuitively sensed his reticence and helped him along. "You know, Brad, I called you because you are such an incredible friend to Norton and me. But that's not the only reason I called."

Brad looked at her with question in his eyes. "I'd be hurt if you didn't call but you're going to have to help me out because I don't know what you mean."

Through her exhaustion, Cassandra's eyes managed a beguiling expression of mischievous taunting. She wore thin-rimmed glasses that served to magnify the depth of brown eyes that twinkled at Brad's mystified look. "You're losing your old cop's edge, Brad. I recall the days when you could smell something rotten like this without being told the details at all."

"My so-called friends tell me regularly that I'm losing more than an edge. Most folks tell me I'm blunt as stone these days." Brad laughed softly.

Cassandra returned his laugh. "I'm only kidding you because I need a little fun. This has been an awful experience, Brad, and I'm not sure I'm even thinking clearly. Anything to laugh about feels good right now so I'm trying to tease you a bit. But, I'm not teasing when I say I think something is terribly wrong."

Reaching to touch her hand, Brad spoke. "Hell, yes, it's been an awful experience and you don't owe anyone explanations about your mental state right now. But, what's wrong? Tell me what's on your mind."

Emotion constricted her throat as Cassandra's eyes filled with tears. "I don't know where or how to start. All I've wanted to do is stay close to Norton but I've had to spend some time with the police, try to answer some questions. They're trying to do their job and they can't just sit around and wait until it's a convenient time for me."

Brad nodded that he understood as he searched her face, seeing exhaustion and agony in her eyes. He remained silent, waiting for her to continue.

"But really, Brad, I ended up asking as many questions of them as they had for me." She paused, wiping her eyes with a tissue. "And the really sad part is that I have no answers for them and they certainly have no answers for me."

"Just tell me what you can." Brad leaned closer, grasped both her hands and held them. "When you've had enough, we'll stop talking and you can go back to Norton. There's no rush on anything here except taking care of Norton." Brad looked straight into her eyes and held her hands even more tightly. "And don't forget to take care of yourself also."

Cassandra smiled and returned the pressure on his hands. "No, Brad, I want to talk to you. This is important. I want you to know everything there is to know. I've had to piece things together a bit at a time. Some of what I have learned comes from doctors and some from the police." Her shoulders sagged. "And, after it's all been compiled together and I try to sort things out, I find that all I have is a ton of questions with no answers." She choked on her next words. "There are no answers to my questions and my heart is broken into a thousand pieces." Tears streamed with no attempt to wipe them from her cheeks.

Speaking softly, Brad kept his face close to Cassandra and forced his own tears into retreat. "Okay, let's try this. Tell me first what you know for sure and what the doctors are saying. Let's start with facts, something solid. Then, we can talk about other stuff, all those things you're not sure about. There's bound to be a lot of conjecture at this point."

"Oh, you're absolutely right on that. The only thing that isn't con- jecture is that my husband is up there in that intensive care unit." Cassandra sounded defeated. "Nothing makes any sense at all." She pulled her hands away from Brad and straightened her body. With a sigh, she gathered herself and began speaking. "Okay, here's what I know. Norton was leaving a local high school that doubles as a com- munity center where he coaches league basketball in the summer. He's done this for years, not a penny for it, all volunteer. After dec- ades of coaching at the high school level and turning out some pretty remarkable teams, he says he will never just walk away from this program that was set up to help struggling kids. Everybody loves him, parents, kids, everybody. There are practically fights each sum- mer with parents willing to do anything to get their kids on Norton's team."

Brad smiled. "I can only imagine."

"The games had gone pretty late into the night and, of course, Norton always loved to hang around just to talk with people. Then, after the crowd had left and almost everyone was gone, he helped shut the place down. He called me and said he was leaving and would be home in thirty minutes. The next telephone call I received was from an EMT person in an ambulance telling me that my husband was being rushed to the hospital and that I should get there as fast as possible." Cassandra's voice cracked and she shut her eyes. Her body swayed back and forth as she struggled with her thoughts, searching for her voice. The silence was agonizing. "Thank God Norton's wallet was still in his pocket and they were able to identify him and find his personal contact information. If not for that bit of luck, heaven only knows when I would have learned anything." Tears openly fell and Cassandra made no attempt to wipe them. "Norton would have laid there on the ground all night in an empty schoolyard and, no doubt, died but for a janitor who just happened to come along and find him."

Giving her time, Brad sat in silence, his insides churning and bile in his throat.

Finally, Cassandra reached for a handful of tissues, held them to her face and wiped moisture from her cheeks. "All right, I made it through all that just to get to the medical part." With a deep breath she continued. "Of course, Norton has never regained consciousness so he hasn't been able to help in any way. The doctors are pretty sure he was beaten with some sort of metal object, probably just a plain old pipe. With all the digging, cleaning and sewing they've done all over his body, it's clear that whatever instrument was used, it was pretty heavy. But the injuries are indicative of something smaller than a baseball bat. No splinters or fragments of anything else were found so they're thinking the probable culprit was a metal club or pipe."

Brad blinked hard not wanting to hear what he knew must be coming next.

"The docs are confident that the attack came from behind. From the nature of his injuries, the way things cracked and broke, someone must have come from behind and delivered a blow to Norton's head that probably put him down almost instantly. Then, multiple blows followed, more to the head and others to his upper body. He was beaten ruthlessly, Brad, without mercy." Tears again streamed. Burying her face into her hands, sobs erupted, escalating to convulsions as she rocked her body back and forth. Brad placed his arm around her shoulders, holding tightly, allowing her emotions to gush while he struggled with the horrible images whirling within his own mind.

After seconds, Cassandra recovered and grabbed another wad of tissues to cleanse her face as she spoke again. "His skull is cracked and they aren't sure yet about the extent of head or brain damage. The blows to his upper body broke ribs and bones in his shoulders. There's been some internal bleeding and they're waiting for him to stabilize further before they can accurately determine if he has internal injuries or how serious they might be." Cassandra halted her dialogue and looked at Brad with a faint smile. "And that, my dear old friend, is what I know and those are the medical facts."

"Jesus." Brad slumped back into his chair, placed his hands over his eyes and shook his head in disbelief. They sat in silence, each lost

Dale Lovin

in their own thoughts. When Brad again looked at Cassandra and spoke, his words carried the exasperation and utter bewilderment they both felt. "What are the police saying to you? Does anyone have any sort of explanation for what in the name of heaven is behind this?"

"Not at all, Brad, not at all. It doesn't take Sherlock Holmes to figure out that robbery wasn't the reason because his wallet was left in his pocket, untouched. The police are asking me about enemies Norton may have had, any recent disputes, that kind of stuff. They're even asking if there are recent basketball games that could have angered somebody, you know a controversial loss or something. I've told them that's crazy, everybody liked Norton."

"What about witnesses, anything there?"

Cassandra moved her head from side to side. "No, when Norton left the gym he had to walk a graveled pathway through some trees and bushes to get to the school's parking lot. It was very dark and, except for the janitor, Norton was the last person to leave so there was nobody else around." Cassandra narrowed her eyes as she delivered her next statement. "But that sure makes it look like someone was waiting for him. Someone who knew he was coming. The police say they think his attacker simply hid in the bushes and struck when he walked by. From the way I understand things, I agree with that theory. But that's not what is really important. What I want to know is why. That's the question, why and who? The police are talking with parents and kids from the gym, trying to find something that will shed light on this." Cassandra shook her head, "I can't fault them for doing that, it's simply logical investigation. But that's not where the answer lies, I'm sure of it." Cassandra brought her body forward, leaning close. "Listen to me, Brad, what happened to Norton has nothing to do with kids, parents or a silly summer league basketball game. Believe me, Brad, that's not the place to be looking. I'm positive."

Brad looked hard at Cassandra. She looked back and their eyes locked; an entire conversation took place without a single word being spoken. Understanding what her eyes had said to him, Brad leaned back, contemplating. He spoke slowly, "Did you tell this to the police?"

Cassandra's mouth turned into a slight smile. "Yes, of course I told them. I told them the entire story." She gave a laugh. "They were all so young they don't even remember reading about it in the papers. They were school kids back then, maybe just beginning to dream of being police officers."

"Did they listen to you, pay any attention?"

"Oh, yes, they have been absolutely professional and are more than willing to consider the possibility. But let's be honest about this, Brad. They have the same questions that are undoubtedly going through your head right now. It's been fifteen years, Brad, fifteen years! And, he's still in prison. Why now? Why Norton? I'm the one who prosecuted the case. Norton had nothing at all to do with it."

Brad shrugged his shoulders, "If you're going to go down the road that what happened to Norton is a result of that case, then those are certainly the questions that scream for an answer." He paused, "You have any ideas?"

Cassandra sighed and shook her head in discouragement. "No, I don't suppose I do. I've been too overwhelmed to give it a lot of thought. But you tell me, how can I not at least consider the possibility? The sneak attack: creeping up from behind, no warning, wham, take out the victim and run away. Come on, Brad, you're not going to sit there and tell me you didn't feel something stir when I told you the story? While I sit up there with Norton, just sitting and crying, something keeps nagging at me that this wasn't random." Cassandra looked at Brad, her eyes brimming with tears and questions.

Brad returned her intense gaze. "Yes, I thought of the similarities, sure I did. But, those questions you mentioned, like the fact that it's been fifteen years, why Norton and not you, those are pretty darned relevant. And no logical answer seems to be jumping out."

Cassandra merely shook her head up and down in slow motion. The simple gesture spoke volumes of her bewilderment.

Brad dropped his eyes and was silent for moment. "Cassandra, let me tell you something. Ever since I came to know you, really saw what made you tick, I have been certain that when you came along the world was getting two for the price of one. You are such a beautiful woman. You are a caring mother and wife and just an all-round, wonderful and fun-loving person. But when you flip the switch, oh, my goodness, beware. That legal mind of yours is as sharp as any I've ever known." Brad forced himself to look straight into Cassandra's eyes. "But you need to know that there is something that I've never had courage to mention."

Question filled Cassandra's face as she looked at Brad without speaking.

Brad took a breath to summon courage before he spoke. "Elizabeth is the only person I ever spoke to about this and that was many years ago." Brad looked to the ceiling, taking himself back in time. "I'll never forget the day you delivered your final argument in that case. What a closing! But, let me clue you in on a little secret. I'm quite sure that I was the only person in the courtroom that day whose eyes were not completely fixated on you. You had total command over every eye and every person who was there."

Cassandra smiled ever so slightly.

"Oh, don't worry. I listened to every word you spoke. I didn't miss a syllable. But the entire time you were talking, I was watching that son-of-a-bitch. I watched him sitting there. He knew what was coming. I'm telling you he knew exactly what the verdict was going to be. He knew full well he was going to prison and that you were the person sending him there. He had to sit there on his rotten, smelly, racist ass while an articulate, black woman stood up and peeled away every phony layer that he had used for cover since the day his mother took him off her breast. You stripped him raw-assed naked and put him on display before the entire world. Jesus, did I ever love it! I loved every word you spoke." Brad paused and leaned closer to Cassandra, his eyes speaking just as fervently as his voice. "But I'm telling you, I watched him, Cassandra. I watched him close. His hatred for you virtually radiated while you were delivering that closing argument. I could feel it, see and smell it. I've sat through dozens of trials for all kinds of really bad people but I never felt anything like I felt during those moments with Vincent Perkins."

Cassandra remained silent, her eyes unrelenting, slicing a line straight to Brad.

"When I went home that night, I told Elizabeth there was no way he was not going to seek revenge against you in some way. I was as sure of it as anything I've ever been sure of." Brad stopped speaking but an air of self-doubt and regret lingered in the wake of his words.

Cassandra sat in silence, staring at Brad, her brown eyes were piercing, but not revealing the thoughts behind them. Seconds passed. Squaring her shoulders, she removed her glasses but remained silent, her face clearly indicating that she was waiting to hear more.

Brad shifted nervously within his seat. "I don't know, Cassandra, it just never seemed like the time was right to say anything. The jury returned a guilty verdict, the judge hammered him, threw away the key and you were an overnight star. Both prosecutors and defense attorneys were singing your praises. News articles from all over the country featured you. It was a big case. Race relations in America were in the spotlight. A white jury convicted a white man of a crime against a black man and white supremacist hate groups were thrust into public scrutiny. All the stuff that reporters and talk show hosts love to pontificate about was in one clean little bundle. It was your big day. Who the hell was I to come charging into the midst of your well-earned acclaim and throw water on everything because I didn't like the way a punk racist named Vincent Perkins looked at you in the courtroom?" Brad paused, meeting Cassandra's incisive eyes straight on. "And, if you want to know the truth, Cassandra, I honestly think that at the time you were feeling invincible. I think that even if I had said something, you would have blown me off like a used Kleenex."

Brad shook his head and raised both arms into the air in a gesture of exasperation. "Now, here we are fifteen years later, your husband is fighting for his life, you're thinking the exact thoughts now that I was thinking back then and I've turned a hospital cafeteria into a frigging confessional." He placed his hands over his eyes and his shoulders drooped, "God in Heaven, Cassandra, forgive me if I screwed up. There just never seemed to be an appropriate time or place to bring it up."

Cassandra sat for some time, her eyebrows coaxing thoughts that were seemingly lost somewhere deep within. She sighed and voiced a reply. She spoke softly and with the tone of one who makes an admission after repeated denial. "Take it easy, Brad, there is absolutely no need to be so hard on yourself. You are one hundred percent correct in how I would have responded to your concerns, no matter what you might have said to me."

A smile appeared as her mind drifted to a life she had known; a life fifteen years in her past. "You know, Brad, it was no accident that the Vincent Perkins trial was assigned to me. Everyone knew what a national lightning rod the case would be and the powers in charge made a very calculated decision to have a black woman take the helm. I could have turned it down. I could have given any reason and no one would have forced me to take it on."

Brad gave a subtle nod of acknowledgement.

"But I wanted it, Brad, oh, how I wanted it! I honestly didn't care about the personal publicity. I wanted it for the reasons you just stated; I wanted to be the one to publicly flay him. I wanted to skin him alive and expose him and all like-minded ilk for the despicable cowards they are. I needed that moment in the spotlight. I needed it not only for me, but also for my parents, my family and all the people who had helped to shape me." With a gentle laugh she added, "And, I suppose there was some of that complicated, 'my great grandfather was a slave' social justice stuff that seems to worm its way into so much of our society." She smiled. "No, my friend, you weren't wrong fifteen years ago and no need for a confessional today. I was riding very high in the wake of the Vincent Perkins victory and I probably would not have listened to your concerns at all. That case was the highlight of my career. It defines the very essence of why I knew I wanted to be a lawyer since I was a little girl." Then, with soft eyes and a genuine smile, Cassandra continued, "Besides, Brad, that's how I met you. If Vincent Perkins hadn't come along, Norton and I would not have met you and Elizabeth and a treasured friendship would never have even happened."

Brad returned her smile and shook his head. "Oh, yeah, how many times I've thought of that. It's unbelievable how so many times in my career that tragedy for others led to something wonderful for me. Friendship with Norton and you is the perfect example. After the dust of the trial settled and we began to see you from time to time over dinner or at a movie or something, Elizabeth would always tell me at the end of the evening how much she enjoyed you. And then she would ask me if I was ever going to tell you about my bad feelings. I just always put her off." Brad leaned forward, elbows on his knees, looking at the floor.

With a sigh Cassandra stood. "Well, enough of this. You did nothing wrong and we are today where we are today. It's crazy and a waste of time to sit here and analyze history. I want to go back to

Norton and my daughter and you need to get to your hotel so you can fly out of here in the morning. There is nothing more for you to do right now and I don't want you to miss even a minute of your vacation. We shall stay in touch and see what the police learn. I'll let you know everything I know as soon as I know it."

Brad followed her lead and stood. "Okay, I suppose you're right. I'll call in the morning before I leave, just to touch base, see if anything has changed. I'll be home a full day before I leave for New Mexico and I'll have my phone with me every second."

"Thank you, Brad." Cassandra replaced her glasses and gave Brad an intense look that spoke of simple, understood facts mingled with obvious affection. "When the reality of everything that happened to Norton sunk in, I quickly realized that I really needed you to be here." She paused and smiled. "Norton and I have many wonderful friends who I could have called in a heartbeat. But, Brad, you were with me when this story began fifteen years ago. You were with me back then and I knew for certain that I needed you here, standing right beside me today." A tone of acceptance and resignation came with her next words. "Something has happened here. I can't explain it and I suppose it's just like those feelings you had in the courtroom fifteen years ago. Please hear me, Brad, I have my own feelings talking to me right now. I'm telling you, Brad Walker, our journey with Vincent Perkins is not yet over." She was quiet but her gaze intense.

Brad stood in awkward silence, a dumbfounded look upon his face.

Cassandra's face and eyes spoke more clearly than her voice as she whispered her final thought. "I needed you to come and be with me today and I thank you from the bottom of my heart. But, it's not over, Brad, and I am absolutely sure that I'm going to be needing you again before this is ordeal ends."

There was nothing to say. Brad stood before Cassandra in silence, a barely discernable nod his only acknowledgement.

Cassandra gave her own silent response. She shook her head that she understood and circled her arms about Brad. They held each other tightly before walking away in separate directions, both seeking to conceal their anguish from the other. Brad listened to her footsteps fade. He wanted to turn, go back and run after her, but he kept walking. The distance between them grew but he could still feel her torment. Wiping his shirtsleeve across his eyes, he thought to himself, who the hell ever said tears were silent?

\* \* \* \*

In quiet and darkness, Brad lay in the bed of his airport hotel and re-lived the events of the evening. It was as though he entered a corridor of time, connecting the past with the present. He saw Norton Roberts, his body swathed in gauze. He could still hear the beeping monitors and see the maze of tubes that violated his friend's body. As he envisioned the face of Cassandra Roberts standing over her husband's hospital bed, his mind drifted back in time, taking him inside a courtroom. There she was, fifteen years younger, standing before a jury. As if it were yesterday, he saw her impassioned face, heard her voice. Every word she had spoken and every movement she had made again unfolded and resonated within his consciousness. He saw the shaved head and sneering face of Vincent Perkins. He felt the hatred that had emanated from the man. Brad lay in his bed and everything happened all over again. It was just as clear at this moment as it had been on that morning fifteen years ago.

Like sand from a dust storm, the cacophony of noise from the airport and sprawl of the city seeped through the hotel's sealed windows; Brad could feel the grit. Tomorrow he would fly home. He would pack up and prepare for his long-planned trip to New Mexico. He thought of the old friends he would visit and how he yearned for the gentle embrace of New Mexico. He thought of early mornings on small streams with his fly rod, warm tortillas and cold Moosehead beer each afternoon. He listened to the city's clamor and longed for the soft breath of the Sangre de Cristo Mountains.

Brad thought of Norton Roberts. He thought of Cassandra Roberts. Brad thought of Vincent Perkins. Then, for a long time, Brad thought about words he had failed to speak fifteen years ago. Would things be any different tonight if he had voiced his concerns to Cassandra years ago? Would Norton be lying in a bed, fighting for his life, if somewhere during those fifteen long years, he had simply talked with Cassandra about what he had felt so strongly that day in her courtroom?

The final words that Cassandra had spoken to him in the hospital still rang within his mind. What were these feelings she now felt?

Were they any different from those that had at one time spoken so loudly to him? How could he explain what seemed to be a full circle of premonition? From an electrified courtroom to a dark and lonely schoolyard, a foreboding of evil hung like a shadow over the future.

As the unsettling hand of the past shooed sleep away, Brad recalled a literature class from college. At the time, within the shroud of youth, words of William Faulkner had been mystifying, even sounded silly. Now, years later, the words returned to him in the solitude of a Los Angeles hotel room. They spoke to him with startling clarity: "The past is never dead, it's not even past."

## CHAPTER FIVE
### July 10, 2012

Earl Sampson parked his car up the street from the bank as he had done so many times before. He took his usual spot at the crest of a hill that offered an unobstructed view of the area, including the bank and the street that plummeted down a steep incline to the Willamette River. He turned off his engine and settled in for a wait. Typical of almost all summer mornings in Oregon, the sky was azure and Portland's skyline seemed to sparkle. When an oil tanker appeared on the river it seemed surreal, out of place in such a pristine setting. Its bow slicing the water like a razor, Earl felt as though he looked at a giant bathtub toy.

Earl watched as the ship passed by. Any second now, he thought, any second. Rolling ridges from the ship's wake undulated across the river until they finally cascaded onto the rocky shoreline in a playful slap. "Any second," Earl whispered, "Any second." He held his breath. "Got ya baby!" Earl did not even realize that he was whispering to himself. He watched as the armored truck made its turn at the bottom of the hill and nosed a course up the steeply inclined street, heading straight toward him. The truck's engine growled a protest as it lumbered its steel body and bulletproof windows up the steep street in a tug-of-war between machine and gravity.

Lettering on the truck was now clearly visible. Earl could see that it was the same driver as last week. The truck parked in the same place as it had parked last week and the week before that. The driver killed the engine and gave a careful look in his mirrors; nothing behind him. He opened his door as his passenger simultaneously did the same. The two uniformed men scrutinized their surroundings, looking in all directions before they walked to the rear of the truck. As they approached, the back doors swung open, having been opened from within. A third uniformed man in the back of the truck handed a freight dolly to his colleagues and then proceeded to unload white canvas bags from inside the truck, passing them to his associates who placed them onto the dolly. When finished and the truck's doors were closed and locked, all three men stood together. Firearms strapped to their hips hung in plain view and the empty truck sat like a stolid, impenetrable giant in the morning sun. Again, the men looked up and down the street, evaluating vehicle and pedestrian traffic. Satisfied, two men walked toward the entrance of the bank, pushing the loaded dolly. The third man remained with the truck, his eyes scanning the street.

Earl was ready. He watched as the men hauled their load. At the moment the men reached the bank's entrance, he slid out of his car and swiftly strode across the street. Earl entered the bank within seconds of the uniformed men. His eyes darted, everything was exactly as it was supposed to be. Perfect. Then, in a flash he realized it was not perfect, not at all. The girl, where was she? She wasn't there. Earl scanned the lobby. She was not at her desk, not behind the teller's counter nor in any of the other side offices. Earl watched as the uniformed men, still carting the canvas bags, were met by the bank's manager. Together, they walked in a short parade until they disappeared through a door that led to a secluded area behind the teller's counter. The door slammed shut behind them; opportunity gone.

Earl scanned the entire bank again, still no girl. He stood at the customer service counter, pretending to fill out paperwork. He waited but she did not appear. He looked into her office again and observed that her desk was unattended, its surface clear of papers. There was no indication that she had been there at all. Then, with a last look around, Earl finally smiled as he realized his own foolishness and walked out of the bank. Of course she would be away from work today. He should have expected it. He also knew that she would be back. Everything was fine, just fine.

After returning to his car, Earl sat for a moment reflecting on what he had seen and thinking of how things would be in the very near future. He bowed his head, closed his eyes and whispered a short prayer, "Oh, God of my fathers, be with me. Guide me with your wisdom, carry me with your strength, allow me to do your will." He opened his eyes, looking down the street to the river. The ship was gone. He saw nothing but glassy water, a beautiful river that coursed through the city as glistening jewelry. He watched the armored truck pull away from the bank.

The day would soon come when he would not be alone and things would be very different.

\* \* \* \*

Brad stepped into his house and, dropping his bag onto the floor, headed straight for the deck. He put a finger to his lips and transferred a kiss to Elizabeth's photograph as he crossed the room. Standing outside, his eyes drifted over rocky mesas and brush-covered foothills that lay tucked in beneath the big mountains to the west. It still seemed strange to come home to this place, but yet it also felt so right. He had left his home in the mountains and moved closer to Denver. It was something he had felt compelled to do. Memories of Elizabeth never dimmed, but here in a new place, the memories were fresh and pleasant; in the house where they had lived together, memories were almost haunting. He had never regretted the move. He pulled a Moosehead from the special refrigerator that he kept on his deck for moments like this. He plopped into a chair and punched numbers into his telephone. Fry answered on the second ring. "What the hell you want?"

"As soon as I drink some of this Moosehead I'm holding, I'll tell you what the hell I want but I have priorities here." Brad took a long, exaggerated pull from the bottle leaving Fry in silence. After an appropriate amount of time he exhaled a satisfied breath directly into the phone before he spoke. "I always have to have some Moosehead to make it through a conversation with you. You're borderline illiterate and you have no social grace. In fact, if I weren't such a magnanimous person, I would say you are a certified pain in the old wazoo."

Brad took another pull from his Moosehead.

"That's one of the nicest compliments anyone has ever paid me. I've worked all my life to earn that reputation. Thank you, Brad, thank you. Now, when do you plan to get your bony ass down here so we can hit the trail? Your brothers and their wives are already here. They're actually quite pleasant to be with. Whatever happened to you is sure as hell a mystery."

Brad took another long Moosehead draw before he replied. "I'm packing my gear today and will be on the road tomorrow before noon. Why don't you plan on buying me a big plate of enchiladas to celebrate my arrival and for bringing a touch of class to the scene."

"You got it. All the Mexican food and Moosehead your little tummy can hold. It's on me."

"I'll take it gladly. Hey, Fry, I gotta ask you something. Remember that bank robbery case we worked in Los Angeles about fifteen years ago? The one where we hit the house full of those white supremacists idiots and then it turned out we were in the middle of a murder investigation that LAPD had going?"

"How could I forget that morning? That was as big a collection of shitheads in one place as I've ever seen. Oh, excuse me, Brad, did I say shitheads? I'm so sorry. I meant to say skinheads, skinheads of course. None of those bald-headed clowns were shitheads, now were they?" Fry started laughing and Brad was right with him.

"Well, take a listen to this and tell me what you think." Brad relayed the events of his trip to Los Angeles and his time with Norton and Cassandra Roberts.

Fry was silent for a few moments. "I'm not sure I can follow you with this one, Brad. You're thinking that all you just told me goes back to a nest of vermin with shaved heads that we arrested fifteen years ago? I don't know. This is a horrible thing that's happened out there and I feel sick for Norton and Cassandra. But even though those guys we arrested were mighty bad characters, it seems a stretch to take what happened to Norton all the way back to a case from such a long time ago."

"I don't know either, Fry. But I'm telling you it was a hell of a trip and it about ripped my heart out to see Norton lying there with tubes and wires everywhere. Cassandra won't leave him. If this ordeal goes on for a long time, and I'm pretty sure it will, I'm afraid she's going to practically kill herself. Their daughter is with her now and giving some relief but Cassandra's taking this all on herself and it's mighty hard. I don't know if her suspicions are founded or simply the result of not knowing how else to confront such a tragedy." Brad was quiet as he searched his own thoughts. "I hate like crazy to say this but I had very bad feelings about Vincent Perkins fifteen years ago. I said or did nothing about it and, now, I'm wondering if the chickens have come home to roost."

"Who can blame Cassandra or you for being upset?" Fry was thoughtful in his tone. "I will have to think about this one. I only worked the bank robbery end of that case. I didn't get involved with Vincent Perkins and the murder case like you did. But I sure remember how upset you were at the time, once you got wrapped up in that trial and got an up-close, personal look at that twisted guy and the people who were his associates."

"It was awful, Fry, it really was. That was the only time in my career where I really got down in the trenches in all that white supremacist garbage. Talk about sickos; those guys take the prize. I mean they talked about black people and Jewish people like they're something other than human. Their jokes about concentration camps and lynching people were as sickening as anything I've ever heard. Vincent Perkins was right in the middle of that rotten melon. He lived and breathed that stuff."

"I don't argue that for a second but, come on here, Brad, the guy's been locked up for fifteen years! Does he really have the juice to direct other people to go out and do a hit on Norton Roberts so many years later? And, why the hell wouldn't he go after Cassandra? She's the one who prosecuted him?" After a pause, Fry continued. "As far as that goes, you are the one who arrested him. It was your courtroom testimony that really nailed his ass and sealed his doom. The way I see it, you are a much more likely target for revenge than Norton, for heaven's sake."

"Well, I have to admit that I don't have an answer for you. Vincent Perkins was sentenced to something like one hundred years, so I know he's still locked up. But, I can sure as heck tell you that Cassandra thinks there's some sort of connection. And after thinking about it for a while, I can't say I think she's wrong. Maybe she influenced me, I don't know, it's just one of those feelings."

"Okay, maybe it is some sort of a revenge hit. I hope to heck the investigation shakes it all out." Fry spoke to conclude the conversation, "But for now, why don't you get on down here to the great state of New Mexico and we'll solve these problems the way problems are supposed to be solved - over Mexican food and beer."

"You're on, my friend," Brad said with a laugh. "I'll see you tomorrow."

Brad looked from his deck out over the landscape. He had fallen in love with this place the first time he had seen it. The surrounding mesas rose in walls of rock. They looked just like what he had grown up with in New Mexico. He never looked at the ancient formations that he didn't think of home. Tomorrow, he was off to visit that wonderful place. He was so ready. It was what he had looked forward to every day since last winter. As far as he was concerned, the entire year hinged on this trip.

Brad stood up and stretched. It was time to pack.

* * * *

Pre-dawn light was blue-grey over the mountains. Walter was tired, stiff and pissed off. He took exit 251 off of I-70 and followed signs to El Hacienda, a classic log cabin structure that offered dining and a large parking lot. Walter parked at the far end, away from any other cars. The drive from California had seemed endless and there was no part of his body that didn't hurt. He had stopped for only a few hours of cramped sleep inside his car and his vehicle was littered with remnants of fast food and emptied water bottles. Walter walked around the parking lot for a few minutes, stretching his legs, before leaning into the passenger compartment of his car to clean out the trash. He dumped everything directly into the parking lot and gave the empty water bottles a healthy kick. Feeling satisfied, Walter propped his body against the hood and opened a notebook. After a few seconds he unfolded a map and studied it, crosschecking with his notebook. Feeling confident, he tossed everything into the passenger seat and opened his telephone, pacing the parking lot as he waited for the voice of Earl Sampson. When he heard Earl's sleepy voice, Walter grinned to himself. "I'm just outside Denver, been driving the entire night while you slept in your feather bed and sucked your thumb; so sorry to bother you. Those banking hours are tough aren't

Dale Lovin

they?" Walter laughed into the phone.

Earl did not acknowledge the humor. "I got plenty to do without listening to nonsense from the likes of you. Are you in Colorado?"

"Yeah, I finally made it and I'm planning to get started right away. I'm probably 20 minutes from his house. I think I'll get everything spotted then maybe find a motel and grab a wink. It was a hell of a drive and I'm exhausted. Anyway, I doubt that he will be up this early. My guess is that he's probably like you, early to bed and late to rise." Walter laughed again.

Earl still showed no sense of humor. "As I remember things, you specifically asked for this job, said you wanted the FBI guy up close."

Walter smiled into the phone. "Yep, that's right. I asked for him. I fully intend to do the same to him as I did to that buckwheat out in Los Angeles."

"Well, it sure as heck took a long time before you and Nolan made your move in Los Angeles. I hope you can get it done faster out there in Colorado. You need to get back here. We've got all kinds of business to handle and I need your help."

"I know, I know. I'll handle it fast as I can. From what that ace investigator you hired tells us, the goofy shit is always out running or hiking. Plus he goes to some damned gym a bunch at night. Now, wouldn't that be sweet." Walter laughed. "Can you imagine how much fun it would be to catch Mr. FBI in his pretty little jock? We'll see how all that healthy exercise shit works with a pipe to his fucking face. The only way this could be better is if his name was Goldstein or something. "

Earl finally chuckled. "Just do it and do it good."

"Oh, don't worry. In fact, I plan to use the same pipe I used on that goddamned nigger in Los Angeles. It's still got his blood and hair stuck to it. I ain't never gonna clean it. And, after doing the same to FBI boy, I just may mount the beautiful thing in a frame. That way both of them fuckers can hang up on the wall together. I'll probably pass it on to my own kids some day." Walter and Earl both laughed. Walter continued, "I love that pipe. It's so much more up-close and personal than a gun. When I whacked that coonrod behind the school, I could feel his bones crack. It was just like fucking with no rubber."

"Yeah, I hear you. Plus, if you get pulled over by the cops, there sure isn't anything illegal about a pipe that gives them a reason to mess with you."

"You have that right. When I'm on the road traveling, it's a pipe for me. " Walter changed his tone. "Everything going okay with the bank job and the girl?"

"Yeah, it's like clockwork and gonna be the best one we've ever done. But, with the girl, it will definitely give us the shock factor that we're looking for. After we take her out, alarms will sound and the country is going to realize who we are and see where we're going. I'm looking forward to getting this entire show on the road. When everything hits the press, it will be July 4$^{th}$ on steroids."

Walter rolled his eyes. He hated it when Earl talked this line of crap but he played along. "I know, it's almost time and it will be very interesting to see how all this falls out."

Earl's voice was calm. "That is so true, but one day at a time, my friend, one day at a time. The girl wasn't there yesterday but I'm not worried. Just think about it. We were brain dead to even expect her, but she'll be back. And then, let the Lord's will be done."

Walter thought for a second. "Oh, for Christ's sake, of course she's gone right now. Hell's bells, it'll probably work out perfect. By the time I handle dickhead FBI man, she'll be back to work and we can rock and roll." Walter paused before he began to sing in an artificially deep voice, "*Swing low sweet chariot, coming for to carry me home.*" Even Earl allowed a degree of amusement at Walter's antics. After their bout of laughter, Walter spoke again. "How about the barbeque, everything all set for that?"

"Yeah, we're almost ready. It will be an event to remember, a real turning point for us, and all believers who are with us. Wish you were here, I could use your help."

"Me too, but I'm sure I'll hear all about it."

"I have no doubt you will hear about it. Travel safe and I will be praying for you."

Walter closed his phone and walked toward the restaurant. He shook his head and mumbled to himself. "I probably disturbed his morning prayers. He carries a Bible in one hand and a gun in the other. What a weird fucking duck." Walter was chuckling to himself as he entered the restaurant. *I need a good strong coffee before I meet Mr. Brad Walker.* Minutes later, coffee in hand, Walter got back into his car and sat quietly. He popped the lid from his coffee cup and watched steam swirl up and over the rim. Feeling the hot brew soothe his insides, Walter thought about Brad Walker. He also thought of Earl Sampson and wondered how in the world he and Nolan were going to keep on working with the crazy guy. This couldn't go on too much longer.

## CHAPTER SIX
### July 10, 2012

The morning was bright and pleasantly cool. Brad had grabbed an early morning workout with a run along the creek, followed by push-ups and crunches. Now, he enjoyed a savored ritual of sipping on a mug of coffee while he soaked the potted flowers that he had arranged on his patio garden. It was a much different garden than what he and Elizabeth had enjoyed in the mountains, but it was beautiful and enough to make him happy. He glanced to a sky of indigo blue that held promise of a great day for a drive to New Mexico.

The instant he felt his telephone vibrate, he knew it was Cassandra Roberts. For some inexplicable reason he could just feel her on the other end. He glanced at the caller identification screen and grinned when his clairvoyance was verified. "Good morning to you, Miss Cassandra, how are things?"

Her voice sounded strong and cheerful, "I'm doing better this morning. How about you, Mr. Brad?"

"It's always good to hear from someone out there in the kingdom of Oz, the land of fruits and nuts, otherwise known as the state of California. You are just the person I was hoping to hear from." Encouraged by the sound of Cassandra's voice, Brad spoke in a light-hearted tone, thinking she needed to hear something cheerful come her way.

"Hey, Brad, I imagine you are getting ready to leave and I don't want to mess with your vacation but do you have just a second?"

"Of course, I have lots of seconds. How's Norton this morning?" Brad held his breath waiting for her answer.

"Actually, Brad, Norton seems to be doing better. His vital signs appear to have stabilized and traces of strength are showing up. Since you left, the doctors decided to take him off the meds that were basically paralyzing his body and, so far, so good. He's not awake but he's moving his fingers a little and occasionally opens and closes his mouth like he wants to talk. His brain is not swelling and the doctors say these are very encouraging indicators. So far, they aren't finding evidence of serious internal injuries and I'm trying to believe them and keep a chin-up attitude."

"Oh, my gosh, Cassandra, that's wonderful. Thank you for calling me. Is your daughter still with you?"

"Yes, and what a God-send she has been. I don't know what I would have done without Amy. She gives me emotional support and stays with Norton while I get away for a badly needed break every few hours. But that leads me to why I'm calling you, Brad. Are you ready for some ranting from a hysterical woman?"

"Women are always hysterical. What's new, my dear?"

"I'll ignore that Neanderthal remark simply because I don't have time for idiots like you at this stage of my life." They both laughed. "Okay, Brad, here I go. After you left the hospital, Amy was with Norton so I stepped outside for a walk. I just had to get some fresh air. Darkness was approaching and I walked about two blocks from the hospital to a coffee shop. It felt wonderful just to spend some time seeing other people who weren't a part of the hospital.

While standing in line, I was enjoying my people-watching experience and had a clear view out the window onto the street. Brad, you're going to think I'm crazy but, all of a sudden, I saw this guy standing across the street, directly under a light, and he made my blood run cold. He was just standing on the sidewalk, not doing anything or going anywhere. He just stood there and every so often he glanced toward the coffee shop. Now, Brad, I know I'm an emotional wreck and maybe I'm not thinking clearly, but I would swear it was Vincent Perkins. I saw him standing there. It was his face, his body and that hideous shaved head." Cassandra halted and Brad knew she was waiting for some sort of reaction.

"Good grief, Cassandra, keep talking. I'm listening."

"So help me God, if it wasn't Vincent Perkins it was a clone of the man that sat in the courtroom with me fifteen years ago. But, what is inexplicable and completely crazy is that he hasn't aged one second! He looked just exactly as I remember from the trial. I'm shaking all over just thinking about it, Brad. I can't begin to tell you how terrifying it was to see whoever or whatever I saw." Cassandra was quiet. Brad sensed that she was crying.

"Hey, come on, Cassandra, I'm not thinking for a second you shouldn't be upset. You have every right to be upset. But help me out here. What happened next? Did he follow you? Did you see him again?"

"This part is also what scares me so darned bad. I held my composure and placed my order. Then, you know how you always have to stand to the side while your drink is being prepared? Well, while I stood there he really started to stare. I mean he never took a step and he never took his eyes from the coffee shop. I was watching him through the window and not believing my eyes. The person called out from behind the counter that my drink was ready and, in the two seconds it took me to reach for my coffee, when I looked up again, he was gone. Vanished like a puff of smoke. Brad, I looked in every direction and he had simply disappeared. I have no idea where he could have gone in such a split second."

Brad was quiet for a moment. "Okay, what then? Did you see this guy again?"

"No, I walked back to the hospital straight as an arrow. I was too upset to even turn and look over my shoulder. But, Brad, I could feel him. He was there. I know he was."

Brad could now clearly hear that she was crying. He allowed a few seconds to pass before speaking again, softly and deliberately. "Okay, Cassandra, let's just think about things a second. I don't question what you saw at all and I don't second-guess your feelings one bit. I just want you to be smart about how you proceed from here. Have you mentioned this to anyone else?"

With a deep breath, Cassandra composed herself. "No, I certainly don't want to upset Amy and who else would I tell? The police would

Dale Lovin

be kind enough to listen and then just dismiss me as a distraught woman with an over-active imagination. And, I think you know, that's being polite."

Brad didn't say so aloud but he agreed with her assessment of how police would likely react to the story. He fired his next question. "Is there anyone else to help you out while you work through this mess? You're going to have to go home and get some real rest, in a real bed, sometime soon or else you are going to collapse."

"You're right, I'm smart enough to recognize my own exhaustion." Cassandra sounded conciliatory. "My sister is on her way up from San Diego. With her and Amy both here, I plan to go home for some time in my own house and bedroom."

"That's great. Now, please listen. You can direct the conversation with your daughter and sister any way you choose. You tell them that you simply don't want to be home alone. That's all you have to say. They will understand, no questions asked. Have either your daughter or sister go home with you, take a pill and get some decent sleep. After that, keep your eyes open and see how you feel about this whole thing." Brad hoped that his words did not divulge his own skepticism about what she thought she had seen.

Cassandra posted no objection. "I know you're right and I will do just that. Maybe I was hallucinating. My sister will be here in plenty of time for me to go home tonight. I'll get some rest and call you. Thank you again, Brad. I needed to talk this out and you are the only person who understands what I'm feeling right now."

"You know better than to even think about this, Cassandra. You call anytime. I want updates on Norton and, just as much I want to hear how you are doing. I'll drive to New Mexico today and be in Taos tonight with my brothers and another old Bureau guy. They've all got their wives with them so I'm feeling like a third wheel. I plan to blow out of Taos tomorrow morning for some fishing time by myself before the rest of the guys join up for our big horse adventure. You call anytime. Whenever I'm in cell range, I'll check messages. When we get to camp, all I have to do is climb to the top of a mountain that sits right above our lake and I'll have cell service. I'm not leaving you, I promise."

"Oh, Brad, get going and have a blast. Everything will be fine here. I feel better already just talking with you." Cassandra paused.

"Maybe I should back off that medical marijuana I've been relying on. If I do that, I'm pretty sure there will be no more sightings of Satan until after your trip." Cassandra laughed. Brad wasn't sure how genuine it sounded.

"Okay, you're on." Brad spoke with confidence in his voice. "I'm not going to call you tonight because you will be sleeping, just like you are promising me right now. So, I'm leaving it up to you to call me when you can. Got it, young lady?"

"Got it! Bye for now and have fun. I'll be looking forward to your usual bucket of fishing lies."

Brad pocketed his phone and paced. Was Cassandra suffering from way too much stress and plain old exhaustion or could she actually have spotted someone watching her? He stepped into his house for another mug of coffee and carried it back outside. Cassandra's words and the image of what she had described were haunting. Brad then did as he always liked to do when something really gnawed at him. From his deck, he looked to the west, to the mountains. There they stood, foothills shouldering the big mountains, rock and soil bolting earth to sky. For Brad, mountains were one of the few things in life that he could always rely upon. Mountains were unpredictable as hell in their weather and appearance, even from hour to hour. But their strength and character were always there, reliable as a trusted friend.

He studied the mountains. Whether Cassandra had seen a threat or not, she was experiencing her own kind of hell. He had no doubt that most people would dismiss the coffee shop episode as perfectly understandable but without substance. He thought about what he had seen in the hospital, remembering Cassandra's eyes. He envisioned the face of Vincent Perkins and thought about Cassandra's expression of the sinister feelings that had gripped her after the attack on Norton. Brad shut his eyes and gave a deep sigh. He wasn't sure about anything.

With a last look at the mountains, he turned away to gather his gear. It was time to head for New Mexico.

\* \* \* \*

From a block away, Walter sat in his vehicle and memorized the look of Brad Walker's residence and the surrounding area. Unexpectedly, the garage door of Brad's house opened and a tall, thin man stepped outside.

Walter took his first look at the man he intended to kill. It was a very different feeling to see him in person and not just a photograph. It felt good.

He watched Brad carry bags from inside the house and place them on the ground, at the rear of his SUV. A sinking feeling gripped his insides as he realized that the bags were luggage and that Brad Walker was preparing for a trip. Walter slumped into his seat, moaning out loud, "God in heaven, show me some mercy." Walter beat his fist against the steering wheel. This was just exactly what the hell he did not need, another God-forsaken road trip around the world and back!

He continued to watch as Brad arranged bags on the ground before placing them into the back of his vehicle. But, as he observed, a slow realization of what was happening developed and the sinking feeling he had initially experienced transformed into elation. He was absolutely sure that fishing rods and packs were being loaded into the SUV. His anger evaporated like vapor and a smile began to appear. This could be exactly what he needed. Oh, yeah, he thought, this is too good to be true. He smiled as his understanding solidified and his mind raced at the possibilities. It was now perfectly clear that FBI boy just might be preparing for what would literally be the trip of his lifetime. Walter's body no longer felt stiff and the thought of more driving did not even register. He watched as Brad continued to load gear into his car. Walter leaned back into his seat, placed both hands behind his head and exhaled a sigh of relief. *Come on you skinny fucker, let's go fishing.*

## CHAPTER SEVEN
## NEW MEXICO, 1864

*It was over. Overcome by military might, hunger, despair and worst of all, broken hearts, the Navajo nation surrendered. There was no longer strength or will for continued battle. Dressed in little more than threads, their stomachs empty and bodies weakened by disease, the Navajo placed their future at the feet of the very people who had driven them to their wretched state.*

*The hands of United States Army General James Carleton held the fate of the Navajo people. From his quarters in Santa Fe, New Mexico, Carleton issued orders that the surrendered Navajos be treated with "Christian Kindness" and force-marched from their traditional homelands of Arizona and New Mexico to an area of eastern New Mexico known as Bosque Redondo. For months during the year of 1864, caravans of Navajo people, men and women, young and old, walked eastward. Every day they walked, herded by soldiers on horses, their home fading into distant memory. New Mexico winds swirled, lifting hot dust or freezing snows into a hovering cloud, a drifting beacon by which to track the trail of human sorrow.*

*Each evening at sunset, they turned their faces back to the west. Mount Taylor, one of their four sacred mountains, grew more dis-*

*tant each day until finally it was gone. Their homeland had disappeared. Still they marched, day-by-day, step-by-step, further eastward. The last portions of the relocation were the most difficult. The Navajo now found themselves in alien surroundings. Cactus, mesquite and sunbaked soil tore at their feet. The air they breathed, filled with foul dust, felt as mud in their lungs. Finally, at the end of the torturous march, columns of broken people shuffled their way through the gates of a military complex that had been erected to stand guard over them: Fort Sumner, New Mexico.*

*The march was over.*

*Approximately nine thousand Navajos made the walk to Bosque Redondo. Hundreds died in the trek. The Navajos had their own name for General Carleton's epic vision of relocation and ethnic cleansing. They simply called it "The Long Walk."*

*From the writings of General Carleton: "The exodus of this whole people from the land of their fathers is a touching sight. They have fought us gallantly for years on years; they have defended their mountains and their stupendous canyons with heroism; but at length, they found it was their destiny, too, to give way to the insatiable progress of our race."*

*Manifest Destiny marched on.*

## CHAPTER EIGHT
**July 10, 2012**

Brad drove on C-470 until he intersected Highway 285. Heading southwest, he climbed upward, leaving rocky, sparsely vegetated foothills for ponderosa and spruce forest. After a few miles of twists and curves, the road leveled into a sprawling mountain settlement. He had driven this route countless time on his way to trout streams and the sights were familiar. Old mountain homes with log walls reflected years spent beneath harsh sun or driving snows. As always, when he drove through this area Brad contrasted the fast food restaurants, coffee shops and day spas that now sprouted among the old structures, choking the landscape with bursts of modernity. Brad shook his head and spoke to himself, "I think I like the old stuff better."

Soon after entering the confines of development, Brad left the main highway and, with a couple of quick turns, made his way to a timbered street that was steep and straight. For those who made it to the top, the reward was a panoramic view of fourteen thousand foot Mt. Evans. Poised at the crest of the ridge, as if in command of the valley below, was Fox Cove Inn. The old, Victorian style house had been converted into a bed and breakfast and it stood like a gingerbread daydream, with promise of pampered luxury within its threshold. Brad parked in front and walked the flagstone pathway to the entrance. He felt compelled to stop when only halfway to the entrance, completely taken by the columbine and lupine that lined the walkway in floral brilliance. Vicki's handiwork was everywhere. Brad marveled at the manicured gardens that cast a magical spell for all who walked the path. As he stood in admiration, the inn's front door flew open and a flash of energy burst through with a shout, "Who is this trespassing on my property? Brad Walker, I'll call the police and have you arrested!" Vicki moved toward Brad, her eyes sparkling beneath an effervescent purple hat perched on her head.

"Well, if it ain't the Hat Lady herself," Brad grinned as Vicki threw her arms around him and pecked his cheek. "When you gonna get out here and pull these weeds and do something with this mess?" Brad arched his hand in a sweeping gesture over the garden. "Looks to me like this place is going to hell in a hand basket."

"Zip it, you old goat. You don't know the difference between orchids and thistle stalks. Come on over here and sit by the fountain. Suzanne is inside brewing up a fresh pot of coffee right now. She can't wait to make fun of you so you just as well settle in and take your medicine."

With a shrug of resignation, Brad walked with Vicki to a table beside a small waterfall surrounded by botanical beauty. Vicki and Suzanne had been his friends from long before Elizabeth had passed. Vicki owned and managed the Fox Cove Inn and was never seen in public without a brightly colored hat as accompaniment to the turquoise and silver jewelry she loved so much. Suzanne had walked away from a booming interior design career in Chicago so that she could be close to her children and realize her dream of living in Colorado's mountains. Vicki and Suzanne had been inseparable friends since the day Suzanne had begun to help with decorating the rooms of Fox Cove Inn. With Vicki's crafting of exquisite gardens and Suzanne's uncanny eye for antique furniture with a Rocky Mountain flair, Fox Cove Inn was recognized as one of the most beautiful and gracious bed and breakfast resorts in the state.

Brad had no more than taken his seat before Suzanne walked out and fired her first shot. "Who let you out this morning? I heard you were still in charge of bubble blowing over at the state nut house for the criminally insane." Suzanne carried mugs of coffee and her short hair and slender body gave the look of a model right off the cover of a runner's magazine.

"Suzanne, my dear, have you ever spoken a civil word to me? If you have, it had to be after downing a pitcher of margaritas. I'm not sure even that would soften you up." Brad stood up and gave Suzanne a one-armed hug and kissed her forehead as he accepted the mug of coffee she extended to him. "Thanks for the coffee, but I probably better run a quick check for arsenic before I take a sip."

Suzanne rolled her eyes. "You're so old and mean, a cup of arsenic would only make you feel better."

"Love you too, darling," Brad replied with a wink as he sat down again. Vicki joined him as Suzanne returned inside for cream and sugar. Brad looked around with a questioning gaze. "I thought this was a bed & breakfast. Where the heck are your guests? This place is empty as church on Monday morning." With a wink, he added, "My guess is that Suzanne ran everybody off with her charm?"

Vicki laughed. "Not that it's any of your business, wise guy, but I've closed for two whole weeks to re-do this place, top to bottom. It's prime season for tourists but I don't care. Suzanne and I started planning this long ago and she agreed to take some time to help me. So, last winter I decided to shut the place down for two weeks and 'just git er done,' as they say. We're starting work this very morning and we are going to have ourselves a blast. Suzanne is staying here with me for the entire time and we're going to work all day and then indulge in a buffet of fattening food and fine wine every evening."

Suzanne returned with more coffee, sugar and cream, speaking as she sat down. "How's that for a grand plan? A little work, lots of play and no nonsense from the likes of you to bother us."

Brad shook his head and chuckled. "I'm not sure at all about this. The two of you here, alone, two weeks in this big ole house with a well-stocked wine cellar? This could be one for the books. I sure as heck want to see those redecorated rooms when you finish. Design by Lois and Louise on libations." Brad laughed out loud.

Vicki made a 'you've-got-to-be-kidding-me' face as she spoke. "We could drink that cellar dry and still work circles around you. Two Moosheads and you're finished. I've seen you in action and you are pathetic, an absolute amateur."

A sheepish grin admitted the truth of Vicki's accusation. Brad reached into his pocket and pulled out an envelope. "Okay, ladies, here is the key to my house. I suppose I should be thankful that one of you wild women plan to drop by and water my flowers while I'm gone. Something tells me that I may live to regret this but it's too late to turn back now." Brad ceremoniously tossed the envelope onto the center of the table.

"Whoowee!" Suzanne laughed, "Let the party begin. After we wreck this place we can just move down the road to fresh digs and start all over again. This is going to be a week to remember! Way better than Disneyland."

Brad laughed with them. "Go for it. Give my neighbors something to talk about. That neighborhood is way too boring anyway, nothing but a bunch of stiff old straight and narrows. I hope I read about your escapades in the paper when I return."

They all laughed and continued conversation laced with jokes and insults. After a few minutes of the banter, Brad stood up. "Enough of this nonsense already. I have horses to ride, fish to catch, enchiladas to eat and beer to drink. I darned sure have no more time for your hurtful insults and mockery. I'm outta here."

Vicki and Suzanne walked Brad to his car. He gave both of them a hug and kiss before getting into his car and starting the engine. He spoke through his lowered window. "Oh, my Lord, I can't believe I'm leaving the two of you here all alone, a key to my house and not even a hint of adult supervision. What in the name of heaven is wrong with me?"

"Get over it and get out of here. We're ready to begin the party and you're cramping our style. Beat it." Suzanne's eyes laughed as she spoke and Vicki gestured with her thumb as if to say 'hit the road.'

They all waved as Brad pulled away.

\* \* \* \*

Walter watched Brad drive his SUV back toward the highway and he saw Vicki and Suzanne return to the entrance of Fox Cove Inn. He allowed Brad to drive a short distance before turning his own vehicle to fall in behind his prey. He settled in for what he felt was going to be another long day of driving but he didn't mind. This was what the weeks of planning had been about. Finally, it was all coming together. *Got ya in my sights, you nigger-loving Jew whore. Come on.*

*Let's take us a road trip, just me and you.*
Once Walter was again positioned behind Brad and comfortably cruising southwest on Highway 285, he punched the keypad of his telephone. He had some things to say to Earl that needed to be said and now was the time. Walter always made it a point to speak profanely to Earl simply because it aggravated the man's religious personality and it was fun to mess with the holy-roller guy. But this was one time he didn't have to pretend. Walter's anger was real and Earl needed to get his nose out his Bible and face a dose of reality.

When Earl's voice came onto the telephone, Walter wasted no time in getting straight to the point. "You paid that tinker-toy investigator way too much money. You're getting fucked out behind the hen house but you just keep on smiling."

There was no response and Walter could sense that Earl had no clue as to what had prompted such an outburst. Plus, the silence confirmed that his vulgarity had delivered its intended effect.

Walter continued with his rant. "Investigator my ass! I've done more good since I pulled into Denver this morning than that lizard brain did for us in a whole damned month."

"What are you talking about?" Earl finally responded.

"I'm talking about the boat load of money you paid that bloated little faggot, that wanna be detective, to come out here to Colorado and spend a month snooping around to find out what the hell makes this FBI idiot tick. Next time just call Nancy Drew. At least when it's all over you might get a blowjob outta the deal!"

"Where in the world are you coming from?" Earl's voice was measured, frustration bubbled just beneath the surface. "I thought he gave us very good information. His report was long and detailed."

"Maybe you think so but from what I'm seeing, we paid him a ton of money and all we got was an address of where he lives and a bunch of mumbo jumbo. You know, all that crap about when he goes to the gym or takes a hike to smell fucking flowers and count fluttering little butterflies."

"What exactly is your point?" Earl's response was slicing. An edge of exasperation betrayed how much he disliked Walter's tone.

"My point is, I don't think we got near enough solid information for all the cash we dished out to that porky little turd. Remember how he told us he thought FBI boy might even be a faggot cause he never went near any women. He made a big deal about how he never saw him go to a bar, nightclub or a whorehouse to get his wiener polished."

"Yeah, I remember."

"Well, I just watched Mr. Clean slobbering and pawing away on two bimbos and they were winkin' and blinkin' like the Vegas strip on New Year's Eve. For Christ's sake, my own balls were getting steamy from just watching the tender scene."

"No kidding?" Earl now sounded interested.

"Did you say no kidding? Gimme a break. No kidding my beautiful, shiny ass! Come on, Earl, quit reading the Bible for few minutes and wake up! We told that sorry bastard detective that we wanted to find FBI boy's weak spot. We were clear as hell that we were looking for somebody that we could use to get to that FBI prick, make him hurt. And what did we get for our trouble and money? We got nothing but a bucket of horseshit, fresh, out-of-the-ass horseshit. We got a long report, a bunch of fancy words about what a boring existence the silly fucker lives. No women, no romance, no nightlife, nothing at all to help us out." Walter had to stop and take a breath before continuing his tirade. "Bite my balls, Earl, I've been here half a day and I already got two little twats that I promise you we could use to put his nigger-loving, FBI nuts in a vise." Walter paused. "No wonder LAPD fired that fat little weasel fucker. I'm figuring he came out here to Colorado, sat around in his room, watched porn and spanked his monkey all day. Then he sent us a bill. And it was a damned big bill in case you didn't notice." Walter was shouting into the telephone.

"Calm down and give me a break. He got fired because he talked too much about how much he hated niggers. Why do you think he works with us now?"

"Well, he might like to thump on niggers but that ain't what we hired him for. In thirty days, Earl, thirty fucking days that we paid him big money for, he doesn't come close to finding what we needed most. I guarantee you, I could have found out a whole bunch more, a whole bunch faster and done it with my eyes shut, for Christ's sake." Walter paused again, letting his words soak in. "Not to mention that I could have done it a whole lot cheaper. He took you to the cleaners. He took all of us to the cleaners and my ass is smoking diesel. If you open your eyes, you're gonna be smoking too."

Earl forced a calm voice. "Okay, okay, that's an issue we can deal with later. Whatever happened has already happened. It is what it is. But for right now, we have to slow down and think." Earl was quiet for a moment before he spoke again. "What else have you seen and what's your plan so far?"

"Jesus on a bicycle, you ain't gonna believe this. I get to FBI boy's house early this morning thinking I'll just spot the place and then go crash for a few hours. I've been driving all night and the crack of my ass has practically grown shut. But, I decide to watch his place for just a little while and damn, I hardly get settled down before I see our boy walking to his car with a bunch of suitcases and shit. I about croaked cause I'm thinking he's gonna take a road trip and I'll be following his boon-loving ass to the equator and back. But then, after loading up some regular luggage he goes back inside his house and returns with a ton of fishing gear. I have no idea where he is going but some fishing is definitely in his plans. From all that damned luggage he's toting, it's plain he isn't going for just a day trip. I have no idea how this is gonna shake out, but if I could catch that asshole by himself, out in some remote area, I can handle this job Jack-Sprat quick."

Earl did not immediately respond. Finally, he spoke. "That's fine if you can do it safely and quickly. Just don't take any chances and get jammed up. We have some big stuff coming up and we need you here. We'll make it okay without you for a while but, you really do need to get back here to help handle some of this other business we're looking at. The bank job and the girl are critical. You have to be here for that one."

"Yeah, I know. If I can get even a little bit of luck, I'll wrap this up in a hurry. It just might work out perfect."

Feeling and sounding in control again, Earl continued. "Let's see how this goes for you and we'll play it by ear. If things don't move really fast, then you will simply have to come home to do the bank and then go back out there to finish up."

"I understand. But after we make a couple more hits out there on the coast, this FBI goof might begin to get a little concerned and start paying attention to what's going on around him. Right now, he's completely brain dead. I could bumper lock the moron and he wouldn't notice me. Once we do the bank and the girl and all the other stuff, even this guy might have enough smarts to figure out some-thing's going on. He's bound to get hinky and a simple job will get a whole a lot tougher."

Conviction resounded in Earl's voice. "You are absolutely right and we all have to be careful here. Everything needs to be finished quickly but not at the cost of getting caught. You get jammed up out there and we all get hurt. Be smart and be careful."

"Don't worry, I don't plan to do anything stupid."

A sense of excitement now rang in Earl's voice. "Once people real-ize what's going on, the press will go nuts. That just means this sleep-ing nation of ours will finally begin to wake up and figure out who we are and what we're doing. Once we get big publicity, then big dona-tions will follow and we grow in numbers and in strength. America will rise to join us. That's what this all this is about. Our time is near and our work will pay off."

Walter wanted to laugh out loud but instead gave a short reply, "You're right, Earl."

Earl spoke somberly, "Of course, the FBI and police will also at-tempt to conquer us but we're just going to have to handle whatever they throw at us. God will lead us and give us strength. I feel his pres-ence each day."

Walter shook his head to himself in complete dismay. There was no way he was going to endure another one of Earl's rants about how God was in charge. Short and curt, he ended the conversation. "Got ya. I'll stay in touch and let you know what's happening."

Walter shut off his phone and wondered at the mystery of Earl. The guy was smart as hell and had a way of recruiting all kinds of people to work for the cause. His followers were devout in their con-victions that God directed them to rise up against Jews, blacks and queers in order to save America. And, he somehow managed to con-vince people to donate tons of money. Yet, Walter knew that Earl had only a handful of followers who actually had balls to take action. It was always the same few who stuck out their necks to do the bank jobs and risked prison or their lives for the cause. Walter was con-vinced that Earl needed to handle things more like a business and not so much like a church service. All the constant talk about how God would show the way was wearing mighty thin.

With Brad Walker a comfortable distance ahead, Walter cruised.

He thought about Earl and he thought about Brad Walker. One thing was for absolute fucking certain; God wasn't in charge here. Walter had a score to settle with the FBI asshole and he would handle business with or without God's help.

\* \* \* \*

Landscape drifted and Brad was engulfed in a deluge of memories of Elizabeth and his children as he passed through valleys and mountain ranges that had shaped his family's life: South Park, Buena Vista and the majestic Collegiate Peaks. Then it was due south through the gun barrel, a stretch of arrow-straight highway slicing the San Luis Valley. Farmland seemed to extend forever, bordered on the east by jagged peaks that reached far above timberline. Music of Emmylou Harris, *If I Could Only Win Your Love,* The Eagles, *Desperado* and *Take it Easy*; a hamburger in Antonito, reminiscences of fishing the Conejos River with his brother and his sons. He left Colorado, crossing into New Mexico; Credence Clearwater Revival, *Proud Mary* and *Bad Moon Rising;* through Tres Piedres, piñon forests, rolling hills and regal displays of stone. Patsy Cline, *Faded Love.* Then, a cut across the lonely, sage-covered emptiness of New Mexico Highway 64; the Rio Grande Gorge, a six hundred foot sheer chasm crafted by the Rio Grande River over countless centuries. Finally, New Mexico's evening sky ended the day in a grand finale. The sun smoldered, blood red, across the desert and its glow seeped like mercury over the mountains. Brad entered the town of Taos, the site of ancient pueblo dwellings and the home of Kit Carson, one of the architects and enforcers of "The Long Walk."

\* \* \* \*

Walter drove into Taos. He had made the trip, hour after long hour, in absolute silence.

## CHAPTER NINE
July 10, 2012

Portland, Oregon, basked in late afternoon sun. Earl Sampson held his face toward the sinking fireball, his eyes closed as he moved his body back and forth in an old, wooden rocker that had sat on his front porch for as long as he could remember. Earl savored the fading warmth on his face, felt its glow all the way into his marrow. A sheaf of papers rested in his lap. Typed and handwritten notes were clipped together, maps and photographs were labeled and cataloged. Resting on top of everything was the opened family Bible, its cover frayed and pages yellowed with oil from innumerable caresses of human hands. Earl prayed. He prayed for himself and for those he knew. He prayed for his country. He prayed for what he was about to do.

Earl's time of introspection was shattered by the sound of a pickup truck arriving in his driveway. Seconds later, four more vehicles arrived, pulling on either side of the pickup to park on Earl's neglected yard of dirt and weeds. Men, aged twenty to fifty, got out of the vehicles and milled about, shaking hands and making small talk. Earl stood, taking his Bible and papers into the house before returning to join his visitors. Conversation continued among the men. They spoke of wives, children, automobiles and jobs. Occasional jokes and laughter were tossed about. The men were a mixed lot, some clean-shaven, some with short, goatee-type beards. Neatly trimmed hair was most prevalent but some wore ponytails while others had bandanna wraps about their heads. Some of the younger men wore their heads shaved.

After the time of give-and-take had continued for several minutes, Earl spoke. "Come on in boys, we need to get started." In unison, the men quieted and followed Earl, single file, through the door into Earl's home. Earl's wife, a small brunette with a quick smile and dimpled cheeks greeted each of the men. To some she gave a hug, others a warm handshake and to all a friendly laugh. "There's lemonade, iced tea and cookies in the kitchen if any of you supermen think you can afford the calories." A few of the group accepted her offer, others politely declined. It was understood that no alcohol would be served and that Earl's wife would not be joining in the meeting that was about to begin.

Like a column of ants, the men followed as Earl led the way downstairs into the lower level of his home. They were now hushed. If they spoke, it was only in a soft whisper. Each man was familiar with the surroundings, as they had done this before. In orderly fashion they assumed traditional places, standing to form a semi-circle about a long, wooden table. Earl dimmed the lights to near darkness. On the table, a crest of candles stood in precise order beneath an elevated pedestal that dominated the room; a pedestal that held a three foot, framed photograph of Adolf Hitler. All conversation ceased as sacredness seemed to whisper and the men became subdued. In deliberate execution of hallowed ceremony, Earl solemnly illuminated the candles, one-by-one, pausing between the lighting of each in a display of piety. Ignited wax sputtered, flames spiraled and a sense of sanctity swelled. Finger-like shadows fluttered over the men's faces and the walls seemed to sway in flickering light. The room became deathly silent. Worship service had begun.

Earl reverently stepped away from the table. He moved to take his place before a cloth-draped lectern that stood before the table and altar. He faced his audience and swept his eyes over the gathered men. Each man returned his gaze; expectancy in their faces. Earl raised his arms in a gesture of heavenly embrace to those before him. His voice was just over a whisper. "Thank you for being with me tonight, my brothers. In our time together, we have broken bread, we have laughed and we have cried. But on this night, on this night of everlasting consequence, we have gathered together to seal our bodies and our souls in a unison as never before." Earl's eyes glistened.

No one so much as blinked. Every eye was fixated on Earl.

"If a man fights for land, wealth or power, he is weak, not even a real soldier and he is easily defeated. But if a man stakes his life in a fight for family, heritage, country or choses to fight for God, then that man becomes a terrifying warrior and is invincible." Earl looked at the faces before him. "We, my brothers, are invincible. No cause has ever been more just, more urgent or more favored by God."

A subtle nodding of heads responded.

"The battle we face is noble and it is righteous. To do anything but fight the battle until victory is attained would be to defy our Heavenly Father." Earl paused and looked about the room. "What has happened to our nation? What has happened to our countrymen? Who among us has doubt that the land we love knocks upon the door and seeks entrance into the kingdom of Gomorrah? Can there be any doubt? Is the United States of America still a land of freedom and opportunity or has it become a land of regulations and oppression, governed by homosexuality and deviancy of every contemptible breed?"

Silence.

"Jews, niggers and homosexuals have wormed their way into the fabric of our lives and our government. Jews and niggers gnaw at our bones, sucking marrow to fill their fat stomachs. If you listen to them, they will tell you that the strength of America is because it is a melting pot. They tell you that a melting pot of races, languages, cultures and sexual deviancy is what makes us strong." Earl paused and looked at his audience. "My words to you on this evening are that those who talk in this manner speak in lies, lies, and more lies. What the demons of deceit call their melting pot of strength is actually a cauldron of poison. A cauldron of poison seasoned with Jews, spiced with black, yellow and brown poisons. They stir the cauldron with glee, knowing that millions will drink its putrid juices and then die from the cancer that follows."

Again, heads nodded, attention rapt.

Earl's voice escalated. Each word carried fervency, vehemence.

"This does not have to be. No one forces us to drink the poison. Invading warriors have not conquered us. We have not been forced into submission by some mighty army. If only that were the case! My brothers, what I speak to you about is far more tragic than succumbing to a conqueror. Our people have made a deliberate choice, a choice that stems from the free will granted by our Creator. But what a tragic choice; America has simply chosen to become weak. Our fellow citizens have made a choice to drink the poison of the black, the toxin of the brown, the disease of the yellow. They deliberately choose to wallow in the fungicide of the Jew. Our people do this because they have been brainwashed that the poison is what makes us strong. Like hypnotized rats they drink the poison, then proudly look at each other and say, 'Look at me, I am stronger, I am better.' Like sheep, our nation follows the brown, the black, the Jew and the repugnancy of homosexuality. They simply follow to slaughter with pride that they have forsaken what our forefathers discovered with bravery, explored with bloodshed and built with backbreaking labor. As a nation, we have forsaken all of this, forsaken our very heritage so that we can fall to our pathetic, weakened knees and worship before the altar of the almighty melting pot."

Sweat trickled from Earl's brow. Even in candlelight, his cheeks showed flush.

His voice rose, becoming slightly shrill. "There is no more time, my brothers, my fellow soldiers. Tomorrow will be too late. The time is now, this very evening. We must take our stand to defeat the noxious evil of black, brown, yellow, the Jew and the homosexual." Earl held his voice as his eyes darted across the faces of the men. "Do we swear allegiance to one nation under God? No we do not. No thank you, Mr. black-ass President! No thank you, Jew government of the United States. We reject your offer!"

The men breathed heavily, their hearts pounding.

"The time has come for us to tell the world how we swear our allegiance. Let us tell all men that we swear allegiance to one Aryan nation, one ARYAN nation under God is our allegiance. One ARYAN nation under God is what we demand and that is what we shall fight for. Take heed, Jew government of the United States. We shall fight you until we have no breath. We shall fight you until we have no strength. And, we shall fight until either you have no life or until we, the Aryans, have no life!" Earl stood in silence. When he finally spoke, his voice was once again soft. "Nothing less, my Aryan brothers, nothing less!"

Earl stepped back from the lectern and wiped tears that moistened his cheeks.

The men stood in electrified silence. Eerie flickers of light from candle flames caused shadows to contort on the walls until they were swallowed by gloom of the basement's darkened corners. The photograph of Adolf Hitler surveyed the scene from its elevated throne and, to the gathered men, the image assumed life. Blood rushed through his veins, his breath blew hot and his eyes gleamed, brighter than anything else in the room.

Earl stood without movement, gathering himself. He spoke again, his voice calm. "We have been brothers for a long time now. We have robbed Jew banks and taken their filthy bags of money. Up until now, we have performed our duties without violence. We have never deliberately or intentionally caused another person harm, not even a nigger or a Jew. But that has changed and will continue to change. You know what our brothers Walter and Nolan have done in Los Angeles. Even tonight, they are on yet another mission. We pray for God's protection over our brother Walter who is in the Rocky Mountains. We pray for God's protection over our fellow soldier, Nolan, who tonight remains in Los Angeles as our work there is not yet finished."

Earl held his voice, looking at the men, allowing the gravity of the moment to magnify. "All of us now stand on the brink. Tomorrow night everyone in this room will cross the threshold into a new realm of battle. There is no turning back. It is an eternal decision." He again paused, searching every candle-lit face. "Tomorrow night people will die. You, my brothers, will be the Angels of Death. It will be your hands that cast the shadow across the door of those who must die. Are you prepared? Is your heart right?"

Silence.

"Very soon we will rob yet another Jew bank. A young woman is going to die. Are you prepared? Is your heart right?"

Silence.

"Our battles will not be without risk or pain. The police and FBI will summon all the forces of our nigger and Jew government. Homosexuals will draw up battle plans against us. They will swarm like lice to destroy our cause. They will invade like maggots to suck life from every one of us. I now ask you to listen to your hearts and to look deep into your souls. Are you prepared? Is your heart right?"

Silence.

Earl opened his Bible and lifted his arms in a beckoning manner, "Gather close, my brothers." The men about the table locked arms, tightening their circle and drawing closer to the presence of Hitler. Intensity and strain on their faces was not hidden by the near darkness of the room. Earl spoke, "My brothers, in the black days of the First World War, a unit of the British Infantry faced a terrible battle. Many of those brave men knew that they would not survive. On the eve of their rendezvous with death, those courageous soldiers gathered together and read a scripture. They read a scripture that, centuries earlier, had been written especially for them. My brothers, they read the 91st Psalm. Tonight, I give this same scripture to you. God gave every one of us gathered here this scripture. He gave it long before his Son walked upon the earth." Earl took a deep breath and held his Bible. He lifted the holy book to read from its pages, but as an afterthought, he placed it on the lectern, shut his eyes and proceeded to quote from memory. "God is a refuge and a fortress. He that dwelleth in the secret place of the Most High shall abide under the shadow of the Almighty. I will say of the Lord, He is my refuge and my fortress. In Him I will trust. Surely He shall deliver thee from the snare of the fowler, and from the noisome pestilence. He shall cover thee with his feathers, and under His wings shall thou trust. Thou shalt not be afraid for the terror by night, nor the arrow that flieth by day."

Earl bowed his head in silent prayer. Those gathered about the table bowed their heads, offering their own prayers.

As a summer night settled over Portland, Oregon, prayers rose up to the darkening sky. The prayers found their way past evening's first stars, made their way through the void, reaching the gates of heaven and the presence of God: prayers of abhorrence and abomination, prayers of hate and unspeakable evil.

God heard. God looked. He saw Adolf Hitler smile.

## CHAPTER TEN
### July 10, 2012

The restaurant was crowded but Brad, his brothers, and his old friend Fry were able to snag a patio table. A round of margaritas with chips and salsa was ordered and all seemed right with the world. Tourists and locals alike shared the magic of a Taos evening after the day's heat had evaporated into cool enchantment. Margarita glasses clinked in toast to the long anticipated horse trip and fly-fishing adventure that had finally arrived. As usual, Fry was a never-ending joke machine, howling with laughter as he leveled threats of all that he planned to do around the campfire during the coming week. Fry, Patrick and Brad had worked together in the FBI, while Matthew had been a professor and university president. Love of riding horses into a wilderness area for camping and fishing was their common bond.

Their wives had chosen a different restaurant for the evening meal and the guys welcomed an opportunity to get a male-only jumpstart on the week that lie ahead. Plus, Brad was keenly aware of Elizabeth's absence and he felt more comfortable with just his brothers and his old Bureau friend. That was also why he had decided to leave the next morning for a day of fishing alone while his brothers and Fry joined their wives for a day in Taos, doing what tourists do in Taos.

With another round of margaritas and salsa on order, crude humor settled a bit and conversation turned to catching up on their lives and all that had transpired since their last meeting. Fry asked Brad about his recent trip to Los Angeles and Brad related again the details of the attack on Norton Roberts and the premonition of Cassandra Roberts that the attack on her husband was in some way related to a trial fifteen years in the past. This time, Brad was able to include the part about her suspicion that she was being watched by a person who looked exactly like Vincent Perkins. The men listened attentively, especially Patrick. When Brad had finished the story everyone was silent except for Patrick. He leaned across the table to speak, directing his words specifically to Brad. "Well, brother, I sure as hell don't think you should blow her off in any way. Her sense that after all these years some of those people might seek vengeance in some way is absolutely believable to me. Now, whether or not she actually saw someone watching her, who knows, but I sure as heck think those people are vicious assholes and are capable of lying in wait for a long time. I wouldn't dismiss her feelings. Not for a second."

Everyone at the table knew that Patrick spoke with authority. He had worked in the Pacific Northwest for much of his Bureau career and had been deeply involved in investigations of white supremacist groups. All eyes turned to Patrick. Only a few minutes earlier he had been wiping tears of laughter from his face. Now he was dead serious as he spoke. "I'm telling you, boys, I had a couple of close calls with those guys and they are not the kind of folks to take lightly."

"Oh, yeah, I remember," Fry leaned forward, interest written on his face. "You got into some serious shit with that Robert J. Matthews character. But what the hell happened? I never did know exactly how that case went down."

Patrick shook his head as he spoke. "Serious shit you say? That's an understatement! I'm lucky as hell just to be here." Patrick spoke quietly as he began to tell his story.

"During an armored car robbery down in California, Robert Matthews dropped one of his guns and left it at the scene." Extending his index finger for emphasis, Patrick spoke with a tone of amazement. "Because of that one single mistake, Robert Matthews gave us the break we needed. His gun was recovered and that single piece of evidence led to a boatload of information on Matthews and his gang.

Simply because of recovering that gun, an arrest warrant was issued and the hunt for Matthews and his boys was underway. We chased leads all over the place for a while without any luck until we finally caught a break. We found out that Matthews was scheduled to meet with a bunch of his associates in a motel not far from the Portland airport. We wanted to grab his sorry ass but what we didn't know was the identity of the people who might be meeting with him. We had hopes that other guys with outstanding arrest warrants would also show up."

Patrick paused, re-living in his mind the events of that day as he spoke to the men about the table. "We were all set up and ready when Matthews arrived but we held tight, allowing time to see if we could spot other members of his gang. I was in a room just down the hall from Matthews and we kept the surveillance all night, trying to figure out what he was going to do and how to arrest him without endangering a whole bunch of innocent people. Early the next morning, we saw him step out of his room and start walking away. We decided to be safe and grab him while he was outside. But, he was cagey as the dickens and spotted us as we moved in. In a flash, that guy was off and running like a damned rabbit. We had a hell of a foot race. I was gaining on him and screaming for him to halt. He ran around the corner of a building and, in a heartbeat, he turned and opened fire on my partner and me. My partner took a round in the leg and went down but I managed to crank off a shotgun round in return. We found out later that my shot pretty much shattered his hand but he sure as hell kept running."

The table was silent as Patrick's words and the expression on his face spoke to the harrowing nature of split-second decisions that determined life or death.

"My partner was on the ground so I stopped to check on his condition. He turned out to be okay but that few seconds was all the time needed for good ole Robert Matthews to get out of my sight. The lucky bastard ran up to some innocent guy on the street, showed him his wounded hand and said that he had been injured and needed a ride to a hospital." With a rueful shake of his head, Patrick continued. "So a Good Samaritan, trying to do the right thing, ended up driving the guy right our of our grasp."

In the quiet that had settled over the group and with a look across the table at his brother, Matthew leaned back in his chair and let out a long breath. "You've told me this story before but that certainly doesn't make it any less frightening."

Patrick gave a half smile as he continued. "Somebody was watching out for my partner and me both, no doubt about that."

Brad had never taken his eyes from Patrick during the entire story. The table remained subdued and quiet before he directed a soft-spoken question to his brother. "How long was it after that morning until the big firefight up in Washington?"

"Oh, it was a few days of some pretty wild-assed investigation. We were aware of an associate of Matthews who we were able to jam up on a weapons charge. We put some serious pressure on the shitbird and the guy finally rolled. He told us that Matthews was hiding out off the coast of Washington, in a place on Whidbey Island." Patrick chuckled. "It was like the invasion of Normandy all over again. About half the damned Bureau showed up. After hours and hours of negotiations on bullhorns and telephones, the sorry SOB started shooting at us with all kinds of automatic weapons fire. We went right back at him and pumped enough tear gas into the place to float a ship." Patrick shook his head in amazement as he recalled the incident. "But, that damned guy never stopped shooting at us. He just ran from window to window, blasting the ever-living hell out of anything he could see. Finally, something ignited a fire inside the house and the whole place went up in a billowing mass of flames. I had never seen anything like it." Patrick again shook his head, a look of reminisce and amazement on his face. "Even as the building burned right down on top of him, he never stopped shooting at us. Things didn't get quiet until the building had collapsed."

Once again, a church-like silence hovered over the table as the images and sounds of such an event played through the minds of each of the listening men.

"It took hours for the house to burn completely to the ground and then cool down enough for us to get close and take a look." Patrick was quiet for a moment. "Matthews burned to death in that house while shooting at us. He didn't stop shooting until he was dead."

No one spoke or moved for seconds. Patrick took control of the moment by continuing. He looked straight to Brad as he spoke. "Very few people grasp the lunacy of those people and how quickly their philosophy can turn violent. Public awareness of all those groups seems to come and go like the wind. Every so often some big shooting occurs or some other type of high-profile incident takes place and they get plastered all over the news for a while. Then things settle down and nobody pays attention until the next blow up and it starts all over again. But those crazy bastards are always out there. They never go away, never stop scheming and never stop hallucinating about how they're going to lead the way into some separate, white utopian nation. They're always out there. The crazy bastards are always out there."

"Wow!" Matthew spoke softly.

Fry spoke up. "I don't have any particular expertise in these groups, but I do know that while many of them are no more than simpletons just following the lead of morons, some of those guys are darned smart customers. They have some members with military and business backgrounds who are intelligent and articulate. I've read some of their writings and they can advocate their philosophy quite well and make a case for everything they do. I suppose it's those smart ones who become leaders and attract so many followers to their cause. Not to mention God knows how much money gets donated every year." Fry laughed. "And that's on top of what they get from robbing banks. Those boys may be a whole bunch smarter than what we give them credit for."

Brad decided to lighten the mood a bit. He gave Fry a skeptical look as he licked salt from the rim of his glass and took a sip of margarita. "I don't know that I would call any of those jackasses smart. No doubt, they are several notches above university presidents, but to say they are smart is a considerable stretch. Let's not get carried away here."

Everyone laughed but Matthew. In an air of pompous indignation, Matthew leaned back in his chair and peered over his glasses, scrutinizing the disdainful dregs of humanity with whom he was forced to associate. His eyes shifted from man to man, as if calculating some lurking, unseen danger. Fry, Patrick and Brad held their breath, anticipating the oratorical deluge they knew was fermenting in Matthew's mind. Finally, as if speaking from an ascending balloon, Matthew addressed the table, his voice resonating with an air of condescension. "Rest assured, you vociferous, obstreperous amalgamation of neurological void, you are reptilian to the core, supercilious in demeanor and lacking in jurisprudence of universal matters."

The table was silent. Fry, Patrick and Brad simply looked at each other in a mixture of amusement and bewilderment. Finally, Fry broke the spell. "You know, just last week my wife and I went to one of those foreign restaurants. I'm pretty sure that a whole bunch of that shit you just talked about was on their menu. We didn't eat none of it, though. We had ourselves a burger and fries instead." The table erupted in laughter, with Matthew laughing the hardest.

Brad turned to Patrick with a look of absolute sincerity. "Tell me something, brother, when you were handling that surveillance of Robert Mathews at the motel, would he have been able to get away from you if you hadn't been having relations with a blow-up doll while you were spending the night, on the government's tab, in a room next door to good ole Robert Matthews?" The entire restaurant looked to the table where so much laughter was taking place.

After more margaritas, a dinner of blue corn enchiladas and sopapillas drenched in honey, the men stood to say goodnight. Fry, Patrick and Matthew were staying with their wives in the old, historic inn directly above the restaurant. Brad had arranged separate lodging. They promised to meet Brad, morning after next, at the cabin where he would be staying after his day of solo fishing. They would then drive to the horse corrals to begin their trip.

As the men parted, Patrick indicated to Brad that he wanted a private conversation. Patrick and Brad excused themselves and began to stroll. The brothers wandered aimlessly for a distance, moving away from the restaurant and busy street. As they walked, streetlights became scarce and the night seemed darker. They passed art galleries and Kit Carson's home and museum. Noise from the heart of the town faded and chirping crickets ruled the night. Patrick and Brad stopped walking and looked up to the stars. As they stood, the history of the ancient town seemed to be alive, breathing through twisting walkways and crooked alleys of adobe. They savored the magical moment, neither wanting to break the spell.

Finally, Patrick spoke. "Listen, Brad, this is a vacation and not a time for a bunch of old Bureau nonsense. But I listened to you back there, talking about your friend in Los Angeles. Say what you will, but I know you better than you know yourself, kid brother. You're worried about her and you've got a bad feeling about what's going on out there in California. I wasn't in that hospital room and I didn't look into your friend's face, so I'm not close to it like you. But I don't like it one bit and I share your feelings. Something smells bad. That asshole that you took to court fifteen years ago has plenty of friends that are very likely still around. And, if they aren't around, I can damned well promise you that their cousins or brothers or somebody has taken their place. They're like cockroaches, impossible to exterminate. After you spray them, they just come back stronger and immune to the spray. If they did what your lawyer friend is thinking, after all these years, then I'm telling you, Brad, they aren't finished. There are going to be more problems ahead. If those slimy bastards have surfaced to take vengeance out on whoever they see as responsible for how that court case turned out, you have every right to be concerned for your friend. You might even watch your own backside a bit."

Brad was quiet. He held Patrick in great respect. His brother had done more in his career than most guys could do in ten careers. "I hear you, bro. I'm trying not to be Henny Penny the sky is falling. But damn, this thing is eating on me. You know, this probably sounds crazy but I learned something in all those years working cases. There comes a time when you have to simply ignore individual facts, think broadly and look at what the collective facts tell you. It's sort of like looking past trees to see the forest. That's what I'm feeling right now. I want to be smart enough to look for the big picture." Brad exhaled a sigh. "On the other hand, what the hell can I do?"

Patrick shook his head. "I know, it's a helpless feeling, but for Christ's sake don't ignore it."

"Okay, I hear what you're saying and I appreciate your counsel. For the time being, Cassandra has some family around and her husband's going to be in the hospital for quite awhile. There's some time here for things to settle and get this figured out. I think a few days of camping by a lake and fishing on a stream are exactly what the doctor ordered. After this trip, I'll probably shoot back out to Los Angeles. By then, Cassandra will have her feet on the ground and, with another visit, we can evaluate all this with a clear head."

"Okay, Brad, sounds like a plan. I'm looking forward to this week more than you know. Just understand that I'm in your corner on this one."

Brad placed his hand on Patrick's shoulder. "You've always been in my corner. I couldn't have made it without you."

Patrick and Brad were quiet again. The spirits of Taos drifted about them, their presence undeniable. "Okay, thanks millions." Brad extended his hand to Patrick. "I'm going to walk a bit before turning in. I probably had a little too much margarita so I'm hoping a walk tonight will pay benefits in the headache department tomorrow morning."

Patrick laughed. "We all had too much margarita but that's okay by me. Hell, give me enough margarita and I can speak three languages and read the minds of women!" Patrick gave a wave as he walked away. "See ya in the saddle, John Wayne. Take care."

Darkened streets somehow felt comforting as Brad ambled. This was his first time back in Taos without Elizabeth. He was glad to be here with his brothers and Fry but so many strange emotions tugged. He sauntered in the general direction of the square and the inn where he was staying, realizing just how much his head was still swimming from the margaritas. *Oh, Margarita, you marvelous, wicked woman.*

Brad felt the presence of adobe houses all about him. There was something about adobe that captivated him. To live in a home constructed of simple mud, the very material that constituted all humans, seemed to draw life closer to the soul. When surrounded by adobe, Brad felt a nearness to the very womb of creation. He stood still and allowed these feelings to envelope him. He again looked at the sky. There were so many mysteries in the stars and so much history in these buildings. With a sigh, he resumed his slow walk through the streets of Taos.

Brad stepped from secluded shadows of side streets back into the lights of Paseo Del Pueblo Norte. He crossed over, heading in the direction of the square. His eyes were still adjusting when it happened. It was over in a flash but his heart raced and his head was instantly as clear as a winter morning. Brad froze and felt his blood run cold. He had just seen Vincent Perkins. *What in the name of God?* Brad blinked, looked hard. Whatever or whoever he had seen was gone, but still, he had been there. Vincent Perkins had been there.

It took some effort but Brad forced himself to run things through

Dale Lovin

his mind, deliberately, slowly. Vincent Perkins was in prison. He had been in prison for fifteen years. Brad had helped to send him there. Even if he were somehow to be out of prison, he would now be close to forty years old. Brad swallowed hard. He had just seen Vincent Perkins! He had seen a Vincent Perkins in his twenties, exactly as he had looked in court years ago.

His eyes darting, Brad surveyed the area as he slowly walked toward the big cottonwood tree where he had seen the face. He searched the crowds, nooks and crannies. He peered through shadows. Nothing. How could this be? The man had just been standing there, looking straight at Brad. He had been there one second and then gone the next. Brad walked a lap around the square trying to make sense of what had happened. *Jesus H. I just saw that rotten son-of-a bitch and it was no damned margarita. He was right there in front of me.* His last conversation with Cassandra and her similar experience kept rolling through his mind. He felt his own racing heart and considered what a terrifying experience it must have been for her to face an encounter such as the one that had just happened.

Brad reached the bed and breakfast inn where his room was located. Before entering, he turned and did a complete scan of everything in his field of vision. Nothing. He walked through the lobby and down a hallway to his room. As he stood in front of his doorway, a surge of uncertainty prickled his skin. He struggled to admit his fear but damn, he dreaded entering the dark room. He quickly visualized the floor plan; ground level, single bed, bathroom to the left. It was the ground level back door that was the source of his concern. The inn was old and built around a courtyard of flowers and trees. Brad remembered that he had left his backdoor unlocked and opened because he loved the beauty and fresh air of the grounds. It would be a piece of cake for someone to have entered his room.

Brad stood at his locked front door, cursing himself for being so careless but accepting that it was too late to correct his act of negligence. *Okay, you idiot, you can't stand here all night.* In a flash he had the door unlocked and he entered, stepping quickly to the side so that he would not be silhouetted in the threshold. His hand slid down the wall, searching for the light switch. Brad overreached and missed the wall plate. The room remained black except for opaque light that filtered from the hallway. His hands swept up and down the wall in a frantic search for the light switch. *For God's sake, where's the damned light?* Finally, his fingers brushed over the switch and the room burst into light. A leather couch, Indian pottery lamps and rough pine bed, all in perfect order, sat like a welcoming committee. They seemed to laugh at the fool who had entered their domain with such angst. He eased the door closed and latched the chain. Calming with each second, Brad walked the length of the room, his eyes on the back door; no sign of anything out of place there. He turned to the bathroom door. It was almost completely closed, ajar by less than an inch, darkness on the other side. *I sure don't recall closing that door.* He stood motionless, trying to retrace his last moments in the room before leaving for dinner. It wasn't clear in his mind but he could not imagine why he would have closed the bathroom door. He visualized the bathroom; toilet, sink and mirror on the right, tub and shower to the left. In a single motion, he threw the door open, turned left and this time his reach was perfect, the light was on in an instant. Absolutely nothing. He returned to the back door and made sure that it was now securely locked. Nothing had been disturbed. He was alone in a wonderfully decorated and welcoming room.

Brad slumped onto the couch, not certain if he felt relieved or simply foolish. He placed both hands over his face and thought back to what had happened. He replayed everything, made it move slowly. Nothing changed. He had seen Vincent Perkins. He stood up and began to pace, thinking how he longed for the glow of the margaritas that had vanished in a blink. He stepped into the bathroom and doused cold water over his face and neck. Nothing changed. He had seen Vincent Perkins.

He turned out lights and stretched out on his bed. He wanted to be able to see outside so he left the drapes over his window open. Elm and willow trees were like shadows in the dim, outside light but at least he could see the sky.

What in the world had happened? Could it have been the margaritas? He couldn't make sense of it. Brad thought of Cassandra's similar and inexplicable tale of seeing a man that she could swear was Vincent Perkins. Deep inside, Brad had dismissed her story, attributing the incident to the horrible nightmare she was living. Now, here he was with an almost identical experience and he knew he could not tell a single soul. All he would hear in return would be endless harassment about his inability to enjoy a couple of margaritas without joining the society of little old ladies. He closed his eyes, trying as he did every night to make the memory of Elizabeth's face to be the last thought of each day. This time it simply didn't work. Images of Norton Robert's broken body and Cassandra's tortured face shoved Elizabeth aside. The haunting image of Vincent Perkins, standing beneath a tree, overpowered them all.

## CHAPTER ELEVEN
## TAOS, NEW MEXICO, 1847

*As a result of a treaty between the governments of Mexico and the United States, Mexico ceded the territory of New Mexico to the United States. Santa Fe and Taos were soon staffed with military and government officials to oversee the newly acquired land. Angered by their loss of sovereignty, Pueblo Indians and Mexican citizens rose up in rebellion against the white-skinned men who now governed their lives. In pre-dawn darkness of a freezing January morning, a group of rebels broke into the house of Territorial Governor Charles Bent. The Governor and his wife lived in the house but, on this particular day, they shared the house with other family members, servants and Josepha Carson, the wife of the famous scout and military advisor, Kit Carson. In the initial moments after the invasion, Governor Bent attempted to deal with the attackers while the women frantically attempted to dig an escape tunnel through adobe walls into an adjoining residence. Ultimately, their efforts were futile. Family members and Josepha Carson watched in horrified terror as the rebels stormed into the house and unleashed their fury upon Governor Bent. He was shot with arrows, scalped alive and his body mutilated.*

*A taste of blood and revenge, along with alcohol, whetted the ap-*

*petites of the rebels and their rampage continued. Taos Indians, fighting with Mexican allies, set upon government officials in a torturous and murderous campaign. They traveled beyond Taos, killing gringos and confiscating supplies and animals from anyone with white skin. When word of the atrocities reached military officials in Santa Fe, a responding force was quickly assembled and deployed. Government soldiers soon located the rebels between Santa Fe and Taos and engaged them in battle. The superiorly armed military forces quickly overpowered the Indians and Mexicans, forcing them into retreat. The rebels fled back to the village of Taos and to what they thought was safety in the Taos Pueblo.*

*The Native Americans of Taos Pueblo had inhabited the village for centuries. It stood as a complex of adobe houses that were structured in layers, reaching several stories in height. A series of ladders provided access from level to level, giving those who lived within an ability to move about their village. If enemies appeared, the ladders were retrieved to halt access.*

*In a corner of the pueblo village, a Catholic mission had been constructed. The Native Americans worshiped in the mission while, at the same time, maintaining their traditional beliefs and customs. Twin towers on either side of the mission's entryway doors hoisted crosses high above the ground, making them visible from a distance. Walls six feet thick were the muscle of the church. The rebels congregated within the mission and lit candles that cast a feeble light against freezing shadows. They bored holes through nooks and crannies of the mission from which to fire their weapons and waited for the soldiers to arrive. Surrounded by artifacts and symbols of holiness, men prepared to fight and die.*

*Soldiers encircled the mission. Heavy cannons were wheeled over frozen ground and their barrels positioned. When men and artillery were adequately prepared, command was issued and a barrage of artillery was unleashed. Cannon shells slammed the mission walls in thunderous bombardment and smoke hung like an acrid veil. But the mighty walls held. Withering blasts continued, providing cover for soldiers to advance directly to the mission where they began to pound upon the mud walls with axes. Finally, a small breech was achieved, allowing a limited opening through the thick adobe. Shells with lit fuses were hurled through the opening while other soldiers placed ladders against the walls and ascended with torches to set fire to the roof.*

*A giant cannon was pulled to within yards of where the soldiers had fractured the wall and, once again, deafening explosions shattered the air. Shrapnel-filled balls flew through the mission in a storm of fiery metal slivers. Human bodies were sliced into shreds and the ignited roof collapsed, consuming the doomed rebels within a screaming inferno.*

*Fragrance of piñon smoke had hovered over the Taos Pueblo for centuries. No such fragrance filled the air on this frigid day.*

*In following weeks, Pueblo Indians who had survived the battle, only to be taken captive, were publicly hung in the village of Taos.*

## CHAPTER TWELVE
### July 11, 2012

Deep night fell over Taos. Streets that only hours earlier had brimmed with life now lay quiet. Midnight's lullaby resonated with an orchestra of unseen crickets in harmony with an occasional barking dog. Behind darkened windows people slept, breathing in, breathing out. The New Mexico night sky shimmered. Brad Walker did not rest; sleep was lost somewhere between a Los Angeles hospital and a man with a shaved head standing beneath a cottonwood tree in Taos. The night dragged. He yearned for Elizabeth but she refused to come.

Finally, hints of eastern light brought Taos Mountain into silhouette. Brad watched from his room's window as grey sky became pink and sleepy homes of brown adobe took on a glow of rose-tinted gold. He rolled off his bed still fully dressed, threw on a jacket and walked to the inn's lobby. Thankfully, coffee had been brewed. With fingers wrapped about the mug, he felt warmth creep through his body, softening the tension that had plagued through the night. He stepped outside to the crisp air of a Taos dawn and felt his senses begin to stir. He strolled groggy streets, savoring the flavor of morning. Perfume of last night's piñon smoke occasionally floated. "Only in New Mexico," he whispered as he walked. "God, I love it here."

Brad returned to the cottonwood tree. He stood where he had seen Vincent Perkins; or had it been the ghost of Vincent Perkins? Just exactly what the hell had he seen? Was he really so jumpy that a margarita and a nighttime walk could trigger such a mirage? Last night's episode in some ways seemed a lifetime ago. Was the remedy for his goofiness as easy as a walk on a cool morning with some coffee? The one thing he knew with certainty was that whatever had happened, what he saw or thought he had seen was going to remain his secret. There would be no discussion about any of this with the guys.

His coffee mug empty, Brad returned to his inn. Maybe some breakfast and more coffee would complete his recovery and he could get his mind back to trout steams and his fly rod.

\* \* \* \*

The sun had risen high enough to melt away morning's chill as Brad drove out of town. He cut through Taos Canyon, heading toward Angel Fire. He passed the time in silence, not caring about news headlines of the day and music held no appeal on this particular morning. Instead, he drove lost in thought, relishing mountain air and conjuring images of the stream where he would soon stand. Brad intuitively understood that, whatever disquiet might persist from last evening's episode the river would swirl away with the ease of wind clearing a morning mist. Rivers always made him feel better. They somehow brought peace while delivering strength. When standing in a river, he faced upstream, muscle against water, moving forward to the next boulder or the next riffle. Trout had to do the same. They must swim upstream to survive, holding against the current. Trout live their lives looking forward, never backward. In so many ways, Brad saw fly-fishing as an imitation of life, or at least how life should be. Life should be experienced looking ahead, facing upstream and not reaching back to what has already drifted past. *A whole lot easier said than done!*

With Wheeler Peak and the Moreno Valley in his sights, Brad approached Angel Fire. He spotted the dirt road he needed and made his turn. Three miles of twisting, rough road later and the stream that he sought came into view. Brad parked and got out of his vehicle. Stretching, he gulped deeply, filling his lungs with air sweetened

Dale Lovin

by mountains. He studied the water that would be his companion for the day. It was a small stream. Its crystal water scampered over boulders and meandered lazily through stands of willow brush. He loved small streams. They were so much more intimate than large rivers. Small streams quickly became friends. Two magpies bounced along the ground near the water's edge. For Brad, it was sight and sound like no other. With a longing wish for his sons to be with him, he got ready to fish.

In twenty minutes, Brad was geared up, standing in mid-stream and casting. The fish were exactly what he had anticipated, small cutthroats and brookies, and it was pure magic. He methodically worked the stream. Every boulder, pool, riffle and bend held trout. Each time his fly drifted, his senses went to high alert, anticipating the split-second he would have to react when a silver body flashed and his rod bowed. Entranced in the beauty of his surroundings and feeling the spirit of each fish he caught and released, morning quickly passed into afternoon. It had been perfect. Brad felt twinges of hunger. Thoughts of a sandwich and Moosehead became persistent. After his sleepless night, even the notion of a nap crossed his mind.

As he hiked back to his vehicle, the feelings began. There was nothing specific on which he could put his finger, but a sense of unease began to gnaw at the serenity that he had felt since arriving at the river. He couldn't say if it was a feeling of premonition or simply a result of being bone-assed tired. Whatever it was, something didn't feel right. He reached his SUV and prepared to ditch his boots and waders for jeans and running shoes. He sat on the bumper of his vehicle, felt the air and hesitated. He always changed out of his gear before driving away from the river but today it didn't feel right. At the moment, the thought of stripping out of his clothes brought a sense of vulnerability.

Brad closed the rear hatch of his SUV and walked a circle around the vehicle, keys in hand, ready to leave. He stood by the driver's door, feeling an odd sensation that another person was nearby, that he was being watched. He made another trip around his vehicle, surveying the landscape. Nothing. He grinned to himself and wandered what the hell he expected to see. An entire army could be hidden in the dense forest and he wouldn't be able to see a single person. Brad shook his head, tossed his keys into the air, grabbed them on their way down and spoke out loud, "Brad, you are frigging pathetic and it's way past Moosehead time." He got into his vehicle, started the engine and drove away from his beautiful stream.

It was a twenty-minute drive to the cabin and the rutted dirt road was rough but passable. The cabin belonged to Fry's cousin who owned and managed several properties at nearby Angel Fire Resort. Brad had stayed in the cabin on previous occasions and knew that he would find a refrigerator filled with Moosehead, along with a fully stocked kitchen. As he bounced over the road's washboard ridges, he thought to himself how nice it was to have friends like Fry: friends who had wealthy relatives.

As he approached the cabin, he broke out of the dense forest and entered a small clearing. Brad pulled to the side of the cabin and parked close to the tree line. Rays of afternoon sunlight slanted through the trees and dust stirred by his SUV hung in the air like specks of weightless gold. By the angle of the sun, Brad realized it was later in the day than he had thought. He got out and walked around the cabin, savoring the memory of past trips and experiences that had been enjoyed here. He felt the temperature already dropping and knew that night would descend quickly. There wasn't a bunch of time. He would change clothes and settle on the cabin's porch to soak up the last remnants of day. With a sandwich and Moosehead thrown in, it would be a perfect ending to the day. He stood quietly. No bad feelings, no premonitions, no sense of ghosts, goblins or boogeymen. It was time to enjoy his evening.

**CHAPTER THIRTEEN**
**July 11, 2012**

The aging warehouse was empty and silent except for the group of men who gathered in a small room that had at one time been used as an office. A single window provided a view outside into a crumbling parking lot. On the inside, beneath the window, a rickety, metal desk sat on the floor with a semi-circle of folding chairs arranged within the room. Earl Sampson sat behind the desk and the same group of men who had been inside his house the previous evening occupied the chairs. Final glimmers of Portland's setting sun filtered through the dust-coated window, casting a pallor of grime over the room and its occupants.

Beyond the office, a cavernous warehouse held remnants of what at one time had been thriving industrial activity. Decaying in abandonment, naked light bulbs suspended by skinny strands of wire dangled over an oil-stained concrete floor. Their glow was sallow and dim. A disintegrating Pepsi machine lay overturned on the floor; a discarded oilcan with a smashed spout kept it company. Just outside the office space where the men were gathered, a giant canvas, brand new and spotless, was spread across the floor. The crisp, newness and cleanliness of the canvas were glaringly out of place in the dust and neglect of the remainder of the warehouse. The canvas obviously covered an array of materials and, even though nothing was visible to indicate what was concealed, the men knew exactly what was hidden beneath.

Seated at the desk, Earl Sampson sat in apparent concentration of documents that were spread out before him. An opened Bible lay to his right. The men were quiet, their nervousness hung thick in the air. What little conversation that took place was carried out in whispers or an occasional, inappropriate laugh that was forced from one of the men in an attempt to feign a calmness that did not exist. Mostly the men just sat, elbows on knees, eyes focused on the floor. They rubbed their thumbs over palms that were becoming damp with perspiration, wishing to somehow speed up time.

Earl looked up from whatever had held his attention. With only a glance and no word spoken, Earl nodded toward the window. The man sitting closest to the window rose from his chair and unfurled a homemade drape that had been rolled above the window. The covered window brought a sudden darkness that seemed to startle the men. Light from the naked bulbs hanging throughout the warehouse now seemed even more inadequate than before. The men became absolutely quiet. Some of them stole a quick glance toward the desk where Earl sat but their eyes quickly dropped again to the floor, not really wanting to meet his gaze. Feet began to shuffle. Nervous bodies shifted in their chairs. Someone coughed.

Finally, Earl switched on a lamp that sat on the desk. Intended or not, the effect was to cast the room and the seated men into shadow while Earl's face seemed to radiate. His hair, coal-black and combed straight back, glistened with oil. Weathered cheeks crafted a frame for his slender face and startling blue eyes pierced the darkness, captivating his audience. "Good evening, brothers and fellow soldiers. It is always a blessing to be in your presence. If only our fellow warriors who are in New Mexico, Los Angeles and other cities across America were with us, our brotherhood would be complete." Earl looked to his Bible and shifted it to sit directly beneath his face. He appeared to read the Bible for seconds, not speaking. The ensuing lull only heightened the tension that gripped every man in the room. When Earl again looked up his blue eyes seemed even brighter and he began to speak. "God has given us his commandment. We are here on this night to obey that commandment. Last evening we prepared our hearts; tonight we don armor and prepare our bodies. Tonight, we hear the Lord's trumpet calling us to battle. Tonight, we look into the eyes of our enemy. We must swallow our fear and march into the very mouth of the evil that seeks to destroy us."

Bowing his head, Earl again looked to the Bible. No one moved. His voice softer than before, Earl lifted his Bible and continued. "I am reading of the night that our Lord spent in the Garden of Gethsemane. I have read how he prayed for deliverance from the terrible fate that awaited him. But when God spoke, telling his Son that there was no other way, no escape, Jesus quietly accepted his destiny and began the road to his cross." Earl became silent, his blue eyes now on fire. "How dare any one of us fear what lies ahead. How insignificant are the sacrifices we may make when compared to the sacrifice that was offered that night, two thousand years ago, in the solitude of an olive garden."

Closing the Bible, Earl stood. His face was now above the desk lamp and became lost in shadow. When he spoke, it was as if his words came from a blackened shroud. Earl's pronouncement was brief. "It is time."

The men stood. They shuffled through dim light without conversation, each making his way through the door that opened into the main portion of the warehouse. They gathered about the canvas that lay spread upon the floor, staring at the rectangular shape as if it were a holy shrine. From somewhere in the darkened room, Earl's voice commanded, "Load up, men." In perfectly unified choreography, the men stooped to pick up the canvas. With military-like precision, it was folded and set aside. Each man took what was assigned to him and left the warehouse. Night had fallen. The men drove away, lost in the darkness of their own thoughts.

* * * *

With Moosehead and a sandwich under his belt, Brad stepped from his cabin onto the porch for a last look at the sky before turning in. He left the porch and walked a few paces before lifting his face upward in anticipation of the heavenly marvel that never disappointed. There it was, the Milky Way. Like a bridal veil that obscures but allows beauty to radiate, the mist of light stretched horizon to horizon. When he stood beneath such splendor, Brad always felt overwhelmed with the immensity of what he saw. But the vast sky had another effect; it always left him with a sense of loneliness and made him think of Elizabeth. How many times had Elizabeth and he taken walks beneath a sky such as this? How many times had he slept outside with his children on nights just like this? He longed for those moments, telling stories while waiting for a shooting star to streak across the sky. He dropped his head. Elizabeth was gone and his children were away, one in the Navy and two in college. With another look to the sky, he marveled at the beauty but cursed the loneliness that it spawned.

He turned his body to search other parts of the sky. It was difficult for Brad to admit but other feelings also stirred somewhere deep within at these moments. When standing as he stood now, his eyes to the heavens, he knew that he would never again be able to contemplate a night sky without recalling the night he had crawled from a cave in Colorado after a powerful storm. On that night he had marveled at the beauty of clearing skies, and then, he had made one of the worst mistakes of his life. Defying every instinct within his body, he had walked away from a lonely cabin, unknowingly leaving an abducted woman, bound and staked to the floor. He had walked away that night, only to later return and face the harsh consequence of his blunder. *I suppose that mistake will live with me forever.*

Taking a deep breath, Brad brought his thoughts back to the present. He listened for sounds and heard none. At nine thousand feet, night sounds were rare but the silence resounded like a symphony. He admired the silhouette of a dead aspen tree that stood in front of the cabin. A gust of air moved through the ponderosa pines and blue spruce, the towering giants swayed in a waltz of treetops. *No moon, one hell of a dark night.* Brad felt a chill and turned to go inside. The guys would be here early in the morning and another horse trip would begin. He could hardly wait.

Closing the door behind him and turning off lights as he walked across the floor, Brad stepped into the single bedroom at the backside of the cabin. Still chilled, he threw on a sweatshirt and pulled its hood over his head. As he always did on trips like this, Brad planned to sleep on top of the bed, fully clothed. He reached to turn off the last light, a small lamp that sat beside his bed, but his fingers never made it. With his hand still inches away from the switch, the room slammed into darkness. Initial surprise subsided within a moment as he stood still, giving his eyes a chance to adjust.

He thought about previous visits to the cabin and recalled that loss of electrical power was relatively common. It was not a big deal, just an aggravation. The cabin's breaker system was located within a weatherproof box on an outside, rear wall. Thoughts about just letting it go until morning crossed his mind, but concern for food in the refrigerator made that option unacceptable. Brad accepted that he would have to go outside to re-set the breaker. "Now, what in hell could have caused that damned thing to trip?" Brad muttered to himself as he fumbled in darkness for the bedside table. "Only one lousy little lamp was burning when it died. Makes no sense." He couldn't use his cell phone for illumination as he had left it in his SUV since there was no service at the cabin. He cursed his foolishness. But, he was almost sure that the bedside table held candles and matches. Groping blindly, he finally found the drawer he sought. "Thank heaven," he mumbled as his fingers felt waxy cylinders and the welcome touch of a matchbox.

Holding a lighted candle, Brad left the bedroom, turning into the main room of the cabin. The first thing he saw was his own reflection in the cabin's window. He had to laugh at what he saw. With the hood of his sweatshirt over his head and holding a candle as he walked, he felt as though he observed a monk in solemn procession through a darkened monastery. *I wonder if those poor old monks ever even get themselves a cold Moosehead?* He moved to the kitchen to where he tried other light switches, nothing. The refrigerator sat in stone silence. *This place is deader than Kelsey's nuts. Guess I'm taking a stroll outside.*

As he made his way toward the door, in the glow of his candle, he heard it. Brad had spent much of his life in the mountains. He knew the sound of critters. He also knew the sound of deer or elk. He even knew the sound of a marauding bear. What he had heard was none of these. Hair at the nape of his neck charged.

Brad knew with absolute certainty that he was not alone.

* * * *

Oregon night had descended in full force. Clouds from the Pacific drifted overhead, allowing only an occasional glimpse of stars. The upscale neighborhood was home to spacious houses on substantial acreage and residents who chose to live in this enclave of rural seclusion frowned upon streetlights. It was easy for Earl to pull his black vehicle off the road, almost completely concealed beneath a canopy of low-hanging trees. A passing vehicle would have to aim its headlights directly at Earl to spot him. But Earl was not worried about that. It was almost eleven o'clock and the house that he watched was the only one situated on the long, dark street. The lights within the house had been turned off over an hour ago.

It was almost time.

As Earl sat in night's blackness, he thought of Walter and Nolan and what they had done in Los Angeles. They had spent countless hours waiting and watching for just the right moment to attack the husband of the nigger prosecutor that had sent a good man to prison. He thought of the work that was still being done there by Nolan, keeping an eye on the lawyer and following local news reports, while Walter had moved on to the next task; he would kill the FBI agent who had also been a part of sending that good man to prison. Walter and Nolan were both solid men, maybe the best he had. But they were involved in the movement for reasons that were so different from his. Earl could easily reconcile everything he did in two words: God's will. It was God's will that Earl should lead the revolution to rid America of sub-human creatures of color, Jew swine and homosexuals. It was as simple as that. No reasons existed beyond his devotion to God. Earl was convinced that the men with him tonight shared his dedication to carrying out God's will.

But Walter and Nolan were mysteries. Earl had no doubt they held similar convictions and they shared his views of what needed to be done to restore America to the right path. But, devotion to God or His will had nothing to do with their motivation. They were driven by a fierce, internal hatred. Earl understood their hatred, he even agreed with them. That wasn't his issue. What aggravated him was how they took delight in ridiculing those who felt a love for God. They wanted everyone to know that they were different. They seemed to enjoy making Earl and the other members uncomfortable by their irreverent and vulgar mannerisms.

Yes, Walter and Nolan were two good men. But Earl recognized that controlling them was becoming difficult. Lack of control was bound to become a real problem unless he was smart, really smart. It had taken some time but he had decided upon his strategy; he would make them indispensable members of the cause. He would elevate them to be his right hand men, sharing his knowledge and power with them. There was one other thing he would do. He would simply bribe them. Big paydays were on the horizon and fat wads of cash went a long way with restless, young warriors like Walter and Nolan. He knew these things because he had talked with God about Walter and Nolan. God had told him what to do.

Earl listened to the night and kept his eyes on the black shadow of the house at the end of the street. He thought more about Walter and Nolan. He wished for them to be with the group tonight. Whether he understood them or not, they were reliable. They were fast-thinking and without fear. And Walter and Nolan had another quality, a quality that Earl knew his movement needed; they were ruthless. As long as they understood who was in charge, and he would make sure they did, he could utilize their ruthlessness to his advantage.

For the hundredth time, Earl glanced at his watch. The dial's faint glow told him it was eleven o'clock; the hour had arrived. Earl felt his chest tighten. He thought of Jesus Christ praying in the Garden of Gethsemane: praying for deliverance, a deliverance that would not be granted. There was no choice tonight. No reprieve would be given. This was God's will. Whispering a prayer as he did so, Earl made the telephone call.

One-quarter mile away from Earl, a man quietly raised the door on the back of a rental truck. In only seconds, a wide wooden ramp was slid and locked into place. Golf carts, rolled out of the truck and, like black ghosts, moved in silence through the blackness of the night. Even though he knew they were coming, Earl still did not see or hear the carts approaching from behind. He was aware of their presence only when they seemed to glide over the road, passing only a few feet from where he was parked. As quickly as the phantoms approached, they passed, disappeared, swallowed by the night. Earl waited, now counting seconds that dragged as minutes. Twenty seconds. He could see or hear nothing. Thirty seconds, thirty-five seconds. He heard the first glass break. Forty seconds, the first flame erupted. Time became a blur. Glass shattered, flames exploded and orange tongues catapulted upwards, searing the black sky. Night disappeared. Surreal incandescence revealed golf carts racing back towards Earl, passing in silence.

The inferno was now in full force. Flames appeared as a writhing, orange serpent clawing its way into the sky. Sparks, launched by the thousands, streaked upward into the night, only to become eerily beautiful as they fluttered to the ground.

Earl started his engine. As he turned his car onto the road to drive away, he heard the first scream.

* * * *

Candle in hand, Brad momentarily froze, then quickly extinguished the flame as he realized it made him an easy target for whoever was outside. A quick drop to his knees took his silhouette out of view of the window. His mind raced, calculating what to do. He crawled across the floor to the fireplace and felt in the dark for the heavy poker that he recalled seeing. His fingers wrapped about the cold, sooty rod as he made his way back across the floor to the cabin's door. Crouching beside the door and listening, no sound broke the night. Brad thought again of his previous evening in Taos and the sight of the Vincent Perkins clone standing beneath a tree. He remembered the inexplicable sense of alarm that had gripped him earlier in the day as he finished fishing. Was all of this some sort of providence?

It was time to go through his options. He could sit here all night and take his chances that whoever was outside would go away, or he could go outside and confront the threat. Brad considered the possibility that an errant camper or hiker, someone simply passing by the cabin had been responsible for the noise. *Bullshit.* Sounds of a person had been clear. Someone had been tampering with the breaker box on the back wall. No way was it an inadvertent hiker who lurked outside.

There really was no choice. It wasn't in him to remain hunkered all night long, hiding in wait for another person to make a move or call the next shot. Brad straightened from his crouch and stood by the door, back to the wall. With his heart kicking like a mule and a death grip on the fireplace poker, he opened the door and swung it open. He held his position inside, against the wall, straining to hear. Absolute silence. Seconds passed, still nothing. With a sharp inhale

Dale Lovin

Brad rolled his body through the opened door in a quick step to stand on the porch. Quiet as a mouse. His eyes literally hurt as they struggled to see into the darkness. Nothing had changed; stars by the thousands, tree tops in gentle seesaw. The dead aspen tree, with its white bark, appeared as a skeleton in the night, leafless branches flaring like gnarled fingers.

Brad was satisfied that he was alone on the porch. The noise he had heard came from the back of the cabin. He softly stepped off the porch, his running shoes soundless on dusty, dry soil. He decided to circle the cabin, starting on the side where his SUV was parked. If it felt right, he would have an option of getting into the vehicle and drive about the open area of the cabin, illuminating the grounds with his headlights. He began a slow and steady walk toward the side of the cabin and the tree line, looking to where he knew his SUV was parked. His vehicle was black in color and completely invisible in the night. *Damn, it's dark!* His feet shifted cautiously, sweat gathered on the shaft of the fireplace poker resulting in an even tighter grip. As Brad approached the forest's edge, the blackness seemed to deepen even more. Finally, the outline of his SUV took shape. Once the vehicle came into sight, his decision was made. Getting inside as quickly as possible to gain some protection and access to light was his best bet. Within the security of his SUV, he would be able to illuminate the clearing and woods. Then it would be time to decide what the hell to do next.

Stopping again to listen, Brad could not hear a sound, not even the wind. His stomach tightened as he approached his SUV, realizing that he would be opposite the driver's door. *Great! What a perfect place for someone to hide, just on the other side of the damned car.* As he stepped closer to the SUV, its outline seemed an optical illusion, ink-like fluid, inseparable from the blackness. Another step. The vehicle sat like a nighttime mirage and Brad's instinct began to waver. Should he continue to move slowly or should he rush to the other side of the vehicle, confront his enemy in an aggressive charge? Which method gave him the greatest advantage?

At first, the sound didn't even register, was not audible over the pounding of his heart. But when his brain finally comprehended what his ears were hearing, Brad was stunned; it was the sound of an automobile. *What in the name of God?* It was definitely a car approaching the cabin from the road. He turned toward the sound. Brad would never remember what his eyes had to see in a thousandth of a second; automobile headlights appearing on the road, breaking out of the forest and heading toward the cabin and a split-second reflection of light reflecting off a metal pipe; a pipe that sliced the air, enroute to his skull.

\* \* \* \*

Dim lights still burned within the warehouse. Earl unlocked the door and made his way to the office, followed by a parade of silent men. Each man again took a seat in the array of folding chairs and Earl seated himself behind the desk. No one spoke. Earl switched on the desk lamp leaving the men in shadow. Earl looked through the dark room to his followers. Their eyes remained dilated and a sense of intoxication filled the room. Hearts continued to pound and breathing remained rapid. Earl reached for his Bible, slid it under the lamp and turned pages until he found the passage he sought. The men waited as Earl read to himself. After moments, Earl bowed his head and all present knew that he was praying.

Earl lifted his face to the seated men. "The book of Samuel, chapter 17, tells us a story that we all know from our childhood. Our parents and teachers told us the story to teach us courage, to help us to always do the right thing. It is a story of long, long ago but it is also a story of what just transpired with us on this very night." Earl lifted the Bible but kept his eyes focused on the men in the room. "The army of the Israelites faced their enemy, the Philistines, and the two armies camped on opposite mountains, a valley between them had become the battleground. Twice a day for forty days, a fearsome Philistine giant named Goliath appeared on the line that separated the armies. Twice a day for forty days, Goliath stood before his enemies, clothed head to toe in armor of bronze. Goliath delighted in taunting the Israelites, displaying his awesome strength and mocking their weakness. Goliath challenged them to send their most championed warrior, a warrior with adequate courage to face him in a single battle that would determine the outcome for both nations. But the Israelites had no such champion. The soldiers cowered in terror, who among them could dare stand up to this giant?"

After drifting his eyes over the room and the seated men, Earl looked down to his Bible. "There was a young man whose job was to simply deliver food to his older brothers who were soldiers in the army of the Israelites. The name of this young man was David. As he made his way through the encampment, he listened to conversations of the soldiers. David heard discouraged and frightened men as they sat about their campfires and talked of the fearsome giant called Goliath. He learned of the challenge that had been made to the Israelites and that no soldier had volunteered to face this giant. Now, David was a special sort of young man and he was appalled at the fear of the men around him and that in an entire army, not one soldier had courage to face the challenge."

Shadows obscured men who sat in rapt attention, waiting for Earl's next words. Earl paused and shook his head as if he too felt shame in the fear of the Israelites. "David went to the tent that housed the Israelite King and, before a group of speechless generals, he offered to accept Goliath's challenge. The King looked at David and saw that he was nothing more than a young lad. This mere child was not a soldier. He did not even possess a sword, shield or armor. The King offered David armor to wear but David declined, saying that the Lord God was his armor. And then, this young, brave man, taking only his staff, a sling and some stones he had gathered from a river, walked across the battlefield to face Goliath."

Earl laid his Bible on the desk and leaned forward. His face was now fully illuminated, only inches from the lamp. "Gentlemen, I want you to know that David walked completely alone that day. No other soldier volunteered to accompany him. Imagine how he must have felt as he approached that massive warrior. No trumpets sounded and no throngs cheered as he took his position before Goliath, a colossal behemoth of strength, heavily armed and eager to kill."

The room was deathly quiet as Earl ceased speaking. Naked light bulbs from the empty warehouse cast a pathetic illusion of light into chambers of darkness. Earl's voice rose. "Goliath roared out to the Israelites in contemptuous mockery of their cowardice. How dare they send a mere boy to engage in battle with a warrior such as he. David stood alone, the battlefield became hushed and armies watched in amazement."

Earl looked at his followers. "My brothers, can you picture how this must have appeared? David had to tilt his head. He had to strain as though he wanted to look at the sky in order to simply face the giant before him. And then, the voice of a boy rose up. Yes, my brothers, it was the voice of a boy that carried over fields, over camps, over swords, shields and spears. David looked up to Goliath and this is what he said." Earl lifted his Bible, placed it close to the light and he began to read, "You come to me with a sword, with a spear, and with a javelin. But I come to you in the name of the Lord of hosts, the God of the armies of Israel, whom you have defied. This day the Lord will deliver you into my hand and I will strike you down. I will give the dead bodies of the host of the Philistines this day to the birds of the air and to the wild beasts of the earth; that all the earth may know that there is a God in Israel, and that all this assembly may know that God saves not with sword and spear, for the battle is God's and he will give you into our hand." Earl became quiet. "Men, you must understand that the words of God were delivered that day through the voice of a boy. Remember, my brothers, we never know how God may speak to us. Be vigilant, listen for the words of God."

The warehouse had become a cathedral. The men felt God's presence. They could hear his voice and feel his holy breath stirring in their midst. Earl continued, speaking softly, "And David hurled a single stone from his sling. The stone struck Goliath in the head, killing the giant. His huge body tumbled to the ground like a felled tree. Gentlemen, can you imagine how those armies must have felt? Don't you think they stood in unbelieving shock at what they had just heard and witnessed? As both armies watched in stunned silence, David stepped right up to the dead Goliath, the giant's body still thrashing in the throes of death. Lifting Goliath's sword from the ground, David sliced the tempered weapon across Goliath's throat, severing the head from a mammoth body." Purple veins throbbed across Earl's forehead. "Can you imagine the sight? Blood must have gushed in a spring of red liquid, soaking the earth, spilling onto David's hands and arms. David grasped the lifeless head, its eyes still open in disbelief, and held it high for all to see." The room remained hushed as Earl again leaned over the table and scarcely whispered, "The Philistines fled in fear."

Earl reverently closed the Bible. He looked at the men, his eyes like coals. "My brothers, we are David. We will deliver dead bodies to the birds of the air and to the beasts of the earth. But I caution you that our enemies will not so readily flee. They will be shocked, they will cry out and they will grieve, but they will not flee. The Goliath we face is wounded but he is not dead. The first stone has been cast and found its target. Unfortunately, more stones will have to be thrown before we sever the head and hold it high, for the world to see. Our hearts are right, our minds and bodies are prepared." Earl folded his hands beneath his chin, "Gentlemen, the battle is upon us, let us pray together."

\* \* \* \*

A murmuring voice seemed to float, a distant sound. Words were spoken, but sounded as an echo traveling through a canyon, fading before they could be understood. The single voice became several voices, soft and caring but strange sounding. The voices came closer. Brad felt a touch, a hand on his shoulder, followed by a man's voice. But this time Brad understood the words, "Ah, compadre, you are alive." Other voices spoke again, strange words, voices still soft. He could not open his eyes but he felt people close by, sensed their presence. Brad felt as though he was suspended in a slow motion drift through a dark tunnel. Another touch, this time a hand on his cheek. He opened his eyes.

Nothing seemed real. Brad saw black sky and obscured faces. Everything was blurred, rotating. He blinked his eyes several times and became aware of horrific pain in his head. Another blink, the rotation ceased. Another blink, the sky now had stars and the faces hovering over him took on features. He had no idea where he was or who the people were that gathered over him. A face came closer; the smell of smoke and sweat came with it. "Hey muchacho, somebody doesn't like you so much, maybe your wife? Did she catch you with a little chili pepper?" A soft laugh followed. "I hope it was worth it." Even in the darkness Brad saw the smile, white teeth flashed behind a huge, bushy moustache.

Other faces bent close, strange words again. The veil of confusion gradually lifted as Brad realized some of the voices he heard were speaking Spanish. "My gringo friend, you need help," It was the bushy moustache again. Brad tried to move his head but an explosion of pain commanded that he not move. He managed to slide his tongue between his lips, his mouth burned. *God, I'm thirsty.* As if he heard Brad's thoughts, the moustache turned to one of the other faces, "Agua, agua!" Brad heard rustling sounds and could have sworn he heard a horse neigh. Somewhere, a few feet away, more conversation in Spanish was carried out before the moustache again came close. "Agua, mi amigo, agua." Brad felt a strong hand gently work fingers underneath his head, then a slight elevation as Moustache tilted Brad's head to a clay pot that dripped water. The pain was horrendous but water trickling over his lips and into his mouth was heavenly. After Brad had swallowed, Moustache gently helped to lower his head, positioning it on some sort of soft cushion that did wonders to relieve the agony.

Brad was still, his breath coming in short gasps. Moustache came close, whispering, "Mi amigo, I can not leave you here. You must have help." A slight eye movement was Brad's only response. He intuitively knew he could not speak. Moustache continued, his voice strong but compassionate. "We shall take you to Manuel's house. His sister, Juanita, she will care for you. Juanita knows much, she will care for you."

Brad made no effort to respond. Moustache stood up and spoke in Spanish to his companions. Within seconds, Brad was positive that horses were present. The smell of dust, sweat and manure that comes only with horses was unmistakable.

Moustache was over him again. "Now, mi amigo, now is the hard part. You will not like this but there is no choice." Moustache spoke in Spanish, his tone commanding. Brad saw other men kneel beside him and felt arms slide beneath his body. Pain augured through his head and bursts of white light exploded within his eyes. He felt his body being lifted from the ground until he stood upright, completely supported by the men around him. He could see and smell the horse, a massive rump pressed against him. Again he was lifted, again the pain. He felt his body astride the horse, behind a man seated in the saddle. Someone wrapped a rope about Brad's body, cinching it tightly to secure him to the saddled rider. Reality of what was happening began to register. More words in Spanish and Brad heard the clopping of hoofs. He felt the horse sway beneath him. A journey was underway.

Moments of pain with interludes of numbness and even some sleep followed. How far they traveled or to where, Brad had no idea.

Dale Lovin

After time, he became aware that the horse's movement had stopped. He opened his eyes and, finally, he saw something besides darkness. The light was dim, but at least it was light; it illuminated at least five horses, all with riders. The light had movement, causing shadows to dance about the restless horses. Brad realized that it came from flames that burned in a fireplace from within a small, log cabin structure that was little more than a hut.

A wooden door was opened wide. Moustache stood outside while a woman remained inside as Moustache spoke to her in Spanish. They conducted their conversation in gentle tones that Brad could scarcely hear. Moustache returned to the horsemen and issued in Spanish what were obviously commands. All riders except for the one on Brad's horse dismounted. Once again the men surrounded Brad and, with a few tugs, the rope about his body was removed. Arms and hands eased him from the horse and mercifully the pain was not nearly as intense as when he had been mounted onto the animal. He remained upright but was carried toward the doorway. The opening was way too small for even a man of average height. The men struggled to get Brad past the threshold into a single room structure where Brad saw a crude, solitary bed on a dirt floor. In only a few steps, the men carried Brad across the room and eased him down onto a mattress. Brad was feeling pain again and the softness of the bed wrapped about him with blessed relief.

With a clomping of boots and soft mumbling, every man left the room except for Moustache who stood nearby and whispered to the woman. When they had finished speaking, he walked to the bed and, as he came close, Brad saw brown skin with black hair falling over the man's ears. A leather thong held a sombrero over his shoulders, his clothing was worn and dust-covered. Moustache knelt beside the bed and placed his hand upon Brad's shoulder. For a long moment he was quiet, looking at Brad, seeming to study every detail of his face. When he spoke it was with a tone of solemnity "In this place, I leave you in good hands, mi amigo. Juanita will make you well. She is a good woman. Do as she says and let her care for you." Moustache remained close, his eyes never ceased their searching and his hand maintained pressure on Brad's shoulder.

Brad managed to turn his face toward Moustache. He wanted to say a simple thanks to this kind man but not even a whisper would come from his lips. No matter how hard he tried, Brad could not speak.

Just as Brad had witnessed earlier, when Moustache first spoke to him, the smile appeared. His teeth glistened in the firelight and a smell of pure humanness wafted from his body. Brad felt the grip on his shoulder tighten as Moustache spoke softly, "Dios me ha mandado a ti (*God has sent me to you*)." His smile faded and he spoke with an urgency that had not been present in previous words. "Tienes mucho que hacer (*You have much to do*)." Moustache paused and repeated, "Tienes mucho que hacer (*You have much to do*)."

Brad could only look at Moustache. Not understanding the words being spoken, he had no idea how to interpret the surreal scene unfolding before him. The woman stood behind Moustache, watching. She remained silent.

Moustache gave a final smile. "Vaya con Diós, mi amigo. Vaya con Diós." Moustache stood and, with a nod toward Juanita, walked across the floor, stepped outside and closed the door.

# CHAPTER FOURTEEN
## PORTLAND, OREGON

*Excerpts from the Sunday edition of The Oregonian, April 28, 1985, which offered brief descriptions of extremist right-wing groups with membership in Oregon and the Northwest.*

*"The Order: Also known as Bruder Schweigen (Silent Brotherhood), The White American Bastion, the Underground, The Aryan Resistance Movement and The White American Revolutionary Army, it is a violent offshoot of the Aryan Nations, which has given at least verbal support. Twenty-three of its members have been indicted by a Seattle federal grand jury on racketeering charges that include two murders, several attempted murders, two armored car holdups, counterfeiting, various arsons and weapons violations. One of the suspects, David C. Tate, 22, of Athol, Idaho is accused of murdering one Missouri highway trooper and wounding another April 15 in southern Missouri. The Order was co-founded in the early 1980s by Robert J. Matthews, who was killed in a December firefight with FBI agents on Whidbey Island, Wash. Documents from the group show it has declared war on the United States government.*

*Aryan Nations: Headquartered on a 20-acre tract of forested land near Hayden Lake in northern Idaho, the group's formal name is Church of Jesus Christ Christian Aryan Nations. Its compound includes a church, guard towers, printing presses and a firing range. It is headed by Rev. Richard A. Butler. Founded in the 1940s, it was established in Idaho in 1973. It is anti-Jew, anti-Catholic, anti-black, anti-Hispanic, anti-homosexual, anti-Communist. Members are trained and urged to commit acts of violence, and some have been convicted of carrying illegal weapons. It has a national white supremacist computer bulletin board. ......"*

## Excerpts from The Oregonian, Tuesday, November 19, 1985

*"SEATTLE – In many ways, The Order sounded almost like a secret club for pre-teen boys.*

*Members had secret names and passwords. They met in a clubhouse they built for themselves on the property of the group's founder, Robert Jay Matthews.*

*Some – those who came from the Aryan Nations compound near*

*Hayden Lake, Idaho – wore "pretend" military uniforms that were modified from clothes bought off-the-rack at J.C. Penney.*

*They made up oaths and designed medallions to be worn only by other members. They declared that their fellow members were life-long friends.*

*It was there that the innocence stopped.*

*According to the government, The Order established hit lists of persons it considered enemies of the white race, and established a separate cell to carry out gruesome assassinations.*

*It used submachine guns, grenades and mock bazookas to pull off a string of armed robberies that netted the group more than $4 million, much of which was donated to other racist and anti-Semitic groups.*

*And it publicly declared war against the U.S. government and drafted an open letter to Congress, vowing to murder members of that body by hanging them by the neck until dead...."*

## CHAPTER FIFTEEN
### July 11 – July 12, 2012

After his jolting horse journey, a soft bed and warmth from the fireplace beckoned sleep like a siren. Brad tried to gauge his surroundings through a haze of pain and exhaustion. More like a vision than observation, he registered a tiny room with a ceiling so low he knew he would be unable to stand. Tiny windows of a translucent material revealed darkness of the outside night. A fireplace constructed of stone and mud, with cooking utensils arranged on either side, was on the wall opposite his bed. He felt in another world, another time. The woman lit a lantern and placed it on a table near his bed. He watched as she heated water over the fireplace and dipped a cloth into the water. The last thing he remembered was the feel of the woman's hand placing a warm cloth over his eyes.

\* \* \* \*

Brad awakened having no sense for how long he had slept. Seconds passed, as he lay motionless with his eyes still closed. He tried to think and sort out the muddle within his head. Gradually, memory of the previous hours seeped into his consciousness. He remembered lying on the ground, men bending over, talking to him. He summoned recollections of being strapped upon a horse, indescribable pain and riding through a night darker than anything he had ever before experienced.

He breathed deeply, inhaling a mysterious mixture of smoke and the fragrance of baking bread. Whatever it was, the aroma was absolutely heavenly. Brad remembered Moustache. He thought of the woman named Juanita and how gentle her touch had been as she placed a warm cloth on his brow. With this in his mind, he made a cautious, uncertain movement. Lifting his hand to his face he felt that the cloth was gone. He heard voices. They were muffled, definitely coming from somewhere outside. He strained to hear the words but could only determine that what he heard came from a man and a woman. Not knowing what to expect, Brad opened his eyes, blinked, and surveyed his surroundings. The room was just as he remembered except that light now poured through the windows. It was daytime.

He glanced about and saw that he was alone. The ceiling he had seen the night before was made of mud and timbers and was every bit as low to the floor as he remembered. Along the wall, next to the fireplace was a wooden table. Clay pots of various sizes sat on the table. He saw that there was no sink, no source for running water, no electricity or no bathroom. Brad knew that rural New Mexico held pockets of extreme poverty but there were also settlements of people who simply chose to live a frontier lifestyle. He was obviously in one of the two. He heard the voices again, a man and woman speaking Spanish.

*Where in heaven am I and what the hell am I doing here?* Pain began to throb within his head and his throat suddenly felt parched. Thirst took control of his thoughts and his mouth felt as though it was filled with sand.

The door opened and Juanita stood in the threshold, holding an armful of logs and sticks. When she saw that Brad was awake and looking at her, she quickly dumped the wood outside the door and entered the room. Through the opened door, Brad had an unobstructed view of the outside. He saw a day that was bright and clear with blue sky above and a green forest encircling the cabin. Juanita walked toward him. She wore a dress made of a simple brown material that reached to the floor. Coal black hair was tied into a ponytail that draped over her shoulder. She seemed uncertain and shy as she stopped a few feet from his bed. "Buenos dias." Her voice was soft. "How are you feeling?" She spoke with an accent that Brad knew well from his days of growing up in New Mexico. She preferred to speak in Spanish but would humor him and converse in English.

Brad opened his mouth to respond but no words would come. He moved his lips but nothing happened, he had no voice. Panic burned within his chest. Why could he not speak? Juanita's eyes radiated caution and she immediately placed a finger over her lips and shook her head from side to side. "Do not try to talk. You must rest in quiet." She stepped closer and scrutinized his face. After a moment of her eyes taking in every detail and with no other communication, she spoke. "You are thirsty, let me bring you water." He watched her walk to the table where she poured water from a clay pot into a smaller cup. When she returned, she sat on the side of the bed and, with one hand helped him raise his head to accept the cup she lifted to his lips. He had never tasted water so cold, so pure or so utterly wonderful. The water touched his throat and a sense of cool intoxication flowed through his body. Within seconds, the pain in his head vanished, simply melted away.

After he finished drinking, Juanita lowered his head back onto a pillow as she spoke. "I met you last night but I will give you my name again since you may have no memory. My name is Juanita, do you remember me?"

A nod of his head and expression in his eyes answered her question.

"I am told you found big trouble last night." She smiled. "You are the lucky one to see the sun in the sky another day." She reached for the cloth that lay beside Brad's head. "You must keep this over your eyes, injured one, it is very important." She walked to the fireplace and doused the cloth in heated water. She again seated herself on the edge of the bed and leaned over his face to place the cloth. As she came close, their eyes met, only inches apart. It happened so fast Brad could scarcely comprehend. With an abrupt jolt, Juanita jerked her body away. Her eyes opened wide, startled, and she stared at Brad's face as if she only now saw him for the first time. She sat, seemingly frozen, never taking her eyes from his face.

Brad could not interpret what he saw and he had no idea what had happened. He was afraid to move. What had she seen? He held his eyes on Juanita, completely mystified, unable to fathom what was wrong or what had triggered such a reaction. Their gaze held and Brad saw her swallow hard. Juanita held her body perfectly still, her expression seemed desperate, almost wild as her eyes locked onto his.

The moment was broken when, from outside the door, a man's voice called out. Juanita seemed startled at the sound and her eyes finally diverted from Brad's. The voice called out again, speaking in Spanish and calling Juanita's name. Her face relaxed and composure returned as she again smiled. "That is my brother, Manuel. He needs me. I must go. Here now, keep this over your eyes and sleep again." She placed the warm cloth over his eyes. "I have made bread for you. You must eat soon but for now, rest. I will visit you when it is time."

Juanita was gone, the door closed and Brad was alone again. What the hell had just happened? Furtive feelings stirred within. What had Juanita seen? She had not appeared frightened but what was that expression? What had she felt? He tried to stay calm. He wanted to think about what had just happened. Why could he not speak? Where was he and why was he here? There were so many questions in his head, so much to sort out. But sleep came quickly. His sleep was deep and carried him away, taking him into another world where dreams became life. Brad saw his children, heard them laughing and the sound of their small feet scurrying as they played hide-and-seek. Elizabeth came to him: her smile, her eyes and her touch. They stood together and watched their children play. She tossed back her head and her laugh, that beautiful laugh, wrapped about him like a blanket. Brad dreamed of rivers. He listened to their sounds and felt the strength of their crystal currents flowing past, enroute to infinity. He dreamed of sunlight on water, his fly rod and the magic of trout rising. He saw white, billowing clouds rolling across a tapestry of blue; he saw black clouds, boiling with anger and hurling fingers of fire. He heard wind as it talked with trees, sweeping through their branches, causing them to sway in a ballet. Brad saw a man in the trees; a man with a shaved head, holding a pipe in his hands. The man smiled at Brad.

* * * *

A voice called but it was too far away, too faint. Try as he might,

Brad could not make out the words. The voice came closer and a hand touched his forehead. The voice, now close to his ear, brushed sleep away and ushered him into a surreal sense of being awake but still within a dream. He felt the cloth being lifted from his face and he opened his eyes to see Juanita sitting beside him. He looked about and realized that it was once again dark. Night had fallen. Could he really have slept all day? The lantern was lit and sitting close to his bed. He heard the fireplace crackle and smelled the same wonderful aroma of smoke and bread that had so enticed him earlier in the day.

"I told you to sleep, but not like a bear in winter." Juanita smiled, her hand still on his forehead. Brad moved his head lightly and tried to smile. "It is time that you eat. You must have food for strength." She looked toward the fireplace, "I have made bread for you." Juanita placed a larger cushion under Brad's head before she rose and went to the table. Brad watched as she worked and returned with a plate holding bread and a bowl. She sat beside him again, and with a smile, dipped bread into the bowl, soaking it in broth. She brought it to his lips. "Come now, fierce one, eat, make yourself strong for the next time you let some fool try to take your head off." Juanita laughed. It was the laugh that did it. What a beautiful sound. That's when Brad recognized her incredible beauty. How had he not noticed sooner? It was in her eyes, her smile and the flesh of her cheeks. He could not take his gaze from her. The beauty was not only in her face; he could feel it radiating from her heart.

Brad accepted the bread. It felt soft on his tongue and a bitter, earthy flavor burst in his mouth. He winced and his eyes widened.

Now, Juanita really laughed. Her head came back, her ponytail in a swish and her teeth sparkled against brown skin. "Poor bambino. I have no sugar to give you so you must suffer." Her entire face smiled as she looked at him while placing more food into his mouth. Fire-light from across the room danced in her dark eyes.

Brad was mesmerized, intimidated by the closeness of her body. He wanted to talk to her. He desperately wanted to ask what she had seen earlier that caused such a reaction, what had stunned her so. He could do nothing but move his lips. No sound would come.

Juanita continued to dip bread into the broth and lift it to his mouth but she spoke no more. Juanita simply looked at Brad and he at her. The intensity of the moment filled the room and was not lost on either of them. She sat the food aside and then extinguished the lantern. The only light came from the fireplace, causing her skin to appear as soft bronze. Brad had never seen such beauty. Juanita placed her hand on Brad's cheek and stroked him softly, looking directly into his eyes. Brad felt his heart thundering. He had not been touched in this manner since Elizabeth. She brought her face close, "Nuestro tiempo ya casi ha llegado (*Our time is almost here*). Hemos esperado tanto tiempo (*We have waited so long*). Sé paciente, mi amor, sé paciente (*Be patient, my love, be patient*)." She came closer, her lips brushed his forehead. "Sleep, my love, sleep." Juanita walked away.

Brad lay in near darkness, his mind spinning. *God, please help me. Where am I? Why can't I speak? Who is this woman? What did she say to me? What is happening?*

Within seconds, Brad was asleep.

# CHAPTER SIXTEEN
# PORTLAND, OREGON


**Excerpts as recorded in *The Oregonian*,
Wednesday, April 10, 1985**


*"One of two Portland homes raided by the FBI Saturday morn-
ing reportedly was being used as a meeting place by members of a
radical right-wing group planning either to murder judges or burn
their homes, according to information contained in an FBI affidavit.*

*Members of the Posse Comitatus Chapter for Multnomah County
reportedly were planning attacks for last Friday night on the homes
of state Judges Charles S. Crookham, Phillip J. Roth and Clifford B.
Olsen; and U.S. Magistrate William M. Dale Jr., according to the
affidavit filed by Special Agent Robert A. Kellison. The affidavit was
filed in support of a search warrant.*

*A law enforcement source, who asked not to be identified, said
members of the group allegedly had planned to burn four more
judges' homes last Saturday night.*

*He would not say who the other judges were, but he said they all
lived in the Portland area. The Posse Comitatus had a "long list"
with the names, addresses and telephone numbers of judges
throughout Oregon, the source said.*

*He did not know why some judges were targeted and others
were not.*

*The group had planned to throw glass containers of gasoline into the judges' homes and then ignite the gasoline with a flare gun, according to the affidavit.*

*Crookham's home reportedly was the first target, with an attack scheduled after 11 p.m. Friday. Members had planned to go to an alley in back of Crookham's home, start the fire and then flee in a waiting car, the affidavit said.*

*Area law enforcement authorities who worked closely with the FBI on the case had Crookham's home as well as Posse Comitatus members under surveillance, said an FBI spokesman.*

*When no one showed up at Crookham's home, the FBI decided to shut down the operation and make Saturday morning raids on the two homes, the spokesman said.*

*'Our concern was for the lives and safety of the judges,' he said. 'We had to move and do the searches as a preventative measure to stop the plot. Although no one has been arrested, we are continuing the investigation to develop probable cause for the arrests.'*

*The spokesman said agents had seized a large number of firearms, including rifles and handguns during simultaneous 6 a.m. raids on homes...."*

*"...On Tuesday, authorities searched a car that had been seized Saturday in connection with the case. They found a 5-gallon container of gasoline, four glass jugs, a list of judges that included their names and addresses, six terry cloth rags, a map and a knitted ski mask...."*

## CHAPTER SEVENTEEN
## July 12, 2012

"Dr. Owens to the nursing station, Dr. Owens to the nursing station."

*Who the hell is that screaming woman?*

"Hey, guys, I think he's coming around."

*That voice sounds familiar. I should know it. Oh, for heaven's sake, it's Matthew.* Like cold water on the face, harsh light stung as rows of fluorescent lights on a white ceiling came into view. That woman's voice again. "Doctor Owens to the nursing station, Dr. Owens to the nursing station." A flimsy, green curtain came into view, Matthew's face materialized. His brother was standing directly over him. What was that stinging sensation in his arm? Brad rolled his head to the right. He lay on a bed with crisp, white sheets. A needle protruded from his arm. He rolled his head back. Now he saw Patrick and Fry. *What in the name of God is happening?*

A woman rushed to stand beside Brad, her face holding an expression of astonishment. "I can't believe you're awake, Mr. Walker. How do you feel?" Brad appraised the woman's loose fitting, blue top and matching pants; *Doctor or nurse, gotta be.* The woman concentrated on a bank of machines that Brad now saw beside his bed: green lights, red lights, beeping sounds. The woman again looked to Brad.

"This is amazing, Mr. Walker, I can't believe you are not sleeping." She turned her attention to the monitors once more as if they held magical answers.

What happened next jolted Brad. He opened his mouth and the sound of his own voice absolutely startled him as he looked to the woman and spoke, "Who are you?" The woman turned her eyes from the equipment that had so fascinated her and looked at Brad. She seemed unsure about how to respond but a smile came to her face as she replied, "Mr. Walker, my name is Charlotte and I'm the nurse assigned to take care of you. I expected you to be sleeping for a much longer time. Please, tell me how are you feeling?" She stood with an expectant look on her face.

Brad ignored the nurse and her question. He turned to his brothers and Fry. They stood side-by-side in a neat row, each wearing a look of total bewilderment. After a second of awkward silence, Brad spoke to them. "You idiots look like the three stooges at the county fair." He turned back to the nurse and said, "I'm sorry, I don't mean to be rude to you but those guys look so pathetic, something had to be said right away. I feel great. Thank you for asking. My only issue is that I have no idea what's going on. If you can tell me where I am or what I'm doing here, I will love you forever."

The nurse stood dumbfounded and simply stared at Brad. Finally, a snicker from Matthew broke the silence "You took quite a blow to your head. Fortunately, no vital organs were struck or you might have been injured in a really bad way."

Now, all the guys started to smile, but still looked at Brad as if he had just arrived from outer space. The nurse looked at Brad with her mouth hanging open. She turned on her heel like an Army sergeant and with a curt, "I'll get the doctor," and she vanished.

Patrick, Matthew and Fry appeared to relax a bit with her departure. They moved to spread out, positioning themselves to stand around the bed but none of them ever took their eyes from Brad. Fry was the first to speak. "I'm glad to see that getting your head bashed in hasn't changed your charming personality one little bit. You're still the same senile, old horse's ass we've always known. You about gave that poor nurse heart failure." The guys shuffled nervously, a forced laugh rippled among them.

For several seconds, a beeping monitor was the only sound. Brad simply looked about the curtained cubicle, trying to wrap his mind about what was going on. He looked at Matthew to speak but his question was meant for anyone who would listen. "Come on guys, I need some help here." His voice began to escalate as he spoke. "What the holy hell is going on? I'm in a bed with clean sheets and I assume that I'm in a hospital. I got a needle bigger than a horse's dick sticking in my arm, some crazy-assed woman tells me she's a nurse and then runs away like Frankenstein is trying to get in her knickers."

Brad continued to take in his surroundings, absolute frustration in his face and eyes. He lifted his head from his pillow as he continued with what was becoming a tirade. "And then, to make things really neat, you bozos stand there like you all got a railroad tie jammed up your ass. Can anybody here speak fucking American? I'm looking at my two brothers and a shithead who's supposed to be my friend. All three of you are standing there, stiff as a post, looking like you just had sex with a sheep in the church library. For Christ's sake, will one of you morons give me just a tiny little hint as to what in the name of God is going on?" Brad was in a full shout as he concluded.

After a couple of seconds to see if Brad's tirade would trigger a reaction from other patients or medical staff, Patrick placed a hand on the rails of Brad's bed and spoke softly. "Take it easy, Brad, take it easy. Of course, we'll talk to you but just slow down a bit. Are you telling me that you honestly have no idea where you are or why you are here?"

Brad looked at his brother and saw dismay and concern written on his face. He looked at Matthew and Fry and realized they had the exact same look. He shut his eyes, trying to calm down and think. When he closed his eyelids, it brought darkness and that made him feel better. He forced thoughts through his mind, really concentrated. What were all these crazy feelings that were bombarding him? He remained perfectly still and kept his eyes closed for several seconds. No one made a sound.

When he opened his eyes again, he took a deep breath and spoke to the ceiling, not looking at his brothers or Fry. "Okay, maybe I'm getting my bearings. I remember dinner in Taos. I went on ahead of you guys to fish for a day by myself." Visions of the stream clarified in his mind. "I remember being in the cabin and the lights went out for no reason." Brad closed his eyes again. It was taking tremendous effort to retrieve thoughts and images, to force them back into his head. Without opening his eyes, he continued speaking. "I heard something that I was certain was a person." Brad breathed deeply and held the air in his lungs. This was difficult. Images and sounds were slow to come but he could feel something stirring inside his head. He gave it a few more seconds before opening his eyes and looking directly at Patrick. "I remember going outside to check on the noise and I recall that I was kinda jumpy because there was no doubt I had heard someone." Brad shook his head slowly. "I have memory of a very dark night but that's where it ends. I have no idea beyond that. Please, tell me right now, what the hell is going on?"

Patrick nodded that he understood. "Okay, baby brother, here's what I can tell you. But you have to understand that there's plenty we don't know. We were supposed to come to the cabin the day after you fished alone. We had a horse trip planned for Emerald Lake. Do you remember that?" Brad shook his head, acknowledging that he did. "Well, after a day in Taos doing women's shit with our wives, we were about to go stark raving mad. So, we decided to drive on to the cabin, sleep there and be ready for the horses bright and early," Patrick grinned, "And believe me the women didn't protest, they wanted us out of their hair like a whore wants out of Sunday school."

Brad smiled. "What if the preacher happens to be a paying customer?"

Everyone chuckled as Patrick continued. "We pulled onto the dirt road that leads to the cabin about ten o'clock or so. We were smoking and joking, deciding if we should sneak up on you and give you the scare of your life. Matthew here talked us out of it because he knows what a pussy you are under any circumstances, much less when you are by yourself and after sundown. We figured that the Lord himself couldn't predict what might have happened if you got scared out there in the wilderness all by yourself." Patrick grinned and Brad managed to roll his eyes and smile back. "All we know is that just as we made the curve in the road right in front of the cabin, our headlights caught a flash of someone taking a whack at your head. This was just a split second deal so none of us saw clearly enough to know what the guy was holding. But, from the way our headlights reflected, we think it was something metal, maybe a pipe."

Brad's face registered a look of shock as he spoke. "I have no idea or recollection about anything like that." He let out a deep breath and stared at the ceiling.

Matthew leaned over the bed and placed his hand on Brad's shoulder. "Don't worry about trying to remember. Just relax as best you can. I'm sure all of this will come back to you with a bit of time."

With a weak grin, Brad shook his head. "Maybe I don't want to remember getting hit. It sounds like that could hurt and I don't do well with pain."

Everyone chuckled as Patrick continued with his story. "We saw you go down like a rock. The asshole ran like crazy off into the woods. I caught a very brief glimpse of the guy but I couldn't take my eyes off of you. I mean you were on the ground and you weren't moving. God, I was scared! I thought you were a goner."

Brad listened in disbelief. He could think of nothing to say.

Matthew continued the narration. "We just had to let whoever the hell it was make a run for it. Our first concern was for you and we got to you within seconds. We had to keep the headlights on you to see what the hell to do so there was no chance at all of giving pursuit into the woods. After things settled down, Fry told us that there is an old fire road that cuts through not more than a quarter mile from where you went down. Whoever was after you must have had a vehicle parked in that area."

For a moment, no one said a word as Brad looked at his brothers and his friend, seeing the concern in each of their faces. This was surreal. Gradually a level of understanding developed in his face and eyes as he spoke very softly. "So, if you guys had been a minute later, I probably wouldn't be here right now." Every one was quiet until Brad whispered, more to himself than to anyone else, "Jesus H."

Matthew broke the silence. "Patrick and I got you into the hospital here in Taos as fast as we could. Fry got your gear out of the cabin and followed us in your vehicle. We've been right here ever since. Patrick made a police report over the telephone. The sheriff's department sent a unit out and searched the area all around the cabin. They didn't find anything that looked like it would help. Honestly, I don't know that there is much of anything they can do beyond what they did. Of course, they want to interview you but we told them you probably would not be too talkative for a while. They were very understanding and want you to call when you're up to it."

Brad gave a slight nod.

The curtain opened as a man wearing hospital garb entered and stepped to Brad's bed. Charlotte, the nurse, followed and quietly stood close by. "Mr. Walker, I'm Doctor Owens." The doctor spoke with pleasant authority as he leaned over Brad, scrutinizing his patient. "You've caused quite a stir around here this morning."

Brad looked at the physician with the embarrassed smile of a child caught telling a lie and gave a slight shrug.

After a cursory look at Brad and a glance at the monitors, Dr. Owens stood straight and crossed his arms over his chest. "Let me tell you, Mr. Walker, I've been an ER doc here in Taos for many years. I've seen a bunch of folks who were very lucky and a bunch who were mighty unlucky. You made it into in the first group last night." Dr. Owens was quiet and gave Brad a stern look. "You, my friend, are an official member of the lucky-as-hell club."

Brad looked up to the doctor and nodded that he understood. "I guess I'll have to take your word for it, Doctor. I don't remember a damned thing."

Dr. Owens gave a short laugh. "Oh, you were lucky alright. In fact you were lucky twice. Your first stroke of luck was that whoever did this to you didn't manage to lay a solid hit on you. Either his aim was bad or you ducked in just the right direction because you took the blow in kind of a glancing manner. Whatever was used to hit you just glanced off your skull and then slid down the right side of your head. One single inch closer to the middle of your head and I'm not sure that you and I would be having this conversation." Dr. Owens allowed the gravity of his words to sink in.

Brad was silent. He could only lie still and listen.

Dr. Owens spoke again. "You were lucky a second time when these men here showed up the moment they did. They did everything right and delivered you here in record time. I don't think you would have lived had you been left to lie out on the ground until the next day. The night temperatures are way too severe where you were assaulted. That area is over nine thousand feet and, after midnight, it gets cold as whiskers. The combination of your injury, shock and hypothermia would have been too much for survival. These men saved your life, Mr. Walker."

Somber moments passed in silence. Dr. Owens again leaned over

Brad and looked into his eyes with a flashlight. He checked the bandage that was wrapped about his head before he straightened up and looked down at Brad in a stern manner. "I'm not sure what to think about this, Mr. Walker. These men brought you in here right about midnight. While I was assessing your condition and figuring just how to patch you up, you began to convulse. At that point I made a decision that you needed to be sedated so I gave you some pretty powerful stuff. You got another weaker dose at 6:00 this morning and a mild sedative is dripping into you as we speak. I fully expected you to sleep through the entire morning and well into afternoon. But, from my observations, along with what Charlotte tells me and from the shouting I heard a few minutes ago, you are absolutely alert and your vitals are strong as can be." The doctor was quiet and appeared contemplative. "Some memory loss is quite normal and I'm not too worried about that, at least not yet. But I need to know if you are experiencing any pain or do you feel dizzy?"

"No, doctor, no pain at all. I'm not dizzy and I feel fine. But, I sure have a couple of questions for you."

"Fire away."

"What time is it?"

The doctor glanced at his watch, "Eight-thirty on the nose."

"It's eight-thirty in the morning and I came in here at midnight. You're telling me that I've been here just over eight hours, that's all?" Brad sounded incredulous.

"Not only are your vitals excellent, your arithmetic's pretty good too." The doctor shot Brad a smile.

Brad rolled his head to stare at the ceiling once again. How could this be? He closed his eyes. Everything was there, inside his head, clear as a bell. He could see Moustache. He could feel movement of the horse beneath him. He saw the tiny dwelling with its dirt floor and the bed where he had been placed. He could feel the fireplace and the scent of smoke and bread still lingered. He carefully calculated every detail in his mind. He had seen at least two nights and one day pass while in Juanita's room. Brad did not want to open his eyes and see the face of Dr. Owens. Not just yet. The dark world within the depths of his mind was what he preferred, where he wanted to be. He summoned it all again: the voices, words in Spanish and the icy cold water that Juanita had given him. The thought of

Juanita caused him to suck his breath short. He felt her hand on his cheek. She had actually swept her lips across his forehead! She had spoken to him in Spanish. The words that Juanita had spoken, what were those words? What had she said?

Harsh hospital lights remained and quizzical faces peered down when Brad opened his eyes. He did not move a muscle as he tried to understand what he was being told and what he saw, as opposed to what he felt inside and what his memory told him. What he did know with complete certainty was that all of his unexplained memories and feelings weren't confined to somewhere within his head. He knew this because, with his eyes wide open and Dr. Owens standing directly before him, thoughts of Juanita caused some sort of quiver inside his body.

Brad again closed his eyes, as tightly as he could. *Please Lord, you gotta help me here. Something wild and crazy is happening.*

"I guess I'm just a little confused on the time but I promise, I feel fine." Brad spoke softly as he opened his eyes and addressed Dr. Owens.

Dr. Owens gave Brad a long look, evaluating his options. "I'll tell you what, Mr. Walker, I had every intention of hospitalizing you today. We've got ourselves a full house at the moment and I was simply waiting for a room to open up. One hour ago, I had no doubt that you were going to be our guest for a while." He was quiet again and scanned the monitors as a stall tactic while he thought before continuing. "You definitely suffered a concussion and you came within a hair of critical injury or quite likely even death. However, in light of your miraculous recovery, I'm going to unplug the sedative and the fluid drips. I want you to stay right here until noon where Charlotte and I will be keeping an eagle eye on you. If by noon you're still doing as well as you seem right now, I will release you as long as you will be in town for a few days. And after you leave the hospital, it is absolutely imperative that you take it easy for several days."

With a nod, Brad acknowledged that he understood.

"I know you guys had a big fishing trip planned but that is out of the question, no way at all. You do understand that, don't you, Mr. Walker?"

Another nod from Brad.

"It would be way too risky for you to ride a horse and get that head of yours jostled all over the place. And, I sure don't want you hours away from civilization if you have any complications. Can you live with that?"

Brad gave a sigh of resignation. "You're the doctor and yes, I'll live with everything you say."

"Okay, Mr. Walker, I'll keep checking back with you throughout the morning." The doctor reached down and patted Brad's shoulder. "You were mighty lucky but don't go charging out of here and do a bunch of crazy stuff. Your guardian angel might be on coffee break next time around." Dr. Owens walked away.

\* \* \* \*

Walter gulped a last swallow of coffee as he hustled through Albuquerque's airport terminal. His flight was boarding and he had barely made it from the parking lot in time for coffee, much less a bite to eat. This was not what he wanted to do but he knew it needed to be done. Some things had to get resolved and a face-to-face with Nolan was the only way to do it. They had to make a plan for themselves and figure out how they were going to handle Earl and his lunacy. Did Earl hold a place in their future or was it time to break away? After his debacle with the FBI fuck, right now was the perfect opportunity to take a day for some conversation with Nolan.

The airplane was packed and he dreaded the two hours it was going to take to fly to Los Angeles. Walter sat in misery, listening to babies cry and endless clatter of people gabbing about nonsense. Walter was exhausted and had been able to think of nothing but the botched job on that goddamned FBI agent. How could things have been so perfect and then gotten so fucked up so fast. Where in hell had that car come from in the middle of the night? His mind could still see those frantic seconds. The bastard had been in his reach with no chance for confrontation or resistance. And then, things had fallen apart in a second. Walter re-lived that critical moment. He had known the instant he swung the pipe that it wasn't a perfect hit but it sure as hell was good enough to put the fucker down. It would have been a piece of cake to follow up with a couple more swings and poof, no more Mr. FBI. Then that damned car had showed up out of absolutely fucking nowhere. How could his luck be any worse than that?

Walter sat in his seat with a rigid body and his eyes focused straight ahead. The airplane was almost filled and takeoff was hopefully only minutes away. He desperately wanted to hear those engines roar. He needed to get his ass to Los Angeles, talk with Nolan and then get back to finish what he had come out here to do. Walter shut his eyes and thought about the seconds immediately after he had run away from the FBI guy to escape whoever was in that damned car. The woods had given him cover, no more than fifty feet from where he had clobbered the shithead. He had laid there on his stomach, and watched from the forest. He had been close enough to even hear some of the conversation of the people who had driven up. He sure as hell could see and hear enough to know that they got the fucker to stand up and load his ass into a car. There was no doubt in his mind that they had made a desperate run for Taos and a trip to a hospital.

Finally, the jet accelerated and Walter felt his body being pushed into the back of his seat. He paid no attention as the jet ascended over Albuquerque's sprawl and the Sandia Mountains. The Rio Grande River twisted through the desert, fading as the aircraft climbed higher. Walter went through it all again, the whole episode, every detail passed through his mind. He could not have done anything differently. If that car hadn't appeared from nowhere, a dead-ass FBI agent would be rotting in the dirt right now.

He felt his eyes grow heavy. Vibration of the aircraft's engines moved through his body with the effect of a lullaby. He felt drowsiness creeping. *I'll be back, FBI boy, It's a personal thing. You owe me a life and I will collect. You can fucking count in it.*

The voice of the pilot came over the aircraft's speakers, "For the passengers on the right side of the aircraft, you have a wonderful view of the Acoma Pueblo, one of the most historically significant sites in New Mexico."

Walter pulled the shade over his window and closed his eyes to sleep. *If you wanna be a goddamned tour guide, get a job at a fucking museum.*

\* \* \* \*

The hotel room was quiet, maybe a little too quiet. Brad had followed the instructions of Dr. Owens and had done nothing but lay around since leaving the hospital. His brothers and Fry had taken their wives to dinner and had begged that he join them. But Brad had needed some time alone and declined. The guys and their wives had all spent the afternoon with Brad, discussing and analyzing the details of his assault and he was simply tired of talking about it. He continued to feel perfectly fine but nothing had changed with what he remembered. The fishing cabin, the dark night, the noise he had heard, everything was crystal clear right up to the moment that he had been attacked. That's where things got screwed up. The details of their miraculous decision to drive to the cabin ahead of schedule, and how it had ultimately saved his life, had been told and re-told. But their story of rushing him to a hospital in the backseat of a car bore no resemblance to what he recalled with vivid detail. For the hundredth time he closed his eyes and lived it again: Moustache, horses, men speaking Spanish, the fireplace and the tiny room. He remembered Juanita. He could see her face, hear her voice and feel her hands. It was like it had all happened two minutes ago. He didn't know if it was shame or thrill, but he sure as heck felt something wonderful deep inside when he thought of Juanita.

After talking with the group all afternoon, he had reluctantly made a decision to break his vow of silence. He described his experience of seeing a man standing under a tree, a man who appeared to be Vincent Perkins. His story had been met by a very long and a very awkward silence. The expressions that had greeted him were almost humorous. The women in particular had given him that look of, "Oh, you poor, poor man. Will you ever get over this horrible experience and regain your sanity?" The guys had simply stared at him, not knowing what to think or say. That type of reaction sure as hell made the next decision easy. There was no way on God's green earth that he would share some wild-assed fantasy of a horseback rescue that delivered him to a beautiful goddess, who nursed him and even lightly kissed him. *Jesus H*. No way in hell was that story going anywhere! Brad laughed to himself. If he were to talk about these things, the group would have him back at the hospital in a flash, and probably with good reason. He lay on his bed and covered his face with his hands. He preferred the darkness and his own version of the rescue. *It just feels so darned real. And, it sure as heck feels better than the clinical bullshit version coming from my brothers.*

Since nothing was making any more sense by just lying around and thinking, Brad stood up and moved about the room. He had to do something. He was desperate to get his head back into something that he knew was real, something that he could control. For one thing, he had to talk with Cassandra. She thought he was off somewhere in the middle of nowhere camping and fishing. He owed her a telephone call but, in the wake of all that she had endured with Norton's attack, he could not even consider telling her the truth about what had happened to him. Yet, he had to check with her, see how she was doing and learn if there had been any developments in the investigation with the attack on her husband.

Back and forth, wall-to-wall, like a caged tiger Brad paced and concocted a story for Cassandra. He punched her number into his cell phone, quickly rehearsing in his mind what he would say. He just hoped that she would believe him. After all, much of her life had been spent dissecting lies and bullshit. That's what prosecutors do every day.

"Brad! I didn't expect to hear from you for another day or so. Between Moosehead and the Rocky Mountains, I wrote you off as one of the lost boys. How's your vacation and how are you?" Cassandra's voice was happy.

"Hey there, lovely lady, I don't have much time to talk. New Mexico is a third world country, you know, so I'll probably run out of electricity any second. They have no modern gadgets such as televisions and they've never even heard of the Internet. There is absolutely nothing that is even remotely civilized in this horrible place."

Cassandra started laughing.

"I've been living a stark existence of tortillas, beer and gorgeous women who need me desperately. This is no way to spend a vacation and I'm so damned miserable I don't know what to do." Her laugh sounded wonderful and Brad hoped it was an omen for the rest of their conversation.

"In your dreams, at least the gorgeous women part. Now, the tortillas and beer, you have a good chance of convincing me with that part of your fairytale." Cassandra continued to laugh as she heard Brad groan. "Honestly, I've been dying to hear from you. Tell me about everything. I want to hear your lies of life in the frontier. Give me details."

Brad took a breath and began his story. "Okay, here we go but I'm warning you, as they say out here in the Wild West, you better hang on to your spurs cause I have a story to tell you."

Cassandra laughed again. "I love stories, especially when they're as full of BS as yours."

"I'm going to make you feel terrible for saying that, young lady. No joking, Cassandra, I had a little problem. Leave it to old Brad to screw things up. I'm afraid me and my horse, well we had a little problem." Brad paused. "Of course, it was a damned woman horse. It would be easier to say the horse was a mare, but since you're a lawyer from California, I'll try to use words that you are able to understand."

"How is it possible to love someone as much as I love you and at the same time hate them as much as I hate you? What's wrong, what happened?" Cassandra's voice was urgent.

"Okay, don't get all excited. I'll give you the embarrassing facts so you can ridicule me to your heart's content." With a quick breath, Brad began his story. "We had just taken off on our trip up into the mountains. We were all riding along, tall in the saddle, thinking we were real cowboys and feeling pretty good about ourselves. I'm still not sure what exactly happened, but all I know is that I looked up to see an eagle the size of the space shuttle headed straight for my horse. I just sat there like a dummy. I had absolutely no idea of what was happening. My horse didn't know what the hell was happening either but, unlike me, she took evasive action. She did a couple of complete circles in about a half second and then commenced to buck like she was a rodeo horse."

"Oh, my God!"

"It was very much like that line from an old country song describing a horse, 'She had lightning in her eyes and thunder in her hooves.'"

Brad could envision Cassandra's face as nothing but silence came from the other end of the call. With a tone that he hoped was convincing, he continued. "I probably don't have to tell you that I didn't manage to stay on that wild beast for even close to eight seconds. The next thing I remember is waking up, flat on my back, looking up at a blue New Mexico sky. Apparently, I landed headfirst on a rock and it really knocked me to the Twilight Zone. They had to get me off the mountain and down to a hospital in Taos. I'm going be fine but I have a concussion and there will be no more horse riding and no fishing this week." After a second without speaking, he concluded, "So, Miss Cassandra, that's how I spent my summer vacation."

There was a half-second of silence before Cassandra erupted. "Oh, my God, Brad. I'm so sorry. Are you all right? Why did the eagle do that? Are you still in a hospital? Did the horse run away? How did you get off the mountain? Are you hurting?"

Brad laughed. "Objection, counselor, objection. You are badgering the witness. Another outburst like that and you will be removed from the courtroom."

Cassandra didn't miss a beat. "Objection overruled! You are a hostile witness and you will answer every one of those questions. And, may I remind you that you are under oath!" They both enjoyed a laugh before Cassandra continued. "Honestly, Brad, I'm heartbroken for you. I know how much this trip meant to you."

"Hey, I know you are and I appreciate it. But, things could sure as heck have been worse. I really got off lucky with only a slight injury. We think the eagle was going for a little-assed dog that the guide had brought along with him. That's all we can figure. But everything is going to be fine with me, I promise. Now, you've heard enough of this idiocy about my life as a cowboy. I need to hear from you. How's Norton?"

"Oh, Brad, the doctors are amazed. He hasn't actually regained consciousness and he hasn't spoken yet. But, as far as I'm concerned, there is some great news. He has started to squeeze my hand as a way of communicating. I feel like we are actually talking with each other. Tubes are still in his mouth and throat but he's getting better faster than the doctors ever expected. It looks like he has some optic nerve damage and his face and eyes remain covered with bandages except for when they examine him. He has a ways to go, for sure, but the doctors are incredulous that he is doing so well."

Brad thought of his own incident and couldn't help but wonder to himself if maybe Norton had taken a trip to some mystical place while he was unconscious. "That's the best news I've ever heard. I am so happy for both of you. Maybe that miracle we all prayed for is actually going to happen."

"I've never hoped and prayed so hard in all my life."

"I can only imagine and it sounds like someone just may be listening. But, you have to talk to me, Cassandra. I'm dying to hear straight from you, have you experienced any more problems with bald-headed creeps spying on you?" Brad held his breath.

"No, I've had no more issues. I did exactly as you suggested in our last conversation. My sister came home with me and I swallowed a couple of pills that allowed me to really sleep. It's amazing what sleep does for a person. Even after some rest, I still think I saw what I saw but I'm handling it better and keeping my eyes open. There have been no more incidents and I don't intend to bother you again with such helter-skelter. I'm going to be a big girl now and that's all there is to it."

Brad sensed a reticence in her voice as she finished speaking. He knew she wasn't being completely forthright and he suspected that something more was coming.

"But, Brad, something horrible has happened and I'm more certain than ever that something is terribly wrong with what happened to Norton." She stopped. "And I'm thinking it may even be related to what I saw outside the coffee shop."

All kidding was over. Brad could feel anxiety through his telephone. Cassandra was dead serious. "What in the world happened? What's wrong?"

"Do you remember the judge from the Vincent Perkins case?"

"Of course I do. That was Judge Christopher."

"You're right, it was Judge Sherman Christopher. I don't think you were in the courtroom on the day that Vincent Perkins was sentenced but let me tell you, it was a day to remember. Not only did Judge Christopher come down hard on Vincent Perkins with the sentence he imposed, he also delivered the most blistering oratory I ever heard from the bench. He went on the record with a withering personal condemnation of Vincent and then he continued with a castigation of the ideology that personifies Vincent and his breed. It was a real barnburner. The entire courtroom was shell-shocked and Vincent Perkins had to stand there and just take it."

"No, I wasn't there but I wish I had been."

"Well, Judge Christopher retired a few years ago and moved up to Portland. Shortly before he left Los Angeles he told me that he had purchased some land in Oregon so he could tinker around with gardening and enjoy some privacy. That was the last I knew of him until the news hit today. Oh, Brad, it is so awful. Judge Christopher's home was the target of arson. It was a coordinated attack with Molotov cocktails and gasoline materials tossed into virtually every window of the house, at least the ones that were on ground level. His entire house was consumed in seconds."

Cassandra stopped speaking and Brad just held the telephone. This was unreal. He was trying to process the human aspect of what he had heard but, at the same time, his mind felt a blur with the significance of the attack. This pushed the envelope way too far to be considered coincidence. Too much was happening and bells were sounding. Brad knew Cassandra had to be thinking the same things. Then, he asked the hanging question that he dreaded to ask; "Did people die?"

"Oh, my Lord, talk about miracles. The Judge and his wife had three grandchildren staying with them. If you can believe this, the judge had taken everyone outside for a little camping type experience. The entire family was in the back yard, sleeping in a tent when the attack took place. If they had been inside the house, like all other normal nights, every one of them would have died a horrible, horrible death."

"Holy Jesus." Brad was silent and he listened as Cassandra struggled through tears.

Her voice collapsed as she gushed her next words. "And, I just as well go ahead and tell you. You know all that silly stuff I told you about being brave? Brad, I'm terrified. Everywhere I go, I'm in fear of seeing that man again. I feel like I'm losing my mind. The police have absolutely no leads or ideas that they can follow and I'm just living every day in fear for Norton and fear for myself."

Brad said nothing, his mind was spinning as to what he could or should say.

Cassandra spoke in a choked tone. "Do you remember what I told you while we were in the hospital cafeteria? You know, about my feelings that what happened to Norton was connected in some way to Vincent Perkins?"

"Of course I remember." Brad scarcely whispered into the telephone.

"Once I heard about the arson on Judge Christopher's house, there was not even a shred of doubt. Brad, this is real. This nightmare is real. I can't begin to explain how this is happening, but I promise you, Vincent Perkins is here. That horrible man is back!" Cassandra let go, completely breaking down into sobs.

Listening to a friend of years cry from deep in her soul was killing Brad. He could only hold on to the telephone and say nothing. Somewhere between shock and heartbreak, he quickly resolved two things within his mind. This was not the time to tell Cassandra his own experience of seeing a man that looked to be Vincent Perkins. And, he knew with certainty that he was going to Los Angeles.

He gave her some time to gather herself. An extended silence on the telephone was perfectly comfortable given the depth of their shared experiences and friendship. When the time seemed right, Brad spoke, announcing his decision. "Cassandra, as soon as we hang up, I'm going through my camping gear to pull out some clean jeans and a few things. I'll be on a flight out of Albuquerque to Los Angeles tomorrow. I have to see you and we have to talk, face-to-face. Can you hold it together for just a few more hours?"

Sounds of crying persisted but Cassandra replied. "Oh, my goodness, Brad, I would love for you to be here but you were thrown from a horse, remember? You're a broken cowboy. You can't be running off to Los Angeles until you have some time to recover from your injury."

"I got a little bandage around my head, that's it. This conversation is over. I've got stuff to do so I'll see you sometime tomorrow. I'll shoot you a call or text with my arrival info."

Cassandra was quiet. "You have no idea how much I appreciate this."

"You have no idea how badly I want to see you and Norton so stop fretting." After a brief thought, he added, "I do have one favor to ask. Will you call Dan Wright for me? I don't have his number in my phone. Please call him and set up a time for us to get together. Maybe we could go back to that little place where we used to go when we were preparing for trial."

"This is the best thing I've heard in days." Cassandra's voice sounded strong again. "Since you don't yet have an arrival time, how about breakfast morning after tomorrow? Will that work?"

"Perfect. I could use some pancakes and ham. Being a rodeo star makes a man hungry, you know."

Cassandra took the opportunity for some humor. "You and your appetite. Some things never change, not even after fifteen years." She laughed.

"I have no intention of ever changing, Miss Cassandra. I plan to remain immature, hungry and horny until I'm too damned old to die young." They both laughed as their conversation concluded. Brad was happy that things were ending on a lighter tone. "Bye, Cassandra, see you real soon."

## CHAPTER EIGHTEEN
## July 12, 2012

Even in the anonymity of one of the world's major transportation hubs, Walter and Nolan were difficult to overlook. As throngs of humanity in all shapes, sizes and colors streamed through Los Angeles International Airport, countless travelers cast a second or third look at the two men who sat dining on a sandwich and iced tea. Whether by casual glance or close scrutiny, it appeared that a single individual occupied two chairs. They looked identical; their physical stature, facial features, shaved heads and tattoos were mirror images. The only discernable characteristic was that they were dressed differently. One of the men wore jeans and a white t-shirt while the other wore shorts and a red shirt.

Nolan had met Walter in the terminal upon his arrival from Albuquerque and they now had an opportunity for a long overdue conversation. Walter related his story of locating Brad Walker in Colorado and the subsequent surveillance to Taos, New Mexico. He detailed the incredible stroke of bad luck that had befallen at the very moment of his attack. He told what he had seen and heard in the aftermath that let him know he had failed to end the life of the FBI agent.

Their discussion continued as Nolan walked Walter through local news coverage of the attack on Norton Roberts and how attention to the story had diminished dramatically after the first couple of days. There was way too much crime and too many boiling political issues in Los Angeles for a simple assault to receive much attention. Newspapers had mentioned that the victim was the husband of a former, high profile Los Angeles County prosecutor, but there had been no significant speculation that the incident may be related to her days in the courtroom. The best news was that reporters had identified the specific hospital where Norton Roberts was being treated and that he was in intensive care. Nolan told Walter of how he had gone to the hospital just so he would know what the place looked like and how he had been lucky enough to spot Cassandra Roberts walking to a coffee shop.

"That hospital would be a good place to start if we decide to go after the lawyer," Nolan observed. "There's a lobby that she has to pass through any time she enters or leaves the intensive care unit. Just sit there and keep your eyes open and she has to walk right past at some point."

"That's good to know and we'll keep it in mind," Walter replied. "But before we start talking about whether or not to hit the lawyer, let's slow down and talk some things over. Me and you have to make some decisions about how we're going handle our lives and finish all this business. We've been able to see some problems coming for a long time and we need to figure out what to do."

"You're right. Let's do it."

"Earl wants to direct everything so he can make a big splash with some high profile crime wave that he thinks is going to start his pie in the sky revolution."

Nolan nodded his head in agreement.

"In my opinion, Earl is thinking only of Earl. He has illusions that he will become famous overnight and that he can draw followers like the Pied Piper from all over the country to support his cause." Walter made a sneering expression. "I don't see it that way. I don't give a damn about his fame or his fucking revolution. Me and you have different priorities and I think we've used Earl for about all the good he can do us."

Nolan shifted his head up and down but did not reply.

Walter sipped his iced tea as he continued. "I can't explain Earl. He's totally dedicated to his ideas of revolution and a nation without nigs, Jews or queers. But the guy doesn't seem to have any kind of a memory inside that religious head of his. He's forgotten how many good men have died or gone to prison because they ran off half-cocked, thinking they were going to be famous and change the world. Ain't nobody going to make any real changes in this country no matter what. But sure as hell, if Earl gets some guys to do a couple of high profile crimes somewhere and a bunch of publicity comes out of it, he has done nothing more than invite the FBI and police to his party." Walter sneered again. "And I say that's a losing game every time."

Nolan nodded again, still listening.

"I'll hand it to the guy though, he's made a hell of a good start cause he's got money rolling in from all over. I don't know how he does it but, by God, he's doing it. He gets some support because lots of people are mad as hell about all the goddamned dogs from Mexico taking our jobs and the Jews, niggers, queers and Federal Government that are destroying our country. But no matter how many people agree with him, he's nowhere close to leading some silly revolution."

This prompted Nolan to break his silence. "I agree. He's going to fantasize himself and a bunch of other folks straight to jail. We have to be sure we aren't a part of that crowd."

"You nailed it on the head. It just doesn't make any sense to start taking credit for robbing a few banks or burning down a house or two." Walter lifted his arms in exasperation. "For Christ's sake, is the guy a total loon? Just when we're starting to get a decent organization going, he wants to go public cause he thinks thousands are going to rise up and follow." Walter grinned. "He's got it in his head that Gabriel's gonna blow his trumpet and the Lord will come riding out of heaven to ride side by side with General Earl. I think that idiot lies in bed at night dreaming about him and Jesus, white stallions and all, leading Christian soldiers in a march straight to Washington to cast thieves from the temple." Walter threw his head back and laughed. "What that fucker is going to get is about three hundred SWAT teams from the FBI and every police department in the country to start smelling his cute little ass every time he blows a bubble in his underwear. It's just a matter of time till he wakes up dead as Mozart's dick or he becomes the private, jail house squeeze of some dope-dealing buck named Leroy."

After Nolan stopped laughing, he agreed. "You're right but we've done pretty damned good by Earl. It was him and his organization that located the lawyer and the FBI agent for us. We can't forget that it was Earl's money and private investigator that got us started. But that doesn't change the fact that he's lost his grip on reality. Outside of the money he brings to the table, I'm not sure why we should stick with him. I'm so sick of his Bible thumping and glory of God bullshit, I'm about to explode."

"I'm up to my ears with his religious stuff too." Walter drained his iced tea. "But, the guys is sure as hell being smart about some things. He's bought several houses and he's got cars and fake IDs stashed away. But, I say that's just a good start to make life tough for the police, not a reason to start talking revolution right into the government's fat, ugly face."

It was Nolan's turn to make a face of disgust as he took a bite of sandwich and was silent for a moment. "Money is not why me and you are doing this but it sure has been nice to have some in our pockets for a while. I sure don't want to walk away from a good thing before we absolutely have to. But this can't go on forever. Something is telling me that things are going to get pretty wild with Earl. And, I think it's going to happen sooner than later. I'm not sure we want to be around for the party."

"I agree. Torching the house of that judge up in Portland is going to stir the pot and make some damned cop somewhere get curious and take notice. We don't have a lot of time before Earl's going to be front-page news."

After another bite of food and looking thoughtful, Nolan spoke again. "But as long as we're talking money, what about the big bank job? Earl's excited as hell over that and he indicates it's going to come up right away. He's talking a really big payday and he sure as hell wants us both for that one."

Massaging his brow as he spoke, Walter spoke to himself as much as he spoke to Nolan. "Yeah, you're right about the money but he wants us there to whack the girl. He plans to make a big headline with her. He intends for her murder to be a part of his big public splash." Walter put his arms on his knees and looked right at Nolan. "That's a tough decision we are going to have to make. The chances are good that a bunch of money is going to come out of that job and I love the thought of getting paid to whack niggers. But, I don't know for sure about this one. I think Earl plans to start making his revolution moves pretty soon after that deal goes down and I don't want to be too close to him."

Nolan crumpled the wrapping papers of his sandwich before he spoke. "I've listened to Earl's sermons and fairy tales till I'm sprouting pimples. I just want the money and if we take out the girl, that's fine. Outside of that, I'm over him."

Walter stretched his arms over his head and laughed. "I think we agree, this Sunday school picnic is about over and we both know how it's going to end." Walter leaned close to Nolan. "And once those government fuckers start taking a close look at the Reverend Earl and his apostles, me and you are going find ourselves in their cross hairs just like the rest of his flock. The more daylight we got between us and them, the better off we're going to be."

Nolan nodded his head in agreement.

"But the question is, what do we do right now? Do we try to string Earl along? Do we stick with him through the next bank deal and make ourselves one hell of a good score before we ditch his ass and go our own way? If what he says is true about this next job, we're talking big money. We stick with him long enough for that and we can disappear."

"I can do that," Nolan nodded his head.

Walter looked hard at Nolan. "But one thing is not negotiable with me. I'm going to finish what I started with that FBI fucker. All I ever wanted when we started this whole deal was to get that goddamned nigger woman lawyer and the FBI agent. I'm satisfied with the lawyer. I think her life has been turned upside down so I don't care about spending any more time trying to do something to her. But I'm not finished. I'm going to do the same to that FBI fuck. I'm going to kill his ass or kill somebody really close to him." Walter paused, "Once I get that French fried faggot handled, I'll be happy as a goddamned clam." Walter grinned. "And our friend Earl can sing hymns with the heavenly host till the world spins backwards."

A smile and a nod was the only response from Nolan before he slowly spoke. "The lawyer and FBI agent put our brother in prison for the rest of his life. Vincent sits in a box every day because of them. That nigger bitch lawyer and Jew-loving FBI agent destroyed our family. Revenge for what they did to Vincent and our family will always be our number one objective. If there's a way to get our own justice and still help a cause like Earl's, then I'm all for it. But I don't intend to throw my life away or go to prison myself just so some religious idiot can be famous for ten minutes."

Both men sat quietly. Finally, Nolan spoke again. "You came all the way out here cause you said we needed to talk. I think our minds are made up so what the hell do we need to talk about?" Nolan shrugged his shoulders in a questioning manner.

Walter leaned back in his chair. "I want to kill that FBI son-of-a-bitch but I don't want to get caught or killed myself in the process. After what I did to him, it's going to be tough as hell to sneak up on him again, at least for a long time. He's going to be watching every corner and shadow. But, I think I know his weak spot. I think I know how to get him."

Nolan leaned forward, "You've got my attention. Talk to me."

Walter related the story of the morning he had followed Brad Walker to the Fox Cove Inn. He told of the two women who had greeted Brad and the obvious affection they had for each other.

Realization showed in Nolan's eyes as he spoke. "Sounds good to me. It would be the same as we did to the nigger lawyer. We hurt her just like she hurt our family. I like that. Doing the same to the FBI guy sounds good to me."

"Well, I'm not sure yet. But once I get back there and look things over, I'll decide. I sure do want to kill that fucker but it isn't worth getting caught and going to the joint. I'll make my move when I'm sure I can do it without getting caught."

"I say hit the broads and get it over with. This shit can't go on forever."

"You may be right. I'll figure it out as soon as I get back out there and take a look at things." Walter paused, "Now, let's get back to the ground floor for a second. I say we play Earl just a bit longer and leave our options open. If we get this FBI bastard handled out in Colorado and want to come back for the bank job, do the girl, pocket some cash and have some fun in the process, what the hell, let's do it. But if we're not finished with what's important to us and Earl wants to charge off with the Mormon Tabernacle Choir to overthrow the government, then we break off and go our own way."

"I am absolutely fine with that."

"Look, my car is at the Albuquerque airport. I'm going to go back out there and head for Denver. Who knows how long it will be before that FBI goof returns home after the headache I gave him. While I'm waiting for him, I'm going to take a good look at those two twinkle tit broads and decide how to make my move. If I need you, I'll call in a heartbeat. Otherwise, you stay here in Los Angeles like Earl told you and make him think everything is fine. Every time you talk to him, pump him for what's happening in the news about burning that house down and what he's planning next."

"Got ya."

"Probably the biggest thing to get straight is to find out when he will be ready to do the bank job. Let's make some cash and send that black-assed girl to the big cotton plantation in the sky. After that, it's hasta la vista to Earl and his revolution."

Nolan gave his twin brother a grin. "I'd rather help you turn that FBI guy's head into hamburger but I can hang out here a few more days if it means we can milk Earl one more time. Now, let's find us a bar and get something besides iced tea. What is that Earl calls it when he preaches about the sins of alcohol and drinking?"

Walter laughed. "Oh, yeah, water of oblivion. Great idea. I have two hours before my flight back to Albuquerque. Let's find a place with a good-looking barmaid in a short skirt and get some of that wonderful water of oblivion. We might even drink a toast to Earl and the apostles."

## CHAPTER NINETEEN
July 12, 2012

Taos was behind him. The historic town had faded from Brad's sight but not the disappointment of recent days. He drove south, taking the high road to Santa Fe on his way to Albuquerque for a flight to Los Angeles. Reality had hit hard as he left Fry and his brothers. It was a bitter pill that there would be no horse adventure, no campfire escapades, no fishing an alpine lake at sunset and, most important of all for Brad, no memories. Instead, he left the company of treasured people with stitches in his head and a tumult of emotions. He would be back in a couple of days to see Dr. Owens and the guys but it wasn't the same. The magic of horses, rivers and friends had been lost in a wave of furtive apprehension over assaults, arsons and sinister encounters with a face from the past. Only days ago he had left his home for a fishing trip, but now, here he was heading to Los Angeles to formulate a strategy dealing with some sort of deadly conspiracy. *Is this upside down or what?*

What made this drive different from when he had traveled from Colorado to Taos was that he now frequently checked his mirror for the possibility of being followed. From time to time he pulled over and waited for traffic to pass, paying attention to what was behind him and vehicles that drove past him. His gut told him that he was wasting his time and that whoever had attacked him was nowhere around at the present time. Still, he exercised caution. As the morning passed, nothing but New Mexico scenery came into view.

Brad drove on New Mexico Highway 518 heading to the settlement of Peñasco, nestled beneath the impressive frame of Jicarita Peak. From there, he would pick up Highway 76 to Truchas and then on to Chimayo. His flight out of Albuquerque was not until late afternoon so he had time to take this scenic route and remind himself why New Mexico is known as the Land of Enchantment. He wanted to make this particular drive because it would give him time to go over things in his mind and prepare for his meeting in Los Angeles. But more importantly, it was a route filled with nostalgia. It seemed that every twist or turn in the road delivered a spectacular vista along with a pleasant memory.

Elizabeth and he had made this drive countless times. Autumn had been their favorite time. They had cherished the warm days and cold nights of changing aspen and cottonwood leaves, hay meadows and chamisa. Gold seemed to burst from every hillside. And the sky, it had always been so blue that Elizabeth would simply laugh out loud in sheer joy of the beauty. It was mid-summer now, too early for the changing leaves but blue sky was in abundance. Puffs of clouds drifted like tumbleweeds.

He cruised with no music; just quiet time with his thoughts. After leaving Truchas, the mountain landscape gave way to vistas of near infinity as he dropped into the hills of Chimayo. This too was part of the reason he had chosen to travel this specific route. There was an old mission church in Chimayo that he felt a compelling desire to visit. Elizabeth and he had been there several times and the wonder never diminished.

El Santuario de Chimayo had been a site of holiness since the early 1800s and a pilgrimage destination for thousands. Countless people trekked to the small mission each year in a belief that the soil under the adobe structure held healing powers for physical or spiritual afflictions. Brad was not a religious man but the old mission had always touched him in a way he could not explain. Whenever he entered the sanctuary, he was always blessed with a reverent and contemplative peace; a sense that people he loved or things that really mattered in his life were somehow there with him, their arms about

him. As Brad neared the church, it crossed his mind that perhaps today was his own private pilgrimage to seek answers to the extraordi-
nary events of recent days.

Typical for a summer day, tourists and worshipers alike crowded
the area about the mission. Brad parked a distance away and began
walking toward the sanctuary. He was still at least fifty yards from
the courtyard that served as the entrance to the church when he saw
her. It was Juanita! She stood just outside the mission doors,
sunlight directly on her. It was the same dress she had worn, her
skin, her hair, everything exactly as he recalled from when she had
tended to him. Juanita looked in Brad's direction and their eyes met.
Her arm shot into the air, her hand waved, and her smile, that beautiful smile, radiant even from the distance. *Oh, my God! Oh, my God,
it's her!* Brad started running and he saw her watching him, laughing
at his frantic efforts. A car honked. In his frenzy, he had stepped directly into the path of oncoming traffic. He darted across the street,
into the courtyard. Juanita was gone.

Heart hammering, he stepped into the church. She would be waiting for him inside. Adobe walls shut out the sun and it was suddenly
dark. Candles flickered and his eyes struggled. The chapel was filled
with people, some kneeling, others standing. Brad walked through
the sanctuary. Juanita was not to be found. *No, God, please, don't do
this to me. Juanita, please don't do this to me. Please Juanita!* He
walked to the front of the sanctuary and stood before the altar: so
much history, so many had knelt here to pray, so many had talked
with God. Brad had always felt that at this altar one could feel centuries of mortals yearning to touch the immortal. But today, at this moment, the statutes and artifacts that had in the past embraced and
offered a sense of welcome, now seemed to mock his presence. His
breathing became labored. How could this be happening? *Where are
you now, God? Oh, Juanita, where are you?*

He turned left, stepping through a threshold into a side room of
the sanctuary. The ceiling was so low Brad could hardly stand
straight. He scanned walls that were covered with photographs of
soldiers along with letters to God pleading for protection while in
harm's way; no Juanita. He had to stoop to peer into the tiny room
that held the healing soil; believers stepped past with small bags of
the holy earth. No Juanita.

A doorway led back outside, into the courtyard. Bright sunlight blasted his eyes again. He felt something near panic. He walked around the entire church, back to the courtyard where he stood so that he could easily be seen. He waited. Seconds dragged. Nothing. No Juanita. He continued looking with a sinking realization that his efforts were futile. Those wonderful moments of anticipation, from when he had first seen her, had so quickly turned to desperation. Now, all emotion ebbed into a simple sense of loss. He waited. Juanita did not come. Loss became betrayal. Brad walked away.

Time seemed suspended as he sat behind the wheel of his SUV, simply staring in the direction of the mission. He replayed everything, every frame, scrutinizing each one until the point where she had seen him. At that point, he froze the scene. It was Juanita. It was her dress, her hair, her skin and her smile. She had waved to him. He had seen her eyes.

Burying his face behind his hands, Brad spoke out loud, "What the hell is happening? How could a simple fishing trip have turned into this?" From the moment he had seen Vincent Perkins standing under a tree his life had been caught in some sort of surreal, translucent, twilight zone. Was there really a bandage about his head, covering stitches in the skin of his skull? Had he really stepped from a cabin, in the middle of nowhere, to encounter someone who attempted to murder him? Had his brothers taken him to a hospital in an automobile or had a mysterious man on horseback rescued him? Had he been treated by a physician utilizing modern technology or had he been healed by a sensuous mystique within a rickety cabin from an age long past? *Jesus H, what the hell is happening?*

Brad started his engine and drove away, leaving El Santuario de Chimayo behind. He left Juanita behind. The earlier peace he had felt while driving through mountain scenery was gone. He no longer saw beauty in the world around him. Descending out of Chimayo's hills, he entered the city of Espanola and turned south toward Santa Fe where he would grab the interstate on to Albuquerque. He ignored the landscape. The only emotion he now felt was anger. The hell with frigging ghosts, dreams and visions in the night. It was time to get his head out of his ass and face reality. It was time to get on an airplane for Los Angeles where he would visit with a dear friend who was in a hospital bed; where he would look Cassandra in the face, and together, they would talk with a real, live police officer. It was time to confront whatever was happening.

\* \* \* \*

Evening was imminent as Walter paid his parking tab at Albuquerque's airport and followed signs to Interstate 25, the road he would drive all the way to Denver. He had managed to grab some badly needed rest on the airplane and he felt energized after talking with his brother. He was now ready to roll. Heading out of the desert city, a setting sun transformed the Sandia Mountains into a mile-high inferno of blazing orange with purple shadows. By Santa Fe, early stars shared the sky with the sun's final remnants. Twilight melted. By the time he passed through Las Vegas, a black sky, adorned with millions of sparkles, embraced the mountains and plains of New Mexico. Walter saw none of this. He followed the beam of his headlights, driving north.

## CHAPTER TWENTY
July 13, 2012

Inching their way through rush hour of a Los Angeles morning, Brad drove his rental car and listened as Cassandra brought him up on the latest from Norton. They made small talk and avoided discussion of what was pressing on both their minds. They shared a silent understanding that the conversation was being manipulated to remain artificially lighthearted until they met with Dan Wright. That's when real talk would begin.

It was just like nothing had changed in all the passing years. It was the same restaurant, same time of day and the same smells. Dan Wright even sat at the same table. He first hugged Cassandra and then warmly shook Brad's hand as they seated. It was easy to see that even in retirement, Dan was the same old Dan. Trim and sharp, he wore the standard slacks and loose fitting shirt that had always been his choice when he wasn't on duty with a suit and tie. Dan had been the lead investigator for Los Angeles Police Department in the Vincent Perkins investigation. Brad and Dan had spent weeks, side-by-side, digging through a trash bin of humanity that constituted the life of Vincent Perkins. The bond that germinated in those ugly days had developed into a lasting friendship. Then, as charges were filed and trial preparations began, Cassandra had stepped into the picture as the prosecuting attorney. The number of hours the three had spent together could not be counted; many of those hours within this restaurant, at this very table. It was here, with breakfast and coffee after another midnighter, that much of the strategy for the trial of Vincent Perkins had been formulated.

Dan silently took in the bandage about Brad's head with a somber expression. "So, Osama, what's with the new threads? After chow, you planning to head off to Mecca?"

Brad rolled his eyes in exasperation. "Okay, let's just spend a few minutes to get it all out. Make jokes, be your usual juvenile self, make certain that you become the center of attention at another person's expense. Sure as hell nothing's changed with you. I see you are as obnoxious as ever."

"Hey, hey. Come on now." Dan threw his hands in the air in feigned indignation. "I just want to know if you need a table facing the east or have some special dietary concerns. Last time I looked, they didn't have figs or camel's milk on the menu. This is all about you, Brad, all about you."

Turning to Cassandra, Brad spoke in exasperation, "Cassandra, you're the hot shot lawyer. You respond to this feeble-minded donkey. All I want is coffee and some breakfast."

They all laughed as Cassandra related her own amplified version of Brad's dismal failure as a cowboy and wild bronco rider.

Dan looked to Cassandra and with a roll of his eyes and dry voice pointed out the obvious. "If our friend here had been riding a camel, he probably would not have had his ass tossed to the ground." Dan shook his head in bewilderment and concentrated on his coffee while Cassandra threw her head back and laughed out loud.

After placing their orders, Dan was the first to bring a serious note to the conversation. "I hate to be the grownup here but, Cassandra, I've got a bone to pick with you. My wife and I went up to Lake Tahoe for a little vacation and we very deliberately chose not to watch television or follow any news out of Washington, DC, or Los Angeles. So, yesterday, I get home and find your message waiting on my home telephone telling me about Norton. A voice mail for heaven's sake! Why in the world didn't you call my cell, Cassandra? I would have dropped everything and been here in a flash."

Reaching across the table, Cassandra grasped his hand and

smiled. "I'll tell you why I didn't call your cell. It's because fifteen years ago, almost to the day, that we sat at this very table. It was just a few days before the trial and you talked about how the Vincent Perkins case had caused you to miss your wedding anniversary and your yearly trip to Lake Tahoe. I remembered, Dan, I remembered. You see, I remember everything that happened around that trial like it was yesterday. I knew it was your anniversary and no way was I going to call you." Cassandra smiled at Dan with a "got ya" look.

Dan stared at Cassandra in astonishment. "I don't know whether to kiss you or strangle you."

Cassandra laughed. "Buy me breakfast and we're even."

"That's an easy one but I still may strangle you." Dan turned from Cassandra and spoke to both of them. "Okay, my old friends, I desperately want to know what's going on here. Brad, you didn't climb on an airplane to fly across the country just because you think it's fun. And, you sure as heck didn't bring Cassandra away from the hospital just for a couple of pancakes. There's something cooking here. Tell me what's on your mind."

A quick glance passed between Cassandra and Brad before Brad leaned forward in his seat and began to speak. He gave a recap of the assault on Norton Roberts, pointing out Cassandra's intuition that there may be a connection with the Vincent Perkins trial. Cassandra then told her story of how she felt that a man who was identical in appearance to Vincent Perkins had watched her. She was totally honest in that she admitted that recent stress she had endured could have influenced her perceptions.

Dan Wright sat quietly, listening with no reaction.

Cassandra then continued with her narrative. She told of how she had learned from former co-workers about the arson in Oregon and the catastrophe to Judge Christopher's home. As she concluded, her eyes were moist and she fought to maintain composure.

They sat at the table in silence for a few moments, each of them attempting to fathom the realities and significance of what had been discussed. Dan Wright broke the silence. "Wow, I didn't know the awful details about Norton's attack and this is the first I've heard about the arson on Judge Christopher's home." He looked introspective, as everyone was again quiet, paying little attention to the food that had been placed on the table. "I think I understand what the two of you are driving at here and I guess I can't say that I disagree with you. There sure as heck may be some connection to Vincent Perkins. However, the three of us lived and breathed that case for weeks and any one of us could be accused of not being completely objective."

Dan leaned back and a skeptical expression crept over his face. "If you step back and look at this more like a judge who has to evaluate an affidavit for a search warrant, I think it's pretty thin. Why someone would attack Norton is a complete mystery but there are hundreds of unexplained attacks in Los Angeles every year. This is a crazy city. And as for the arson on Judge Christopher's home, you have to remember that the man was a judge for many years. He conducted trials of every stripe and color and sentenced hundreds of really bad people to prison. He's handled murder cases, rapes, drugs and gang bangers. You name it and Judge Christopher encountered it. There's no end to the possibilities of creeps who have an ax to grind with the judge." Dan looked across the table at Brad and Cassandra, "Not to mention that all kinds of those cases are a heck of a lot more recent than our case with Vincent Perkins."

Dan turned to Cassandra. "I have no explanation for what you saw at that coffee shop but I honestly don't think it moves the needle. You were coming off an incredibly traumatic experience and seeing someone like that guy could easily trigger a very upsetting reaction." Dan was quiet again before he softly spoke, "I know that's not what you wanted to hear, but I'm being brutally honest with you." Dan stopped talking and looked to Cassandra and Brad for reaction.

Cassandra gripped a coffee mug in her hands, her eyes still holding a reservoir of tears. She dropped her gaze, unable to look at either man. Her head shook in acknowledgement, as she spoke, not much more than a whisper. "I suppose you're right, Dan. As a lawyer, I can step back and be analytical, just as you suggested. And if I do that, I reach the same conclusion as you just articulated. But, as a wife to Norton, a friend to Judge Christopher and simply as a woman who has lived a whole lot of life, much of it as a pretty darned good criminal prosecutor, I'm telling you there's something here." A single tear trickled down her cheek. She made no attempt to wipe it away.

Neither man could look at Cassandra. They suddenly decided they were hungry and concentrated on their food. After moments of silence, Brad took a deep breath and spoke. "Okay, Dan, I think you have sized this up absolutely correctly. But, as you said earlier I did-n't fly out here just to chat with you and take Cassandra away from Norton without good reason. I have something more to add to this story."

Dan simply nodded with an "Okay," but Cassandra's head snapped to attention and her eyes flared with puzzlement. Brad squirmed in his chair, obviously uncomfortable, all eyes suddenly upon him. With a gulp of air for courage, he faced Cassandra and spoke. "Cassandra, before I say what I have to say, I apologize to you right up front. Please hear me out and try to understand why I have-n't told you before now what you are about to hear."

It was her prosecutor's face. Cassandra's eyes augured straight through Brad. Her defenses were on high alert and Brad sensed that counter attack was imminent.

With his face looking as though he had just swallowed something terribly bitter, Brad began to talk. He told of his nighttime walk in Taos and his haunting encounter with "Vincent Perkins," who ap-peared to have somehow defied the aging process. Brad was aware of the dumbfounded facial expressions coming from Dan and Cassan-dra but he did his best to ignore them as he continued. He related his tale of the night at the fishing cabin and the assault he had suffered. He told of rescue by his brothers and friend and about being trans-ported to a hospital in Taos. He matter-of-factly relayed his doctor's words about how a fraction of an inch had saved him from horrible injury or death. Brad glanced across the table to Dan and spoke in a tone that brought conclusion to his chronicle. "So, that's the story, Dan. We have a crazy son-of-a-bitch traveling around the country using a pipe to smash the heads of people who are connected in some way to the Vincent Perkins trial. And then, just for fun, somebody burned the house of the presiding judge."

Brad stopped talking and the table was silent before he made his last statement. "Now you know why the hell I flew all the way out here to see the two of you. It damn sure wasn't just to be sociable." Brad leaned back in his chair, exhaling a sigh of frustration and re-lief. Then, he had no choice but to wait for a response.

Dan simply looked amazed as he absorbed what he had just been told without saying a word. Cassandra was more difficult to decipher. Her face was transfixed in astonishment but her eyes burned with indignation. Brad saw her shoulders come forward as her voice delivered a mixture of harsh judgment tempered with caring relief. "My God, Brad, how could you have lied to me about this? How could you have withheld something so consequential?" Cassandra's brown eyes held his gaze and telegraphed her inner thoughts: should she sob or scream, slap him or hug him?

Brad had no idea how to respond. With an expression of one who begged for mercy, he turned away from Dan and focused upon Cassandra as if she was the only person in the restaurant. "Come on, Cassandra, I had no idea what to think about what I saw, or thought I saw, that night in Taos. I had downed too many margaritas and I was upset over you and Norton. And think about it. Even if I had told you, what was it going to accomplish?" Brad shrugged his shoulders and lifted his arms to indicate his own exasperation. "Then, I blink twice and wake up from some sort of coma to find that I'm in a damned hospital not having any idea what in the world had happened. I've been trying to figure things out myself. It's not like I've got all the answers. It wasn't until our telephone conversation when you told me about the arson on Judge Christopher's home that events seemed to solidify. That's when I finally began to see things with clarity."

Brad looked to Dan Wright for support but none came. Dan listened to the conversation of his friends but had been a cop way too long and was far too wise to get involved with this one. This was one time that Brad was going to be on his own.

Cassandra finally took her eyes off of Brad but she had no idea where else to look. Her gaze drifted about the café, as if she was looking for herself. For the second time in minutes, a tear streaked her cheek, catching light as a prism against her dark skin.

Brad felt his heart about to explode. He stood up from his chair and went to Cassandra. He stood beside her chair and simply said, "Cassandra, please." She looked up into his face, deliberating. It took a few seconds but Cassandra stood up to face Brad; their embrace was spontaneous and fierce. The crowded café became awkwardly quiet as dining patrons were treated to the sight of a six foot three, grey-haired white man locked in an embrace with a six foot black woman, while another grey-haired white guy sat with a goofy grin on his face, seeming to take great delight in the spectacle.

Finally, with everyone again seated and the restaurant back to a buzz of conversation, Brad looked to Dan with a sheepish grin. "Okay, I think we need to get busy."

"No shit, Sherlock." Dan laughed and reached across the table to give a squeeze to Cassandra's hand.

Turning his eyes to Cassandra, Brad began. "I've got all kinds of stuff running through my head. First, let's talk about you, Cassandra." With a no-nonsense tone, he leveled his comment directly to her. "I don't want you in your house alone at all, especially at night. Not only that, you shouldn't be out and about anywhere at all unless someone is with you. You have an issue with that?"

There was no opportunity for Cassandra to even respond. Dan interjected authoritatively, "We're not even going to waste our time on that one. While you two children were making up after your little spat, and providing some great entertainment for everyone's breakfast pleasure I might add, I was sitting here thinking like a cop. I may be retired but I still carry some weight downtown. The moment we finish up here, I'll be talking to some folks and I can promise a female officer will be with you, twenty-four seven, starting this afternoon."

Both men turned their eyes to Cassandra. Her relief virtually radiated. "Thank you, thank you. You have no idea how terrified I've been."

"One more thing," Dan continued. "Talk with your doctors and see when they think it will be safe to move Norton. The newspaper has identified the exact hospital where he is located and that is absolutely no good. If he can't be moved for a while, no problem, I'll get an officer to be posted in the hallway outside his room. If the doctors say he can't be moved, don't worry, you've got someone with him all the time."

Cassandra merely nodded, her gratitude and relief obvious.

"Good, that part is handled." Brad shoved his plate away and leaned over the table. "The way I see it there are a couple of things that need to get done right away. First, I say LAPD needs to dig up the Vincent Perkins case and review every detail about that shitbird. Just think back to when you and I were putting that case together. We found all kinds of associates and connections for that knucklehead. He ran with common street punks but he also was entrenched with some well-organized white supremacist groups. I can't begin to remember them all. Someone needs to be tracking down every person who ever so much as said good morning to Vincent Perkins. And then, every one of them deserves a really hard look."

"Without a doubt." Dan rubbed his forehead. "I flat don't remember too many specifics about his family and associates but all of those records need to be reviewed."

"Absolutely."

Dan pulled a pen and pad from his pocket and began to write. "And since he's locked up here in California, let's find out what Corrections can give us. Visitors, mail, telephone calls, all that stuff."

"You bet your ass. And I was thinking on my flight out here that we need to determine if he had any friends in the joint who have recently been released. Vincent Perkins is never going to change; he is what he is. My money says that if he has any friends in the joint, they're all going to be made of the same muck. Any of those guys who have been recently released and are back out on the streets need to be considered as real suspects."

"Consider it done." Dan was jotting notes as he spoke. "And, another thing. I'm going to ask around headquarters about what's going on with the various hate groups that are scattered over the region. I'll see what old timers are still hanging on and if some new talent has moved in."

With a headshake to signify his agreement, Brad continued. "I plan to call the Bureau office in Portland and do the same thing up there. That whole area has been a breeding ground for losers like Vincent Perkins for years. With the arson of the judge's home, the Bureau and every police department up there will already be on high alert and shaking things up. I'll give them a heads up about everything that has happened down here. That should initiate communication between the Bureau and LAPD."

Dan closed his note pad and looked at Cassandra and then to Brad. "Okay, this is a good start for old retired folks but I need to go over this once more. Let's talk about what happened to the two of you so I'm sure I've got this straight. First, Cassandra sees Vincent Perkins, or his ghost, on the streets of Los Angeles. Then, Brad, you have a very similar experience when you also see some bald-headed fruitcake. And, just like Cassandra, you swear that this phantom is a dead

Dale Lovin

ringer for Vincent Perkins."

Brad caught the twinkle in Dan's eyes and grinned as he looked across the table but Cassandra looked serious as a funeral, adamantly nodding her head up and down. Dan laughed out loud as he spoke to Brad. "I can promise you one thing, you worn-out old goat, if it weren't for Cassandra's story as corroboration, I'd look you right in the eye and tell you that you were chewing on peyote buttons. However, with someone of her credibility backing you, I'll give you benefit of a doubt and move on."

Dan tossed a wink toward Cassandra as he continued speaking to Brad. "You're telling us that you are out in frigging New Mexico, not exactly the commerce capitol of the world under any circumstances, and you are in a cabin way the hell up some mountains. And somehow, someway, a villain with a club apparently beams himself to your location and waits for your ass outside this cabin that nobody else in the world knows about. And then, you're stupid enough to go checking out noises in the night and some shadowy phantom knocks the ever-living hell out of you." Dan took a breath and leveled his eyes at Brad. "Now, I'm sitting here across this table from you, looking at your busted head all wrapped up like silly-ass Lawrence of Arabia, and somehow all this is supposed to make sense? I think you should have stuck to your story about getting bucked off a horse. It was sure as heck more believable and I just plain liked it a lot better."

Cassandra was smiling now, loving the old humor that she missed so much. After Dan finished his soliloquy, they all laughed. Cassandra leaned close and spoke directly to Brad, "Now, Mr. Honest Abe, is there anything else in this story that you have fibbed about or parts that you are conveniently leaving out? You know, something like the courtroom line: the truth, the whole truth and nothing but the truth." She was smiling, but half serious.

It took less than half a second for Brad's decision. He would tell the truth but not the whole truth. He lifted both hands into the air in a gesture of surrender and honesty, "You know the hard facts as I know the hard facts." No way in hell was he going to tell them about the night rescue by Moustache, a tiny house from the past century or the tender touch of Juanita. Brad could only imagine the response he would get from Dan Wright. He could almost hear his friend laughing and making some wise-assed comment like, 'When do I get to ride on that magic carpet? A low level cruise over Hollywood sure would be nice!' Some parts of this story would remain his and his alone.

Brad offered his response. "The two of you go ahead and bust my chops and have your laughs. But don't think for a second I haven't racked my brain about how someone found me at that cabin. There's only one way that this thing could have unfolded and I don't like the conclusion one little bit." He paused, crafting his thoughts before speaking. "Somebody followed me from my house in Colorado. That's it. The only people who knew my plans were Cassandra, my brothers and an old Bureau friend. Some people in Colorado knew I was going fishing but they had no idea where I was headed."

Cassandra and Dan listened but offered no judgment.

Brad gave a curt laugh. "How some dredge found out where I live is troubling but not all that mysterious. Anybody with a computer and a few dollars can find just about anyone who's living a normal life and not making a real effort to hide. Hell's bells, I'm so open that my name is right there in the phone book, the good old white pages. I'm easy to find." He shrugged, "This is no big mystery. Someone found me, someone followed me and someone tried to take my head off."

The entire table was quiet for a second before Brad made his final point. "All that has to be done is to look at everything that has happened in its entirety. Consider what happened to Norton by somebody using a pipe. Think about what Cassandra saw outside the coffee shop and the guy I saw in Taos. Then, add to the mix the arson of Judge Christopher's house and the assault on me by a pipe-swinging lunatic. To think that all of these things are random and unrelated is lunacy. Everything here is planned and deliberate. And once that is acknowledged, it would be insane to deny that it is all related to Vincent Perkins. If the assault on me is related to Vincent Perkins, then so is Norton's and so is the arson. It's like that circle of life stuff." Brad sat back, obviously finished.

Both Cassandra and Dan talked over each other in their rush to agree with Brad's assessment. They finished their meal and finalized details of what needed to be done and promised to keep in close contact. Dan and Brad shook hands as Dan departed, heading to police headquarters to track down his contacts in LAPD. Cassandra and

Dale Lovin

Brad left the café enroute to the hospital for a visit with Norton.

\* \* \* \*

The scene that confronted Brad as he entered Norton's room was very similar to what he had seen days earlier. Fewer bandages were wrapped about Norton's head but his face remained covered. A small area of skin was visible around his chin and neck but the tubes and monitors had not changed. Amy sat beside her father. Cassandra and Brad entered the room and Amy stood, hugged her mother and extended her hand to Brad. "Hi, Mr. Walker, thanks for coming out again. Mom and I appreciate your help more than you know."

"Oh, my goodness, Amy, it's my pleasure. Thank you for helping out here. This is going to be a team effort for a while."

Cassandra stepped around Amy and Brad to reach Norton's bed. She leaned over to address her husband and spoke in a whispered tone. Amy and Brad stood in silence, giving her time. Brad could hear some of her words, enough to know that she told Norton that she had been with Dan Wright and Brad Walker. Cassandra stood straight and beckoned for Brad to come close. "Here, Brad, hold his hand. He will respond to you by squeezing. He'll be thrilled to talk with you."

Brad leaned close to Norton and grasped the hand that extended from under the bed sheet. He spoke softly of how everyone was pulling for him and that he was way too strong to let a little thing like this keep him down. Brad felt pressure on his hand. He told Norton that he was a lucky man to have a wife as wonderful as Cassandra and he talked about the beauty of Amy; she was an absolute ringer for Cassandra. Brad again felt pressure. He brought his mouth even closer to Norton's face. "I'm making you a promise my dear friend. I promise you that I'm going to find the son-of-a-bitch who did this to you. I'm going to find him and see to it that he hangs by his balls. You have my word, Norton, you have my word." Brad felt the strength of a bull squeeze his hand.

Amy, Cassandra and Brad stepped out of Norton's room into the hallway. Emotions were high and they made small talk, each finding their own way through the moment. Turning to Amy, Brad inquired as to how long she would be able to stay with her parents. "I'm planning to leave tomorrow but I'll be back soon. I need to get home for just a few days to make some arrangements at work and then I'll hurry right back." She was dabbing remaining tears with a tissue as she spoke.

"Amy, please forgive my forgetful old brain but I've lost track of you. Back when I saw you frequently, you were in school. You're all grown up now and I don't even know where you live or what you are doing." Brad seemed a bit embarrassed.

Amy laughed. "Oh, no worries. I live in Portland, Oregon. I absolutely love it there. It's such a change from Los Angeles. I'm engaged to be married next spring and I have a wonderful job as a certified financial planner. You wouldn't believe the great office I have. It's in a bank and, from my desk, I have a phenomenal view of the Willamette River."

\* \* \* \*

Albuquerque's airport felt like a graveyard after the pandemonium of Los Angeles International. Brad stopped in the terminal to inhale an enchilada before his drive back to Taos. This time, he drove a faster route. He shot up the interstate to Santa Fe where he took Highway 68 north to follow the Rio Grande River all the way to Taos. Night had fallen and traffic was minimal as he made his way past strip malls and fast food restaurants of modern day Taos. He felt relief when he finally reached the old, historic district. As soon as he set foot inside his room he made a beeline to the small refrigerator, thanking the gods that he had chilled some Moosehead before he left. Dr. Owens had cautioned him to avoid alcohol until his follow-up visit that was scheduled for the next morning. *Rules were made to be broken.* Brad popped a Moosehead and silently toasted Dr. Owens. It would be coffee with the guys in the morning, a quick visit with Dr. Owens and then time to get busy.

## CHAPTER TWENTY-ONE
July 14, 2012

After a restless night, Brad was glad that only a handful of people sat in the restaurant as he sipped his coffee and perused the morning's edition of the **Albuquerque Journal.** Matthew and Fry were the first to join him. Fry quickly informed Brad that the previous day's fishing had been a tough day for Matthew as both Patrick and he had caught more fish than the esteemed professor. Matthew's face looked like someone had squirted lemon juice in his eyes, instantly confirming to Brad that Fry spoke the truth. Within seconds, Patrick approached. He glanced at Matthew and reacted with a startled expression. "What in the world is wrong, Matthew? Why the sad face? Did you get your ass spanked on the river yesterday or did someone take a shit in your cornflakes?" Even Matthew had to laugh.

After a quick rundown on the previous day's fishing, Brad passed on the highlights of his Los Angeles trip. "I'm outta here to go see Dr. Owens," and with a glance to Patrick, "I sure would like to see you when I get back."

"You got it. Sounds like we need to talk."

After a few more minutes of jokes and some good laughs, Brad excused himself and left for his doctor's appointment. He was back and sitting with the guys under a shade tree in just over an hour.

They sat within a stone's throw of Governor Bent's House and Museum, the site of the Taos rebellion. It took a few minutes to relate that Dr. Owens was absolutely pleased with how well he was doing. Brad laughed when he talked about how he had simply forgotten to tell Dr. Owens about his whirlwind trip to Los Angeles. He explained that the doctor had insisted that a bandage must remain about his head, mostly as protection for the area where stitches would remain for a few more days. The doctor had told Brad that even an accidental bump on the wound could be serious, so a padded bandage would remain a part of his wardrobe for a while longer. Fry suggested that some feathers tucked into the bandage would not only be quite festive but might cause tourists to think Brad was an important chief of some sort. Brad suggested that Fry engage in a sexual act.

"Hey, Patrick, I need to call the Bureau out in Portland. Wouldn't Lynn Everett be the person to call? I'm thinking he's going to be the guy who will be on top of the arson case up there and really have his finger on the pulse of things. I know him but just not as well as you." All humor had left Brad's voice.

Without thought Patrick replied, "No question. Lynn Everett is the man to call. He's one of the best men I ever worked with and he'll be your man. He will know all about the arson and anything related to it. He's the guy who put together the case on that royal jerk, Bhagwan Shree and the Rajneeshees, in their commune out east of Portland."

Brad looked thoughtful for a second. "Oh, yeah, those were those people who tried to poison the food supply for attorneys, politicians and about half of Oregon so they could have their own little utopia out there in the friggin boondocks with free sex and meditation for everyone."

Patrick gave a cynical, half laugh, half grunt. "You got it. It was another one of those cult scams. And the majority of the imbeciles who followed the Bhagwan were the same old usual suspects: doctors, lawyers and Indian chiefs. We even spotted Fry running around the compound. He heard about the free sex part so he came running. You should see him in a thong, sandals and headband. He fit right in with that distinguished crowd." Everyone laughed.

"Do you have Lynn's number in your phone? I sure would like to talk with him."

"You bet, I have it right here." Pulling his phone out, Patrick had the number up and ringing in a heartbeat. Brad listened as his brother conversed with Lynn for a few minutes and then handed the phone to Brad.

"Hey, Lynn, thanks for your help here." Brad got straight to the point. "I think we've got ourselves an issue that could get out of hand pretty darned quick."

Lynn Everett listened as Brad explained the events that had led to the call. After Brad finished speaking, Lynn was quiet for a moment as he thought about Brad's story. "Wow, that's some tall tale. If it were your brother telling me this, I would know right away that it was simply the result of way too much beer that finally ate up his brain. However, since you're the one telling the story, I guess I'll have to believe you." Brad laughed as Lynn continued. "Well, let me tell you what's going on with this case up here. You already know about how lucky we were that the judge and his family weren't killed. It was one heck of a fire and it spread through that house really fast."

"That could have been one major tragedy."

"That's an understatement, my friend. I have the ticket on this thing for the Bureau so I'll be handling the case and I'm really glad to get your call this morning. Of course, the folks from ATF are also on it big time. They are out there working hard and killing themselves to find some sort of evidence. But that place is nothing but a big pile of ashes. Those poor people are digging through everything, piece-by-piece and ounce-by-ounce. They're doing a great job but based on what the judge and his family saw and heard that night, along with how the whole place went up in seconds, there's really very little doubt that it was a well planned arson carried out by several people. ATF figures at least ten people had to have been involved. Every window in the house was shattered, practically simultaneously. And then, it appears that gasoline bombs were thrown into the house. Whoever the heck did this, they were dead serious about killing everyone inside the house." Lynn was quiet.

Even though this wasn't the first time he had heard the story, the reality of the callous nature required for a person to actually perpetrate such a hideous crime triggered a sick feeling in Brad's stomach. "For heaven's sake, Lynn, just when a guy thinks he's seen it all, something like this happens. How in the name of mankind could someone try to murder an entire family, especially in that manner?"

"I know, Brad, it's an absolute mystery to me. I don't see how people could be so demented but we sure as the dickens have us some twisted minds out there on this one." Lynn's voice sounded discouraged. "What I've been doing is taking a look at everything and everybody who has been in the judge's life since he moved to Oregon. But I really don't think that's where the answer lies. It's just something that has to be done. Los Angeles is the key. I've felt that way from the start but now, after hearing your story, I'm even more convinced.

"Yep, this will all go back to Los Angeles."

"We're already working with LAPD and the Bureau in Los Angeles but we will definitely concentrate more diligently in that regard now that we have this new information. We're trying to find someone from the Judge's days on the bench who might be likely suspects for something like this. We started by going back through the last five years of the Judge's career, you know, the usual crowd, dopers, street gang people, really neat folks like that. With each case we have to dig through the files of the principals who were involved and then look at all their associates to see if anything jumps out as a possibility. It's one heck of a monster job. But after hearing your wild story, I've got a feeling we've been fishing in the wrong pond. We need to be looking way further in the past."

"I think that's correct, Lynn, I really do. There's just way too much here for this to be coincidence. It has to go back to Vincent Perkins in some way. Now, the question is whether this a story of pure revenge for something that happened fifteen years ago, or are we dealing with more complicated reasons that indicate another chapter of supremacists is back to their old tricks. Who the heck knows?"

"Okay, Brad, you have no idea how much I appreciate your call. I'm going to hop on this the second we hang up and I'll keep you in the loop."

"I sure would appreciate it. Somebody needs to get caught in a hurry on this one."

"Absolutely, Brad, we're on it starting right now."

Two hours later Brad stood with Fry, his brothers and their wives. Everybody hugged and said goodbye after luggage was loaded. It was the end of what was to have been the best week of the year. But now here they stood, tears in all eyes, to bid farewell in an emotional con-

Dale Lovin

coction of disappointment and uncertainty.

Taos faded into Brad's rear view mirror. The warmth of friends and the magic of New Mexico evaporated and landscape passed by unnoticed. With melancholy his companion, Brad made the drive in silence, heading for home. He remained vigilant for surveillance but his gut told him this was not the time or the day that his enemy would make another appearance.

* * * *

Long before the familiar landmarks that signaled he was getting close to Denver, Brad made his telephone call. He had been thinking about it for the past hundred miles. Kurt Riddle answered right away and the moment Brad heard the voice of his friend, he knew that a conversation with Kurt would be of more benefit than a dozen sessions with Dr. Owens. After Kurt's predictable onslaught of insults, an agreement was reached to meet for coffee as soon as Brad reached the outskirts of Denver. "I need a friendly face for a while," Brad muttered to himself as he hung up the telephone. Kurt was a sheriff's investigator just west of Denver and had been Brad's friend for years. Time with Kurt was never wasted.

Kurt's car was supposed to be an unmarked unit but Brad was still able to spot it as a police vehicle within seconds of pulling into the parking lot. Kurt was standing outside the coffee shop and gave a wave as Brad parked his SUV. Kurt's easy smile traveled all the way across the lot and Brad knew he had done the right thing by calling.

With black coffee and a plate of cookies between them, they enjoyed their usual back-and-forth over who was the best looking and who had solved the most cases. Kurt had planned to go on the New Mexico horse trip with Brad but a subpoena for court testimony had forced him to cancel at the last minute. He listened in amazement as Brad related the events of the past days and told of why he had returned home early, wearing a bandage on his head and no tales of a campsite in the mountains.

"Unbelievable," was uttered numerous times throughout the story as coffee was sipped and the cookies disappeared. When Brad had finished telling of all that happened in Los Angeles, New Mexico and Oregon, Kurt grinned with his response. "You and I worked together for years, but it wasn't until you stopped being a Fed that life with you really became interesting."

Brad laughed and shook his head in a bewildered agreement. "Is that ever the sad truth!" Years of working together had led to volumes of shared experiences but it was what had happened after Brad had left the FBI that really stirred their emotions. Through sheer happenstance, Brad had stumbled into a heartbreaking case that involved a kidnapped woman and an organization of human traffickers. Kurt had been a key player in solving the tangled web that had ensued. Brad spoke, half-laughing and half-serious as he thought back to the events of those days. "What the heck is it with me and fishing trips? I took a day to fly-fish. What's wrong with that? But do I just go fishing and have a good time like everyone else we know?" Kurt was laughing out loud, knowing what was coming. "Hell no," Brad said as he thrust his arms up in exasperation. "I go fishing and stumble into a kidnapping that leads to Washington, DC hotshots who are involved in human trafficking. Now, months later, here we go again. I sneak off to New Mexico for a chance to fish and wham; a bald-headed monkey damned near kills me. And, it sure looks like I'm in the middle of another wild-assed investigation. Why can't I simply go catch a few little trout, drink a Moosehead and go home like a normal person? "

Kurt loved every word of Brad's rant. "Maybe you should take up bowling or playing the trumpet. Hell, anything to get that silly old fly rod out of your hand. If you give up fishing, there's a chance, a very slim chance, that you might live long enough to find yourself some romance in a nursing home one of these days."

"Maybe you should sit on a chili pepper." After a good laugh Brad became serious. "Really Kurt, what do think about this crazy stuff? This entire episode has a feel about it that reminds me very much of the deal with the woman who was kidnapped over in Aspen. That was a case for the police and FBI, not a guy like me with absolutely no authority. But, when that whole thing started, you were the first person I called. I trust you more than anybody I know. And what you told me that morning was the best advice I ever had. You told me to have adequate courage to follow my gut instinct. And, you stuck with me from start to finish. Thank the Lord in heaven I listened to you. I credit anything good that came out of that case to you and your counsel. If I had not listened to you, that poor lady would never have been found and those Washington shitheads would still be trafficking people. So, here I am again, hat in hand, you old sage. What's your advice this time?"

Kurt leaned back and gave a Brad a thoughtful look. "Well, apart from suggesting that you give up fishing, I'm not sure what to say to you. There is no doubt that you're smack in the middle of something." Kurt grinned. "That goofy patch on your head is proof of that. But this is different than your last big Tom Sawyer adventure with the kidnapping in Aspen. Most everything that developed in that case was right here in Colorado, pretty much in your own back yard." Kurt shook his head slowly. "This time around, it appears the action is going to be out on the West Coast. The big thing for you is that somebody with ties to those creeps went to a bunch of trouble to hunt you down. And they obviously had intentions to put you out of your misery."

Brad gave a slow nod that he agreed with Kurt's assessment. "That's what has been so frustrating. I feel like I'm at the mercy of the police or FBI in Los Angeles and Portland. They are all great people and they'll work hard to put everything together but it doesn't sit well with me to lay around and scratch while someone else figures out who almost killed my very good friend and who tried to nail me."

"I absolutely understand. I would feel exactly the same if I were in your shoes." Kurt hunched his shoulders toward Brad. "Listen, I don't have an easy answer for you but as I've listened to you talk, something keeps coming up and I suggest you think about this."

"That's why I called you, Kurt. Tell me what you think."

"Don't get excited. What I have to say is certainly no magic bullet and it may sound trite but here is what strikes me." Kurt gathered his thoughts. "You speak about the ominous feelings that you experienced fifteen years ago when you were in that Los Angeles courtroom and how they lingered, but you swept them aside, year after year."

"I'm listening."

"Then you told me about your friend, Cassandra, and how she told you that immediately after the attack on her husband, she had strange feelings that what happened to her husband was related to this big case that the two of you worked."

"I'm still listening."

Kurt smiled and shook his head as if he wasn't sure how to proceed. "Then I hear your stories of how both you and Cassandra have inexplicable encounters with phantoms from your past. Some person, or ghost or something keeps popping up thousands of miles apart and making life miserable for you. And, let me add to the mystery here by saying that I absolutely believe it when you tell me how you felt someone was watching you when you were by the trout stream in New Mexico. I've had those same feelings myself and they usually turned out to be accurate."

"Oh, hell yes, Kurt. What I felt at the river that day was real. I was just too stupid to pay attention. And I agree with you, those feelings serve us well all through life. I don't know if it's the human body, the mind, the soul or what it is but sometimes there is simply something inexplicable out there. Something that is completely invisible but can sure as heck be felt, just like the wind."

"No doubt." Kurt nodded his head as he contemplated Brad's words.

"Especially, when we're dealing with something really evil or really good. You know, Kurt, it's almost like evil and good have their own unique odors or energies. If a person simply pays attention, those sensations are right there, a part of our senses. Sometimes our intuitions are felt subtly and other times they're more like a flashing strobe. What's amazing is that since we don't really understand the phenomenon, we so often tend to stick our heads in the sand and ignore those signals."

"Absolutely. I agree completely. But no matter, I sure think that some person was watching you that day in New Mexico. But here is something important, Brad." Kurt directed his eyes right into Brad's and spoke with feeling. "I'm convinced that whoever it was, they didn't want to face you straight on. They weren't willing to chance a confrontation with you. They waited for an opportunity to take you from behind. You were dealing with evil, my friend, a damned evil person. But worse than evil is cowardly evil. Don't underestimate what this guy or these people can do to you." Kurt pointed his finger at Brad for emphasis. "But, I'll lay you dollars to donuts that if you ever find yourself face-to-face with this no good bastard, and the odds are even, he will fold like a wet rag. Cowards are weak. They think only of themselves."

"I guess I hadn't thought about it in those exact terms but I think you are right on."

"Okay, let me wrap this up. I've listened to you lay out an incredible story and woven throughout are these mysterious feelings shared by a veteran prosecutor and a veteran FBI agent. My vote is that your feelings are not hocus-pocus at all. I think that there is a reason for your hunches. There is something very real here. Something solid is triggering your feelings. You just haven't yet put your finger on that certain something. That's what's missing."

Brad nodded his head, taking in every word spoken by his friend.

"You are overlooking something that is tucked away in the cracks of that old brain of yours. Cassandra is doing the same thing. The two of you must get inside your heads and dig around. You have to find that little nugget. It's there, you've simply misplaced it or you're overlooking it. But, it is still in there and you must find it. Once you do that, you will understand the strange feelings and they will no longer seem strange."

Kurt leaned back and gave his big smile. "Now, you old knucklehead, if I was a licensed shrink I could charge you a fortune for this advice. Instead, I'll let you pay for my coffee and cookies and I'm getting back to work. Then, you need to get your ass out of here and go figure out what you're missing. If anything comes up that you need a hand with, give me a call. I'll come running."

The men stood and shook hands. Nothing more needed to be said. Decades of experience and years of friendship did the talking for them as they bid farewell and went their separate ways.

Before he had made his way out of the parking lot, Brad knew exactly what he had to do. Why in the world had he not realized this sooner? He thought back to the matter of the woman who had been abducted near Aspen. When he had felt so much tumult in the early days of that incident, he had gone to the Frying Pan River to sort things out. It was time on a river that had cleared his mind on that difficult day. It would work again.

*I sure as hell don't have anyone at home waiting for me.* Brad turned from the parking lot and headed southwest, away from Denver. There was a special place on the North Fork of the South Platte River that would work perfectly.

Thirty minutes later Brad was walking. It was a short hike to the place where he had spent so many magical hours, fishing with his sons. When the water came into view, an ocean of memories flooded. He sat down and looked at the river. He recalled every boulder and knew each riffle. He knew where the water held hidden deep pockets and where sand bars rose to create soft shallows that begged for a graceful cast with a tiny fly. He listened and watched. Evening was approaching and shadows were already beginning to fall across the river. Sparkling water rushed from areas within bright sun to shadowed bends that were dark and grey. He thought of Elizabeth. They had loved to share evenings like this together.

Brad closed his eyes and took his mind back to Cassandra's initial telephone call telling him of the attack on Norton. He moved his mind and body through a re-play of every word and expression he and Cassandra had shared. He sat through the trial again. He listened to testimony of police officers. He recalled his own words that had been spoken from the witness stand. He brought back every face that had been in the courtroom: the reporters, the court staff and the family of Vincent Perkins. He concentrated to see them all. He was in Taos again, walking with Patrick. He listened once more to their conversation and felt the margarita buzz that had been so wonderful. He saw Vincent Perkins standing beneath the tree. Brad stopped everything right there and examined the face he had glimpsed on that night. Nothing had changed. It had been the exact Vincent Perkins from the courtroom. Every word spoken over breakfast with Dan and Cassandra, he listened to again.

He opened his eyes and looked at the river. Shadows were growing longer. He couldn't find what he was looking for. What was missing? He returned to the world within his mind. He lived it all again: the cabin, Moustache, Juanita, his brothers in the hospital, every detail, inch-by-inch, moment-by-moment. Nothing came to him.

He looked again at the darkening water and could swear that he heard Elizabeth's voice and her beautiful laugh. Light was fading. He envisioned his sons in the river. They had loved to stand side-by-side, passing a rod between them, taking turns with their casts. They had been so small when he taught them to fish. He had watched them grow up and mature on a river.

Darkness was near. Nothing was helping. No ideas were taking shape. *No great revelations on the river this time.* The temperature had dipped into a chill. It was time to go. Brad stood up, disappointed in his failure to identify what eluded him. He turned to leave and gave a last look at the river. He wanted to picture it one more time, the image of his young sons, Cody and Michael, standing in the water, making the last casts of the day. They had been so small, now they were grown men. *Where does the time go?* Brad bid a silent farewell to the river and this special place and stepped away.

It hit him! *Oh, my God, how could I have missed this? It's been right in front of me all along.* His heart raced and elation surged through his veins as he sprinted to his SUV. As darkness fell, Brad was headed home and making telephone calls to Cassandra and Dan Wright.

* * * *

Dogs barked and Walter pushed a button to silence the howling. Nolan started chuckling before he even spoke. "Maybe it's a good thing we had a talk when we did. Earl just called me and is he ever fired up. He was huffing and puffing and is insisting that I get up to Oregon immediately. He's mighty excited about something. The guy sounded like he had a light bulb up his ass. I guess I'll be driving up there today."

"You got any idea what's causing his heartburn?" Walter's voice became sarcastic, "Maybe one of the boys skipped church to worship the naked body of some long-legged woman. Earl don't seem to understand that sometimes heaven itself can be found right here on earth."

"Beats me what's wrong with the guy," Nolan replied with a laugh, "but I'm going up there to find out and get a feel for just what's happening. Who knows, this might turn out to be a good thing. If we're gonna ride in his wagon for a bit longer, we need to know what the hell the guy's got up his sleeve. I sure would like to know a little more about the bank job." The tone of his voice became sarcastic, "You know the basic stuff like when and where. For some reason he won't say too much about that job. He says his investigator found the girl's bank and that we're going to have hell of a payday when we get her. But the old reverend Earl ain't talking beyond that. He's keeping this one close to his vest."

"You're right that he's being mighty secretive but if he's relying on the investigator, we got problems cause I don't think that guy can find his own ass after sundown. I say it's time for you to tell him we want no part of it unless we get a personal look at what he's got planned. We need to start shoving back a bit and let him know we aren't his little puppets for him to dangle on a goddamned string."

"I agree and will do. What's happening with you? Any luck out there in Colorado?"

"I'm still working on things. There's been no sign of life at all in the house of Mr. FBI but I have a feeling he'll show up soon. And speaking of long-legged women, I've been thinking. You know how a little pussy talk always gets Earl to start Bible thumping and screaming about how important it is that Christian soldiers have a strong spirit 'cause the flesh is weak and all that holy roller shit?"

Nolan started laughing.

"Well, the more I think about this deal, I believe that those two sweet-puss broads our FBI friend was hugging on are probably lonely ladies. I'm thinking I should do my Christian duty and make them happy women. That might do more damage to Mr. FBI than getting hit on his own thick head. What you think?"

"What's wrong with this picture?" Nolan chuckled as he spoke. "You're having all the fun. While I'm suffering through another Vacation Bible School with Earl, you're going to be soaking your sausage out there in the Rockies."

"You, Earl and Vacation Bible School all deserve each other," Walter laughed. "Besides, when we do the bank, you can have the girl. That should help even things up."

"Maybe so but I still hope you get a disease."

Don't worry, I'll send you pictures and tell you all about how much fun I have." They laughed as Walter ended the conversation. "Be sure to give me a call once you're in Portland. I'll be interested in what Earl is so excited about."

"You got it."

## CHAPTER TWENTY-TWO
## Denver, Colorado
## 1984

*Studios of KOA radio, located in downtown Denver, Colorado, broadcast with 50,000 watts of power and reached vast regions of the United States. A listening audience of thousands was able to tune into the station where Alan Berg hosted a program of talk radio. Berg was a controversial radio personality. He was noted for being brash, outspoken and sometimes rude. Also, Alan Berg was Jewish. Alan Berg's antics offended many people, especially those on the far right such as Robert Matthews and his members of The Silent Brotherhood, or The Order.*

*Laramie, Wyoming, a community just a short drive north of Denver, had survived another winter. Spring was in the air and hope swelled for summer and warm weather. Robert Matthews had driven to Laramie to visit with a woman who was pregnant with his child. While enjoying time in Laramie, Matthews found himself in a most unusual situation. Jean Craig, the mother of his expecting lover, was for some reason bizarrely attracted to Matthews. Even though she understood the nature of the radical views that Matthews held, Jean Craig made it clear that she would do anything to endear herself to this man who so mysteriously captivated her.*

*Robert Matthews was perceptive enough to recognize the vulner-*

*ability of Jean Craig and he was more than willing to exploit her emotional weakness. Sensing opportunity, he took her aside and engaged in private conversation. Matthews invoked a sense of intimacy as he spoke to Jean Craig in a soft, convincing voice. He told her that he needed her help, that he was relying on her and that he had a job for her in Denver. Thrilled with his attention, she assured Matthews that she would help and would do whatever he needed. Robert Matthews told her that he was interested in Alan Berg, a radio person who broadcast out of Denver. Matthews explained that he wanted her to travel to Denver to find out everything she could about Alan Berg and how he lived his life.*

*Jean Craig was an energized and love-stricken woman. She departed Laramie, Wyoming, on a mission that was to have fatal consequences.*

*Upon arrival in Denver, Jean Craig quickly set about her duties with remarkable ingenuity. She approached the offices of KOA radio under the guise of a journalism student doing research on talk radio. The management of KOA turned out to be most helpful and gave her photographs and biographical information on the personalities of KOA radio and a schedule of their broadcasts. With this information in hand, she then initiated surveillance on Alan Berg to develop the information requested by Robert Matthews.*

*After two weeks of tireless work that involved hours of surveillance, during all hours of the day and night, her mission was accomplished. Jean Craig returned to Wyoming where she met with Matthews and gave him a package of materials. Matthew was thrilled. As he reviewed what Jean Craig had accomplished, he saw that he had photographs of Alan Berg, the location of his residence and information concerning the automobiles that Berg drove. Also included were details about Berg's daily schedule and restaurants where he frequently dined. Robert Matthews smothered Jean Craig with praise for a job well done.*

*The deadly mission was completed and had been successful beyond his wildest hopes.*

\* \* \* \*

*The last day of Alan Berg's life was June 18, 1984. It was a typical early summer day in Denver. Warm morning temperatures en-*

*couraged people to enjoy outdoor activity. But as morning became afternoon, balmy conditions transformed into billowing, grey thunderstorms from the mountains. Lightning flashed and thunder rumbled. Drenching downpours and whipping winds charged across the city in brief squalls of fury. Then in predictable fashion, just as quickly as the storms had appeared, the angry clouds dissipated. Wisps of vapor rose from steaming streets and a clear and pleasant evening settled over Denver and the mountains to the west.*

*For Alan Berg, the day began with his usual early morning rise to plan for his daily broadcast. At 9:00 he was behind the microphone at KOA studios where he conducted four hours of banter with callers and guests of notoriety. After his show, Alan Berg left KOA, glanced at the threatening sky and went about his routine.*

*While weather changed and Alan Berg met with friends and handled errands, Robert Matthews and his followers, David Lane, Richard Scutari and Bruce Pierce, sat within the confines of a run-down motel. The men poured over information and photographs that had been given to Matthews by Jean Craig. They had everything they needed.*

*Time dragged. Air inside the motel was humid and stagnant. Curtains remained closed over the room's window and lamps illuminated the array of materials spread about the bed. They heard sounds of rain and felt thunder rattle the walls and windows of the motel. The room smelled of dampness and human bodies.*

*At about 5:30 in the evening, Alan Berg met his ex-wife, Judith, and drove to a restaurant for dinner. The couple had maintained a good relationship after divorcing and had worked out their problems. They felt that they loved one another and were talking of getting back together. Afternoon storms cleared, patches of blue sky appeared and the approaching sunset behind the Rocky Mountains promised beauty.*

*Matthews and his men left their motel and drove to the area of Alan Berg's residence. In their vehicle, concealed within a tennis racket case, they carried a MAC-10 fully automatic weapon with a thirty round clip. As a beautiful summer evening settled over Denver, four men, consumed with hatred for Jews, began a deathwatch.*

*Alan and Judith Berg finished their dinner. They walked from the restaurant, talking of the future. Enjoying the weather and each other, they drove across town in Alan Berg's black Volkswagen. While driving, they talked about the next day's radio show that was to be a discussion on gun control. They stopped at a convenience store where Alan Berg purchased food for his dog. They then drove to where Judith had parked her car. With no idea that they were sharing their last moments together, Alan and Judith Berg kissed their last kiss, said goodnight and parted.*

*Shortly after 9:00, Alan Berg pulled his Volkswagen into a short driveway that led to garage doors directly underneath his residence. He grabbed the recently purchased bag of dog food, opened his door and extended his leg to get out of the vehicle. Bruce Pierce appeared out of the night. He quickly stepped to within only a few feet of his victim and stood over an unsuspecting Alan Berg. From point blank range, Pierce opened fire with his weapon that blasted .45-caliber rounds faster than a human ear can comprehend. In less than a single second, twelve chunks of blistering metal shredded the torso, face and head of Alan Berg. The weapon jammed on round number thirteen. Alan Berg lay dead in the driveway of his own home, one leg extended out and one leg still inside his car.*

*In subsequent interviews and courtroom testimony, it was learned that the men joked about how Alan Berg, "Went down like someone had pulled a rug out from under him."*

## CHAPTER TWENTY-THREE
## July 15, 2012

Suzanne had been merciless with Brad when he called and told her his concocted story of being thrown from a horse as the reason for his early return from New Mexico. Brad saw no reason to discuss the details of what had really happened so he kept the wild horse and cowboy fantasy alive. Suzanne relayed the tale to Vicki, who was working on a ladder with a paintbrush, and the two of them proceeded to tag-team their ambush. Brad was thankful that he had to endure their torment only by telephone and not in a face-to-face assault.

He had hardly put his phone down when it rang again and Dan Wright's voice brought him back to the real world. "I've been pestering the hell out of my old outfit since our breakfast with Cassandra and, of course, your telephone call after you had that big epiphany on the river." Dan chuckled. "You know it sure is nice to be able to get involved with an investigation and not have to do a single piece of paper. Even though relating information to you is pretty challenging, I still think I like being a retired guy."

"You and me both," Brad agreed.

"You have some time for some interesting stuff from California?"

"Heck yes, I've got time."

"Okay, I have some things to tell you that you are going to find most fascinating."

"I'm all ears." Brad knew that Dan Wright was as solid as a rock and if Dan thought something was significant, it was time to listen.

"To start with, both Norton and Cassandra are all set with full time protective company, courtesy of LAPD. My poor old department is like every other police agency. They have way too much to do and not enough bodies to do it but they didn't even hesitate. They were really easy to deal with and are on board one-hundred percent."

"That's fantastic. Cassandra has got to feel a huge sense of relief."

"Oh, yeah, that had to be done and there was no argument at all. Okay, my friend, here we go with the latest info, right off the press. Vincent Perkins remains locked up, parole is not on the horizon and he will likely die in the joint. He's doing his time pretty quietly but the prison staff that has to deal with him on a daily basis says he is one bitter customer. He is a loner by nature but they still take precautions to keep him segregated from most of the population as best they can. The prison folks did a review for us and they didn't find any of Vincent's friends who have recently been released that they consider likely suspects." Dan paused, "Now, that's no guarantee but just their opinion."

"Yeah, I understand. I was hoping that some really logical suspect might pop out of those prison records. But if that's not the case, then we have to keep on looking."

"I agree." Dan shuffled through his notes before continuing. "Here's the part that you're dying to hear. Congratulations you old codger. You actually used your brain and you were spot on the money with your revelation about Vincent Perkins having younger, identical twin brothers. After your call from out there in the mountains, sitting beside some darned river, we all woke up. Every single one of us had forgotten about those two little twins."

"I don't know how I could have been so stupid," Brad moaned.

"Well, I think we all have some egg on our face. But, keep in mind, when Vincent Perkins went to trial those little brothers of his would have been only ten years old. Nobody paid any attention to them at the time and they just slipped through the old memory cracks. Fast-forward fifteen years and we've got ourselves not one, but two twenty-five year old shitheads who are absolute clones of Vincent."

"Jesus H! Why did it take so long to put this together?"

"Thank goodness it didn't take any longer. They both have criminal records and if you look at their photographs, I'm telling you Brad, you're looking at Vincent Perkins all over again."

"What in the world is wrong with me?" Brad collapsed into a chair. "I saw those kids while we were putting the case together. They were in the courtroom several times during the trial. It just never registered with me that those young boys would now be grown men. What finally kicked me in the head was when I sat down by the river and had thoughts about my own sons. I marveled at how I taught them to fish as little guys and how quickly they grew up. Suddenly, the faces of those two little Perkins boys, sitting in the courtroom, just flashed in my head and I knew instantly what was going on. Those boys had grown up and are the faces that Cassandra and I saw." Both men were silent for a moment. Brad voiced his thoughts, more to himself than to Dan, "Now Cassandra and I don't sound so crazy when we both say we saw Vincent Perkins and we were a thousand miles apart."

"I think you've broken the code, G-man," Dan said with a laugh. "Don't be too hard on yourself because I sure as hell didn't think about it and apparently it didn't register with Cassandra either. Both of the little knuckleheads have been in trouble all through their juvenile years. Then, when they were the ripe old age of twenty-two, they both got popped for an armed robbery. They managed to beat the case but at least we have great photographs of them. Neither one of them has had any criminal arrests since then. So, what does that say to you, Mr. Einstein?"

"I can actually give you an answer to that one. It says to me that those boys operate as a team, that they learned their lessons well and that have gotten slicker and more cautious in their old age. They sure as hell haven't seen the light and changed their ways."

"By golly, maybe there's hope for you yet," Dan snorted. "But the story isn't over so keep listening. Both twin brothers, Nolan and Walter happen to be their names, are frequent visitors to Vincent at the penitentiary. That's no big deal in itself but here is the kicker. Two years ago brother Walter happened to be the driver in a traffic accident here in Los Angeles. It was a serious enough deal that police responded to the scene. Walter got rear-ended and the other driver was actually cited as being at fault, so Walter was clean."

"Okay."

"However, brother Walter had himself a passenger at the time of the accident. It was a guy named Earl Sampson. Now, Earl Sampson has no arrest record, at least that we've been able to find under that name. However, get a load of this, Earl has a wife named Shirley. Prison records show that Miss Shirley is a very regular visitor to Vincent Perkins in the joint. But when she visits, she checks in using her maiden name, Shirley Barnes."

"That's pretty odd. Maybe she doesn't want anyone to see a connection between her, Earl and Vincent. What do you think?"

"I think you are right on track. Those were my words exactly when I found out. Plus, the prison staff describes Shirley as one hot lady. She shows up for visits dressed like a hooker and ready for the kill."

"That could be ruled as cruel and unusual punishment to a bunch of poor guys locked up." Brad laughed and Dan joined in agreement.

Dan continued. "But I think this group is a little too tight and the scent of a smokescreen fills the air. I say they're adding a layer to the onion so it is a little bit more difficult to get to the core. You know, the old Indian trick of letting a sweet little lady be the messenger and go-between. When a woman visits a guy in the joint, everyone just figures it's a romance thing. But, if Earl showed up for multiple visits, someone would begin to wonder what their business might be. Shirley could easily be visiting just to carry messages back and forth."

"Never underestimate the power of a woman, Dan."

"Sad but true."

"But just think back to when we were digging up everything we could find on Vincent Perkins before the trial. Good grief, we found all kinds of information that linked him to supremacist groups across the country. We were amazed at the extent of his connections. Do you suppose Vincent is keeping lines of communication open by using Shirley as a courier to this guy Earl?"

"That is exactly what I'm thinking. And, there's plenty more here to thicken the plot, my friend. A little bit of police work starts to make this real interesting. The lovely Miss Shirley is not only married to Earl Sampson but she is the sister of a clown named Stanley Barnes. And, I hate like hell to say this but, Stanley Barnes is well known to LAPD."

After a brief silence Brad spoke up, "What do you mean he's well known to LAPD?"

Dan Wright gave a sigh. "Stanley Barnes is well known to LAPD because he almost became an officer of the Los Angeles Police Department. I'm telling you, Brad, I'm not sure if I'm sick to my stomach because he almost got in or if I'm happy as hell that we caught our mistake before it was too late. He is a sorry, no-good three-dollar bill who actually got hired by LAPD. The jerk just never made it through the academy. He was a disaster in the classroom and a disaster on the range. But what got his ass fired before he ever got to first base was his arrogance and general attitude. He was a smart-ass and just couldn't keep his mouth shut. Once the idiot started talking, the truth came out about what really makes the guy tick. He was a hardcore racist with a hair-trigger temper. Once he became comfortable with a few of his classmates, he dropped his public façade and began to make some really radical statements about minorities. He alarmed his fellow cadets so badly that they reported him. With a little scrutiny and additional background investigation into his past, it became clear that he wasn't just a fruitcake, he was a scary fruitcake with big time racial hatreds."

"Good grief!"

"The academy staff remembers him quite well and said firing his ass was a no brainer once they figured him out. But, apparently the guy was smooth as silk until he showed his true stripes. It took some time and effort but thank heaven he was identified and dismissed before he made it out into the real force."

Speaking as he processed what he had just been told, Brad spoke slowly. "So, we have a police wanna-be in Stanley Barnes who is a racist goof. Stanley is connected to Earl Sampson who hangs with a twin brother of Vincent Perkins. We know Vincent is a hard-core supremacist and it appears that the younger, twin brothers are of the same bolt of cloth. And this guy Earl Sampson hangs with the whole Perkins family, either directly or through his wife, Shirley, who visits Vincent in prison. And Shirley is a wanna-be hooker who is a sister to Stanley." The line was quiet before Brad spoke again and began to laugh. "Jesus H, how did I do, Dan? I've got a headache already from trying to keep the cast of characters straight and I have no idea if what I just said is even close to what you told me."

Dan laughed out loud. "That was very impressive, Algernon. Why did that talent never show itself when we were working together?" After both men laughed, Dan continued. "The way I see it, there is absolutely nothing here that means anything from an evidentiary standpoint. However, it is interesting as the dickens and I think very relevant. The academy instructors say Stanley Barnes is a mighty slick con artist and they view him as capable of doing just about anything. That is anything except earn an honest living," Dan added as an afterthought.

"It sounds like you guys dodged a bullet with Mr. Stanley."

"Did we ever. But the story still isn't finished. To add insult to injury, after LAPD canned his sorry ass, he goes out and starts a new career as a private investigator!" Dan's voice boiled with anger. "And of course, he passes himself off as a former police officer of the LAPD. That kind of shit steams me beyond words!"

"Man alive, think through all the possibilities." Brad was quiet as he contemplated. "No matter how you slice it, one thing for sure is that there's a loose cannon out there that is connected through friendship, blood or marriage to white supremacist shitbirds, one of whom is in prison for a ruthless murder. And, it only makes sense that all these characters are going to be birds of a feather."

"You are calling it exactly the way that I see it and the way everyone downtown at LAPD sees it."

"Does anyone know where Stanley is right now, where he lives, what the heck he's doing, all that stuff?"

"That's the first order of business going on downtown as we speak. I can't imagine he'll be hard to find but everyone wants to move cautiously until we figure out who the hell is doing what to who."

"Absolutely. Do you know if your guys are talking to the Bureau in Los Angeles and Portland?"

"Yeah, I know some conversations have taken place but I don't know exactly what information has been exchanged up to this point."

"No problem. I'm going to give a quick call up to our office in Portland and give them what you just told me. The guy I'm talking to is Lynn Everett. He's a no nonsense investigator and he'll hop right on this and be sure that your department and the Bureau keep an open line."

"Okay, sounds good, Brad, and I'll stay in touch the minute I learn anything. I don't mean to be an alarmist but watch your back out there. This whole thing doesn't smell too good, so be careful. Seeing what these jokers have done so far with assaulting people and burning houses, you can't be too careful."

"Thanks, Dan, and you're not being an alarmist. It took a while for things to penetrate into this old brain of mine, but once that happened, I definitely realized how lucky I was. It's a damn miracle I'm not fertilizing an aspen tree in New Mexico. I'm planning to stick pretty darned close to home for a bit." Brad thought to himself for a moment. "Besides, for the first time since I got out of the hospital, I've been experiencing a pretty severe headache in the last few hours. I sure hope it doesn't lead to something that requires another visit to a doctor. I plan to stay right inside my house and grab some couch time. But when I do go out, you can bet I'll be keeping my eyes open."

"Well, be sure to take care of yourself and your broken head. Don't do anything stupid." Dan paused, "That's a difficult thing for you to do but give it a try." Dan gave a friendly laugh as he wrapped up the conversation. "Well, you old geezer, I've got to get going and solve this mystery. I'll talk with you right away."

"Thanks, Dan, keep me posted."

* * * *

Rhythmic ticking from a clock that hung on the kitchen wall was the only sound. The two men sat across from each other, neither had spoken for seconds. Nolan looked at Earl in flabbergasted silence. Each swing of the pendulum announced the passing of another second and Earl sat with unflinching eyes that bored into Nolan like a drill. He waited for a response that Nolan seemed unable to formulate. Mugs of cold coffee sat between the men. The mountain cabin where they sat had been built with the intention of providing serenity from the rush of city living. Constructed of logs, its multiple windows offered views of meadows and dense forest. A rustic ambiance was the intent but the only ambiance Nolan felt at the moment was isolation. Another living soul could not be found for miles. Nolan's apprehension was growing by the second as he realized that he was trapped. He was absolutely alone in the presence of a man who proudly carried a gun and, as far as Nolan as concerned, was completely crazy.

Time continued to pass with no words spoken as the men sat, looking at one another. The pendulum swung, back and forth, tick tock. Finally, Nolan broke the silence. "You want me to kill your brother-in-law? You're telling me that he is coming here today, thinking we're going to discuss a bank robbery, but when he arrives, you want me to kill him!" Astonishment and doubt were written on Nolan's face.

Earl remained quiet and still. His eyes scrutinized Nolan in a hard stare that was edged like a razor.

"And then, you're saying to me that we're going to drag his ass off, dig a hole in the ground, call it a grave and bury him out there in those woods!" Nolan lifted his arm, pointing through the kitchen window.

Earl's face remained expressionless, his eyes never leaving Nolan's face. The two men again stared at each other in silence. Even the clock seemed to understand the consequences of the moment. Tick, tock, the pendulum swung. Never skipping, it seemed to grow louder with each swing.

"Come on, Earl, you're not talking about killing some damned nigger or fat-ass Jew. You are talking to me about killing one of our own, your wife's brother of all people. I can't believe I'm hearing this." Nolan gaped at Earl, his face registering nothing but confusion and disbelief. "And then, this evening after your own frigging brother-in-law is dead and buried, we are going to have a meeting at your house. You are going to stand up and tell the rest of the group that the two of us just got together for a cup of coffee and calmly decided to kill one of our members." Nolan raised his shoulders and hands in exasperation. "I'm speechless. I have no idea what to say to you."

Earl's response was direct and flat. "I will handle tonight's meeting. That is not your concern." After a pause, with a face void of expression and no emotion in his voice, he continued. "I want you to think about what I have told you. Think it through from start to finish. After you've done that, after you have really run this through your head, you tell me, Nolan, what would you do if you were in my position? You tell me, do you see any alternative?"

Nolan leaned back in his chair and studied Earl's face. Was the man about to laugh and say this was just a big joke? Earl's face remained stoic. Whatever was happening was real and not going away.

Nolan narrowed his eyes and doubt radiated as he moved his head from side to side. "Are you absolutely positive about all of this?"

"Oh yes, my friend. There is no doubt, no doubt at all." Earl leaned across the table. "I've laid it out for you plain and straight. There is nothing more for me to say. Up until the time that I learned the ugly truth, I had placed great trust in Stanley and had given him a critical role in our movement. It was a role he asked for, how he wanted to fight niggers and foreigners. It was his part of our effort to squash the Jews and queers that run our government. This was what he wanted to do as his part to bring our nation back to God."

Finally, Earl shifted his eyes away from Nolan. He glanced to the ceiling and looked about the room as if he sought an elusive answer. When he brought his attention back to Nolan he spoke with sadness. "Stanley Barnes, the brother of my own wife, had unrestricted freedom in managing the donations that believers from around the country gave to our movement. I never questioned him. He had my complete trust. It was simply through pure accident that I talked with a fellow believer in Missouri and things were said that made me realize that I had been blind and that Stanley was skimming the donations for his own pocket. I made calls to other members in other states. They told me that they had held doubts for some time and explained to me in detail the donations they had given."

Earl was quiet, as if he was telling himself the story for the first time and couldn't believe what he heard. Earl spoke again but his voice began to harden. "With a broken heart, I checked Stanley's records and nothing added up. I have talked with believers all over the country and I have talked with God. When it was all over, I had to face the harsh reality that a member of my own family, the brother of my wife, was not who I thought he was." Emotion charged and Earl raised his voice. "Stanley has betrayed me! He has betrayed you, he has betrayed all of us!"

Nolan said nothing but simply stared at Earl. The pendulum swung, back and forth.

Earl looked across the table to Nolan. "Your own brother, Walter, questions whether or not Stanley actually performed the work that he charged us for out in Colorado in regards to the FBI Agent. And, Stanley travels back down to Los Angeles every month saying he has business there. I now understand his business. His business is simply a life of debauchery, whores and liquor. He leads a life of sin and he pays for that life of sin with money that he has stolen from fellow Aryan warriors. Money that was given in good faith."

Earl was quiet. He looked to the ceiling and placed his hands over his face. When he spoke again his voice was soft and he seemed to be far away, not even talking to Nolan. "This is a sad day, a day that I never wanted to face. But I have prayed about this, Nolan, I have prayed hard. I told God that I didn't think I could face this horrible deed." Earl looked straight to Nolan, "And, do you want to know something? God answered me. He answered me all right but his answer was not what I wanted or expected." Earl reached to his side and placed his hand on a Bible that lay in the chair beside him. Lifting the Bible into the air, he continued. "Oh, yes, God answered me all right, he answered me with a laugh! God laughed at me, Nolan. God laughed at me and asked me a question. He asked me, 'Is this all that you are? Is this how you respond when you are asked to do something difficult in my name? What about the cross where my son died? What about the sacrifice I made for you? I gave my son to die on a cross for you and now you struggle with something as simple as this?'" Tears pooled in Earl's eyes.

The pendulum swung, each tick echoed. Nolan looked at Earl's expectant face without offering a reply.

"I want you to tell me something, Nolan. I want you to look me in the eye and tell me what you would do. For years now I have listened to you and your brother telling me that our organization must have thinkers and talkers but it is most important that we have doers. And you and Walter so proudly boast that you are doers. Well, my friend, today is a day that you must be a doer. Step up to the throne of God and make yourself a doer." Earl's voice was growing louder and louder. "What is your answer, Nolan?"

Nolan chose not to speak but slowly nodded his head up and down. The only sound was from the clock, its pendulum swinging, back and forth, tick, tock.

Earl's relentless scrutiny of Nolan never ceased, his eyes continued to drill across the table as he shouted. "I don't want a shy little nod. No, Nolan, that's not good enough. I don't want a little movement of your head. I want you to tell me clearly, shout it out. I want to hear your voice. I want God to hear your voice. What would you

Dale Lovin

do? Would you allow Stanley to continue? Would you confront him and then accept his denial or his apology? Would you expel him from the movement and allow him to depart a bitter man, knowing that he carries the secrets of our brotherhood, that he knows every detail about our organization?" Earl became quiet; his fierce look sliced through the air, straight to Nolan. "Don't sit there in silence, Nolan Perkins, talk to me, talk to God! Would you trust Stanley to just walk away and hope that he will maintain silence about who we are and all of our plans?"

Earl stood from his seat. He placed his hands on the table, leaning across to bring his face to within inches of Nolan. Eyes inflamed with passion, he was now screaming. "Talk to me, Nolan, where is your heart? Show me who you are. Are you willing to trust your life and your future to a man who sells his soul for stolen dollars? Will you place the life and future of you or your brother, Walter, into the hands of this man? Who are you, Nolan Perkins? What are you made of? Are you ready? Is your heart ready? I want to hear you, Nolan. I want to look inside you right now. Open up, open up and show me your heart." Earl's face was hysterical. "Open up, Nolan, not for me but for God. Do you have what it takes to show your heart to God? This is your moment of destiny. There is no tomorrow. Are you prepared?" In a final crescendo, he lifted the Bible into the air, and expelled a desperate shriek, "Are you prepared?"

Breathing in short, struggling gasps Earl held the pose, his face purple. Slowly, he straightened his body and eased back down into his seat, never taking his eyes from Nolan. He again reached to the seat beside him and grasped a small, cloth bag. "No, Nolan, you do not have to dig a hole in the ground and call it a grave. I've already done it for you." Earl opened the bag and, turning it upside down, flung its contents upon the table; clinking metal on wood, silver dollars rolled and tumbled across the table, settling into silence, their faces glistening in the light. "But before you throw the first shovel of dirt on Stanley's face, I want you to place these on his body."

The pendulum swung, back and forth, back and forth.

\* \* \* \*

After passing on Dan Wright's information to Lynn Everett in Portland, Brad placed his telephone on the table and knew something was terribly wrong. Dr. Owens had given him pain pills, but up to this point there had been no need for them. That had changed quite quickly. What had begun as a dull throb, just at the point where he had been struck, had now spread and Brad was beginning to think his entire head was going to explode. He downed two pain pills with water, folded a cold cloth over his eyes and face and eased his body onto the couch that had been his friend for years. He touched a button on his remote for some music. He craved something soft and soothing. What he really wanted was to have his daughter, Meghan, sing for him. *Jesus, I miss that girl.* But the harsh reality was that Meghan was far away, studying vocal performance and musical theater. Without Meghan for comfort, the music of David Lanz would have to do. As he closed his eyes behind the cloth, the piano notes came. They wrapped about him in a warm embrace and the world faded into blackness. Brad slept.

\* \* \* \*

Walter could not believe how rapidly the temperature dropped after sunset. He cursed himself for wearing only a flimsy shirt but he could stick it out for a while longer. Night was different out here. He had never seen so many stars but yet the darkness seemed darker than anything he had ever experienced. "This sure ain't Los Angeles," he muttered to himself. He had found a place where he could pull his car well off the road and park within a secluded stand of trees but yet maintain a bird's eye view of the Fox Cove Inn. Earlier in the day he had walked past the inn and observed a sign posted in the gardens, near the entrance. The sign said the establishment was temporarily closed for remodeling. How absolutely fucking perfect.

The street was dead-ass quiet. Throughout the entire evening only a few people had walked the street with kids or dogs. He had seen only one car drive away from the inn and not a single car had driven past him to approach the now-closed bed and breakfast. From time to time he had seen lights go on and off in different areas of the inn but now, only a single light burned in an upstairs window. Walter checked his watch, ten-thirty. When he saw the last light in the inn go dark he checked again, ten-forty. The inn was completely dark. The street and entire area was totally deserted.

How absolutely fucking perfect.

\* \* \* \*

Wailing sirens, faint at first, grew loud as they passed nearby and awakened Brad from his sleep. He opened his eyes but realization of where he was did not come quickly to his clouded mind. His house was dark and quiet. As his mind cleared, he realized that he had slept through the afternoon into night. A dim blue light from his sound system reminded him of the David Lanz music that had seemed almost euphoric. He rose up, anticipating pain to be in his head but he felt absolutely nothing, no pain whatsoever. He reached for the cloth that had covered his eyes but it was gone, apparently fallen to the floor. Brad pulled his body into a sitting position on the couch and sat in darkness, searching his senses, wondering what the hell had happened. How could he have slept so soundly for such a long time? How could his pain have developed so quickly and then vanished so completely?

He checked his watch, ten-forty, and massaged his forehead with his palms; it had happened again. Moustache had stood over him, spoke to him, wished him well and had given that bright, mysterious smile. Then, Moustache had looked serious and spoken in Spanish, just as he had done in Juanita's cabin. But what were the words, what were the words? Brad concentrated, brought the scene back; "Tienes mucho que hacer (*You have much to do*)." That was it. Those were the words Moustache had spoken. What in the world was he saying to me?

Brad did not have to concentrate to recall the rest of the scene. What had happened was as clear and real as anything Brad had ever experienced. Moustache had stepped aside to reveal Juanita standing close by. She had knelt beside him, touched his cheek just as before. He could feel her fingers as she raised his head and gave him water; the cold, wonderful water he remembered from inside her home. She had given him bread, dipped in the same pungent mixture that he so vividly recalled. Her eyes, her face, her smile, they were all there in his mind. Then, she had laughed. She had tossed her head back, just as before, her laugh filling the air with pure enchantment.

It was all so real. Juanita had spoken to him, her voice soft and with the same smile as before. But unlike the words Moustache had spoken, he had to concentrate to make Juanita's words come back.

She had spoken in Spanish, the same words she had said to him when he had been inside her tiny home. She had spoken the words in a manner that caused Brad to perceive they were important; words Juanita desperately wanted him to hear and understand. Closing his eyes tightly, he saw her face and heard the soft voice. He listened to his memory and slowly, her words sounded again within his head. "Nuestro tiempo ya casi ha llegado (*Our time is almost here*). Hemos esperado tanto tiempo (*We have waited so long*). Sé paciente, mi amor, sé paciente (*Be patient, my love, be patient*)."

He sat on the couch, clearing his brain and listening to his heart. What was Juanita saying to him? Why did she seem so intent that her message be understood?

Shoulders sagging, Brad looked through the darkness of his home. First, he had gone to New Mexico only to be clobbered on the head. Then, he had drifted off to some incredible dream world that seemed more real than life itself and his mind was filled with fantasies of a woman who didn't even exist. Just when some time had passed and the insanity had begun to fade, he took a pill and bingo, it was right back to La La Land and Fantasia. But, God in heaven, it seemed real. Even as he sat alone in his empty house in the dark of night, he could swear that he detected the same aroma of smoke and bread that he had experienced in his last dream within Juanita's cabin.

He stood up from the couch and made his way across the dark room. As he moved toward his bathroom he spoke softly to himself. "Brad Walker, you are one messed up cowboy." As he stepped into the bathroom he reached for the light switch. His eyes startled at the burst of harsh light and he blinked hard. But when Brad looked at the counter next to his bathroom sink, his blinking stopped; lying neatly folded was the cloth he had earlier used to cover his eyes.

\* \* \* \*

That something momentous had happened or was about to happen was unmistakable. As Earl took his place before the altar, the men shared a sense of anticipation. Adolf Hitler oversaw the scene in the glow of candles and words of The Lord's Prayer, which had been uttered in unison, echoed in darkened corners of the basement. Earl had summoned the men with urgency and there had been no graciousness in his words. His wife had been conspicuously absent when they arrived and frigidity hung in the air.

Earl faced the men. To his left was an empty chair, a single candle burning in its seat. Folding his hands beneath his chin, Earl bowed his head in a moment of silence before he addressed his followers. "There are many words in our language that are repulsive. Because all of us are different as human beings and have had unique experiences throughout our lives, some words may be particularly offensive to one man while not to another. But there are some words that we all detest. We all abhor words that take our Lord's name in vain, words that are vulgar or glorify that which is sinful. Those are words that we do not want to hear and we shut our ears when those words are spoken. There are other words that we certainly prefer not to hear, words that we do not want to speak with our own lips but yet we recognize that these words must be spoken from time to time. Words such as 'Negro' or words such as 'Jew' or 'homosexual.' These are words that are bitter on our tongues. They sting our ears and bring revulsion to our souls."

Looking over the candles, peering into the faces of the men, Earl stopped speaking. His gaze was intimidating. He held an inexplicable sway over the men in the room and when his eyes rested upon an individual, that person felt exposed, as if he had no secrets. As Earl's eyes swept over the room, each man looked to the floor, feet shuffled nervously. After seconds of silence, Earl continued. "But hear me clearly, my brothers, there is one word that is vile above all others." Earl's voice rose. "One word that in its very utterance speaks to everything that is noxious and repugnant to people of God. One word whose sound causes rodents to scurry to their nests within the sewer and causes serpents to slither into black holes beneath the earth." Earl held his breath and the assembled men collectively held theirs. In a shrill shout, Earl exploded, "That most despicable of all words, my friends, is Judas!" Earl's eyes were on fire. "Judas, Judas, Judas! Listen to the word. Judas, Judas. What do you feel? Does your heart turn to stone? Does your blood become cold as it flows through your body? Judas, Judas!" Earl was screaming. The stunned and terrified men had no idea of what was happening or what was about to happen. "Judas, the name that betrayed Jesus Christ. Judas, the man whose kiss upon our Lord's cheek sent him to die upon a cross. Suspended by nails driven through his hands, our Lord endured the most horrible death imaginable." Earl's voice quieted, became soft, just above a whisper. "He hung upon that cross because of Judas."

Earl dropped his head as if in defeat. His shoulders raised and lowered in labored breath. Not a sound was made. Even the eyes of Adolf Hitler appeared dazed while men stood as paralyzed characters upon a stage.

Lifting his Bible, Earl continued. "When you go home tonight, there is something I want you to do. I ask that you read the story of Judas. I want you to read how Judas, as one of the apostles, had been delegated to care for the money that he and the other apostles had been charged to administer; money intended for the poor, sick or afflicted. It was Judas, the steward of money for the apostles, who betrayed our Lord Jesus Christ. For thirty pieces of silver, Judas delivered Jesus to his death. With thirty pieces of silver in his hand, Judas stood beside Jesus and kissed the Lord's cheek. A kiss that signaled to soldiers the man they were to arrest and crucify."

Turning to the empty chair, Earl extended his hand as if in an act of introduction. "My brothers, I give you our Judas. I give you Judas who was the steward of our money. I give you Stanley, our Judas, who betrayed every man here tonight by stealing money that had been given for our cause." Earl was silent, looking to the empty chair and the candle that flickered from its unoccupied seat. He turned to again face the men. "On this night, as I speak to you, Judas is in the ground. Judas is buried, alone for eternity. Judas is buried where worms bore into his skull, beetles of the earth feast upon his eyes and varmints of the forest dig his body for their nourishment." Earl leaned his body over the podium, his voice hissed as he spoke. "But let me tell you my brothers, when Judas is gone and nothing - not even a bone - is left, his grave will forever hold the thirty pieces of silver that were buried with him."

Earl stepped to the empty chair and blew out the candle.

## CHAPTER TWENTY-FOUR
## JULY 16, 2012

Sunrise and coffee had always been powerful potions for Brad and today was no different. He sat on his deck and watched the mesa as dawn's light seeped over the horizon. As the sun rose, it was as if the mesa also rose up, awakening from a night's sleep within the earth. Changing colors creeping across walls of stone and earth reminded Brad of flowers opening their petals to light. Once the sun had fully risen, its warmth seemed to soak through Brad as warm water through a sponge. A coffee mug in hand offered the comfortable silence that only genuine friends can share.

It had been another long night after his headache and crazy dream. Everything from thoughts of Cassandra, twin brothers of Vincent Perkins and mystery men named Earl and Stanley kept rolling around in his head. And then, of course, there were the visions of Moustache, Juanita and a neatly folded towel. Finding the towel in the bathroom was no problem to explain. He had obviously gotten up in the night and taken the towel into the bathroom; he just had no memory of doing so. The more difficult part of the puzzle was to explain how it had been folded. Brad hadn't folded anything since he was six years old. He was a throw it on the floor guy. *If Elizabeth had known that sleeping pills could turn me into a neat freak, she would have kept me doped up all the time.*

Miraculously, the aching in his head had not returned. He thought about grabbing a workout but decided not to push it. Yesterday's bout with pain made him cautious. As he rummaged through cabinets for something decent to eat, his phone rang and he immediately recognized the number as coming from Oregon. It dawned on him that it was mighty early on the West Coast, which meant that Lynn Everett had probably worked through the night and must have something significant to report. When Brad answered, Lynn's voice responded, full of energy. "Good morning, Brad. Am I calling too early, interrupting blueberry muffin time?" Lynn paused a second, "Oh, I'm sorry I guess you're probably eating bran muffins at this stage of your life but if you have a second, we need to chat."

"Heck yes, I'm dying to hear from you. Based on this early morning call, I'm betting you've been going all night."

"Yeah, it has been a long one but that's okay because we've made some progress. I've got a little good news and a little bad news, so hang on and I'll give it to you straight. We're talking with LAPD almost constantly and some kind of picture is beginning to take shape. First, I have to hand it to you. That was a good call you made on thinking about the young twins. Everybody seems to have overlooked those young lads."

"I'm still stinging from being so blind and stupid."

"Well, that's okay because the hounds are on the trail now. LAPD found an old, beat-up house that the twins have rented in east LA. So far, there has been absolutely no sign of life. They're continuing to watch the place but it's looking like nobody at all is around."

"Okay, maybe someone will show soon."

"Who knows, but Los Angeles is on it real good. What doesn't seem right to me is that neither of the brothers has a car registered in their name. They've both had cars in the past but nothing registered in the past two years."

Brad thought for a second. "That tells me they're driving rentals or they have other identification that they're using. I'm guessing rental cars. Easier to keep changing wheels."

"I suspect you're right but we simply don't know yet." Lynn shuffled papers and continued. "Next, we did find several cars registered to Stanley Barnes, his sister, Shirley, and Earl Sampson. That was easy. Then, a little more digging turned up an address here in Portland for this Earl Sampson character and we've also located an apartment in Los Angeles for Stanley Barnes. But, unlike the wreck of a house for the twins, Stanley keeps a super nice place. It's more of a jet-set residence and environment. However, just like at the house for the twins, there's no sign of life at the apartment."

"Sounds like everyone is off to enjoy summer camp," Brad said with sarcasm. "Are the LA guys keeping an eye on that place also?"

"Oh, yeah. Those guys are hot. This is a very personal matter with everyone in LAPD. Even though the arson was in Portland, it was the house of one of their judges that was torched and the spouse of one of their prosecutors who was attacked. This is very close to home for LAPD and, I promise you, they aren't taking a back seat to anyone on this one."

"That makes me happy for lots of reasons, but especially for Cassandra."

"You got it. However, there is more to report. We are turning over everything we can to learn more about this guy, Earl Sampson. As we speak, there is a car parked in front of his house. It's a California car that is registered to Stanley Barnes. We have people sitting on the vehicle but so far, it hasn't moved. We're only guessing, of course, but it looks like Stanley might be either visiting or living in Portland. Either way, we have another connection between Earl Sampson and Stanley Barnes."

"What does Stanley's car look like?"

"It's a small little sports car type, I forget the exact make, but it certainly goes with the bachelor pad image of his place in Los Angeles. What's interesting is that every other vehicle we've located so far is just a plain, vanilla type car. They're good cars but nothing at all to draw attention. Only Stanley's stands out as something special, just like his apartment."

"What about Earl's house, what does it look like? I'm trying to get a feel for what these people are like."

"Oh, it's a very middle-class area and a very middle-class house. His yard is pretty neglected but nothing else stands out. Earl is forty-five years old, no criminal history and he used to be a welder. We can't find any record of him working anywhere for the last couple of years."

"It doesn't sound like Earl and Stanley really go together." Brad spoke as he thought out loud.

"I agree. We've talked about that but who knows what we're dealing with." Lynn continued, "I'm sick about this but, I'm pretty sure we missed a heck of an opportunity to figure out a whole bunch of this stuff last night. We were doing a ton of things at the same time and trying to get set up with surveillance on Earl Sampson's house. It was almost midnight and we were scrambling to get people out on really short notice. So, just as the first units got there, they saw a ton of people leaving Earl's house. It was obvious to everyone that some sort of meeting was breaking up but we didn't have adequate coverage to take advantage of the mother lode of information that was probably right in front of our eyes."

"Oh, Lord, that's a heartbreak."

"Yeah, we missed the boat but nothing to do about it now except keep on working." Lynn's voice reflected both frustration and determination. "However, we got lucky as the dickens in one regard and it sure validated that we've got a serious issue on our hands."

"I don't need any validation, Lynn," Brad chuckled. "I've got a crack in my skull and I've seen Cassandra's husband wrapped up like a mummy in a hospital. You've got a house burned to the ground and a judge's family that's lucky to be alive. That's enough validation for me."

"Okay, I'll give you that. You're right, you are absolutely right." Lynn laughed. "I'm not too concerned about your little head but the rest of those incidents are very troubling." Brad joined in the laugh before Lynn continued. "Get a load of this, Brad. For all of the bad luck we had by missing last night's meeting, we did have one stroke of great luck. Just as the surveillance team was getting into place, they were lucky enough to pick up a single vehicle as it left the house. They didn't manage to get a tail on the car but they did pick up a tag number. The vehicle turned out to be registered to a lady named Janice Bowdin. That last name mean anything to you?"

Brad was quiet as he thought about Lynn's question. "No, can't say that it does."

"Well, don't feel bad because I didn't recognize it either. But the good old computers, God love 'em, they darned sure knew a guy named Sam Bowdin. He is a suspect in the murder of a state trooper in Arkansas about two years ago. Janice Bowdin is Sam's mother and she's been dead for years. You know this routine."

"Oh, yeah, here we go with the old trick of multiple identifications."

"I'm afraid so. The murder of the trooper started out as nothing more than a routine traffic violation. But when the car pulled over, apparently several people came out blazing with fully automatic weapons. When it was all over, a young trooper died on the spot. He never had a chance and probably had no idea what hit him. Enough rounds were fired to qualify the scene as a combat zone."

Brad was quiet for a moment. "I hate those stories. Most people just read a headline and go on to the sports page. But behind those tragedies, somebody suffers for years. In the wake of that trooper's murder, someone was left who loved him and depended on him. It happens so often that society has become numb and fails to grasp the suffering that accompanies those horrible stories."

"You are so right, my friend, you are so right. Well, it turned out that the vehicle had been stolen only about two hours earlier and the darned thing hadn't even been entered into the system when the poor trooper pulled it over. Arkansas investigators recovered the car about twenty miles away and they found all kinds of stuff in the trunk. They found every type of gun imaginable, grenades and a ton of ammunition."

"Holy smokes."

"They were lucky enough to recover a bunch of fingerprints out of the vehicle and from the weapons as well. Sam Bowdin's prints were identified from some of the guns that were in the trunk. So, he's a suspect in the murder but no warrant has been issued. He's got a record a mile long and Arkansas authorities and the Bureau have known him for a long time as a supremacist and a crazy. He's one of those guys that thinks he's going to bring down the government."

"Jesus H."

"You got that right. And guess what else? I'm sure this will surprise you. Since the night of that murder, good old Sam Bowdin is nowhere to be found. He's in the wind, gone like a bad smell. So, like I said, we got ourselves even more validation that we're poking around inside a hornet's nest. Plus, someone in the group is using an identification of Sam Bowdin's deceased mother. My money says that with some more digging, we'll find other property under her name."

"Man, you did have a busy night."

"Yes, we most certainly did. But, hang on, are you ready for the bad news I promised you?"

"I already know I didn't win the lottery so if that's what you're going to tell me, save your breath."

"Lottery in your dreams. Your idea of winning the lottery is a gift card for prune juice at Friday night's bingo tournament. Now, shut up and listen, you moron. This is why I called you so early in the morning. LAPD found credit cards for Nolan and Walter Perkins and they're tracking them in real time."

Brad felt his heart compress. Something was coming.

"So far, we are finding very sporadic use of the cards and only in gas stations. Nothing at all has popped up in grocery stores, retail establishments or hotels or motels. Nothing but gas stations."

"That's mighty strange."

"I agree."

"That probably means they're operating with cash."

"I suppose so but motels usually require a credit card. They either have other cards that we are unaware of, they're staying with friends, sleeping in their car or they frequent real dumps that will take cash with no card. For the past several weeks, all we've found for Nolan is an occasional gasoline charge in the Los Angeles area. Then, bam, he starts to charge in northern California and all the way up to his last charge right here in Portland."

"How about that, it looks as though you have some company, Lynn. You guys getting together for a glass of wine any time soon?"

"Yeah, yeah, yeah. Well, before you relax too much, I have even more news for you. When we looked at Walter's records, we found a gasoline paper trail all across the country, from Los Angeles right to the Mile High City of Denver. And then it gets really interesting. We have charges in Taos, New Mexico. I'm thinking that maybe even you might be smart enough to figure this one out."

Brad exhaled a long, protracted sigh. "Well, I guess that nails it down pretty solid. It's not like I didn't already know that somebody had followed me, but this is hard evidence and it sure makes everything real."

Lynn took a second before speaking again. "Okay, Mr. Brad, I hate to be the bearer of more hard evidence but you have to know about this. Last night, Walter Perkins purchased gasoline at a station on the west side of Denver."

Brad did not immediately respond. When he did speak, his voice had an air of finality. "Well, Lynn, it looks like you and me sure as hell are popular with the Perkins Brothers. Since it's doubtful that neither one of them made such long drives to see a hair stylist, I think they must have made the drive just to visit with us."

Lynn started laughing. "I've been thinking about this for a long time and I never once considered they may be visiting with a hair stylist."

Brad laughed also. "It's like this, Lynn, I'm a believer in that old saying that it does no good to cry so we just as well laugh. There's lots of wisdom in that advice so I try to incorporate it into my life." Brad paused, "But as soon as we hang up, I'm going to break down and sob like a damned little baby." Lynn joined Brad in a good laugh. "Okay seriously, Lynn, thanks for the warning. I guess I better think about this, but I'm not going to panic and go crazy. All I know for certain is that he went to a hell of a lot of trouble to follow me all the way to Taos. After that, he stuck with me until he found his opportunity out there at that remote cabin. He must be one patient guy because he waited a very long time before he snuck up behind me in the dark."

"I thought the very same thing myself."

"I've talked this over with a friend who is a mighty fine police officer and we are in agreement on this. Looking back on things, I'm convinced that the person who assaulted me was watching while I fished in the stream earlier in day. I think he made a deliberate decision not to do anything where I might have seen him and been able to fight back. That says to me that he absolutely does not want a face-to-face confrontation and he sure as hell doesn't want to get caught. It also confirms in my mind that he was operating alone. You agree?"

Lynn thought for a moment. "Yeah, that all sounds reasonable but who knows what might have changed in his thinking after he missed you the first time."

"I suppose you're right but my money says he won't change his strategy. He's going to wait for circumstances where he can sneak and run with virtually no chance to be seen or caught." Brad paused, "I'm smart enough to realize that I can't walk around whistling tunes and live forever looking over my shoulder. I'm just sure as hell hoping that you guys are going to blow this case open. I need for something to break out there in Oregon or California and for you to resolve this mess." Brad laughed again. "That's what I'm hoping for, but once again, there is another old saying that I live by. If you have hope in one hand and shit in the other hand, when you put your hands together, all you have is a handful of shit."

Both men laughed, knowing that humor was a great way to mask stress or fear.

"Okay, Lynn. Thanks for the heads up. I sure as heck will be careful and I'll figure out what to do and how to handle things. I'm not planning to even leave my house today. Until I can get back to the gym, I don't really have to go anywhere. I may just find a good book and wait for you guys in Portland and Los Angeles to save my skinny hide."

Lynn chuckled, "I hear you but you can't stay inside your house forever."

"Well, I can promise you something for certain. There sure ain't nothing too exotic in my immediate future. You know, I just do the regular stuff: Caribbean cruises with wild, naked women and lots of booze. Just a hum drum life for old Brad."

"Cruises and wild women would send you into cardiac arrest. Go enjoy your frigging cross word puzzles. I have work to do and I'll let you know when we get new information."

"Thanks, Lynn, talk soon."

With a mug of fresh coffee, Brad returned to his deck for more sunshine. What Lynn had told him was nothing to joke about but he simply wasn't going to work himself into frenzy over the deal. He had to think about this and decide what to do.

He turned his face to the sun and shut his eyes, immersing himself in morning warmth. He thought back to Taos and his recent dinner with Matthew, Patrick and Fry. He could smell the tortillas and green chili that had tasted so wonderful and the thought of salty margaritas brought moisture to his mouth. Brad could see Patrick's face from that evening, the earnest look on his brother's face as he had spoken about the evil of white supremacist hate. Patrick's words were as clear right now, sitting in morning sunshine, as they had been that night when Patrick spoke. Brad listened inside his head to his

Dale Lovin

brother's words: "Very few people grasp the lunacy of those people and how quickly their philosophy can turn violent. Public awareness of all those groups seems to come and go like the wind. Every so often some big shooting or high-profile incident takes place and they get plastered all over the news for a while. Then things settle down and nobody pays attention until the next blow up and it starts all over again. But those crazy bastards are always out there. They never go away, never stop scheming and never stop hallucinating about how they're going to lead the way into some separate, white utopian nation. They're always out there. The crazy bastards are out there."

The sound of geese interrupted Brad's thoughts and caused him to open his eyes. He looked to the mesa where a dozen or so of the flying marvels, in perfect formation, winged across a backdrop of sky so blue it hurt. He loved to hear them. Their honking had always stirred something within his heart. But this morning their song seemed different. Was the sound forlorn or foreboding? "Honk, honk, honk." Brad listened, "Honk, honk, honk. They're always out there. The crazy bastards are always out there."

\* \* \* \*

Multiple locks secured the grey, metal door. Once Earl had completed a laborious process involving keys and twisting combinations, he swung the door open. Nolan's first impression was that he was peering into an abandoned mine pit. Closer examination revealed a darkened shaft that led from the main floor of the warehouse into some sort of underground storage area. "Be careful," Earl admonished as he switched on a flashlight and pointed the way down a narrow and steep staircase.

Nolan grasped the handrail and stepped into the darkness, Earl followed, remaining a step behind holding the flashlight. Feeling as though he was descending into an ancient catacomb, Nolan's apprehension became absolute fear that tightened in his chest. At the foot of the stairwell, Earl motioned for Nolan to make a turn as he cast the paltry beam of his light onto cinder block walls that were green with age and mold. A few steps further and Earl reached up to switch on a lantern that hung from a ceiling of wooden beams. Spider webs hung as rotted silk in air that smelled of abandonment. The lantern's deficient glow created more shadow than illumination, giving the two men an appearance of wax figures come to life. Nolan looked about, realizing that he stood in a man-made cavern with a honeycomb of darkened tunnels disappearing into inky void. Beneath the suspended lantern, Nolan saw a sheet of plywood balanced on saw horses that apparently served as a table. Scattered about were a few chairs and several large metal chests sat on the floor. Each chest was secured with hasp and lock that defied intrusion. Nolan's heart began to pound and he felt his mouth go dry. *Holy fuck, is this some kind of secret torture chamber?*

"Sit down," Earl motioned to a chair. Nolan could not tell if Earl was offering or commanding. They took seats at the same time on opposite sides of the wood table, the lantern swayed over their heads. From the angle of his seat, Nolan could see only the surface of the table and Earl's face, everything else was black as night. Earl did not speak but looked directly across the plywood table into Nolan's face.

Nolan had no idea what to do or say so he attempted to meet Earl's gaze, but he knew that the fear in his gut was bound to be painfully apparent in his face. Just as in the cabin on the day of Stanley's murder, Earl had been most obvious that he was armed. Nolan most certainly was not. Earl had the advantage and was enjoying it.

Earl's face broke into a smile. His teeth appeared unnaturally white beneath the lantern's glow, making the gesture more macabre than comforting. Earl seemed to sense Nolan's discomfort as he spoke in a condescending tone. "Take it easy, Nolan, everything is fine." He swept his eyes over the room. "There is no one here but me and you. It's just the two of us. No one else even knows we are here." His smile broadened. "I think we need to talk, Nolan. Do you have any objection to some conversation?" He paused. "You know, while we're here completely alone, where no one outside could ever hear a thing." Earl continued to smile.

What happened next was going to be important. Nolan knew that if his voice wavered or betrayed fear, Earl would be dealing from a position of absolute power. Nolan summoned everything from within his core to speak with a strong voice, "What's on your mind, Earl? Spit it out."

Earl's smile held and his eyes continued to evaluate Nolan. He made no attempt to break the awkward silence that hung in the wake of the question Nolan had asked.

Dale Lovin

From the shadows came scurrying sounds. Faint at first, the sounds became louder and prevalent, impossible to ignore. Rats. It had to be rats. Nolan hated rats.

Earl's eyes left Nolan and glanced about, peering into various chambers of darkness. "Sometimes we have visitors down here." He smiled again. "They can actually be quite friendly. Maybe they smell food, who knows? Sometimes I think they just get lonely down here in the dark. I've even known the furry little rascals to come right up close. I've had them run right over my feet or brush against my leg." Earl's smile beamed in the lantern's glow.

Nolan forced his eyes to look at Earl. "You called this meeting, Earl. If you want to talk, let's talk." Nolan was pleased with the sound of his voice. At least it hadn't cracked.

Leaning back in his chair, Earl withdrew his face from light, taking it into shadow. The expression in his eyes became concealed and his face looked more like plastic than flesh. "Nolan, I've already had the most important conversation; I've talked with God. He told me to bring you here today. God told me to bring you here because sometimes it is in dark places, down deep beneath the earth where most men fear to venture, that a man's soul is most easily seen. God told me to bring you here." Earl swept his arm beneath the lantern in a gesture encompassing the room. "And he appointed me to be the judge of your soul." Silence followed, silence broken only by rustling of unseen creatures, scurrying about their business. "What do you think of that, Nolan? What do you think about being down here in this hole, just Earl and Nolan? No other person knows we are here. What do you think about God commanding me to bring you here and judge your soul?" Earl looked from the shadows, his face remained hidden but the teeth behind his smile were still visible.

Nolan returned Earl's gaze, his mind a blur of fear and uncertainty. *You crazy fucking lunatic. If you're going to shoot me, you better do it quick cause I'm not going to sit here and let you play your game much longer.* Nolan held his body rigid and looked through the shadows to the outline of Earl's face. "Earl, if God trusts you to judge my soul, then I trust you to judge my soul. I stand before you as I am and I consider myself honored to have you as my judge." Even in the dim light, Nolan saw Earl's face take on a glow that had not been present before.

"Well-stated my brother and fellow Aryan warrior." Earl brought his face back under the lantern. "I've already told God that I had no doubt about you. I told him that you have strayed from the fold in the past but that deep inside, your heart is steadfast and your spirit devout. When I watched you follow my commandment to confront Judas, that's when I knew that my convictions concerning what lies inside you were correct. Judas was your trial by fire and you passed through the flames without being burned. After spending time with you in this darkest of rooms, I am prepared to report my verdict to God, that I have seen your soul and that I am pleased." Earl extended his arm toward Nolan and, beneath the lantern the two men clasped hands and held tightly. Neither man spoke.

The sound of Earl's chair sliding across the floor broke their silence. "Let me show you a few things, Nolan." Earl stood up and turned away from the plywood table. "You are about to see some materials that only a handful of men even know exist." He lifted the lantern from its hook in the ceiling and carried it to one of the chests that sat on the floor. Turning to Nolan, he passed the lantern, "Hold this for me." He dropped to his knees and spent several seconds manipulating the lock. Earl raised the lid of the trunk and then took the lantern from Nolan. "Have a look, my brother." Earl held the lantern low over the trunk, casting light on its contents.

Nolan had never seen so many guns. He knew enough to recognize that he was looking at an assortment of military-style, long rifles along with dozens of handguns of multiple sizes and calibers. He was speechless. He simply stood over the trunk in complete amazement. No words would come.

Earl stood and once again passed the lantern to Nolan. He unlocked and opened another trunk. This one was filled not only with guns but also with a multitude of items such as grenades and magazines designed to hold multiple rounds of ammunition. One end of the chest appeared to hold nothing but boxes of ammunition. Earl reached into the trunk and retrieved a notebook that lay on top of the deadly armament. "Come here a second," Earl said as he took the lantern and again hung it from the ceiling and motioned Nolan to again be seated. "Every trunk in this room is stocked just as the ones you have just seen." Earl looked at Nolan expectantly.

"I had no idea." Nolan spoke softly. He remained in virtual shock at what he had just been shown.

His face now openly beaming with pleasure, Earl leaned across the plywood table and opened the notebook. "These are the things you must know." He slid the opened notebook directly under Nolan's face. Photographs of a bank with an armored truck parked nearby were pasted onto the first page of the book. As Earl turned each page, he became more animated, his eyes danced in the lantern light and his voice sounded electrified. Earl began to speak in a manner that Nolan had never heard before. He poured his heart out. Talk of plans and schemes flowed from Earl's mouth: robberies, shootings and arsons. Earl's voice carried a passion that Nolan recognized from when Earl spoke of Biblical scriptures or commandments from God.

Forty-five minutes later, Earl replaced the notebook. With the chests closed and secured, Earl turned off the lantern, plunging the room into womb-like blackness. Earl switched on his flashlight and motioned for Nolan to follow. In stunned silence, he shuffled behind Earl, following up the staircase as they ascended from the dungeon.

Sunlight filled the sky and warmed the men as they left the warehouse and walked to their vehicle. Neither man spoke as they drove away.

\* \* \* \*

Low clouds thickened and a fine mist threatened to become actual rain. What had been a sunny morning in Denver was now a memory and dampness slickened the roads for afternoon commuters. Walter wasn't sure if Mr. FBI was home or not. The garage door was closed and he had seen no sign of life all day. With cloud cover developing, Walter had hoped to see some lights inside the house, but he had seen nothing yet. Walter was watching out of frustration as much as anything. He wanted to know when the jerk was home but unless something developed right away that would give him another chance to whack the guy, he was simply going to shift his plan to the broads. He felt good about what he had done to the lawyer by getting her husband.

But what was bothering Walter the most right now was not the FBI Agent. It was that he had no idea what had happened to his twin brother. He had called Nolan numerous times in the past day with no response. Walter could not imagine what was wrong or what could have happened to make Nolan disappear like this. He had even broken down and called Earl but there had been no answer and no return call from him either. "Maybe they're off on a religious adventure together, looking for lost souls," Walter muttered to himself.

Mist was now falling so heavily that Walter had to use his windshield wipers to maintain a view of the house. He also felt a chill settling. He had spent enough time in Colorado to recognize that when night fell, it would get cold in a hurry and he would need a jacket. "The hell with this," he mumbled out loud. "I'm going to get something decent to eat and check back when it's dark. At least I'll be able to see for sure if any lights are burning." Walter turned the keys in his ignition and drove away.

Walter paid for his meal with cash and returned to his car. In perfect timing, his phone finally rang and Walter saw that it was Nolan. With no greeting, he curtly spoke into his telephone, "I thought you were dead or had taken off to search the highways and hedges for lost souls with Brother Earl. Where in holy hell have you been?"

The onslaught of profanity that poured from Nolan took even Walter by surprise. He had never experienced his brother in such a state and he had to virtually shout at Nolan to get his attention and tell him to slow down. "Jesus Christ, Nolan, slow down and talk to me. I can't understand what the hell you're jabbering about."

Deep breaths could be heard over the telephone before Nolan finally spoke in a manner that could be understood. "You have no idea how crazy this fucker is! We've always known he had some loose hardware but I'm telling you, Walter, that son-of-a-bitch is right-out-of-the-asylum, cross-eyed crazy." Nolan was still breathing hard.

"God almighty, Nolan, are you okay?"

A healthy pause occurred before Nolan replied. "I think I'm okay. But ever since I arrived up here in this land of lunatics, there's been more than once that I thought I was a goner. I thought for sure Earl was going to shoot my ass and that is God's honest truth."

"What the hell's happened? I was wondering if something had gone wrong. If you were in jail, you would have called so I didn't know what to think."

"It's been a nightmare, a total goddamned nightmare. Remember, I told you how Earl called and that he was all excited about me getting up here to Oregon to see him right away."

Dale Lovin

"Yeah."

"I made it to Portland all right and have I ever got stories for you. Jesus, have I got stories." Nolan took a breath in preparation to talk. "I drive for about a thousand hours and get to Earl's house late at night. He invites me in and he's all super friendly like I'm his best friend since him and Jesus were out walking on water together. I had only been there for a few minutes when his wife comes strolling in. And holy Jesus, I mean she came strolling. You should have seen her. Her entire outfit would have fit into a matchbox. That woman was wearing a skirt that barely covered her ass and a low cut blouse that would have given a faggot a boner. She looked hot as hell. I'm trying not to get a stiff dick while she's making sandwiches and hugging all over me. I'm telling you, she was acting like me and her are gonna make us some Christmas fudge together, right there in front of Earl. I sit like a post with my mouth shut and eyes open, trying to figure what the hell I've stepped into."

Walter snickered into the telephone. "I'm liking this story."

"Yeah, you just keep listening and you ain't gonna like it one bit. This flirting and teasing goes on for a couple of hours before good old Earl yawns real big, scratches his balls a few times, says goodnight and tells me we've got some business to handle the next morning. He just walks out of the room, calm as can be, leaving me there alone with his wife. She's winking and blinking and bending over the table with her tits about an inch from my face. It was plain as day to me that Earl's been spending way too much time following the Lord's footsteps and not his wife's sweet little ass. I stand up and tell her that I'm going out to my car to sleep but she's all over me, begging me to come sleep on the couch where she can check on me during the night to be sure I have everything I need. Jesus Christ, I don't know if I'm gonna get laid or shot. I got myself out of that house and back to my car, not having any idea what the hell was going on."

Walter was starting to laugh. "And you're upset over that! Why didn't you just bend her over the table and show the little lady the Promised Land?"

"Screw you. This story is only just beginning. I stay out in my car the rest of the night. I didn't get even a wink of damned sleep. Sure as hell, not too long after sun-up, out walks good old Earl. He's just happy as a baby robin on a spring morning. He hops in my car and off we go for coffee and biscuits. It was like we were on summer vacation together."

"Damn, I was hoping to hear a little more about Earl's wife."

"Oh, for God's sake, there is nothing sexy in what you are about to hear." Nolan told Walter about driving to a remote cabin and how Earl had announced that he wanted Nolan to murder Stanley Barnes. Stress was evident in Nolan's voice as he related the bizarre details of his conversation with Earl that morning. "I'm telling you, Walter, Earl would have shot me in a heartbeat if I had refused to go along with him. Even while I was shoveling dirt on poor old dead Stanley, Earl just stood back, wearing a gun on his side, and watched while I shoveled. Every time I moved a scoop of dirt, I thought sure as hell I was going to get a bullet in my own back."

"God almighty!"

"But you know something, while I was thinking that that bastard was going to shoot me, what was going through my head was that the last person I would have ever spoken to would have been goddamned Earl. And then, to make it worse, I thought I was going to end up sharing a grave with that smelly, little fat fucker, Stanley! Nobody deserves that. And then, after Stanley is buried and sleeping with the worms, Earl sticks out his hand and says for me to give him my telephone. He took my goddamned telephone!"

Walter listened to his brother without uttering a sound. When Nolan stopped talking, both men were quiet. Walter finally responded his voice was subdued. "If anybody but you had told me that story I would have laughed and called them a liar."

"Oh, hell yes! If it was you telling this crazy shit to me, I'd call you a liar."

"What the hell is Earl going to say to his wife about all this, for Christ's sake? It's not like he can just walk into his house, sit down at the dinner table and say, 'Pass the ham sweetie. And by the way, I decided to blow your brother's brains out cause I didn't like the way he combed his hair.'"

"Don't ask me what he's going to do about her. All I know is that Earl says his wife will not be a problem and that he can handle her. Beats the crap out of me how that one's gonna play out. I doubt that she even knows anything about it yet. But here's what I'm wondering. I think all that baloney about Stanley stealing from the movement might be just a huge smokescreen for Earl's jealousy over his wife's roving eyes and hot little snatch. It sounds upside-down but I wouldn't put it past Earl to take out revenge on his wife by attacking her brother. I have no idea what makes anybody in that family tick."

"I'm hearing you and I agree."

"There is nothing at all except Earl's word that the guy was stealing. He hasn't showed any evidence to anybody, not one little shred. All those goofballs following him around just take his word for everything and consider anything he says to have come straight from God."

"Jesus, I hate those morons!"

"No kidding. And then, later that night we had one of those holy-roller prayer meetings with the entire group down in Earl's basement. Oh, my God, everybody was lighting candles, holding hands and praying. Holy Mother Mary, it was a wild night! I mean we've seen some of that stuff in the past, but I always thought those idiots were just playing along with Earl. But after what I've seen in the past few hours, I don't think so anymore. Every last one of those silly bastards really believe in Earl and think he is some sort of Messiah." Nolan paused, "And I damned well know that Earl considers himself the Messiah. I promise you, Walter, every man that we have ever met through Earl is crazy as a shit house rat."

Walter cut Nolan off. "I'm glad to at least hear from you, know you're still alive. I couldn't figure what the hell had happened, but in ten million years, I wouldn't have thought of this."

"I was dying to call you but Earl's had my telephone and been following me so close there was no way. There hasn't been ten seconds when he hasn't been stuck to me like bristles on a pig's ass. After throwing poor old Stanley's dead bones in the ground, we drive back to Earl's house to get ready for the big revival meeting. Earl has me park my car in his garage cause he says he doesn't want anybody to know I'm there. But then, the asshole locks the door to his garage so I couldn't leave if I wanted to. That son-of-a-bitch is holding me prisoner!"

"Jesus!"

"I spend the rest of the day with Earl getting his shithole basement all set up for the Last Supper, but this time his old lady ain't nowhere around. After Earl has his church service and everyone has left, it's just me and Earl. No little wife with her boobs peeking out. He looks right at me with a really strange expression and makes sure to tell me his wife will be home soon. And then, just like the night before, he yawns, plays with his gonads for a bit and strolls off to sleepy-weepy land. I mean he walks away and just leaves me there, all by myself in his kitchen. My car is locked in a garage that I can't open and that fucker has taken my telephone! I'm like a whore at a church picnic. I have no phone, no car and no goddamned idea what the hell to do. So, I tiptoe to the couch and lay my ass down."

Walter gave a low whistle to indicate his dismay. "So what now, when you getting out of there?"

For the first time since their conversation had begun, Nolan actually laughed. "Not so fast, Walter, not so fast. This story is nowhere close to being over. I haven't even got to the good stuff yet."

"No way." Walter had no further response.

"Since I'm getting to the part that starts to involve you, you better listen with both your big ears."

A grunt preceded Walter's quiet reply, "I'm not sure I really want to hear this."

"Believe me you want to hear this. You ain't gonna believe it but you sure as hell want to hear it."

"Okay, go ahead and give it to me."

"So, after Earl is off counting sheep or whatever the hell he does, I spend another sleepless night. But this time, I'm all cuddled up on that harebrained fucker's couch. I lay there all night long not knowing if the next five minutes are going to bring me a blowjob from his neglected little wife or a blow to my head from a goddamned, double-barreled, twelve-gauge shotgun."

This time Walter managed a short laugh. "After all you've told me, I think I've lost interest in his wife."

"Thank God she never did show up and I have no idea where she is. He may have killed her too, for all I know. To say they're having marital issues is like saying me and you have bald heads." They both enjoyed a real laugh before Nolan continued. "Okay, you have to hear the rest of this story. Next morning, bright and early with Earl happy as Florence Nightingale, off we go on another road trip. I mean my ass is dragging and my pecker's shriveled cause I still don't know what the hell he's planning to do. I'm telling you, every second I was with that insane man I was expecting a bullet in my head or my back. It would have been God's will, of course, but I would be just as dead."

Walter interrupted with a curt command. "Hurry up and finish this goddamned story because me and you are sure as hell going to do our own killing after this horseshit. That fucker is dead meat. He's going to pray for something as gentle as what I did to that god-damned nigger in Los Angeles." Walter's voice had transformed from dismay to anger. "Where does he get off thinking he can treat either one of us like that? Somebody needs to do the right thing and put that crazy bastard out of his misery."

"I'm not arguing with you and we can definitely talk about how to handle him, but that's for another time. You better hold on cause the rodeo ain't even started."

"My ass is smoking and I'm telling you right now, I'm going to kill him, Nolan. Get used to it."

Nolan laughed again. "You ain't doing so good at killing niggers and FBI shits. Maybe you need some batting practice or something. All you've been hitting are foul balls." Nolan was really laughing and enjoying the moment.

"Go ahead, laugh all you want. If you're not pissed off enough to kill that goofy bastard, then I'll come out there and do the job for you. This is the craziest crock I've ever heard in my life."

Bringing his laughter under control Nolan replied, "Slow down, slow down. Let me finish telling you everything that happened out here. There's a good chance that if we use our heads, we might be able to turn this whole thing our way."

Walter's heavy breathing gave away the difficulty he was having in maintaining composure. "Okay, but hurry your ass up and get this over with. I'm ready to fly to Portland tonight."

"You know something, I don't know whether to feel sorry for you or just laugh at you. I mean, think about it. I'm the guy that's stuck out here with this bean head and I'm the guy who spent hours think-ing I was going to be shot, stabbed or buried alive. And yet, you're the one that wants to come charging out here and start a street fight. Take a pill and calm down for Christ's sake. Now let's get on with this because it's important."

Walter refused to reply and let silence drag.

"Earl takes me out for another lumberjack breakfast and then we go way the hell out to the outskirts of Portland. We ended up at some old warehouse. I had never seen it before and I'm not real sure I could find the damned thing again."

"A warehouse?"

"Yeah, it was old and in terrible shape. We get there and he lets me know that he has rented the entire place for the movement. Earl was proud as hell of the dumpy place. He tells me to come inside with him and once again, I'm thinking he's gonna kill me and throw my body in vat of acid or something. I'm not shitting you. I was scared as hell. I mean that place is old, weird and creepy and Earl just loves it. He's whistling and humming some damned church hymn as we walk around through all that crumbling old shit."

"I can't take much more of this. God almighty!"

"Oh yeah, I know, it was a God almighty moment. But look, I'm sure as hell alive and telling you the story so everything turned out okay." Nolan then related his adventure of descending into the tomb-like cellar with Earl and what had been said and the unbelievable sights once the trunks were opened. Nolan stopped talking, letting his brother think about the tale that had just been told.

"I've already said this to you," Walter was growling as much as talking, "but I have to say it again. If you weren't my twin brother that I've known all my life, I would write you off as a liar and the most insane fool I've encountered since I learned how to breathe."

Nolan chuckled. "Walter, let me tell you something. Both of us have been making a mistake for a long time with Earl. Neither one of us has ever taken him seriously. I now realize that has been a big mistake. We've been so hung up on his religious rants that we have flat been blind to some things that we should have been paying attention to. I say it's way past time to open our eyes."

"I don't think I follow you. Spell it out."

"Okay, up until now we've just played along with him. He brought us in to be soldiers in his holy war against the government. That was fine with us because he understood that it was the government that sent our brother to prison for killing a nigger that had it coming. Earl understood better than we gave him credit for about how much our family lost when Vincent went to prison. He offered us a network that was able to track down the lawyer and the FBI agent, the two people that were most responsible for taking Vincent away from us.

You agree with all this so far?"

"Yeah, I agree," was Walter's grunted reply.

"So, Earl brings us into his private little club. Right away he helps us find the lawyer and FBI agent and we get to pick up some cash along the way in a few robberies that he puts together for the movement. Not a bad deal for us at all. What he wants from us in return is all that holy warrior, loyalty crap that we've always made fun of and never took seriously."

"Yep."

"Well, Earl made a believer out of me in the past couple of days. I sure as hell think he's insane and all those guys following him are insane. But, I'm telling you, Walter, insane or not those guys are about to unleash holy hell."

A long silence fell before Walter spoke, "What do you mean?"

"I have no idea if Earl is being truthful when he talks about having followers all over the country. He may be full of shit as a Christmas turkey. I don't know. But, by God I do know what I saw down in that damned hole in the ground. I guarantee you that all those guns didn't just magically appear when Pixie, the gun fairy, sprinkled a little dust in the basement." Nolan was quiet again.

"All right, you're making sense."

"When me and Earl were sitting there in the dark like a couple of kids by a camp fire telling ghost stories, I began to see what you and I have been blind about all along. This guy has the firepower, the will and enough idiots following him to start some really major shit. He wants to start with the bank and armored car job that he's been hinting at for weeks. The bank and armored car are his real priorities. The lawyer's daughter that happens to work there is just gravy. And he wants either me or you to pop her, just to finish fucking with the lawyer and create a sensational headline for the news shows."

"Mighty Christian of him," Walter growled. "And I'll be happy to do it."

"I agree, but here's the part we didn't know. It was poor old Stanley, dead as a doornail Stanley, who gave Earl all the information on how that armored truck goes to that bank and that they have unbelievably poor security for receiving the money."

"You have got to be shitting me?"

"No, not shitting you at all. Stanley had some connections in Los

Angeles with the armored car company that services the bank. Some guy with loose lips gave Stanley the whole scoop and Stanley passed it right on along to Earl."

"Mother Mary. When is this supposed to happen?"

"In the next few days. He wants you here and he wants us both to go take a look and help him case the place. He wants our opinion about the details."

Walter sighed a deep sigh. "I have no idea what to say or think about all this. This guy is a preacher, a robber, a murderer and flim-flam man. I can't make sense of him at all."

"Who the hell can?" Nolan chuckled. "But here is what is causing Earl so much stress. What Earl has to decide is whether he wants to just rob the bank after the delivery truck has taken a load of money inside. Or, he's considering a robbery of the entire damned truck! According to what Stanley told him, if he goes for the bank only, the take will be close to a million. If he takes the truck, he's looking at several million. But, of course, the catch is that there's tremendous risk in trying to rob an armored truck in the middle of Portland in broad daylight. Just robbing the bank will be an easy, quick hit. Earl wants to take us out there to look everything over and he wants our opinion."

"You can give him my opinion right now," Walter snapped. "Take what can be taken from inside the bank and get the hell away fast. Don't even talk to me about that Hollywood John Dillinger stuff of trying to rob an armored car right out in front of God and every-body."

"Oh, absolutely, that's a no brainer. But come out here and we'll look serious, scratch our ass and pretend like we're thinking about it. When we tell Earl our opinion, he'll think we're calm and thoughtful. My money says he will do exactly what we say." Nolan paused, "That is unless God gets involved and tells him to take down the truck. In that case, we might have a problem." Nolan started laughing. "Who knows, brother, we might even get promoted a rank or two in Earl's holy army of the great revolution. I would love to have some medals and stripes to strut around while we're having church services."

"I like that idea. I want to be a General and I want me a beautiful secretary with big tits and a short skirt to follow me around and write down my orders." Now Walter was also laughing.

Nolan became serious and spoke again. "Look, we don't even have to talk about that crap right now. But, you have to listen to me a minute and then it's decision-making time." Nolan's voice became intense. "This bank job is just the first of many things on Earl's calendar. I had the shitty luck of spending a bunch of hours with him in the last day and this guy is convinced that God is directing him. There is not one shred of doubt in his mind that when he starts his crime wave, white brothers from across the nation are going to rise up and deliver holy hell to Washington, DC. He showed me photographs of other banks he intends to rob. He plans to bomb synagogues and burn more houses down. He's even got himself a hit list of black and Jewish political leaders. He's got people who he intends to assassinate. People all up and down the West Coast. And I swear to you, he's as calm and confident about all this as me and you are about ordering a sandwich."

"This is unbelievable stuff, What's your suggestion?"

It took no time for Nolan to reply. "I say you need to get your tattooed ass out here to Portland. We need to tell Earl we are believers and that we want to serve the Lord. We may have to swallow some shit for a few days but we can do it. I say let's go to work on this bank deal before a wrench gets thrown into the gears and the job gets screwed up before we even get our chance." Nolan gave his brother a chance to respond.

"I'm sure you're right. I hate that fucker so bad I can taste it, but I can go along with your idea."

"Come on, Walter, it will be easy. We only have to put up with him for a few days. Once we do the bank, ice the nigger girl and take our money, we can get the hell out of Dodge. I want as many miles between us and Earl as we can get in a very short amount of time. We pull this off and we've done everything we set out to do. We've avenged our brother by getting the lawyer and FBI agent, had ourselves some fun whacking on niggers and we'll finish up with a pile of money. I call it the American fucking dream."

"Only one thing wrong with your fairytale, dear brother. I've not yet killed that skinny, goddamned FBI agent."

"I have to leave that up to you. I want you to get another chance at the guy, but this is taking way too long. It can't go on forever. You gotta make something happen and make it happen fast." Nolan stopped talking. The ball was in Walter's court.

"Let me work on this and I'll get back to you."

"You got it but let me know what the hell you're doing."

"Don't worry, you'll be the first to know." Walter paused before his voice changed as he spoke. "Hey, Nolan, I don't mean to ask anything too personal but I sure would like to know something."

"What's that"

"You told me that while you and Earl were down there in that dark old cellar, Earl looked into your soul. I've been thinking about that. Just exactly how did he go about looking at your soul?" Walter paused. "Did you drop your drawers for good old Uncle Earl and spread nice and wide so he could take a peek at your soul?" Walter started laughing. "I bet he had himself a special probe, a soul probe he probably called it, just for checking to make sure you're a loyal soldier in the Lord's army."

Silence preceded a torrent of profanity from Nolan as Walter howled. Nolan hung up the telephone and Walter held a dead line in his hand as he wiped tears from his eyes.

Walter tried to look outside through the windows of his car but they were too heavily steamed over to see anything. He rolled down the driver's window. Light drizzle fell and a blast of cool air flooded the car. Walter raised the window and started his engine. His decision was made: get this over with and head for Portland. Walter spoke to himself as he cranked up his defrosting system and pulled away. "I think it's time for me to pay a visit to the Fox Cove Inn."

\* \* \* \*

A dreary afternoon had become an even more dreary evening. Brad was deciding between Cheerios or peanut butter for dinner when his phone rang. A glance at caller ID showed it was Bob Ahrens, an old neighbor from when he and Elizabeth had lived up the mountain. It took Brad less than a second to accept Bob's invitation to drive up the hill to meet for dinner at a restaurant. Several friends would be there and it sure beat anything else he had planned. Twenty minutes and a shower later, Brad was ready to go. He hopped in his car and drove away. Drizzle was steady and the temperature had plummeted. An unusually cold evening was on the way.

## CHAPTER TWENTY-FIVE
## Oklahoma City, Oklahoma
## 1995

*April 19 began like any other day. Alarm clocks roused people from their beds for another day of work or school. It was a new day of life in the largest city in central Oklahoma. Morning routines were ordinary: a cup of coffee, a bite of breakfast and a glance at a newspaper. Lunches were made for a child or loved one and, with a wave to the school bus or a quick kiss to a spouse, a day began that was to be anything but ordinary.*

*By 8:45, parking lots and garages had filled and offices buzzed with activity. A yellow, Ryder rental truck moved through city streets as morning's rush eased. People inside the Alfred P. Murrah Federal Building made routine decisions about whether to sit at their desk or walk down the hall to the copy machine. They made decisions as to whether to ride an elevator or walk stairs to another floor. Routine decisions; decisions that on this particular morning determined life or death.*

*By 9:00 the children's day care center of the Alfred P. Murrah Federal Building was filled.*

*A few seconds after 9:00, the yellow Ryder truck rumbled down the street in front of the Alfred P. Murrah Federal Building, pulled into an unoccupied space and parked. The driver ignited a slow burning fuse, stepped out of the vehicle and simply walked away. At approximately 9:02 the truck's four thousand pounds of explosive materials detonated in a cataclysmic eruption that shredded the north side of the seven story building into flying shards of glass, concrete, steel and human bodies. Upper floors collapsed onto lower floors turning walls, furniture and living people into pulverized rubble. The children's day care center was directly over the parked truck and the epicenter of the explosion.*

*In the ensuing hours, rescue workers scrambled frantically to find signs of life buried beneath tons of rubble. Human agony was unbridled: amputation was employed without anesthetic; parents were rescued only to learn that their children had been killed. Horrible decisions fell to rescue workers in deciding who to save and who to abandon to die.*

*One hundred sixty-eight people died on that terrible morning. Nineteen of them were children who had been in the day care center. Hundreds of people endured injuries; some slight while others were maimed for life.*

*The driver of the lethal, bomb-bearing truck was Timothy McVeigh, a United States military veteran in his mid-twenties. McVeigh carried out his attack because he wanted to strike a blow to a command center of the United States Government. McVeigh was angry about many aspects of the government, including the fiery destruction of a compound at Waco, Texas, one year earlier. The materials he used to construct his murderous device were ordinary farm fertilizer components.*

*An influencing factor in McVeigh's life was a book written by American Nazi Party member, William L. Pierce, titled,* **The Turner Diaries**, *in which attacks are carried out against government buildings.*

*An Oklahoma State Trooper arrested McVeigh, within hours of the bombing. At the time of arrest, McVeigh wore a shirt with a picture of a tree with three droplets of blood and the Thomas Jefferson quote, "The tree of liberty must be refreshed from time to time with the blood of patriots and tyrants."*

*In interviews that took place subsequent to April 19, McVeigh referred to the children's day care center and the nineteen children who died as "collateral damage."*

Dale Lovin

*Timothy McVeigh was executed by lethal injection on June 11, 2001, at the Federal Corrections Center, Terre Haute, Indiana.*

# CHAPTER TWENTY-SIX
July 16 - July 17, 2012

Mist gathered, gradually building into droplets that trickled in miniature rivulets across the restaurant's windows. An air of drabness outside only made the mood inside more cheerful. Brad and his friends sipped hot coffee and savored final minutes of the evening's delightful food and conversation. Handshakes and hugs around the table brought end to the impromptu affair. Brad made a dash through the cold and wet as he returned to his SUV. *What crappy weather.* He started his engine and hit the wiper switch. But, before he pulled away, his telephone rang. It was Vicki. From years of friendship, Brad knew Vicki to be one of those people who could wink with her voice, instantly bringing a smile to everyone listening. But at the moment, Vicki's voice was not winking and Brad was not smiling. As Vicki spoke, Brad could hear anxiety wrapped within each word. He felt his own chest tighten as the reality of what he was hearing hit home. How could he have been so stupid?

Vicki told Brad that in recent days while Suzanne had been outside walking her dog, she had noticed that a car with California tags was parked to the side of the road near Fox Cove. This had happened in late evening or night and the car's windows were tinted so that Suzanne had not been able to get a look inside the vehicle. Initially, this had not been alarming since kids frequently utilized the remoteness of the lightly used street as a place for romance or a sneak rendezvous with beer. But tonight something had changed.

Vicki explained that earlier in the evening, Suzanne had left Fox Cove, planning to spend the night in her own home to pay some bills and catch up on things in her house. Suzanne had left her dog, Gunnar, since he and Vicki's dog, Scottie, had become inseparable friends. As Suzanne had driven away, she had spotted the same California car, again parked near the inn. She had called Vicki to tell her about what she had seen and that it didn't feel right.

A clammy film coated Brad's palm where he held his telephone in a death grip. He wanted to vomit. He knew where this was headed. It hit him like a truck that he had stopped at Fox Cove Inn the day he had driven to Taos. He realized now, with sickening certainty, that Walter Perkins had watched him stop there and meet with Vicki and Suzanne. How the hell could the significance of that fifteen-minute visit have failed to register with him?

Vicki forced her way through the story. "We've been having so much fun. Suzanne just needed one night at her house and she plans to be back here in the morning. So, I'm here alone tonight except for Scottie and Gunnar, who between them couldn't find enough meanness to even bark at Jack the Ripper."

Without hearing any more of the story, Brad knew that he needed to be driving to Fox Cove Inn. Windshield wipers slapping, he headed that direction.

"Now, Brad, I don't know what the weather is for you, but up here it's the worst fog I think I've ever seen. For some crazy reason, fog terrifies me. It makes me feel like I'm trapped in another world. But fear or not, I knew I had to let Scottie and Gunnar outside. The darned fog is so bad, I was actually afraid the poor guys would get lost if I just turned them out. So, I gathered my courage and put them on their leashes. I was actually afraid of getting lost myself so the best thing I could figure was to take them on that pathway that you and I have walked together, the one that cuts through the woods and circles around to the street below the inn. Since the path is made from crushed granite, it feels totally different from the floor of the forest and I figured it would be easy to follow with no way to become disoriented."

"Oh, God, Vicki," Brad groaned, "Why didn't you just let the damned dogs pee in the house?"

"You're right, that's absolutely what I should have done, but I'm glad now that I did what I did."

Brad could only moan into the phone as he drove.

"I went off walking with the dogs and, after I got over the initial creepiness of being out there, it really was kind of nice. It was so quiet, not a sound. Even the dogs seemed to sense it and they were calm as could be on their leashes. The pathway was very easy to follow but even so, I did become somewhat disoriented."

"Vicki, what's wrong with you? What happened? Did you get lost out there?"

In spite of her nervousness, Vicki managed a laugh. "No, Brad, I'm not calling you from a truck stop in Ohio. I didn't get lost so calm down. What I meant when I said I became disoriented is simply that I had no idea how far I had walked or where I was in relation to the inn or the street. I never left the pathway and I knew that I was fine. It was just a horrible feeling to instinctively know where I should be, but since my eyes couldn't see a thing, my brain couldn't verify what my senses were telling me."

"Oh, for heaven's sake. Go on. I'm going to throttle you next time I see you."

Vicki continued to relate what had happened, her voice becoming like a coiled spring. "Brad, I was walking very slowly and the dogs were just padding along with me. All of a sudden a light breaks out right in front of me. It almost scared me to death. No more than ten feet in front of me, this eerie light suddenly just appeared through the fog. I stopped dead in my tracks and so did the dogs. I was terrified and I'm sure the dogs sensed my fear. It took a few seconds for me to realize where I was and what I had done. I had walked further than I realized and was completely surprised when I got my bearings. I had reached the point where the pathway meets the road and I had almost walked right into a car that was parked there. I just knew instantly that this was the car that Suzanne had been seeing. It was parked far off to the side of the road, exactly where the pathway and road come together. The last thing I expected was a parked car and, with it being so dark and the fog so thick, I never would have seen it in a million years except for the light coming on."

Brad was trying to visualize everything that Vicki was saying but he did not readily grasp what had happened. "What do you mean you saw a light? What the heck happened, what were you seeing?"

"The light I saw came from a man who had opened the driver's door of the car, causing the interior lights of the car to come on. He left his door open so the light stayed on and I was standing so close I could almost have touched him. But I was behind him and he had no idea I was even there."

"Holy Jesus, Vicki!"

"Oh, Brad, my heart was pounding so hard and I was praying that the dogs wouldn't give me away. I've never been so scared in my life. I watched him undo his pants and just stand there and urinate in the middle of the street. I could see him and hear him. I swear, I could even smell his urine, he just splashed it all over the street." Vicki became quiet.

Brad sensed that she was struggling and gave her some time. "Okay, Vicki, tell me what happened next."

She took a gulp before speaking. "Nothing more happened, that's all. He did his business, got back into the car and that was it."

Now was time for the hard question. Brad knew the answer before he asked. "Did you get a good enough look at him to tell me what he looked like?"

"That's why I'm so upset. It was no kid drinking a beer and there was no one else in the car with him. He was an adult for sure and maybe the ugliest man I've ever seen." Vicki gulped again, "I can tell you he had a shaved head and, when he got back into his car, I saw tattoos all over his arms." Vicki stopped for a moment. "I know, Brad, I know that lots of men have a shaved head and tattoos and that doesn't mean anything at all in today's world. So maybe it was because of the darkness and fog together with that dim light from his car. I don't know but I can tell you there was something about him that looked hideous to me."

Brad's mind went into a spin. What should he tell her? Vicki knew nothing about what this involved. He had never even told the truth about his own assault, much less the related stories from Los Angeles or Portland.

Vicki was talking again. "But, Brad, what in God's name was he doing sitting out there in the dark on a night like this, only yards from my inn? I guess I can't say for sure but everything in me tells me this was the same guy that Suzanne has seen before." Hard breathing and stifled tears were all that Brad heard for a second. But quickly, the tears were no longer stifled as Vicki blurted in half statement and half sob, "Brad, he's watching me, I know he is."

"Okay, Vicki, cry your eyes out, that's perfectly all right but you have to do something first. I want you to dial 911. You need to get some help as fast as you can."

Through tears and a choked throat Vicki replied, "I've already done that. They're on their way but Highway 285 is completely closed due to a multi-vehicle accident with fatalities. It happened about a half hour ago, just up the mountain, less than a mile from the inn. Almost the entire Sheriff's department is responding to the mess and everything is at a standstill all over the mountain. The police aren't making any promises about when they can get here."

"Oh, for heaven's sake."

"I called Suzanne and she's not answering. I'm worried sick that she might be involved in that horrible accident because that's exactly how she would have driven home. If she went straight home after leaving me, she's fine. But, if she stopped for any reason, she could be in the middle of everything." Vicki's sobs were breaking Brad's heart.

Brad was driving hard and fast as he dared. "Listen to me Vicki, everything will be fine but you have to be smart. Is your inn locked?"

"Yes, absolutely. After I saw him get back into his car, I made it back to the inn as fast as I could move in the fog. The doors are locked and double locked."

"How about windows, back doors and emergency exits. Is every entry point into the inn secured? I'm talking upstairs stuff also, don't forget anything."

"Yes, I'm positive. Everything is locked. I've checked everything daily since Suzanne and I started this remodel project."

Wet streets seemed to have discouraged most people, enabling Brad to maintain a decent speed and he was making good time, given the conditions. As he drove, he tried to visualize the interior of Fox Cove. He had been inside the inn several times but he certainly wasn't intimately familiar with its layout. What he did know was that the inn was an old historic structure. Vicki had maintained it with loving care but Brad doubted that any of the doors or windows would withstand a good hard kick. He thought about whether or not he should mention that to Vicki. He decided not bring it up. "You're going to have to use some judgment here, Vicki. I want you to go to your kitchen and get a knife or something big and heavy that you can use like a club if you have to. Then, you choose what you think is the best room in the inn that you can lock yourself into. Get into that room and go into the bathroom. Lock yourself in again. Don't come out until you know it's me on the other side of those locked doors. Got all this?"

"Yes, I'm walking toward my kitchen right now."

"Okay, great. I'm on my way. I was already up the mountain when you called so I can slip in on Highway 73 and miss the road closure. It's just raining where I am right now so maybe the fog is lifting and the police will be able to get there right away. When I get there, I'll bang and yell plenty loud. You'll know for sure it's me. Got it?"

"I'm almost to step into the kitchen right now. I'll find some kind of weapon and go lock myself up somewhere."

"You're going to have help there before you know it. Come on, Vicki, you've faced worse than this when you were growing up on your farm in Missouri." Brad pressed the phone to his ear, hoping Vicki could not somehow hear his thoughts; *Oh God, if only that were true.*

"I'm going to do what you said, Brad, but please hurry."

"I'm flying, baby, I'm flying. Oh, Vicki, one more thing, be sure to keep your phone with you. Turn off the sound and keep it where you can feel it vibrate if someone calls."

"I'll do it."

"I have to use both hands to drive right now, Vicki. Rain is pouring and I'm driving way too fast. Hang up now and get yourself squared away. I'll be seeing you in a matter of minutes."

"Okay, just hurry."

Brad turned off his telephone, gripped the wheel and pressed the accelerator even harder. Oncoming vehicles cast a vicious glare through falling mist, but fortunately light traffic made such encounters rare. Brad raced his SUV over the twisting ribbon of asphalt. This was a narrow and dangerous road on any night, and even more so when driving too fast in bad conditions. He prayed that this would not be the night a wild animal chose to wander into the middle of the road. *Thank God I came up here for dinner tonight. That had to save me an easy twenty-five minutes.* Any sense of good fortune quickly faded as a more somber reality settled with each curve of the road and splatter of each raindrop: *I am about to meet Walter Perkins for the second time.*

Brad knew exactly what to expect from the road and the topography as he cut through the back way to Fox Cove Inn. However, he did not expect what he saw as he topped a hill just before descending to the road that would take him to Fox Cove; an ocean of pure white billowing in the night. From the crest of the hill his headlights focused down, into a valley of fog that appeared to swallow the road before his very eyes. "Oh, my God," he breathed in disbelief as he hit his brakes. This was something right out of a science fiction movie. The fog was surreal, a masked phantom daring one to enter. "Holy shit!" Brad flicked a switch for the SUV's fog lights and eased his way into the floating shroud. The pressure inside his vehicle seemed to change and Brad felt as though damp mist coagulated within his vehicle.

Peripheral vision was instantly lost. The powerful beams from his fog lanterns scarcely penetrated beneath the fog, illuminating mere feet before they dissipated into nothing. Swallowing hard, Brad slowed his SUV to a crawl. He had been in similar conditions before and knew that he could become hopelessly lost in a matter of seconds. He checked his odometer, guessing he had to travel about half mile before he would need to make a left onto Vicki's street. He crept. His eyes hurt from the strain. Typical of many mountain roads, there were no centerline markings, so most of the time he had no idea if he was in the center of the road or about to drop off the edge. He was passing through rural, forested terrain so there was not even a hint of a house or streetlight to offer a clue to where he was in relation to the turn onto Vicki's street. *Oh, God, this is taking forever!* Quarter-mile to go. *Keep it on the road, keep it on the road.*

Heart hammering, Brad's anxiety increased by the second. The fog was so dense he felt constriction, a garrote about his throat. *Almost there, gotta be.* Fog became a veil over his eyes, everything looked exactly the same; there was no up or down, no straight or to the side. He had no idea if he was even on the road. The odometer progressed, one-tenth at a time. *I'm coming, Vicki, I promise, I'm getting there fast as I can.* The odometer rolled another tenth; half mile exactly! *I'm close, I have to be close. Her street has to be real soon. Please, God, don't let me screw up now.*

He brought his SUV to a complete halt. He needed a few seconds. With both hands gripping the wheel as though his life depended on it, Brad took deep breaths as he contemplated a plan. Vicki's street was going to be a left turn. If he missed it, he was screwed. The most critical thing was to illuminate the left side of the road until he reached her intersection. *For Christ's sake, don't miss her turn.* He began easing his vehicle forward, angled to cast his fog lanterns to the left shoulder of the road. Then, with periodic corrections to the right, he managed to keep the left side of the road illuminated.

More than anything, Brad wanted to jam his foot down on the accelerator, press it to the floor and fly to Vicki. Instead, he crept, five feet, ten feet, frantically searching for a strip of black pavement branching in from the left. Another five feet, ten feet, correct to the right. He repeated the process, again and again. His fog lanterns strained to pierce the murk; it was as though they were submerged in buttermilk. The lanterns illuminated trees and grass but no asphalt. He duplicated what he had been doing; drive toward the side of the road and correct to the right. What he strained to see through the soupy murk seemed never to change: trees and grass, trees and grass, correct to the right; trees and grass, trees and, oh, thank God, there it was, asphalt! Brad made the turn. At last, he was on Vicki's street.

Now, he had to make a decision. He had roughly another quarter mile to go. It was a straight, up-hill climb to Fox Cove. Should he push it hard and fast with his lights on or, should he try to sneak up the hill. If Walter was inside the inn, would he even look out to notice a vehicle approaching? But if he was still in his parked car or remained outside the inn, Walter would definitely see lights approaching and Brad would be at a huge disadvantage. In a split second, Brad made the call. He figured that in the fog, Walter would not be able to spot automobile headlights more than seventy-five yards at best. He left his lights on and pushed his old fishing SUV up the hill, straight and hard. He did his best to watch for Walter's car parked to the side of the road but realized he could easily miss it even if it was still sitting there. When he had driven what he calculated to be half the distance to the inn, Brad killed his lights. He had not seen a parked car but the truth was that he had no idea where Walter's car was located. He had no choice. Brad kept his SUV moving forward.

It was no different than driving blindfolded, Brad could see absolutely nothing. He felt tires on the right side of his vehicle leave the pavement and sink into soft soil., He swerved back to the left and kept going. *Jesus H, I have no idea where I am.* In seconds, Brad had lost all perspective of where he might be; it was madness to continue driving. He stopped his vehicle and turned off the engine. Fog wrapped about the motionless vehicle like a cocoon and squeezed tight. Brad struggled to breathe. *I'm coming, Vicki, I promise. Hang on just a bit longer, I'm coming.* He reached into a side pocket of the driver's door where he kept topographic maps for fishing trips. His fingers found what he needed and had hoped would still be there: his flashlight. He needed light and he needed something heavy. His flashlight was the heaviest thing he could think of that was readily accessible. He pulled it out and felt sweat in his hand as he wrapped his fingers about the cylinder. It wasn't much but damned sure better than nothing.

He sat in the dark for a moment to think and to listen. He could hear only his own suffocated attempts at breathing; a wet blanket seemed to be wrapped about his face. No real plan came to his head other than to just do something. He reached for his phone and hit the button to call Vicki. He heard the ring. *Answer, Vicki, please answer.* The ringing continued. Vicki did not answer. *The hell with this bullshit.* Brad threw open the door and stepped into the fog. All he knew for certain was that the inn was somewhere in front of him. He began a half-walk half-jog, his heart kicking wildly. Watery mist filled his lungs. He kept moving. It flashed through his mind that this must be what it would feel like to drown. He kept moving. *I'm coming, Vicki.*

When he literally stumbled into the parked car, he had no idea what had happened. His fingertips explored cold, wet metal until he realized what he had struck. A quick blast from his flashlight revealed that the vehicle was empty and that it had a California tag. Now, Brad knew for certain that Walter was inside the inn. But where was the inn and where was the pathway to take him there? He kept moving. His eyes felt they were going to explode.

At first, it was just a milky dot, more an eerie presence than any-

Dale Lovin

thing real; the light over the front door of the inn materialized as a tiny ghost, floating in the air. Brad wiped water from his face and kept moving. He was only a few feet way when an outline of the inn finally became visible. He desperately searched for a lighted window. As best he could tell, the inn was totally dark except for a single light on the far right side. *Gotta be the last room at the end of the hall.*

When he finally reached the door to the inn and stood beneath the dim porch light, Brad felt nausea in his stomach. The door was wide open, its jam splintered into shreds. Brad could only imagine the terrifying sounds Vicki would have heard as her door was being kicked in. Looking through the battered doorway, there was nothing but stark blackness. He had to see something. Brad turned on his flashlight. Even in his hypersensitive state, the devastation that greeted his eyes stopped him in his tracks. It looked as though a bomb had exploded inside the inn. In a microsecond, Brad understood what had happened. Gaping holes pocked the walls where Walter had swung his club, into the walls. Pulverized plaster coated the floor like blown snow. Brad stepped through the entryway and swung his light to the left, into the kitchen and dining area. Shattered pottery, annihilated dishes and crystal were strewn like confetti. Chairs were overturned. The magnificent antique table that had been the focal point of Vicki's dining room was on its side, legs broken like straws. Handcrafted china cabinets that had hung on walls lay on the floor in heaps of fractured junk. The demolished dining room mirror, now nothing but slivers of broken glass, glittered like millions of tiny diamonds in the beam of Brad's light.

Brad stood perfectly still as he surveyed the horrific scene. *Holy Jesus, this guy is an absolute maniac.*

Brad switched off his light. Nothing; no light, no sound except for his heart thundering inside his head. What must have this been like for Vicki? Where had she been when this club-wielding monster burst into her home? Water dripped into the kitchen sink behind him. Nothing else. Only the steady drip, drip.

Another sound. Straining, he listened. He heard it again. Was that the whining of a dog? The sound came from the end of the hallway. It was unmistakable, a dog whined pitifully. He flicked his flashlight back on. The beam sliced through a black corridor exposing a row of guest rooms, every door closed. By the time the flashlight's ray reached the end of the hallway, it was weakened, almost to disappear, but powerful enough to reflect a reddish glow: animal eyes looked back at him. Two dogs sat side-by-side outside the closed door of the last room on the right: Scottie and Gunnar. With his light directed at them, their whining increased but neither dog moved. That told Brad what he wanted to know; Vicki was inside that room. Walter Perkins was inside that room.

Closed doors to empty guest rooms stood silent vigil as Brad made his way down the hall. Scottie and Gunnar quieted, lifting their heads as he approached. Expectancy reflected in their eyes but neither dog moved. Brad heard a tail thumping against the floor. Light filtered from underneath the closed door and muffled sounds of a voice reached Brad. He strained to hear; it was a man's voice. He had made it. Brad didn't know what had happened or was about to happen, but one thing was certain: Walter had Vicki on the other side of the door.

The only thing Brad had going for him was surprise. There was no doubt that his single, slim advantage would be gone in a flash once he opened the door. He tried to remember. Vicki had given him a tour of the inn but he simply had no recollection of how the room was laid out. Could he possibly open the door quietly enough to gain entry without Walter knowing it? Would Walter have his back to the door or would he be positioned to see the door open? Was the door locked or unlocked? No answers. Brad cast his flashlight on the door for a quick evaluation: solid wood, old stuff, but no way to tell about the framing. His mind was processing a million thoughts. He couldn't stand there all night. Decision made, go for the shock factor. He stepped back, placing himself directly in front of the door. He focused his light and, with everything in his body, Brad drove his foot into the door, just to the side of the knob.

A detonation erupted within the room as metal ripped through wood and the door flew open. In a blink Brad saw the back of a man, a shaved head, Vicki's face, tape on mouth, hands tied above head. The room spun in a blur. The man turned, a stunned face. Brad lunged, flashlight to the shaved head, contact, both men on the floor, fists, fingernails, blood, spit, gasping sounds expelled from the lungs. Walter broke free and in an instant was on his feet. He held the pipe in his hands and began to swing wildly. The first blow landed on the iron frame of the bed, a deafening twang of metal on metal. Brad rolled to his feet, leaping backwards in desperate retreat as the pipe made another pass, missing his chest by an inch.

Time that had accelerated to light speed now regained equilibrium as gasping men stood face-to-face, circling, calculating. Walter sneered, "If it ain't the nigger-lover his self. What's that patch on your head, you Jew fucking pig?" Sidestepping, the men circled. Walter held the pipe, both hands wrapped about the deadly shaft, coiled, looking to strike. "You must have come cause you want to watch me give the little lady here a real good fucking before I jam this pipe up her twat till it comes out her mouth." Blood trickled from Walter's mouth, giving his smile a hideous effect. "I got me some good nigger hair on this pipe already. Add some FBI brains and juicy pussy hair, holy fuck, what a treasure." Walter's smile widened, his eyes were wild, like burning marbles.

Round and round, each step deliberate, the pipe held high, cocked. Brad knew a blow from the pipe, no mater where it landed, would be his end. He had to get in close, take away Walter's leverage. How to do it? They circled, eyes never breaking contact as wheezing sounds were expelled from the lungs of both men. Rational thought had vanished. Basic instinct directed movement. Whoosh! The pipe sliced. Brad ducked, missing the deadly trajectory by a breath. He lunged, thrusting his shoulder into Walter's groin and wrapping his arms about his adversary's waist in a single motion. Walter gave a violent twist, flinging Brad onto the floor. In a sickening, split second, Brad found himself on his back with Walter straddling over him, the bludgeon in both hands high over his head. The last thing Brad saw was the crazed look on the face of Walter Perkins as the grey pipe arced downward, straight toward his face.

Blackness, hot, heavy and smothering was all he felt. The blackness grew heavier, his lungs screamed, he had to breathe. Brad sucked hard and rolled to his side, the body of Walter Perkins rolled with him. Brad stared into the blood-smeared face of Walter. Less than an inch away, Walter stared back. Brad rolled to his back again and looked up. Frozen in static suspension, stood Suzanne with a ceramic flowerpot in her hands.

A sense of place and time seeped back into the room and focus worked its way through Brad's mind. *Jesus Christ!* He rolled his head. Walter was close enough to kiss. Brad sprung to his knees.

Walter was stunned but nowhere near out. Brad saw his flashlight on the floor just under the bed and reached. Walter realized what was happening but it was too late. Brad raised the flashlight above his head, just as Walter had done with the pipe, and drove it down, straight into Walter's head delivering the blow with all his strength. The flashlight burst apart in Brad's hand, batteries rolled across the floor like marbles and the lens shattered. It wasn't enough. Brad needed something heavy. In a single movement, Brad reached up, grasped the bedside lamp and swept it off the table. The room plunged into blackness but Brad knew exactly where Walter's shaved head was located. Grasping the lamp with both hands, he bludgeoned it into Walter's head and face. In manic fury, the blows continued until Walter's body became still.

The room was silent and absolutely black. Brad could see nothing and the only sound was his own breath. He remained on his knees. *God, it's dark.* Something cold touched his face; a dog's nose. Brad knew that he was still alive and that Suzanne was standing somewhere in the dark but what about Vicki! "Suzanne, turn on a light." Nothing moved. "Suzanne, get to a light, now!" Brad screamed. He heard movement and an overhead light came on. Suzanne stood by the doorway, her hand on the light switch as if she was unable to move her arm or hand. Her entire body was rigid, her face in a daze. Brad looked at her as he stood up. He couldn't wait to hug her but Vicki had to be first. He looked down at the bloody mess that was Walter. He was beginning to stir. A quick look at Vicki confirmed what he thought he had seen when he had first charged into the room: she was on the bed, her hands tied above her head and secured to the metal headpiece of the bed. Grey tape covered her mouth. He took a closer look at her bonds; standard police plastic flex cuffs held her hands together and tied to the bed. *That son-of-a-bitch came prepared.*

He turned to Suzanne. "I need help, Suzanne. I need you fast." He barked the words but he wasn't sure that her face showed response. "Now! Suzanne, come here now!" Understanding flickered in her eyes as she removed her hand from the light switch and crossed the floor to Brad. He dropped to his knees again, grabbed Suzanne's foot and placed it on Walter's throat. "Put some pressure there, Suzanne, and don't let up until I tell you." He glanced up to Suzanne's face and she nodded that she understood. Brad felt pressure in her leg as she pressed her foot down into Walter's throat. "You're doing great, sweetheart, absolutely great. Don't let this son-of-a-bitch move." She nodded again. Brad ran his hands over Walter's body and found exactly what he expected in the pocket of his jeans: an entire bundle of flex cuffs. It took only a few seconds for Brad to raise Walter's arms over his head and cinch them exactly as he had done to Vicki. He tapped Suzanne's foot, "Okay, ease off now." With Suzanne's foot removed, Brad drug Walter toward the bed. He left him lying prone on the floor, his semi-conscious face staring at the ceiling. Brad raised Walter's arms just enough to secure them to the foot of the bed. As he did so, Brad saw the dent in the metal that had been left when Walter swung his pipe. It flashed through his mind what that blow would have done to his head. *Think about that later.*

When he stood up from tying Walter, Suzanne was sitting on the bed looking at Vicki, not sure what to do first. Brad grabbed her by the shoulders, "Go to the kitchen. Bring scissors or a knife. Hurry!" Suzanne gave another nod and ran from the room. Brad worked a finger underneath the tape that covered Vicki's mouth, "Sorry, babe, this isn't going to feel so good," and with a jerk the tape was gone. Vicki did not speak but gasped, air rushed in and out, pathetic moans escaping with each exhale. Brad pressed his hands on her shoulders, "It's okay, Vicki, it's okay."

Scissors in hand, Suzanne ran back into the room and Vicki was free in seconds. She rose up into a sitting position and the three virtually collapsed into each other in a mesh of hugs and sobs. Two tail-wagging, face-licking dogs joined the melee and sobs turned into laughter.

A woozy, but conscious, Walter Perkins lay on the floor, aware of the celebration taking place only a feet away. Blood trickled from his mouth and oozed down his throat causing him to gag and cough. Walter's heave came from deep down as vomit and bile erupted, his throat and mouth boiled in repugnant fluids that dripped from his chin and onto his chest.

Brad stood over Walter and double-checked that he was securely tethered to the bed. He motioned for Suzanne and Vicki to follow him out into the hallway and, along with the dogs, they all left the room and walked down the hall toward the devastation of the dining room and kitchen. Brad opened the door into one of the guest rooms and ushered everyone inside. They all needed to see something other than the chaos and ruin that Walter had delivered.

In the serenity of a freshly painted guestroom, words and tears flowed from Vicki. She told of how Walter had stormed into her house within seconds of the moment she had ended her telephone conversation with Brad. She told of her terror as he swung his club with abandon and the deafening noises as furniture and glass were demolished in explosion after explosion of his rampage through the room. With every swing, he had taken a step toward her, drawing closer second by second. Vicki trembled violently when she told of how he had screamed like a savage and howled with laughter as he swung his pipe, destroying everything in his path, stalking his way straight to her. She had simply collapsed onto the floor, helpless in fear. He had tied her wrists as she lay on the floor and then dragged her the length of the hallway, telling her what he planned to do to her. Vicki was sobbing. Brad and Suzanne both embraced and hushed her. There was no need for more talk.

Suzanne related her story of being trapped in fog that came from out of nowhere and, then, a massive traffic jam. The world had come to a halt in absolute blindness. She had finally managed to turn her car around and struggled to make her way back to the inn. Even in the stress of the moment, Suzanne's sense of humor wriggled its way to the surface. She managed a grin, "And the rest of the story, folks, is all history."

Brad shook his head in disbelief and relief. "Okay ladies, you may have made history but some work remains to be done." He turned to Vicki, "Get on your telephone and cancel that 911 call. Tell them everything is fine, that friends have arrived and you don't want to endanger an officer in the terrible conditions outside. If the 911 operator wants to argue, let me know and I'll handle it. Got it?" Vicki nodded. Brad turned to Suzanne as he powered his phone. "Okay, Wonder Woman, here's what I need you to do." He reached for pen and paper on the nightstand and copied a number from his cell phone. "Call this number. It's for a guy named Kurt Riddle. He's a sheriff's officer and a good man. Tell him that Brad Walker could use some help and tell him to come over here but only if the fog lifts and he can do so safely." Suzanne was shaking her head like a kid who had been

222

Dale Lovin

offered candy. "If the 911 folks are giving Vicki any crap, Kurt can help with that also."

Brad looked at both Vicki and Suzanne. "Then, I want one of you to go out there in that mess," he nodded toward the destroyed kitchen, "Find a bottle of wine, scotch or something and bring it back here. You can cry, scream or do whatever you need to make you feel better. I want your door closed. If I need you, I'll walk twenty feet down the hall and knock on your door. You ladies okay with all this?" Two heads nodded. "Fine, get those calls made and start your cocktail hour."

\* \* \* \*

"My, my, my, Walter, what a mess you've made," Brad spoke cheerfully as he made an exaggerated survey of the wrecked room. "And look at you, Walter, why, I do believe you've been sick. Does Walter have an upset tummy?" Brad looked down at Walter with a patronizing smile. "You would feel better if you weren't such a mess. Let me help clean you up, Walter. I want us to have a gentlemanly discussion and I'm sure that things will go better if you are nice and clean." Brad picked up a trashcan and stepped into the bathroom. He cranked the shower handle and filled the can with cold water. Back in the bedroom, he walked toward Walter. The men eyed each other in silence. Brad didn't just pour the water over Walter; he flung it. The water struck Walter's face with such force that it sounded like a slap. Walter reflexively gasped, his head, face and chest now a smear of blood and vomit. He breathed hard. His eyes burned with hatred.

"That better, Walter? I sure hope so." Brad's voice continued its cheerful tone. He pulled a chair to within inches of Walter's semi-prostrate body. With great fanfare, Brad sat down and shifted back and forth in the chair as if he were in a theater, preparing to enjoy a long performance. After settling into the perfect position, Brad placed his elbows across his thighs and leaned forward, bringing his face close to Walter. "Now, Walter, I must ask that you forgive me a terrible oversight. I think I failed to introduce myself properly. My name is Brad Walker. I spent twenty-five marvelous years in the FBI putting pukeheads like you and your brothers in the penitentiary. I am pleased beyond words to have this opportunity to formally meet you, Mr. Perkins." Brad stopped speaking and appeared thoughtful.

"But then again, you tried to murder me a few nights ago. We were down in New Mexico and you didn't bother to introduce yourself to me either. So, I suppose we're even in the social oversight department." Brad smiled. "By the way, how is that older brother of yours doing? I've heard that they've got themselves a real friendly community in that little prison. It's like a country club with no monthly dues. Now, that sounds like a wonderful deal for someone like your brother." Brad shook his head and smiled at Walter. "Can't beat a deal like that, can you, Walter? No sir, that's better than Christmas morning in a toy store."

Brad stopped speaking and kept his face so close he could feel Walter's breath. Walter glared. Brad glared back. Hatred was palpable. Seconds of silence passed before it happened. The wad of spit came from deep in Walter's throat. He hurled it with force. Blood, mucus and bile splattered on Brad's cheek, just below his eye and oozed downward, creeping toward his lip. Part snarl and part growl came from Walter. "Go fuck a nigger, you filthy Jew-loving pig. Make some babies, just what we need, lots more of them smelly jungle bunnies."

Brad did not move. He held the position, inches from Walter's face, his eyes boring into Walter's. The gelatinous glob trickled down Brad's cheek. Finally, Brad stood and walked into the bathroom. When he returned to Walter, he held a towel in his hand and periodically dabbed at his cheek. He seated himself and resumed the same position, their faces within smelling distance. "Walter," Brad spoke in a fatherly tone, not much more than a whisper, "I'm going to talk to you about two things and you need to listen very carefully. This is important shit. I'm going to talk to you about two things, two things that we all encounter at some time in our lives: missed opportunities and regrets. Missed opportunities and regrets, those are sad words, Walter, really sad words. Missed opportunities and regrets," Brad shook his head in a rueful manner. "Wouldn't it be nice if we could go through life and never experience a missed opportunity or a regret?" Brad shook his head again, "I don't know about you, Walter, but I've missed lots of opportunities and I have a truck load of regrets that I have to carry around with me. Sometimes it's a real burden, Walter, a real burden."

Silence became as heavy as the outside fog. Brad glanced to the window and then brought his eyes back to Walter. "It's a mighty foggy night outside. I am so glad that we are inside this nice cozy room. I think this a wonderful place for us to have a conversation. Do you agree, Walter?" Walter glared as Brad continued, his voice soft and his tone gentle. "You see, Walter, I worked very hard back in my career with the FBI. I worked hard and I was absolutely Mr. Straight. I followed the law to the letter, every day. No fudging, Walter, no fudging. I followed the law. And, let me be perfectly clear, following the law is not one of my regrets, not at all. I'm very proud of how I conducted myself and I would do everything exactly the same again today. But, you know the old saying about how things change? By golly, that sure seems to be the case as we go through life; things do change, Walter, things certainly do change."

Brad pinched the bridge of his nose with thumb and forefinger as if he struggled to find words. "Two really important things happened to me after I left the FBI. Looking back, I now understand that one of those things was a missed opportunity. A really terrible missed opportunity. And the other thing, Walter, well, it has been a huge, huge regret." Brad shook his head, sadness in his expression.

Pulling his face away from Walter, Brad straightened his body and took a more relaxed posture in his chair. "Let me tell you my stories." Brad grinned, "Isn't this just absolutely wonderful? It's a cold, foggy night and here we are in this beautiful inn and it's story time." Brad paused and looked at Walter. "You don't look so happy, Walter. That's too bad. Maybe my stories will cheer you up and bring a smile back to your ugly, fucking snaggle-toothed face."

Walter glared.

"Okay, here we go. I was out fishing one afternoon, not too far from here actually, and I got caught in a really bad thunderstorm. I mean it was a hell of a storm. Lightning and thunder like you would not believe. And rain, man, the rain came down sideways. It was a mess. But I was lucky and I found a cave that I was able to crawl into. I sat inside that cave and waited out the storm, warm and toasty as could be. In fact, Walter, that night reminds me a lot of the way things are right now, crappy outside, nice and dry inside. Well, while I was sitting inside that cave, something very interesting happened. I saw two cars driving around out in the woods. Can you believe that? In the middle of a ferocious storm, two cars were driving off the road in the middle of a forest. Does that sound strange to you, Walter? I sure thought it was strange. But that's not all. I watched a bunch of people get out of those cars and carry something into a rotten, old cabin that was out there in the forest. Then, those people just drove away. They simply drove away into that storm and that dark night." Brad was quiet for a moment, looking straight into Walter's face before he whispered, "Poof, they were gone and I had no idea what had happened."

Taking a pause, Brad looked to the ceiling for a moment. "Now, Walter, let me ask you a question. What would you have done if you had been in my shoes that night?" Brad stared at Walter. "Would you have walked over to that old cabin to find out just what in the hell was going on? Would you have broken into the cabin to see what those crazy people had put inside?" Brad leaned forward again and slowly shook his head back and forth. "Let me tell you something. I didn't do that. You see, Walter, I was still Mr. Straight. It wasn't my property. I had no search warrant. I had no authority at all. So, I was Mr. Straight and I simply walked away, Walter, I just walked away." Brad was quiet for a moment. "And that, my friend, was a missed opportunity. Because I let that opportunity slip past me, a woman suffered and it took a long time to straighten out the problems that were caused by that single, missed opportunity. Missed opportunities, Walter, they change lives. Sometimes the life that is changed is yours and sometimes it's the life of someone else, but lives are changed."

Brad pressed the towel to his cheek and was quiet. "Now, about regret, Walter, let me tell you a story about regret. My story about regret also goes back to a stormy night. It was a stormy night, much like tonight, and I was with a shithead, much like you." Brad looked as though he had just made a discovery and he smiled broadly. "What is it about shitheads and me on stormy nights?" Brad gave a laugh. "Shitheads and stormy nights, hell, that just might be a great title for a country song. Let me ask you, Walter, do baldheaded pukes like you ever listen to country music?" Brad shook his head in a manner of sad acceptance. "No, you probably don't appreciate my kind of music at all. Anyway, 'Shitheads and Stormy Nights,' what a great title for a song." Brad laughed again. "I like it, Walter. Your picture can be on the cover." Brad grinned and leaned closer, "Do you think anybody will have trouble deciding if you are the shithead or the

Dale Lovin

stormy night?" Brad threw his head back and laughed loudly. "How about we take your photograph right now? You look great." Brad continued, grinning as he spoke. "You don't seem to be warming up to this idea, Walter." Brad shook his head, "That's disappointing, especially since we just talked about missed opportunity. Maybe you didn't get the point of my story." Brad leaned close again and spoke earnestly. "You better listen to the next story, the one about regret, more closely. It just might have a whole lot to do with how the rest of your night goes."

Standing up, Brad stretched his arms over his head and swiveled his body back and forth a few times. "Sorry, Walter, sitting close to shitheads on stormy nights seems to tighten me up. And heaven knows I don't want to be tight, not with a world-class shithead like you. When we finish up here, I plan to take a really good work out. Boy, do I need a work out." He dabbed at his cheek again with the towel, "Okay, where was I? Oh, yeah, it was a stormy night and I just happened to find myself in a mountain canyon with a man named King Solomon. Believe it or not, King Solomon was a whole lot like you. He was repugnant, through and through. Just like you, he was such a shithead that people could smell him from a mile away."

Brad paced the floor, hands behind his back. "It just so happened that on that stormy night, King Solomon had some really rotten luck," Brad looked directly at Walter, "Just like your bad luck when that lady came in here and smashed your ugly fucking head with a flowerpot." Brad threw his head back and laughed out loud. "Boy, did she ever nail you! You crumbled like a broken cookie. That should teach you to never underestimate the power of a woman and a flowerpot."

Well, back to mountain canyons and King Solomon. This guy, King Solomon, was lying on the ground and I happened to be standing right over him, very much like you and I are positioned right now. And can you guess what happened?" Brad hesitated, giving his question time to settle. "I kicked him in the balls, Walter. I kicked that miserable, obnoxious fucker in the balls with all my strength. I felt his little balls smash like I had stepped on a beetle. You ever step on a beetle, Walter? Remember that crunching sound as the poor beetle's shell snaps open. That is exactly how it sounded when I kicked King Solomon's balls."

As if he searched for God, Brad looked up to the ceiling and the room was quiet. Brad lowered his head, walked close to Walter and bent over, placing hands on knees. "Doing that to King Solomon, kicking his fucking little balls, felt better to me than anything I've ever done in my whole life. It felt so damned good, I wanted to do it again." Brad sat down, and again drew his face close to Walter. "But I didn't do it. I didn't kick his balls again, not even one more time." Brad leaned even closer. "And that, Walter, is a story of regret. Not a day passes in my life that I don't regret that moment. How wonderful it would have felt to feel his balls smash just one more time. Oh, my God, I can't even imagine. What if I had kicked him three more times, five more times? That would have been enough pleasure to last me a lifetime. I regret not kicking him again. Oh, how I regret that."

Brad strightened and walked the floor again. "Here's the way I see things, Walter. Tonight, I have an opportunity. I have an opportunity to grab hold of an investigation that's going on out on the West Coast. Your ugly, shithead brother, Nolan, is involved in the matter. And, of course, your good friend, Earl, is also a part of the deal. My opportunity is to fast-forward that case at the speed of light. Now, I want you to understand something." Brad pointed his finger at Walter. "All those poor guys out there, the police officers and FBI agents, they are exactly like I was. They are a bunch of Mr. Straights. Every one of them will follow the law, day after day, until they finally catch up with all of your dog shit pals out there. It's a very slow and tedious process when one follows the law. But that's okay, I'm very proud of our system of laws. Now listen closely, Walter, this is where opportunity comes in. I'm going to accomplish in one evening what it will take those Mr. Straights a year to get done. Opportunity is alive and well tonight in this very room." Brad stood directly over Walter. "This opportunity will not escape, Walter, I promise. You and me are a team tonight and we are going to move that investigation along. We are going to move it really, really fast."

In a slow, deliberate manner, Brad continued walking until he stood all the way across the room. His eyes locked onto Walter's face and he began a slow, methodical march across the floor, back toward Walter. "Now, I honestly believe that even that ugly, misshaped fucking head of yours understands what I mean about regret. Someday, when I'm in a nursing home and looking back on my life, I don't intend to have any regrets about tonight. No regrets, Walter, no regrets." Brad stopped walking. Faster than a blink, the toe of Brad's shoe drove into Walter's groin. The thud and ensuing gasp was sickening. With a detached glare at Walter's anguished face, Brad turned, walked away and stepped into the bathroom.

Standing over the bathroom sink, Brad splashed cold water on his face, rubbed it across the back of his neck and sponged off with a fresh towel. Stepping back into the room, Brad's voice was once again light and cheerful. "Vicki runs a great place here. It's a shame that someone made such a mess up front, don't you agree?" He sat down again and continued to wipe his face with the towel. When he had finished, he folded it with precision and placed it on the bed. Brad leaned until his face was only inches from Walter's. "Why, Walter, I think I smell vomit on your breath." He shook his head as if disappointed. "I suggest you carry peppermints with you at all times since you never can tell when you might meet someone really special." Brad paused. "You know what I mean, vomit breath and no peppermints, that can spell missed opportunity." Brad then placed his mouth directly over Walter's ear before he whispered, "Do you understand me? I am no longer Mr. Straight." He pulled back a few inches and looked into Walter's eyes. "Now is your chance, Walter, if you want to spit on me again, let it fly. In fact, I want you to. Please, I'm begging you, give me another good shot. Show me how you can hurl that Aryan warrior manhood right out of your mouth."

Silence.

"This is your moment. Remember what I told you about missed opportunity and regrets. Take your time, I'm not going to rush you."

Silence.

"Think, Walter, think about missed opportunity. Think about regret." Brad stopped speaking but never took his eyes from Walter's face. After what seemed an eternity, he asked softly, "What's your decision, Walter, what are you going to do?" Brad held the position.

Walter did not spit.

Brad and Walter talked. Their conversation lasted hours. The night seemed to be held hostage by darkness and fog as hour after hour dragged. Midnight passed and a new day clawed its way through fog and darkness.

\* \* \* \*

"Fog's gone, it's clear as can be," Suzanne announced from a window as Vicki poured coffee into mugs and carried them back to the chairs that they had set up in the remains of what had been an elegant dining room. Out of concern for Scottie and Gunnar, the ladies had meticulously swept broken glass from the floor and the dogs now joined the group for an early morning treat. Brad had accused Vicki and Suzanne of having more concern for their dogs than for themselves, him or the ravaged condition of the inn. Vicki had simply rolled her eyes with a "Duh" for a reply. Suzanne had made it clear that Gunnar was smarter and better looking than Brad, so why shouldn't she be more concerned for her dog? Brad had been unable to come up with a suitable response.

Brad's conversation with Walter, followed by telephone calls to Lynn Everett and Dan Wright, had taken considerable time. The men in Los Angeles and Portland were relieved for everyone's safety in Colorado and elated with the information that Walter Perkins had provided. Brad could feel the energy that would drive investigators in the coming hours. He would give anything to be with the team that would ultimately search Earl's residence and the warehouse. Once the mystery of Earl, his followers and the weapons buried down in that rat hole were examined, God only knew where the investigation would go.

But by far, the best part of Brad's morning had been his call to Cassandra. Even though the conversation had been brief, it was the best feeling he had experienced in a long time. When she had learned that the same men who had attacked her husband also planned to murder her daughter, Cassandra had become too emotional to continue. That was just fine. Cassandra was going to be okay and Brad told her that he planned to make a trip to Los Angeles as soon as things settled down in Colorado. He would be with her and Norton in a matter of days. When Brad had suggested that Amy remain in Los Angeles for a few days and stay away from Portland, Cassandra had jumped on the idea and assured him that it would happen.

Coffee mug in hand, Brad closed his eyes and took a breath. He thought back to Taos, the guys and the cabin where he had almost died. *A simple little fishing trip, that's all I wanted. How the hell did it turn into all of this?*

Suzanne's sarcastic voice interrupted his thoughts. "Okay, Barney, when you taking me out to dinner for saving your bacon down there in that room?"

Ignoring her question, Brad spoke to Vicki, "Where in hell did that crazy-ass lady go to charm school?"

Vicki didn't miss a beat. She turned to face Brad, took aim and fired. "Well, at least she went to school. After seeing you show up at the party armed with a plastic flashlight, we should be asking where in the world you went to school. The lady you just called crazy-ass at least had enough sense to bring a flower pot, thank God."

Brad could only groan as he lifted his mug. The sound of an automobile pulling up outside the inn saved him for the moment. "That's got to be Kurt." Brad rose and walked to the door that he had managed to partially close in the wake of Walter's destructive foot. He pulled it open to reveal the first hint of dawn. It was still more dark than light but the profile of his friend walking toward the inn was unmistakable.

After stepping inside, Kurt smiled and shook hands with Brad but was visibly taken aback at what he saw. His eyes slowly drifted about the room, taking in the scene of chaotic devastation that greeted him. When he got to Suzanne and Vicki, sitting like schoolgirls in the midst of roll call, he quietly asked, "Who's the owner here?"

With a timid lifting of her arm, Vicki responded, "That would be me."

Kurt seemed not to have heard. He continued to look about the room, completely dumbfounded. Finally, he turned back to Vicki, "Jesus, lady, what did you do, burn the cinnamon rolls and piss somebody off?" Kurt continued his rolling evaluation of Vicki's inn in silence.

"I apologize for the rudeness of these ladies," Brad spoke up. "Would you like some coffee, Kurt?

"If you're not serving whiskey, coffee sounds great." Kurt Riddle's smile finally appeared. "Damn, next time I'm in the market for a bed and breakfast, I'm coming here. You folks know how to throw a party."

"Ladies, please meet one of my truest friends and the best police officer on the planet, Kurt Riddle." Vicki and Suzanne walked to

Kurt, skipped the handshake routine and gave him a hug. Brad handed a mug of coffee to Kurt. "It's been a hell of a night here, Kurt. Everyone will give you statements and be available for whatever you need. But, before you start to figure out what has to be done to sort all this out, come down the hall with me, I need you to meet a guy. He's had a really tough night and will probably be very happy to see someone other than me."

\* \* \* \*

The sun had not yet completely risen into the sky but its early glow illuminated Mt. Evans and the fourteen thousand foot behemoth glowed like a frosted rose. Brad stood on the front porch of The Fox Cove Inn, another mug of coffee in hand. He watched Kurt Riddle's car disappear, following the patrol car that transported Walter Perkins to a hospital for evaluation and then to jail. It was wonderfully quiet at the moment. This was Brad's favorite time of day but he knew the tranquility would not last. The inn would soon swarm with police officers. They would be taking dozens of photographs and conducting interviews. Brad fully expected to spend his morning on the telephone providing details to FBI agents and Portland prosecutors for search warrants.

But for the moment, the serenity was perfect. Brad sipped his coffee. *What an incredible night!* He thought again of Portland and Los Angeles. He thought about the investigation that would roll like a steam engine for a while, then, slow down to a regular old grind. They'll catch a bunch of the assholes, he thought, but just like trout, some always get away. Brad thought about his brother, Patrick. He could hear those prophetic words spoken over dinner in Taos. His brother had nailed it, he was so right: "They're always out there. The crazy bastards are always out there."

## CHAPTER TWENTY-SEVEN
July 17, 2012

Lynn Everett took a walk through Earl Sampson's house. The search team and evidence people were everywhere. The main living areas of the house were gradually being cleared of items that had obvious evidentiary potential. Materials to be confiscated would be placed into containers and logged. Notebooks, file folders and computers would ultimately be removed from the house. The search warrant authorized the search and seizure of every car that had been observed to visit Earl's residence since the beginning hours of the investigation. The process would take hours. After the initial search was completed, days of tedious labor would follow to decipher documents, evaluate photographs, records and information stored within computers. Fingerprint and evidence technicians went about their methodical tasks, painfully slow in every move.

Arrest warrants had been issued for Earl Sampson and Nolan Perkins. Lynn felt certain that additional warrants for numerous people would follow once the evidence had been scrutinized. He had two primary hopes for this search: that specific information would be obtained to identify the warehouse that Walter Perkins had talked about and that something solid would turn up on Sam Bowdin. He thought of his recent conversation with Brad and how they had talked of the unspeakable grief Bowdin had brought when he murdered a young trooper in Arkansas.

It had been a rather easy decision as to whether it was preferable to attempt a continued surveillance on Earl's house before executing the search warrant or to march ahead and serve the warrant. From the time that Brad had made his call from Colorado, Lynn and his team had known it was only a matter of hours before word of Walter's arrest would reach Earl and Nolan. Walter would be on the telephone as soon as opportunity presented itself. Given the severity of the crimes involved, it had been decided that they must hit Earl's house with a warrant and hope for the best. Evidence from inside the house would likely be instrumental in identifying and locating additional members of Earl's group, as well as to disrupt any immediate plans for crimes that the group may have planned. There were times when public safety had to take precedent over gathering evidence or arresting a particular individual and this had been one of those instances.

Lynn had not expected Earl to be inside the house. While warrants were being prepared, agents observed as Earl had left his residence but a discrete surveillance had been impossible. There was no way to know if Earl had learned of Walter's situation in Colorado and fled or if it was merely coincidence that the house was empty when the search team arrived. Whichever it turned out to be, Earl would by now know for certain that law enforcement was on to him.

Lynn knew all too well that when dealing with people like Earl, the chances for a final and violent standoff were very real. It had happened before in places all over the country; supremacists engaged law enforcement in deadly gun battles and then, quite often, the surviving members chose suicide over capture. Lynn thought with sarcasm that their suicide sure as heck did nothing to bring back others who died because of their radical beliefs and actions.

A crew back in the office was desperately conducting investigation to locate the warehouse. They were scouring through public records for every commercial storage and warehouse complex in the metropolitan area. They were searching for owners and lease agreements that might lead them to Earl. It was a big job. Lynn sensed that it was a race against time. If Earl planned to go out in a blaze of glory, the warehouse would be his location of choice. Lynn could feel it.

Dale Lovin

Lynn walked through the house. He wanted to develop a feel for who had lived here, what kind of life had transpired within the walls. He wanted to know his enemy. To escape the buzz of activity that permeated the primary living areas of the house, Lynn quietly walked down stairs to the lower level. The teams had made a cursory sweep of the entire house for safety reasons, looking for traps or explosives rigged to kill law enforcement. They had then decided to search from top to bottom, leaving the basement for last. Lynn wanted to take a look ahead of the evidence guys. He wanted to be alone.

The moment he stepped into the damp smelling room, Lynn felt something so different from the upper floors. He had no idea how to describe what he felt, but twenty-five years of police work had sharpened his sixth sense. That sense had just gone into full alert. There was a smell, a feel or an energy that permeated. Whatever it was, it could not be denied.

A single light fixture hung from the low ceiling, apparently controlled by a dimming switch, and was turned down to a diminutive glow. Shadows seemed to be coiled within each corner, silently eyeing this man who dared to intrude their domain. Lynn stood still and gazed, giving his eyes and his senses some time. He breathed moist, moldy air. He saw a podium that looked as though it belonged in a church. It was draped with a purple cloth that hung to the floor. The rich material was an ornament obviously intended to cast a royal ambiance over the room. It seemed horribly out of place.

Lynn took a few steps forward and stopped as he reached a long table that stood before the podium. Candles lined the table. Their wicks were blackened from use and their scent lingered. Lynn felt his skin prickle. He was face-to-face with Adolph Hitler. One of the most evil men in history was looking directly into his eyes. Lynn was frozen in place. He had never experienced anything like this. The photograph seemed to move as if it had breath; the face was alive, the eyes were alive. Adolf Hitler looked at Lynn and evaluated who stood before him. The eyes smiled mockingly.

His chest constricted and it required courage for Lynn to simply look back into the face in the photograph. Many times, Lynn had stood in the midst of crime scenes that portrayed unspeakable brutality, but nothing had ever affected him quite like this. He remained still, analyzing his feelings. Finally, he stepped away. He had to look through the rest of the room but he was so shaken that he was reluctant to even turn his back on the photograph. Something terrible might happen. He forced his feet to move and he walked to the back of the room. As he moved away, light faded and he stepped into total, obscured shadow. Lynn paused to examine the room and brushed his fingers over the basement's plastered walls. They felt cold, like they had never known heat. Nothing else seemed to be in the room, just dark, empty and cold corners. In a jolt, it happened. Lynn spun his body in instinctive, survival response. Chilling goose bumps exploded. The eyes of Adolph Hitler had turned. They followed Lynn, even into the corners of the room. Hitler looked directly at Lynn, his eyes laughing, still mocking.

Lynn had never wanted to be away from something so badly in his life. He headed for the stairs, up and out of the basement.

Desperate for fresh air, Lynn walked through the front door, leaving the house and moving into the front yard. He wanted to touch the sun. Warm wind and soft light of late afternoon enveloped his body. He bent forward, placing his hands on his knees. As a runner sucks oxygen after a race, Lynn purged his lungs of the poison from the basement. What had just happened? He stood straight and lifted his face upward. He had to see the sky. He wanted to head for home, hold his wife and call his children.

It was not going to happen. As Lynn struggled to understand what had transpired in the bowels of this evil house, his telephone rang. "Lynn, we've located the warehouse! It's an old wreck of a place out on the east edge of town. Earl's cars are all there and a whole bunch of other vehicles are also there. It looks like the whole gang has gathered. Something is definitely cooking to bring all of these jokers together like this. We've got an airplane headed out there and the SWAT team is gearing up."

\* \* \* \*

Earl stood facing his men. Nolan was seated directly to Earl's right and the rest of the men were clustered before him. There were not enough chairs for everyone so some stood while others rested on the locked trunks that were positioned on the floor of the cellar. The single lantern that had previously hung between Earl and Nolan now was called upon to illuminate the entire group. In the inadequate light, men who had never before seen this room stood or sat in nervous wonder. They grasped to understand their sinister surroundings and felt a growing apprehension of why they had been summoned so urgently. The rats, that had at first been intimidated by such a large presence, quickly adapted and their furtive scurrying was incessant.

A floor length robe hung from Earl's shoulders. It wrapped about his body and belts of brightly colored cloth swathed a crisscross pattern over the front. Some of the men had seen the robe before and knew it signified occasions of momentous significance.

As Earl prepared to speak, the men scarcely breathed. The only sound was that of the rats. "My brothers, thank you for coming. Whether it is midday or midnight, I am always honored to be with you. On the night of our Lord's betrayal, he summoned his followers for final hours of fellowship. Can you imagine how the memory of that last evening together must have remained in the minds of the Apostles after the crucifixion? What do you think they talked about as they sat together, breaking bread for the last time?"

The men shuffled as a sense of destiny emanated from Earl.

"Let me tell you what I think. I think that in the midst of the fear and dread that filled the room that night, they all felt a peace. I think that they felt a peace in their knowledge that the love of God was with them and, that no matter the events that were about to transpire, they would always be together. Neither the Roman Army nor Pontius Pilate could separate them." Earl dropped his voice to a whisper. "We will always be together. Nothing, my brothers, nothing on this earth shall ever tear us apart."

Earl's hand was lightning fast. The precise type of weapon that years earlier had killed a Jewish radio talk host named Alan Berg, a MAC-10, fully automatic, thirty rounds, was out from his robe and at Nolan's head. The first bullet shattered Nolan Perkin's skull in a millionth of a second. White hot metal blasted through the gathered men in a spray of gunfire. There was not even time to scream as they entered eternity. Bodies twitched. It was over in seconds. Rats were silent for a few moments, then, went about their business.

Earl placed the weapon on the table, beneath the lantern that had miraculously survived the onslaught. Smoke hung heavy, settling like poison gas over the mass of twisted bodies, some with eyes still opened in disbelief. He quietly stepped over the grotesque scene and retrieved a can of gasoline from behind one of the trunks. As explosive fuel was sprinkled over the lifeless forms, Earl began a low chant. "Our Father who art in heaven..." more gasoline, "Thy kingdom come..." more gasoline, "Deliver us from evil"... more gasoline, "Power and glory forever."

Earl stood over his men. He reached into his robe and removed a small revolver. There was no silencer. A final shot reverberated in a deafening shatter a split second after he tossed the match.

In a wide, lazy orbit, four thousand feet above the warehouse, a single engine aircraft circled through the sky. The two FBI Agents who piloted the craft saw flames erupt into the sky. FBI Agents and police officers, who were just arriving in vehicles, heard the hellish sounds of thousands of rounds of ammunition detonating within the inferno.

No one saw or heard the pitiful, screaming rats.

## CHAPTER TWENTY-EIGHT
### July 19, 2012

Sam Bowdin tossed the newspaper aside. The front-page story of death and destruction in Portland, Oregon, held no surprise for Sam. He had fully expected it to happen. That was part of the reason he had decided to put miles between him and Earl.

It was raining in Kansas City and life outside the motel room was grey and subdued. Shirley Barnes Sampson rolled over in the bed and drew her body close to Sam Bowdin. Her hand reached for his penis.

## CHAPTER TWENTY-NINE
July 24, 2012

It was emotional in ways they could never have imagined when Cassandra, Amy and Brad met in the lobby of the hospital. So much had happened. Thinking back to the night of Norton's attack in the schoolyard, everything since then seemed surreal. Would they awaken to find everything had been nothing but a dream? The embraces, tears and laughter that they shared were very real.

As they made their way through the hospital, Cassandra held Brad's arm and told him of Norton's incredible progress. He was out of intensive care and in a regular room. Bandages covered only his head and his face was completely exposed. The horrible tubes had been removed from his throat and he was swallowing under his own power. He had not yet spoken but the doctors were hopeful.

"Oh, Brad, you have no idea how wonderful it was to see his face again. It was like we have been given a whole new life together just to be able look into each other's eyes. The doctors tell me that after an injury like this, the ability to speak has a very powerful psychological and healing effect. Poor Norton, he is trying so hard. He wants so much to talk and every day we are hoping that this will be the day. The doctors are convinced that once he begins to speak, his progress will take off like a rocket."

Amy smiled with pride. "Look what I've brought." She lifted a fast food bag into the air, "A chocolate milkshake! If this doesn't make Dad start speaking again, nothing will."

Cassandra gave her daughter a hug as they walked. "Oh baby, I hope you are right."

Norton's face looked a thousand times better than what Brad had expected. Swelling was minimal and his eyes had that great Norton shine when Cassandra and Amy bent to kiss him. Cassandra fussed over flowers and Brad felt Norton's grip again. It was strong, full of energy. Amy couldn't wait to share the milkshake and she pulled a chair close to her father. Norton smiled like a kid as Amy began to spoon the dessert into his mouth. It was a slow process, swallowing still took effort. But the entire experience was euphoric as everyone chattered non-stop while Norton enjoyed his milkshake. He wanted to say something to Amy. Norton's lips moved, concentration and effort strained his face but sound would not come. Cassandra and Amy both took it in stride. They never lost their cheerful manner but continued to talk about everything under the sun.

When the milkshake was finished, Brad took a seat close to the bed. They gripped hands as Brad leaned close and looked right into Norton's eyes. In a soft voice, Brad told the story of the past days. He related the events as a story, eliminating many details but unfolding all that had happened in a smooth, easy flow. When Brad spoke of the threat to Amy that had been averted, tears glistened in Norton's eyes. Cassandra stood beside Brad. Her tears did more than glisten; they flowed. Brad told of FBI agents following leads all over the country subsequent to a wealth of information that had come from Earl's house. He concluded the story by telling of the warehouse fire and the death of Earl Sampson, Nolan Perkins and the followers of so much hate. When he had finished, Cassandra and Amy both stood close by. The look coming from Norton's face made further conversation unnecessary.

Brad felt tremendous pressure from Norton's hand. He knew Norton was trying to communicate. Brad returned the grip and leaned close. Norton's lips shifted, his tongue moved. It was scarcely a whisper but he may as well have shouted. Everyone in the room heard his words. "Thank you."

## CHAPTER THIRTY
## 1945

*The United States was heartbroken. Four years of war had left the bodies of fathers, sons, mothers and daughters scattered across the globe and littering ocean bottoms. Adolph Hitler had exterminated millions of Jews in Europe and savage warfare continued with Japan.*

*Night fell over New Mexico on July 15, 1945. Some people slept and some people toiled but practically everyone prayed. They prayed for those lost, prayed for safety and prayed for peace. The planet spun, bringing midnight and July 15 became July 16. Only a handful of people knew that the desert of southern New Mexico, The Jornada del Nuerto (The Journey of the Dead Man), held America's greatest hope to end World War II: sitting atop a one-hundred-foot tower and armed for detonation, was the world's first atomic bomb.*

*A second-by-second countdown led the way into a new age. The voice of a man blasted over outdoor speakers and followed wires into special bunkers, where scientists waited with thundering hearts. "Minus thirty seconds," ... "Minus ten seconds." The voice transmitted in suspense beyond belief. "Minus five seconds." New Mexico, the land of Acoma, The Long Walk and the Taos Rebellion,*

Dale Lovin

*held the final seconds of pre-atomic mankind. "Minus three seconds, minus two seconds." Civilization teetered. "Minus one second. Now!"*

*In official records, a witness to the blast offered this description: "The lighting effects beggared description. The whole country was lighted by a searing light with the intensity many times that of the midday sun. It was golden, purple, violet, grey, and blue. It lighted every peak, crevasse, and ridge of the nearby mountain range with a clarity and beauty that cannot be described but must be seen to be imagined. Seconds after the explosion came, first, the air blast pressing hard against the people, to be followed almost immediately by the strong awesome roar which warned of doomsday and made us feel we puny things were blasphemous to dare tamper with the forces heretofore reserved for the Almighty."*

*Upon seeing the blast, Project Director, Dr. J. Robert Oppenheimer recalled a passage from the Bhagavad-Gita, "I have become death, the destroyer of worlds." Test Director, Kenneth Bainbridge, a physicist from Harvard expressed the moment differently, "Now we are all sons of bitches."*

*Twenty-one days after the test, August 6, 1945, the B-29 bomber Enola Gay dropped an atomic bomb on Hiroshima, Japan. President Harry S. Truman issued a statement to the people of the United States and to the world: "Sixteen hours ago an American airplane dropped one bomb on Hiroshima, an important Japanese Army base. That bomb had more power than 20,000 tons of TNT."*

*The bomb dropped on Hiroshima was code-named 'Little Boy.' Directly beneath the center of the explosion, the temperature is estimated to have been about 7,000 degrees. Heat created was so great that people over one and a quarter miles away had their clothing ignite; roof tiles a third of a mile away melted.*

*The explosion also created ultra high pressure. Wind speed on the ground, directly beneath the explosion is estimated to have been 980 mph. One-third mile distant, winds are believed to have been 620 mph and a full mile from the blast the winds were 190mph.*

*The atomic bombings of Hiroshima and Nagasaki (bombed on August 9, 1945) killed approximately 150,000 people. As a result of radiation and related injuries, the death toll by 1950 was calculated to be approximately 400,000 people.*

*President Dwight D. Eisenhower, in his inaugural address, January 20, 1953, gravely proclaimed, "Science seems ready to confer on us, as its final gift, the power to erase human life on this planet."*

## CHAPTER THIRTY-ONE
### August 3, 2012

When the letter was delivered, Brad was away enjoying solitude in the Flat Tops Wilderness so it languished with bills and junk mail before it was even retrieved from his mail box. Still dressed in camping clothes that reeked of smoke and grunge, Brad carried a bulging bag of mail outside to his deck, dumped it on a table and headed for the beer fridge. His Moosehead was ice cold, the sunset was magnificent and Patsy Cline's voice sounded marvelous as he began the process of emptying the sack of mail. Junk mail was tossed with impatience directly into the trash. His arm was half cocked to toss the letter when something made him stop and give it a second look. It was the return address that had caught his eye: Office of the United States Attorney, Albuquerque, New Mexico. *I don't suppose they are sending me shopping coupons.* Another Moosehead and he slit the envelope. As he unfolded the official-looking letterhead, he felt memories. He had lived half his career in these offices. Working with prosecutors to obtain warrants or preparing for trial had been a never-ending process.

The official purpose of the letter was largely ignored as he read the document and its real implications became apparent; this letter was his ticket to October fishing in New Mexico. Prosecutors and investigators from across the nation were planning a conference for intelligence sharing and tactical planning relating to ongoing investigations into white supremacist organizations. Albuquerque had been selected as a centrally located site for the conference that was to be held the first few days in October at a downtown hotel. The conference would conclude just in time for Albuquerque's famous hot air balloon festival for those who wished to extend their stay. Brad was being invited as a special guest due to his unique involvement in one of the cases that would be discussed. Please RSVP.

*This is manna from heaven!* Brad could not care less about the conference but he cared a great deal about being in New Mexico in October. As far as he was concerned, there was simply no place on earth as magical or enchanting as New Mexico in autumn. Aspen trees of gold, the aroma of roasting chilies and slow-flowing trout streams defined New Mexico in October. Hell yes, he would RSVP. He doubted that he would attend any of the conference beyond initial registration and he would do that only to snag the benefit of a free hotel and breakfast each morning. "Whoowee!" Brad toasted himself and downed his Moosehead.

Brad walked across his living room, put a finger to his lips and touched Elizabeth's photograph. Then, elated with his good fortune, he hit the shower. He knew that this boondoggle had Lynn Everett's fingerprints all over it. Lynn was the only person who would have known about Brad's involvement and he had obviously managed to get Brad's name on the attendee list. *Gotta buy that man some beer and a plate of enchiladas while we're in Albuquerque.*

After his shower, he called Patrick and Matthew. Of course they would meet him in New Mexico. They were still stinging from the loss of their horse trip earlier in the summer and this would help make up for what had been missed. Fry had to decline. His niece was getting married in San Francisco and he couldn't get out of it.

Two hours later, Brad was asleep in his favorite old chair, a copy of *49 Trout Streams of New Mexico* opened across his chest. It was the first time since the night at Fox Cove Inn that Brad did not dream of Walter Perkins and a lead pipe.

## CHAPTER THIRTY-TWO
October 3, 2012

Five o'clock in the morning had been his planned departure time, but anticipation of seeing his brothers and fishing in New Mexico was too much. Brad left at four o'clock instead. It was pitch black and October's chill could be felt as he circled C-470 to Interstate 25 and pointed his SUV south. Long before he hit Colorado Springs, he had heard all of the news he could handle so it was back to the old regulars: Emily Lou Harris, Alabama, Sarah Brightman, Willie Nelson and Nancy Griffith. After breakfast in Pueblo, the morning was crisp and blue. Just what he needed. Another ninety minutes and he was past the Spanish Peaks and through Trinidad, beginning one of his favorite stretches of road anywhere in the country: Raton Pass. As he crested the pass leaving Colorado behind, the vastness of New Mexico stretched before him. Brad had marveled at this vista a hundred times and it had never failed to stir his imagination or fire his spirit. He looked as far as his eyes could reach, to see the land of his childhood home and feel the sadness of his parents' graves.

Brad pulled to the side of the road and got out of his vehicle. He needed to breathe and feel this. From this vantage, he felt as though he stood on the cusp of the world, close to God and close to his home. He could see so much of what makes the very soul of New Mexico:

flat deserts to vertical mountains with ancient Indian worlds that lay nestled in the shadow of Los Alamos, home to the atomic age. Wind blew across Brad's face. Wind that hours earlier had swept over Acoma, to be cooled as it swept over the snowy peaks of the Sangre de Christo Mountains. He breathed deeply. He loved it. This was home. He looked to the south. Thousands of acres of empty land seemed to go on forever.

Brad contemplated that just because landscape is vacant, it is by no means empty of history. Scattered across the prairies were countless pockmarks of black rock that were remnants of extinct volcanoes from when the earth had bubbled. Volcanoes had cooled into habitat for dinosaurs and then served as landmarks for passing wagon trains. Dustbowl days had buried the land in drifts of grit, but interstate highways now sliced the land. Brad could feel the centuries that had blown across this land. In a place like this, how could one not realize the frailty and insignificance of all things made by man? With so much emptiness and so many memories of his youth within this landscape, he couldn't help but think of Elizabeth. She was as gone as the days of the wagon trains that had crossed these prairies.

*Will I ever stop missing her?*

As he prepared to get back into his car, he took a final, lingering look. The land was as still as a painting. The wind, that New Mexico wind, it continued to blow.

Two hours later, Brad stood with his brothers in the Cimarron River. They had driven up from Albuquerque, met Brad in the village of Eagle's Nest and now the stream of their youth rolled over their feet. Small browns, sensing the imminence of winter, fed with urgency. Rods remained bowed and hands were always cold as each fish was held beneath the surface for release, vanishing faster than the eye could comprehend. Chokecherry bushes, stripped clean by bears, shared the banks with willows. Yellow leaves floated through the air, falling onto the water in a farewell gesture to summer. They drifted away like the dreams of a child, gone but not forgotten. The stream seemed to relax, enjoying their human presence. Magic meandered. Matthew, Patrick and Brad stood in the water, casting, breathing, and remembering days gone by.

When the sun was directly overhead, they walked the twisting, old canyon to stand in the clearings where Mom and Dad had brought them as small boys. They could smell Mom's fried chicken and hear Dad laughing. It has been said that heaven is simply going back to favorite times of our lives. Matthew, Patrick and Brad spent a day in heaven. They talked and laughed. Their childhood memories came to life, illuminating roads long forgotten and, with the accuracy of a compass, memories that took them back to where they had been. Brad and his brothers reminisced with stories of raccoons invading their campsite and bears shredding their tent, Dad's stories by the fire and Mom's voice as each night she sang to three, exhausted little boys. They stood beneath the Palisades, sheer cliffs of granite where layers of time could be seen or touched. Sometimes they laughed, at other times one had to turn away. Each brother spent time with his own thoughts: the web of pathways that lead to the future, but the single road that always leads back home. How quickly turning pages of calendars become seasons changed and lives lived.

The enchanted day seemed to tiptoe by and all too quickly it was time to part. Brad headed back to the Interstate for his drive to Albuquerque. The plan was that he would spend one obligatory day in the conference before Patrick and Matthew joined him. Then, they would blow out like the wind for more days of fishing around Santa Fe.

As he pulled into his hotel parking lot, it was dark and Albuquerque sparkled in nighttime, desert air. Brad could not imagine a more perfect day than the one just experienced. The last thing he wanted to do was to sit in a stuffy conference room and spend hours talking about people like Walter Perkins. That man's face would haunt him forever. He didn't need to talk about it.

\* \* \* \*

Blue jeans, cowboy boots, Stetson hats and expensive business suits jammed the hotel's restaurant for morning's breakfast hour. *Just another contradictory wonder of New Mexico.* Brad sat alone at a corner table, sipping coffee as he waited until time for the conference to begin. In the old days he would have recognized half the people in the room, but too much time had passed. Now when he looked at the crowd, all he saw was a sea of strangers. Suddenly, the single familiar face that he had been seeking appeared. Lynn Everett stood in the mass of jabbering humanity. Brad stood up and waved across the room to his friend. It took several seconds of frantic gesturing before Lynn spotted Brad and worked his way through the bustle to join him. They shook hands and exchanged obligatory insults and greetings as they ordered breakfast. Brad told Lynn of the previous day with his brothers and promised that Patrick and he would be sure to drop by for a quick hello before the conference concluded.

"Hey, thanks millions for getting me invited to this thing. I appreciate the heck out of it. But, let me warn you, I'm not hanging around too long so you better let me buy you dinner this evening. This old, retired guy has better things to do than sit on his duff and talk about baldheaded assholes. I'm outta here, my friend, trout streams call," Brad lifted his coffee mug in a toast.

Lynn returned the gesture. "I will be very disappointed if I see your face after today. I wish to heck I was going with you. But, since I'm still official, I suppose I'll hang around. And, if you want to buy me dinner, I'll certainly let you do that. However, I have to tell you that you owe me absolutely nothing. I had not a thing to do with you being invited here. I was surprised as the dickens when I saw your ugly kisser over here in the corner."

"You're kidding me! I was certain it was you who snuck my name onto the list."

Arms raised in surrender, Lynn grinned. "I'm an innocent man. Your presence here, whether reward or punishment, has nothing to do with me, I promise."

"Well, in that case, buy your own darn dinner," Brad said with a laugh. "I have no idea of anyone else around here who even knows me. But, I sure as heck thank whoever it was for the hospitality."

Lynn laughed. "Wow, did I just goof or what. I should have kept my mouth shut and let you buy dinner. I like your credit card a whole lot better than mine."

Brad grinned at Lynn, "Yep, your old brain sure ain't what it used to be."

\* \* \* \*

Tables were arranged along a wall of the conference room, each with a sign providing direction for alphabetical registration. Brad made his way to the appropriate table, still wondering who in hell could have known his name and how he had managed to be included in this affair. A smiling, young lady found his name on the list of registrants and handed him a nametag. She explained that for the first hours of the morning, the conference would be divided by region, with prosecutors and investigators going over cases in their specific regions. She referred to her master list and told Brad that he had been assigned to the Albuquerque region. "That will be conference room G, down the hall on the right. Just check in there." Brad thanked her and worked his way through the chaos of bodies and the energy that first mornings always hold.

As he bumped shoulders with complete strangers and listened to incessant chatter, Brad suddenly felt terribly lonely. In the midst of so many people, he felt alienated, like he didn't belong. His career was in the rear view mirror, a part of the past. These people were here because they were still a part of the race, still mixing it up every day. As always when he felt lonely, thoughts of Elizabeth came to mind. She had brimmed with enthusiasm when she had been a prosecutor. She loved a courtroom and she loved big, exciting events such as this conference. But that was all so far in the past. In a swell of emotion, Brad thought that even making an appearance at this conference had been a huge mistake. *Elizabeth is gone, I'm retired, what the hell am I doing here?*

About a dozen people milled about within conference room G. Brad spotted a stenciled sign, "Check In Here," that was posted on a table in the center of the room. Several people stood behind the table, their backs to Brad, engaged in conversation. He walked to the table and stood patiently, waiting to be acknowledged. That was when he heard it: that beautiful laugh. It sounded so much like Elizabeth. She turned to face him: copper skin, black hair to her shoulders and brown eyes that went straight through him. He couldn't help himself, he had not done this since Elizabeth but it was beyond his control - he glanced at her left hand - no ring. Her eyes found his nametag as she extended her hand in greeting. Electricity jolted as their fingers touched. "Brad Walker," she spoke with a smile, "Thank you for coming. I'm the prosecutor here in Albuquerque. My name is Juanita."

## AUTHOR'S NOTE

Today, Acoma Pueblo awakens each morning and "The City That Always Was" begins another day of life as the sun brings light and warmth. Winds blow over dusty remnants of "The Long Walk," sometimes in a breeze, sometimes in a howl. A menagerie of stars gathers each night over Taos, over the ruins of the mission destroyed on a bitter January day. Beneath these fiery spheres, humanity passes through life. Months, years and centuries are calculated by the swirling of our solar system: a solar system that watched as Spaniards flung Native Americans from a cliff because they followed spiritual beliefs different from theirs; a solar system that watched as Indians and Mexicans slaughtered Governor Bent and convenient gringos in Taos; a solar system that watched as hate-filled men drove from Oregon to Colorado to murder Alan Berg because he was a Jew.

Centuries pass. Galaxies spin. Planets rotate and winds of time blow. Clubs transform to swords, muskets to automatic weapons and trucks filled with farm chemicals become bombs. Winds of time never cease. Winds that blew dust in the faces of the Navajo on "The Long Walk" also blew across Oklahoma on the day Timothy McVeigh parked a bomb-laden truck beneath a day care center; a bomb to be detonated because he was angry with his government.

252

Dale Lovin

Winds of time blew over a desert named The Journey of the Dead Man on the morning of the first atomic bomb. There are times when New Mexico winds blow so long and so hard that they seem to actually stretch the day, make it last a bit longer. But blow as it might, radiation from that fateful morning still simmers in the desert sand.

As winds blow and molecules of time revolve in our mysterious, cosmic carousel, is it possible that they talk of Acoma or the Long Walk? Do they recall Alan Berg or Timothy McVeigh? What must they say? What must they think? Given the galactic perspective they enjoy, can they see into our future? How long will it be before a Timothy McVeigh or an Earl Sampson has access to the horror that was born in 1945 in The Journey of the Dead Man?

\* \* \* \*

To be ignorant of what occurred before you were born is to remain always a child.
Cicero

The past is never dead, it's not even past.
William Faulkner

# About the Author

Dale Lovin was an FBI Agent for twenty-five years, specializing in investigations of violent crimes. In the wake of September 11, 2001, Congress mandated an enhanced Federal Air Marshal Service and he worked in the establishment of this agency. Dale lives in Colorado with his wife, has three children and is an avid fly fisher.